D0043171

THE

VISION OF THE

BLIND KING

By

Ako A Eyong

Dallas Public Library
950 Main Street
Dallas, Oregon 97338

This is a novel. It is a work of fiction. All characters
appearing in it are fictitious. Any resemblance to any person, living or dead is
purely coincidental.

©Ako A. Eyong.

All rights reserved. No part of this publication may be reproduced, distributed, or
transmitted in any form or by any means, including photocopying, recording, or
other electronic or mechanical methods, without the prior written permission of
the publisher, except in the case of brief quotations embodied in critical reviews
and certain other noncommercial uses permitted by copyright law.

ISBN: 9780988830103

FOR IMANI AND ISASIMBA

I Thank you Lord,

I Thank you for this most amazing celebration of love called life. I thank you for the people in my life, some of whom contributed in no small way to facilitating the successful culmination of this book. I thank you for the guidance, the persistence, the wisdom, the inspiration, the joy, the abundance, and the love. And may I always remember that everything is not of me but of you. So help me God.
Amen.

List of Characters:

-Abanda son of Dar- Me.

-Abou Bakar- General of the King's army in   Avaris, Has a son, Iroha.

-Aesare- Current king of Kemet. His father was Neferhotep.

-Aisha- Works with Semon.

-Caliph-Assistant High Priest of the god Kepharra.

-Charlie- My boss, newspaper editor.

-Cikatrix- Current Vizier of border security.

-Hasim- Works for Salatis.

-Iroha- Son of Abou Bakar. Has a girlfriend, Emoon. Mother is S'sara.

-Itzo- Former Vizier of border security.

-Jean Pierre- French man living in Cameroon, his boss is Yves Mammon.

-Johnny Letgo- Brother to the priest.

-Marcus Franken- Paulie's associate.

-Melenoc- Chief High Priest of the god Kepharra.

-Neferhotep- Former king of Kemet. His son is Aesare.

-Paulie Spinelli- Small time thief. Associated to Marcus Franken.

-Queen mother- Mother to the current King, thus one of Neferhotep's widows.

-S'sara- The General's wife. Iroha's mother.

-Salatis- Aamu leader, Abou Bakar's arch enemy.

-Sango- My neighbor, father of two young children.

-**Selena-** Speaker, Paraguayan immigrant living in California.

-**Semon-** Paid to spy and report on Selena.

-**Yao** –Revolutionary.

-**Yves Mammon**- French man living in Cameroon.

CHAPTER ONE

Cameroon, Central Africa

I have heard it said before, that if you are aware, I mean really aware, you can sometimes tell when your own death is not too far away. Like many, it is a saying to which I had never given much thought, because I had never had a reason to, -that is, up until now.

I had known that there was going to be some danger to everything. Of course. But the certainty of death? That was a different issue altogether. It was something for which nothing had prepared me. And the un-preparedness turned the minutes of dreadful anticipation into a barely controlled panic attack. I really did not want to die.

But no matter how hard I tried I could not shake the nagging feeling at the pit of my stomach that the end had come. Death, it seemed, had found me in spite of myself and in spite of my love for life.

Just thinking about it filled me with dread and frantic desperation. But what could I do? What was there to do? Jump out of my own body and run? The facts of the matter were that I was exhausted, aching, and try as I might, I could not go any faster. Every step had become an ordeal, made more difficult by the mass of Jean's unconscious form on my shoulders. Is this how I had imagined my death? No. But the noose was tightening all the same.

With great effort, I shifted the position of the bleeding body as I sought relief from the burning that Jean's weight was inflicting on my tired muscles. But it was in vain. The pain seemed to intensify.

It was a pain that had started as a dull and manageable ache. But five hours of fleeing, carrying the bleeding, gently breathing body, and plodding through dense tropical undergrowth, had slowly evolved into this sharp, biting sting that was now torturing my whole torso. Simple breathing was now a problem. It felt as if my lungs were being squeezed down into my stomach. I could not continue like this. Something had to be done. But what?

It was a question that I had refused to consider up till now, a question that seemed to defile the person that I believed myself to be. And it was a simple enough question:

Should I leave Jean behind? Should I drop his body and move on although he was still alive?

It would make everything easier. All I had to do was lean to the side and his warm, though inert body would slide effortlessly to the ground. Without his weight on my shoulders, maybe I would stand a chance of eluding the men and getting out of this jungle alive.

So, should I leave him behind and move on? Why not? What was the point of trying to save him if I was going to die in the process? And he was not even African.

Forcefully, I tore my mind away from the thoughts that were shouting in my head and limped on into the windy night. This was not the time to give in to such a thought, I told myself. "But why not?", another thought shouted. "Do you want to live, or do you want to die? Is this how you want to end?"

I did not want to die. More than anything, I wanted to get out of this jungle alive. With voices screaming in my head, I pressed on.

By the time I reached the Crocodile infested Manyu River, my whole body was screaming, the moon had disappeared and it had started to rain again. Huge fat raindrops that were coming down on the rainforest leaves with a surprisingly noisy onslaught. *Ratatatatatat* the pelting went, wetting everything and transforming the dark, moist earth into a mushy, slippery paste that rendered progress more difficult.

As I began navigating the slippery incline to the banks of the flooded river, it suddenly became insufferable and I had to stop. Careful now, I told myself, this is definitely not the time to fall. But neither is it the time to be standing around.

My pursuers were not far behind and at the pace I was going, they were sure to catch up soon, that is, if the hyenas did not find me first. I knew they were around as well, and Jean's bleeding was probably leaving an aromatic trail that would lead the creatures right to us.

I peered into the darkness but it was too dark to really see. Everything was a blur and the rain was not helping. I could barely make out the huge stems of Iroko, Ebony, and Sapele trees that went towering high into the night.

5

The moon had disappeared and it had started to rain again.

I cocked my ear and listened, hoping to penetrate the windy rain and hear beyond it. What was that noise? Was it real or was it just my mind? The mental strain was becoming intolerable as well. Maybe I should find a good hide out by the river to rest and consider my options. Who knows? The men may go by without seeing us. It was desperate thinking and highly unlikely, but what other options did I have? Leave Jean behind? That seemed to be the only one. I could drop him right here. Why not? Why was I so concerned with the fate of a French national when his government had caused and was causing so much pain for my people?

So, was it wrong to leave him behind although I believed that trying to save him would kill both of us? Did it amount to abandonment? What if I abandoned him? Did that make me into a coward, or a realist? And if somehow I survived could I live with the fact that I had turned my back on a helpless man to save myself? Why not, I reasoned. He was just a man of white skin that Chance had seen fit to throw into this whole mix and...

Wait! Chance? Was it Chance? Was that what it was? Was it the same thing as Destiny? Did that mean it was my destiny to abandon a helpless man in the depths of an unforgiving rain forest? Maybe so. Do the sages not say that everything that happens was meant to be? Does the holy book itself not say that God saw my substance, being yet unformed? And in his book were written the days fashioned for me when as yet there were none of them? Was that not what Destiny was all about? If not, then what was it? Fate? What about all the many, different, seemingly unconnected circumstances and events that had had to come together for me to find myself in this predicament? Was it Chance as well? Or was it Destiny?

My name is Abanda, Son of Dar, and my father told me that in this life, everything happens for a reason. He also told me that his own father died on the very first day that he was to begin school. At the time he was six and needless to say, his young life took a drastic turn for the worse. You see, his mother, my paternal grandmother, did not have the means to support him and his siblings, so it was decided that he would leave the little village of Obang, and go to the township of Mamfe, where he would find a family to serve in exchange for food and a place to sleep. That meant fourteen hours of work everyday. No time to play.

It was a tough life for a little boy who had recently lost his father and was now forced by circumstances, to live in servitude a long way from home and family. The life was far from steady and he was tossed from home to home, at the whims of factors that were not within the comprehension of his young mind.

As he grew older, he began wondering about himself, about life, about other children... Why was he always serving other people? Why could he not live with his mother and family like everyone else? Why had his father died? Was this all he was going to be? Why wasn't he going to school like other children? Was he fundamentally different? Was something wrong with him?

Out of these questions was born a powerful desire to better himself. And somehow he figured out that the accumulation of knowledge was essential to achieving this dream. But first, he had to learn how to read. So he taught himself. Then, he began entreating his guardian, at the time a Nigerian from the Ibo tribe, to let him attend school. Surprisingly the man accepted and my father proceeded to earn a long overdue standard six certificate, which qualified him to sit examinations for an entry-level position into a local bank! He passed, got the job and his life changed.

With a job he got a little place that was all his own. For the first time he did not have to come home to one thousand and one chores, there was no one to scream at him or beat him up if he made a mistake or became too tired to finish a chore. His mother and siblings could visit him any time and even live with him if they choose. But most importantly, he now made enough money to buy a few books at the end of every month. And he did.

From his meager salary he began reading voraciously, so that by the time I was born twenty years later, entire walls of my father's house had been taken up by bookstands that were struggling to contain an ever-increasing library.

As a toddler I would spend hours and hours poring through these books, searching for beautiful pictures, paintings and drawings. I would stare at the beauty of the lines and marvel at the ingenuity of the artists. I would see myself in dreams, drawing beautiful lines, objects, images, and illustrations like those in the pages of my father's books. The pencil became my best friend as I went about drawing on whatever surface was available to be drawn upon. I could not get enough of the line. I would draw things and my friends and schoolmates would be dumbstruck. Teachers from other classes would send for me if they needed an illustration on the chalkboard. I was soon doing comic books and storyboards and my life was slowly, but surely, being taken over by art. And there was nothing, I, or anybody, could do about it.

Then in June of 96, I earned a bachelor's degree in history. It was a moment of truth, especially for my mother who had made all kinds of sacrifices so I could go to college. It was time to get a job and make a living. But guess what? There were no jobs. Absolutely none.

You see, Cameroon is the classic archetype of a contemporary African nation; extremely blessed in countless natural resources, but exploited and mismanaged into abject poverty, a status quo that gave me, an unemployed graduate, many things about which to be distressed. Being an *artiste*, I began submitting political cartoons to the country's biggest, privately owned, bi-weekly English newspaper. The editors liked my work and I became the official cartoonist.

All of what I have told you so far is important because, now that I think about it, I realize that without my father's books, my imagination may never have been triggered into the world of art. Without that, I would probably never have become a cartoonist. If I had never become a cartoonist, there is no way I would have met Jean. And without that fateful meeting, I would not be in this predicament where I was wondering if I should abandon him in the jungle or not.

Kingdom of Kemet, 1720 B.C

*A*lthough the sun was almost at its highest point in the sky the King had not yet appeared. Like everyone else Ridissi was not certain as to why the monarch was taking so long. No one alive could remember the last time that a celebration dedicated to the sun god had started this late. Ridissi was certain that it had never happened. At least, not during his lifetime and certainly not during the Forty-one rains that he had served as the first royal announcer of the King's court.

Was it not common knowledge? Did children not sing about it? Who in the Kingdom did not know that the celebrations of the sun must always start at sunrise? Had the King somehow forgotten? That would be impossible! The priest of the sun god was a man that Ridissi knew personally. He was not the kind of man who would let the palace forget something as important as this. The King was usually alerted well in advance of such events, and Ridissi was certain that this one had not been an exception.

For the thousandth time, he wondered what the Monarch's excuse could be. Maybe he'd just overslept! But what can one expect? The new King was nothing like his father before him. He was different and in some very unsettling ways.

Since Neferhotep, the last King, went to *be with the gods* five rains ago, the Kingdom had suffered one setback after another: The nation-wide irrigation system needed a lot of repair work, dams were broken, agriculture was suffering, food was getting short, crime was on the rise, the trans-Saharan trade routes were not safe anymore, public infrastructure needed repairs; the list went on and on.

During this time, the new King had been busy with his group of select friends who were always hovering around like an extension of the royal shadow. Nobody outside of this circle could say what they were about. The word was that even the distinguished council of elders that deliberated on all major issues, did not have the King's ear anymore, which was impossible to imagine. But if there was any truth to it, then a major line had been crossed, and Ridissi wondered for how long it could go on before something bad happened. The council of elders was not a group that a man could hide away in his pocket. Not even the King could get away with it. Not unless he was extremely popular and well loved by the people.

With that thought, Ridissi raised his eyes and surveyed the scene in front of him, the sea of faces that were looking up at him and creating a stark contrast to the whitewashed buildings of the city in the background. The turnout was impressive and he estimated that up to Twenty thousand people were present for this Ceremony. There were men, women, and children from all walks of life. Some of them were still standing, but most had given up and found a place to sit on the bare earth, in small family groups, under the shade of date palms.

From experience Ridissi knew that the size of this crowd was not a reflection of the King's popularity. It was more an indication of how worried the people were getting. They could tell that things had not been going well. In fact, some things were going rather badly, and by showing up they felt as if their presence was not only a reminder to the King about his responsibilities, but also an indication of the urgency in the situation. So like obedient children, they had all come into the presence of their father, hoping to hear about a solution to the problem, a solution that would cause sleep to return to the eyes of the men, and bring back food to the stomach of the women and the children.

The size of this crowd was not a reflection of the king's popularity…

Suddenly, a wave of excitement swept through the crowd and a cloud of dust rose as thousands of people, simultaneously, rose to their feet. From his vantage point, Ridissi used his hand to shield his eyes from the sun as he attempted to make out the reason for the excitement. He glanced to his right, where the huge, highly decorated royal platform had been erected. He noted that this particular construction had been raised just high enough to be out of the people's reach.

The platform was filled to capacity and had been so for hours. The chief priests of all the different gods, counselors to the Palace, Nomarchs from all the provinces, Generals of the King's army, ambassadors from distant lands, scribes, praise

11

singers, and the hundreds of uniformed servants that was the trademark of royal events, were all present. And all of them were seated in order of importance, with the lowliest delegations, placed furthest from the raised throne of solid gold, which as yet, was conspicuously vacant.

To Ridissi's left was another raised platform, somewhat bigger and equally decorated. And it too, was filled with fat, oily looking dignitaries and 'friends of the court', who were all accompanied by their own friends, family members, hangers-on and servants in waiting.

On both platforms, everyone had turned out in full ceremonial regalia. There were even matching insignias that served the purpose of identifying the different delegations by function. Most were enhanced with precious metals and stones, displayed for all to see; a symbol of how much power they wielded at court. Indeed, it was raining gold and precious stones.

Finally, Ridissi could see the reason for the excitement. It was coming from the platform to the right, where the Chief priest of the sun god, had risen to his feet. It was an indication that after six hours of waiting, the King was finally ready!

As Ridissi watched, the priest, dressed in shimmering black silk, walked to the edge of the stage and raised both arms, first upwards towards the sun, and then outwards to the crowd. It was the royal salute, and the crowd heaved a small, but audible sigh of relief.

It was also the signal that Ridissi, fifth son of Ngoma, first royal announcer to the King's court, and honorable member of several councils, had been waiting for. He cleared his throat. Then in a rich and powerful baritone that belied his size, he lunged into the royal recitation that would welcome the King onto the platform.

"A long, long time ago," his voice boomed, "far up in the Hutu and Tutsi hills where the great Aur River begins its journey, a great Kingdom was born. It was a Kingdom that was created by the heroes of old, and so from the very beginning it was blessed with great Kings and rulers. These great men expanded the Kingdom, building city after city along the lengthy river, all the way to the sea. People of the Kingdom," he continued, "By the laws of our tradition, we must therefore, always thank and celebrate the gods in honor of all the blessings that we enjoy," he paused. "Today is the day of the sun, and every man, woman, and child in the Kingdom has been celebrating since sunrise," he shouted, pointing in the general direction of the platform. "The sun priest himself, honorable eyes and ears of the sun god, keeper of the sun's secrets, he on whom we all depend for solar transmission, is here. And as expected he will lead the people in the ceremonial rites that will open the heart of the sun god, so that blessings can be poured out onto the land."

From the corner of his eye Ridissi saw the black-clad priest briefly raise the gold staff in his left hand in acknowledgement, as his office was mentioned.

"But before this can happen," Ridissi continued, "We must first welcome the one whose presence is essential to procure the attention of the gods, the blessed one, he who was divinely chosen, he whose word is power, upholder and keeper of our laws, owner of vast uncountable wealth, great warrior whose heart fears no foe, General of a thousand armies, conqueror of endless Kingdoms and ruler of all the world." He paused to catch a breath. "Men, women and children gathered here today, I, Ridissi fifth son of Ngoma, first royal announcer to the King's court, have the honor, to present to you KING NEHESY AESARE, Son of Neferhotep, guardian of Kepharra's right hand, and lord of the great Kingdom of Kemet."

Ridissi had come to the end of the recital and he bowed to thunderous applause as the King, surrounded by a thick phalanx of bodyguards, stepped onto the stage through a side door that had been made especially for the occasion.

Now, with the ceremony underway, Ridissi sat down and turned his full attention to the platform. He had a clear view of the king as he lumbered over to the huge golden throne, and lowered his massive bulk into it.

He was late by six hours. It was a sacrilege that could never be overlooked. But the announcer could not say it aloud. Not if he wanted to live. At this point, no one knew as yet what the gods would decide. It was a prerogative that was theirs, and theirs alone. What Ridissi was certain of, though, was that there would be serious consequences with far reaching ramifications. The sun's wrath would be terrible to behold.

In the blistering afternoon heat, he shivered at the thought.

CHAPTER TWO

Cameroon, Central Africa

I clearly recall that I was drunk on the night that I met Jean Pierre for the first time. I had been drinking all day, going from bar to bar, and I had finally arrived at that place, which most alcoholics call 'no more money'.

It was dark by now and the drunken rollercoaster had led me to this busy side street that was all bars and loud music. There were people everywhere, work- toughened men who had come out to enjoy the evening, beautiful women floating by in colorful dresses that failed to disguise their perfectly rounded derrieres. They were drifting up and down the poorly lit street, guided by the light from the naked electric bulbs and kerosene lamps that were hanging from almost every doorway.

And the men, trying not to be obvious, were feasting their eyes on this plentiful display of feminine voluptuousness. But fortunately for these ladies the eye cannot touch what it sees. So these males, most of them determined to get much more than a visual perspective of feminine sweetness, could be seen taking the first steps, in that ancient, timeless dance, known in English as 'courtship'. And it was happening to the rhythm of irresistible *makossa ndombolo* beat, which is a classic part of the Cameroonian bar scene.

If you have never been to Cameroon, it is a country that has evolved an interesting relationship with alcohol. Cameroonians love to drink. And by that, I mean, really drink: the kind where it is normal to down five liters of alcohol every evening, and never be seen as, or called an alcoholic. Just to make a point, the drinking is so widely established that it is normal to see drivers of long distance public transport vehicles, having a beer or two at rest stops, right next to police and army officers, on duty, in uniform, sometimes armed, getting drunk with everybody else, amidst a lively discussion on soccer, women, men, music, or politics. There is even a school of thought, which argues that this central African nation owes its relative peace and stability to the calming effects of alcohol.

The next bar I chose was a little shack, right next to the spicy roast fish stall.

The bar I chose…

It was a place that specialized in very cheap, and very potent, locally distilled *afohfoh*.

An *afohfoh* shack, like the one I strolled into, is an architectural feat accomplished with building materials that are more often than not, dependent on findings from the nearby refuse dumps. And the dirt floor, which is almost constant, only adds to the crude construction, which in it self, is an accurate pointer to the quality of vino in question. Summarily put, it was a place that catered to the lowest rungs of the alcoholic hierarchy. And tonight, with the rest of my fortune down to a few coins, it was definitely where I belonged. I walked in, sat down and the bar man came over.

"Na matango or na afofoh?" I chose the former and he brought me a five-liter jug in exchange for the rest of my money. Without wasting any time I attacked the jug.

Several hours later I was sitting by myself and staring at the vessel in front of me. The contents had long been dispatched, and my imagination was now engrossed in various creative schemes, calculated to undermine normal business procedure, and get me a refill at *empty pockets cost.* So far it seemed futile and I was about to give up, when out of no where, I mean out of no where, a white man sat down at my table and offered to buy me another *one.* I was not immediately sure if he was real, or if he was just a figment of my drunken imagination. You see, white people are not so common in this country, and definitely, not in a run down matango shack in this small mountain town. Where had he come from and what did he want?

"My name is Jean. Jean Pierre Le sage," he said holding out his hand. "And I am French."

With a name and an accent like that, what else could he be? Saudi Arabian? I grabbed the hand and shook it. It was real. Firm handshake as well. And every eye in the room was on us

"I am Abanda. What do you want?"

"I know who you are," he said quietly, "And I need to talk to you."

"About what?" I was immediately suspicious. After all he was white and this was Africa. Does every one not know that our ancestors welcomed white men into our homes when they first came here? Did we not give them food, and drinks and even a place to sleep with our women? And did many of them not proceed to abuse our hospitality in every way conceivable? I had heard of horrible, horrible things that had happened because Africans had been too trusting of their smiling new friends. So, I was suspicious.

The man did not reply. Instead, from under his jacket he produced a folded copy of *Cameroon tribune* and pushed it across the rough wooden table to me. My suspicion was not allayed.

Cameroon tribune is a government published newspaper, and in my opinion, it is no more than a well-funded praise singer of a corrupt dictatorship that had elevated mismanagement to a very fine art. And little or nothing within its pages could be trusted.

"Page Five," he said. "Read it and give me a call." He pushed back his chair, got to his feet, and with all eyes in the room fastened on him, he made his way out of the bar. For a second I contemplated going after him with the questions that were sprouting in my drunken mind. But that did not happen because at that moment, the barman arrived with my drink. So, instead, I took a long swig and turned my attention to the folded newspaper that the man had left on the table.

I turned to page five and was surprised by what I found. He had circled the heading of the article he wanted me to read:

"*CHINESE DELEGATION TO VISIT CAMEROON.*" I knew about the story and it was not the source of my surprise. It was in the news and had been covered by almost every newspaper, including mine.

The morning before, the corpulent minister in charge of communications had announced in a press conference that a very high-powered delegation from China was expected in the country. The exact date was still a secret but it was hinted to be within the next couple of months. And true to form, *Cameroon tribune* had identified this as a major success, which could only be attributed to the tireless genius of his Excellency the King, I mean the President. That was to be expected. It was *Cameroon tribune* so I was not surprised.

What was surprising was the stack of newly printed One-dollar bills, which were lying next to the article, -about three hundred of them, I 'guestimated'. A piece of paper with a telephone number had been taped onto the topmost bill. Instinctively, I glanced around. The only people remaining in the bar, that is apart from myself, was a rowdy group of men who were trying to get each others money by tossing dice. They were two tables away and none of them seemed to be paying any attention to me.

I picked up the newspaper, careful to shield the action with my body, and staggered towards the door. This was not the time and place to be seen with cash. Especially dollars. Human life had been taken for far less. I was drunk but not stupid. With the paper and its contents firmly in my grip, I lurched around the few tables and emerged onto the street. No one followed me.

Outside, It was still dark but I could tell that this was the darkness that comes to announce the dawn. The music that had heralded my arrival had given way to a silence that was punctuated by the occasional drunken slur, uttered in some local dialect. I glanced up and down the street. Nothing seemed out of place; the drunks were drunk, the women had been spirited away, and most of the bars had closed their doors. Except for a few late nighters on the prowl, the street was almost empty.

My mysterious visitor was nowhere in sight. He had disappeared as quickly as he had appeared and I did not blame him. At night on these streets, he would stick out like a sore thumb. And every one knew that for some strange reason, white people in Africa always had more money, even when everyone else was dying of poverty. It was what it was. So that fact alone would make it very unsafe for him at this hour.

I crossed the street just in time to flag a lone taxi that was operating without headlamps.

"Wosai you dey go?" the driver queried in pidgin. I gave him my destination and watched him mull it for a moment. Luckily he decided that it was worth his salt and I got in. I was going home. For some reason I did not feel like drinking anymore that night. My curiosity was piqued and I couldn't wait for the sun to come up. Jean Pierre the French man had something on his mind and I wanted to hear about it.

We met for a late lunch at a small, well hidden restaurant called *Fufu*. It was a place that was mostly frequented by cheating lovers who did not want to appear on any radar. I had been there before and I knew that at this time it would be empty. Jean Pierre probably knew this too. The man did not want to be seen with me.

He was already there when I showed up. He was sitting with his back to the wall at a small corner table that allowed him to see every one that walked into the place. I walked over to his table and sat down.

"Thanks for coming," he said.

In the light of day I studied the man more closely.He looked younger than I remembered. If I had to guess, I would say forty-two. And he looked very fit. Lean and well muscled. Not an ounce of fat anywhere on him. I decided that if I had to take him on, it would be a really tough fight. That is, if I was not drunk.

"So what is going on?" I asked, signaling the waiter. "Who is the money from and what is the connection to the Chinese delegation?"

The waiter arrived, took my order and left. Jean Pierre did not place an order. He was not hungry. He was here to meet me, not to eat. In the meantime, while I ate he could tell me why he had given me four months salary. What did he want in exchange? You see, I know that the pig who thinks it's owner is overfeeding it out of love, is usually proven wrong on market day.

"The money is from me," Jean Pierre said looking directly at me, "And there is more where that came from. All you have to do is listen to the story that I will tell you. When I am done, I expect you to do one of two things: either walk away or join me."

"Join you?"

"Yes."

"In doing what?"

"You will have to hear me out first. That is not too much to ask for three hundred and fifty dollars is it?" he asked.

I could not argue with that and I did not. But now that I think of it, maybe I should have, because the French man's tale changed my life forever.

In the light of day I studied the man more closely.

CHAPTER THREE

Kingdom of kemet, 1720 B.C.

*A*bou Bakar, from the clan of Abu Ramzi, had just turned thirty when King Neferhotep, father of the present King, appointed him as Nomarch of the northernmost province. It was a decision that caused ripples along the corridors of power, because at thirty, he was viewed by many, as too young for such a position of responsibility, -especially the old guard, who felt that one of theirs would have been more suited for the position. They had argued that with all the trouble that the Aamu immigrants were stirring in the north, a man with more experience was required.

King Neferhotep had disagreed. He had reasoned that Abou Bakar was a proven fighting man, one who had risen through the ranks, and a General whose strength was legendary. Had he not killed a Nephilim? Had he not led several very successful military campaigns against the powerful Kings of Cush? Had he not taken city after city all the way to Mero? This, the King had insisted, was the kind of man who was needed to protect the northern region not only from the occasional barbaric incursion, but more importantly, from the ever increasing and disturbingly violent Aamu uprisings. He was young no doubt, but he was more than capable. Because Neferhotep had been popular and so well loved, the old King's argument had carried the day.

The Aamu, who were immigrants from the north, had begun trickling into the Kingdom a few hundred years ago, during the reign of Amenemhat the Tolerant. At that time they had all been drawn by the dream of a better life, wanting work and a place to raise their children in peace, so the citizens of the Kingdom had not found anything wrong with that. Consequently many of the immigrants had settled in the land, married locally and started a new life.

But with the passage of generations, the situation had changed. Not only had they multiplied in number, they had also become more troublesome, staging revolt after revolt so that by the time Neferhotep became King, their way of life had evolved into a full blown rebellion.

They were claiming to be victims of a state sponsored discrimination that was being enforced along racial and cultural lines. A good example of this, they insisted, was the fact that their own spiritual customs were not legally binding as per the laws of the Kingdom. And successive Kings, they argued, had ignored this problem. But what made it unbearable, they said, was the fact that even though the laws of the land claimed to recognize everyone as equals, in practice it was a very different story. Was the law not provided to protect the weak and minorities?

In a bid to diffuse the tension, the King had called for a meeting with the leaders of the Aamu community. During the meeting, he had listened patiently as Salatis, the self appointed Aamu leader, had presented their grievances.

When it was his turn to speak, the King had acknowledged most of the problems and congratulated the Aamu on their patience, before proceeding to reiterate the age old proclamation which held that it was a crime for any man, woman, or child, within the Kingdom to be discriminated against.

Then, following the proclamation, the King had gone further to explain to the Aamu leaders that they and their people were welcome to live and prosper anywhere in the land as had always been the case. But, concerning the matter of making new laws based on Aamu religious customs, he did not believe that it was acceptable. He did not think it was reasonable for the Aamu to migrate into the land and demand that the religious laws be changed just to accommodate them. He had stressed that having religious freedom within the Kingdom as stipulated by law, was good enough. "If your neighbor offers you a room in his house," the King had argued, "and while living in the room, you realize that you do not like the way your neighbor is managing his household, will you rise up against him to destroy his house? Do you not always have the option of returning to your own house, from whence you came by your own free will?"

Unfortunately the Aamu leaders had left the King's presence looking very disgruntled and positively angry. And shortly thereafter the revolts in the north had intensified to the point where the trading city of Avaris had come close to shutting down.

The King, for his part, had reasoned that if the revolt were left unchecked, it would be interpreted as a sign of weakness from the Palace. And that it would be the wrong message to send. It had therefore become imperative, not only to squash the revolt, but to do so in a decisive manner. And for that, the King had turned to Abou Bakar, who at the time was the youngest General in his army.

...the Aamu leaders had left the King's presence looking very disgruntled and positively angry...

The General remembered the episode with surprising clarity for something that had happened over two decades ago. He recalled that, immediately following the appointment he had traveled in secret to the troubled northern city disguised as a commoner. A week on the chaotic streets had yielded all the needed information.

The Aamu had been building a secret army within the borders of the Kingdom, and they were being supported by one of the bigger warlords in the north. Armed with this information, Abou Bakar had sent a fast rider back to the palace, in the capital city of Itjawy.

The message had requested for reinforcement. The King had obliged, and soon afterwards the young General had confronted the Aamu army in a bloody weeklong battle that had ended with the surrender of the immigrant force.

The King had been ecstatic. Abou Bakar had not. He had been disappointed by the fact that Salatis, the popular Aamu ringleader had managed a miraculous escape. How the man had done it, Abou could not say, but done it, he had -something that had soured the General's victory and made him wonder yet again if his own destiny had been cursed at birth.

Over the years his thoughts had frequently drifted back to that day, and the memory always left him a little uneasy. As he recalled, the immigrant army had been routed, and Salatis had been cornered in a little house on the outskirts of Avaris. So word had been sent to Abou Bakar that the Aamu ringleader was about to be taken. The General had rushed to the site, sword drawn, ready to confront and mete out justice to the man behind the trouble in the northern province.

It was a moment to which he had been looking forward, a fitting culmination to a campaign that had cost the Kingdom in blood and gold. But somehow Salatis had disappeared. Melted into thin air. One second he had been right there and the next he'd been gone. Just like that.

The General's men had sworn that he'd been in the building. They had seen him run in. No one saw him come out. And these were men that the General had known for all his life, men who had fought by his side in different battlefields, men who lived by a strict code of honor and loyalty. And they had not been lying. Of that, he was sure.

So what had happened? Jinx? Or had Salatis really transformed himself into sand and disappeared into the desert as the legends held?

Abou Bakar had wanted the man's head and he had failed to get it. Do the elders not say that when you kill a poisonous snake you have to make sure that it is quite dead by cutting off its head? As far as he was concerned, he himself had failed to get the snake's head when the opportunity had presented itself. And the reptile had survived.

As a consequence, here he was twenty years later, at the age of fifty-one, still fighting with the same snake.

Salatis had returned. With an army.

The word was that he had a bigger, well-trained, and better-equipped army with him this time. So Abou Bakar had every reason to be worried. Even now as he sat there, pretending to participate in the ongoing feast of the sun, he could barely keep still. Impatiently, he glanced at the sky. In another hour the sun would disappear below the horizon. And that would mark the end of the ceremony. Of course it was an important ceremony and he would have liked his thoughts to be more present. But a foreign army, led by a very dangerous man, was marching in secret towards the Kingdom.

The most recent sighting of the mysterious army had been south east of Gaza, in the outskirts of a small isolated desert village that was not on any map. The General knew the area in question very well. On foot, it was an eleven days journey, but he calculated that it would take Salatis slightly longer than that because the man was moving his army only at night.

How he wished he had killed Salatis twenty years ago.

After learning about this new army, Abou Bakar had left the northern province for the capital city, accompanied by his son and a few trusted men. They had ridden for three days and nights, stopping only long enough to water and rest their tired mounts. Upon reaching the city, he had rushed to the palace and demanded audience, only to be told that the King was not available! Even for an emergency! Shocking! It was the first time in his career that this had happened. And it was frightening to think that the palace was that unconcerned. But what else could it be? Was the palace involved in another emergency that was somehow more pressing than the one in the north? It was unlikely, but even if that were the case, would the King not delegate a capable official to attend to a General's pressing concerns? What was going on?

It had been a few years since he had been to the capital city, but things could not have changed that much. Or had they? And what was he to do? Become a town crier now and go shouting in the public square to warn the people? That would be madness! It would cause immediate panic and all kinds of chaos within the capital, -a situation that would play directly into the hands of the foreign army.

He had decided instead to get the ear of somebody who had the authority to bypass protocol and see the King in short notice, -the Vizier of frontier security -a man that he'd known for a long time.

He'd sent his son to the man's office to ask for an immediate audience. But once again he met a wall! The Vizier had agreed to see him, but only after the ongoing feast of the sun god, which had actually started six hours late!

Absentmindedly, the General shifted his gaze from the master of ceremony to the obese individual on the throne. Were the stories about the young King true?

Like everyone else he had heard rumors about the new ruler. But he had not paid any attention to them. Maybe he should have. Had he himself not arrived in the capital city with news that amounted to a most serious emergency? Had the King not *refused* to see him? What kind of man would stay asleep with the roof of his own house on fire?

Something was very wrong!

They had ridden for three days and nights, stopping only long enough to water and rest their tired mounts.

CHAPTER FOUR

Cameroon, Central Africa

"*I* work for my country's secret service." The French man said assessing my reaction. I did not say anything. I already suspected that he was involved in some kind of shady business, so I was not totally surprised. The disgust on my face was obvious and I did not care. In my opinion, most men like him are the scum of the earth, and I will tell you why.

Any political science teacher who is worth his salt will tell you that countries do not have friends. They have interests. And French interests in Africa are a matter of national security to the French government. This is so because without the ruthless exploitation of French speaking Africa, the French economy would be in tatters. And the French know it too. So in the fifties, when it became obvious that Africans were intent on ending the illegal occupation of foreign imperialists, most European governments, including the French, panicked. A possible scenario without African raw material amounted to a nightmare. Automatically, it became imperative that a stranglehold on African resources be maintained.

At all costs.

France and the other European imperialists quickly set in motion a scheme to ensure that the independence of the richest continent on Earth, in terms of raw materials, would be purely symbolic. It would be limited to the political, so to say, and have little or nothing to do with the economic, which was in fact the actual prize in question.

And in the process, patriotic Cameroonian revolutionaries like Felix Moumie and Martin Paul Samba, men who loved their country, men who saw through this and spoke up, were murdered in cold blood by the French secret service.

All across the continent, this same scenario played out and genuine African leaders like Patrice Lumumba, Tom Mboya and Kwame Nkrumah among others, met their deaths at the hands of foreign secret service organizations, while *corrupt and therefore manageable* individuals like Mobuto, Idi Amin, Bokassa, Ahidjo, etcetera, were propped up into positions of leadership.

At the end of the day, after the 'so called independence', the economic policy of African countries, like Cameroon for example, was never relinquished, and is still in the hands of foreign governments who have become the Kingmakers, or better still, the makers of corrupt Kings within African 'democracies'. And this, in summary, is the phenomenon that is commonly referred to as neo-colonialism, -a state of affaires that is calculated to maximally exploit poorer countries by any means necessary. Oftentimes it is carried out through the use of suppression, censorship, blackmail, terrorism, murder, assassinations, coup d'etats, and even engineered wars that make billions of dollars in weapon sales, while claiming the lives of innocent women and children.

And the foot soldiers in these Machiavellian schemes are men like Jean Pierre le Sage, -men who work, sometimes hand in hand with the mostly despicable, greedy, corrupt, vicious, thieving and ruthless traitors of the African ruling class, without whom the whole scheme would not be possible.

Now, I hope you understand my disgust for what the man represents.

I looked at him once more, shaking my head in revulsion, wondering what his cover was. He was not American so it could not be Peace Corps. *Alliance Franco-Camerounaise*? Maybe. People like him usually seemed to be part of some noble outfit or NGO that was usually involved in genuine good work.

Suddenly, my appetite was gone. I pushed aside the half finished plate of fufu corn and asked the waiter to bring me a beer. It was a little early in the day but so what! I felt like a drink and I was going to get a drink.

The bottle arrived and I proceeded to empty it in one go. Jean Pierre waited until I set the bottle down and asked for another before delving once more into his narrative.

"I am sure that you are aware of French designs on your country, *non*?" he asked. I nodded. "The status quo is one that the French government would like to maintain indefinitely. You know that, yes?" I nodded again. "But the landscape is changing. For the French government that is a serious problem. Presently, there is a very strong anti-French sentiment that has been building all over French speaking Africa. It has led to riots in Algeria, Ivory Coast, Central African Republic, Cameroon, Chad, etcetera, and the situation has been compounded by an aggressive Chinese presence which is in competition for the same resources that the French economy so desperately needs."

Jean Pierre, coughed, clearing his throat, and squinted at me. "I'm afraid to say, that the Chinese are making a head way into the continent. They have made considerable gains in Angola, they are in Equatorial Guinea, Ghana, Gabon, and countless other countries. They also are very persistent in their desire to expand, which compounds the problem. Needless to say, the French Government is furious. A lot of sleep has been lost to worries about African energy reserves that are presently in Chinese hands." Jean Pierre coughed again. "So, imagine the panic that hit the French government at the news that a high powered delegation from China is expected in Cameroon. "High powered", means only one thing; people who have the authority to sign on the dotted line. And our sources tell us that this expected meeting might lead to extensive trade agreements between the Chinese and the Cameroonian government. Meaning that, once again, China may very well replace France as the chief *exploiter* in a country that is rich in raw materials. And that, my friend, is absolutely unacceptable to the French government at this time." He paused. "A plan to undermine Chinese intentions in Cameroon has been put into motion. I fear that this plan may go so far as to *destabilize* the whole country," he concluded.

I could not believe my ears. "Destabilize? Destabilize the whole country? You mean war?"

"Yes," Jean Pierre whispered.

Was the man insane? War in Cameroon? Was he lying? Maybe, but what he was saying was not outside the realm of possibility. It had happened before. Dafur was a prime example. So what was I to do? This was more information than I could handle. Suddenly my mind was in turmoil and I needed to think. No I needed a drink. No, to think. War!

"So why are you telling me this?" I asked.

"Because I want you to get this information out. I want you to publish it in your paper. If you can do that in time, it would expose the story. Everyone will know what is in the pipeline. It may forestall the plot and war could be averted. You know, the devil is essentially a coward, yes? Expose him and he runs away. Yes?" There was truth to what he said, but it did not explain everything.

"But why are you telling me?" I asked again. "You are French. You work for your country's secret service. And you are telling me, a Cameroonian, about a secret plot that has been hatched by your own Government? I do not claim to have an understanding of French law, but does that not amount to some kind of treason?"

"People are people," Jean Pierre said looking away. Imagine what would happen if all the patriotism on the planet, from all the nations, could be turned into love for people. Just people. What a change that would make." A distant expression had come into his eyes. It was an expression that was suggestive of deep peace, -an understanding that, without more words from him, I could not fathom. The man was in contemplation and his thoughts seemed far away. After a long moment of silence, he spoke.

"Sometimes in life, for whatever reason, we human beings are subjected to particular experiences which force us to re-evaluate our belief systems," he said. "And occasionally it would lead to paradigm shifts that can transform us into new persons, with new sets of priorities."

"Is that the case with you?"

"I believe it is," he answered, looking straight into my eyes. "Twelve years ago I had an experience that, shall we say, contributed to altering my view of life." He paused for a sip of water, took a deep breath and lunged into another narrative.

"My whole family was driving on vacation from Calais to Marseille. My girlfriend was with us. She was six months pregnant with our twins. Two boys. And I was the happiest man in the world," he said with a small rueful smile. "Then, we had an accident. My father, a sixty-year-old man who had been in perfect health, had a heart attack at the wheel and the van went off the road. They all died, -my parents, my brother, my sister, my nieces, my nephew, my fiancé, our babies, everybody. And I, the only survivor, was left in a coma that lasted for weeks!" He cleared his throat. "As if that was not enough, when I regained consciousness the doctors informed me that as a result of extensive corporal damage, I would never be able to father children. That, my man, was a cruel blow. It meant that my family's bloodline would end with me. My existence had become a curse, and living in France with all the memories was a nightmare. So I resolved to go as far away as possible from France. I decided to go to a place where no one had heard about me, or my accident. And since I did not have any money at the time, I joined the French Foreign Service and thankfully they shipped me off to this country, where I buried myself into my work. But unbeknownst to me, another strange set of events was waiting to unfold."

Jean Pierre took another sip of water before going back to his narration. "Two years ago, I was driving from Douala, to meet a French operative who was stationed in the southwest province. It was at night and it was raining heavily. About a mile away from the Mongo Bridge, the car in front me, a Peugeot 504, lost control, rolled over several times and crashed into a tree. Mine, was the only other car around so I pulled over to the side of the road and ran over to check. There were five people in the wrecked car and four of them were dead. Then I noticed that the driver, a graying man, was clutching his chest in death, as if he had been having a heart attack at the time of the accident. But he was dead, so I turned my attention to the only survivor who was a woman in her early thirties. She was unconscious but I could tell that she was alive, so I pulled her out of the car first. When I saw her face, my heart almost stopped. Her resemblance to my late fiancé was shocking. From the full lips, the long eyelashes, the heart shaped face, everything was almost identical. The only difference of course, was her complexion. She was African. Needless to say, my curiosity was piqued, so I stayed in contact with her while she recuperated, visiting her in the hospital and getting to meet other members of her extended family.

...the car in front me, a Peugeot 504, lost control, rolled over several times and crashed into a tree.

In the process, I learned that the driver of the car had been her sixty-year-old father, a man who had been enjoying vigorous good health. He had had a heart attack at the wheel and the car had lost control and driven off the road. The other people in the car, who also had died, had been her mother and her brothers. Miraculously, she had survived, and all the doctors agreed that her recovery would be complete. Except for the fact that she would never be able to bear children. Now I was more than intrigued. The circumstances around the accident were just too similar to be dismissed out of hand, so I kept on seeing her after she left the hospital. We developed a friendship that was based on a mutually experienced phenomenon, which to us automatically qualified as a mystery worth exploring. So we connected on a deeper level and eventually we fell in love. Then three months ago she found out that she was pregnant!"

He stopped to survey my reaction. "Can you imagine? We were both shocked out of our minds. So we went to a hospital where a *docteur* confirmed that she was actually pregnant! With twins! Two boys. Can you believe it?" His eyes were moist and he was smiling. "*C'est incroyable!*" he whispered. "For the first time in my life, I am convinced that there is something out there that is bigger than we are; call it God if you want. This has forced me to acknowledge the possibility that my beliefs up to this point have been based on a rather shallow understanding of life. Even my job does not make sense any more. Working to undermine Cameroonian interests has become unacceptable. Now, it amounts to working against my own children and my wife-to-be. So, at the end of this month I plan to tender my resignation to the French government, marry my girlfriend, buy a little house on the beach, where we will raise our children and nurture the happiness and understanding that we have found in each other."

"If there is no war," I reminded him.

"Yes, if there is no war," he agreed wistfully. "Which is the reason why I am talking to you right now."

"And what stops you from driving across the border with your family," I asked. "You could go to Gabon, Congo, Equatorial Guinea, or back to France, where you will be out of harms way. Obviously, you can afford it."

"Yes, I can. But there is a problem. My girlfriend will not leave. Her grandparents are still alive and they depend on her for a lot of things. They are both old and she would never abandon them. She is stubborn like that. Apart from that, how do you think I would feel, living in another country with her, knowing that the rest of her extended family and friends are being wiped out in a war that I could have done something to prevent?"

"And what if we fail?" I had to ask.

"Then we would have failed," he said. "But at least we would have tried. I'd rather try and fail than not to try at all. You see, my friend, the world is full of people who fail because they never try. I used to be one of them, but not anymore."

CHAPTER FIVE

Kingdom of Kemet, 1720 B.C.

$\mathcal{M}$elenoc, High Priest of the god Kepharra, took a deep breath, exhaled slowly and closed his eyes. Immediately his hands stopped shaking and his whole body relaxed.

For a moment, as he knelt on the moist earth, he felt himself become one with the sounds of the darkness around him, -a loud silence that was punctuated by the flapping wings of hundreds of bats that were obviously angry that he had invaded the privacy of their underground dwellings.

But that was the least of the man's concerns as he raised his closed eyes and listened to the atmosphere in the cave. The silence seemed to grow louder, almost as if it were defying him to do something. Nervously he licked his lips, wishing there was some way of knowing how everything would go. He so desperately wanted nothing to go wrong that he had spent many a night thinking about this day. This moment. The moment of truth, that he, Melenoc, son of Andala, had been destined to walk through. But this did not make it any easier. He had to be extremely careful.

If the palace got wind of his intentions, it would be the end. Even the council of a thousand shamans that he had led for many rains would not stand by him. They had attempted everything to achieve what he was about to do, and failed. At great cost too. But their anger will be more about the fact that he had not intended to share the benefits of this venture. His position as High Priest of Kepharra would be forfeited and he would be accused of treason, which was a line that one did not cross and expect to be pardoned. Death would be slow and especially painful.

But it was a risk that had to be taken.

He was not going to shy away from his own destiny. Not now, not ever. Hopefully by the time anyone knew what was really going on, it would be too late. And by then, he should be in position to kill several birds with one stone, -an opportunity to teach the Kingdom a lesson that no one will be able to forget for many seasons to come. He could hardly wait. Finally, his father's spirit would feel avenged enough to sleep in peace.

For a moment, as he knelt on the moist earth, he felt himself become one with the sounds of the darkness around him,..

When he'd first been sworn in as the new head of the shamanic council, he had been a mere boy of no more than ten years of age, and it had happened because his own father, who had been the High Priest, had just died and under circumstances that had left Melenoc very traumatized.

Shortly after his father fell ill, the members of the shamanic council, of whom young Melenoc had always been in awe, had begun paying frequent nocturnal visits to the house. In silence they would file into his father's room, close the doors and be in there for hours with the ailing man, whose situation did not appear to be improving.

Then one day, while tending to his sleeping father, Melenoc had heard the familiar steps of the shamans as they walked into the house. More from fright than anything else, he'd scuttled under the bed just in time to avoid detection, as the group of frightful looking men walked into the room and roused the sick man from sleep. The conversation that ensued had shocked the boy beyond words. He had listened to his father, pleading and begging the men not to do something to him. But they had been adamant.

"The gods have decreed that you must go on this journey. It is the only way to retrieve the information that we seek."

"And what if I cannot find my way back," his father had pleaded.

"You will. We are sure of it. Once you find the stone and the elixir, the way back will become clear to you."

"But what if there is no stone or elixir? What if the wise ones were mistaken?"

"Mistaken? Do you really think so? What about all the people that you yourself have sent into the afterlife in pursuit of these same things?"

"But none of them ever came back. You all know that..."

"Probably because none of them had your wisdom or power. You are both High Priest of Kepharra and head of the shamanic council. It is the first time that one such as you has had to go."

" Please my friends, do not do this to me, please."

"Hold him down."

From under the bed Melenoc had listened to what had sounded like a struggle.

"Swallow it. If you dare to spit it out, the gods will put an eternal curse on you and yours. Think of your son."

After the Shamans left, the boy had crept out from under the bed to find his father asleep once again, -a sleep from which he had never awakened. Slowly, it had dawned on the boy that his father was not coming back. He had lost his way on the journey back from the spirit land just as he himself had feared. A week later the council of shamans had collected the body for burial.

In accordance with tradition the boy had been sworn into the office that his father had vacated. At the age of ten he had become both the head of the shamanic council and the High Priest of Kepharra. And he had hated it all. The only thing that had made it bearable was the power that the position provided and the plans he had made.

His existence as the young head of the ancient priesthood had drifted into a phase of partial seclusion, -a time during which he had made several secret attempts to connect with his father's spirit in an attempt to guide him back to life. But his efforts were met with disappointing failure, time and time again. The powers that he was rumored to have as High Priest had failed to steal his father from the cold clutches of the afterlife. For the first time he had begun to consider and question the very nature of death. Why was it so powerful? Could it be vanquished? If that were the case, why had he not succeeded?

The questions had pushed him into further action and he'd begun seeking out other corpses on which to experiment. He would slip out in the dead of night to scour the countryside where the tombs of poor citizens were readily available to those who had the courage to go looking.

What he'd found had traumatized him even more than his father's death, - rotting, smelly, maggot infested bodies which were crumbling before his very eyes. But how could that be? How could these people be in the next world when their bodies were rotting right here? Was this supposed to happen? Was it because these people had been too poor to afford the preservative process of embalming? With no answers to pacify his quest, the young High Priest had become even more consumed by an intense fear and hatred of death.

Tormented by this fear, he would stay up all night, afraid to fall asleep lest he failed to wake up. And that had only been the beginning. It had spurred him on. He had dedicated lengthy hours into researching an idea that had begun to gnaw its way into an obsession. From the temples of Kepharra to the shrine of Anubis, he had searched, searching with a determination that could only be born of extreme paranoia.

By the time he was twenty, his persistence had turned up a few treasures, chief amongst which, was an old stone tablet, about which almost no one seemed to have heard. As unfamiliar as the script had been, he had not been discouraged from working at it, even going into trances for spiritually mystical translations, until finally it had begun to make sense. By the time he'd turned forty he had found some clarity. He had known what he was supposed to do, but it had not made anything easier. First of all because, even though he'd learned what to do, he did not yet have everything that was needed to make it happen. Which was why it had taken him such a long time just to get to where he was.

Again he licked his lips in nervousness, and then quietly, almost silently, he mouthed the sacred words paying particular attention to enunciation. For a moment nothing happened and his heart did a little skip. Had he missed a word? Had he gotten them wrong? No, that was not possible! For most of his life, he had been preparing for this moment, and he had rehearsed it too many times to make a mistake now.

Suddenly the fluttering in the air was intensified and the dark cave was filled with an airy scream, a sound that bat wings would make if they were forced to fly at the speed of the rain wind. The creatures were soon screeching in pain and several wings were forcibly torn off, as muscles struggled to keep up with the unnatural increase in speed.

Melenoc felt the wetness of their bodily fluids spray across his upturned face as his nostrils were simultaneously assaulted by a disgustingly foul odor. With characteristic discipline he resisted the urge to take the hem of his flowing, priestly robe, to clean the mess. At any other time that would have been fine. But right now he had to stay focused. Very focused. Any sign that he was distracted could upset the Belial-based energy field in the cave and he did not want that. No, he did not. Instead, he forced himself to listen harder, even as the blood began pounding in his temples.

A few moments later, the thirst came.

He had been warned about it, but nothing had prepared him for the sudden dryness that wasted no time in assailing his senses. He felt it creeping into his soul even as his body began heating up. Damn! What a thirst! It was carving a hole on his tongue and inflicting arrows of need down his throat. It was even vibrating the eye of his mind! Now, that was unexpected. What to do? What to do?

His mind's eye had been opened before, but this was different. With little or no time to reflect, he decided to let the vibrations in, and the eye of his mind flew open.

As always, it took him a moment to adjust to the change in

light and scenery. With his eyes tightly shut, he could see a beautiful meadow that was bathed in bright sunlight. Green hills rolled off into the distance in every direction for as far as he could discern. There were trees of all kinds, huge ones, little ones, thick ones, and thin ones. Lianas, heavy with colorful flowers, were lazily draped on the branches, curling, twisting, and rolling onto the rich and dark earth. There were birds and animals here and there. But there were no men and there were no women. Just the happy laughter of children.

With his eyes tightly shut, he could see a beautiful meadow…

Then suddenly, a partially transparent being, bathed in blindingly bright light, materialized into the picture and beckoned to the High Priest. He had never seen anything like it. But he was not frightened. Was it not all in his mind? So he saw himself take a few steps forward as the creature turned around and began leading the way to a brook that was streaming down a lush hillside about a hundred paces away. At the banks of the stream, it indicated that it wanted Melenoc to take a drink from the shimmering waters. So the High Priest bent low, but instead of drinking he dipped his right hand into the cold water. Almost immediately his hand picked up the worded vibration in the stream. Its message was distinct.

"Drink of my living waters and forget the ancient tongue O man," the stream vibrated. "Nothing good can come from it. It is a language that is spoken only by spirits who seek power for reasons that do not prosper the soul. And men like you who are given to understand a few words, are just pawns in a game that even these spirits do not fully comprehend. Beware O man, for you can do everything, but not everything is beneficial."

Impatiently, almost angrily, Melenoc withdrew his hand out of the water and looked at it. It was dry and he was not surprised. He had chosen not to drink.

Yes, he had willingly accepted to live with the thirst, which was actually a very ancient curse and would now be with him for as long as he lived. That meant water had now become his number one enemy, and his number one friend. From tonight he would have to carry as much of it as he could, wherever he was, wherever he went, irrespective of where he was or what he was doing. It was a lot of weight to carry on a permanent basis but he had known all along that there was going to be a requirement. There always was. With the spirit of Belial, everything always comes at a price. He would carry the water. Even to bed. It was a small price to pay for what he was getting in return.

He straightened up and turned around only to realize that the creature had disappeared. So be it, he thought, impatiently. After all, it could only offer him an option that he found unacceptable. Ridiculous at this point, actually. Instead he focused his energy into the job at hand.

He willed his third eye shut and almost immediately the vibrations ceased. The sunlit picture vanished from his mind, and his spirit rejoined his body in the dark cave, on its knees, still listening to the fluttering movements all around.

The number of bats seemed to have quadrupled, and the dampness in the air was suddenly down to almost nothing. Even the airy scream had acquired a distractingly eerie octave. He did his best to ignore it, wincing in discomfort from the headache that was pounding his skull like the drumming from some demonic circus.

Then, out of the bloody whirlwind of bats, a whisper issued forth, words that had not been spoken by a human tongue for a thousand years, words that could choke a grown man to death if uttered on the wrong occasion, words that meant everything and nothing, and they were manifesting out of the melee of a thousand, foul smelling bats, and the damp but rapidly drying cave air.

'*Wayi wayi sisiloko. Ira san amaya, wayi motay, man ghar*'

The words were in the ancient tongue of the dead and Melenoc heard them very clearly, listening to each syllable and then mouthing it in repetition.

He smiled. At last everything was making sense, or almost everything. His understanding was near complete, his power was also growing, and the next move in his path was now crystal clear. There was just one more task. Just one more. And compared to everything else it was not that difficult. He felt confident that if he played his part right the items that he sought would soon be his. This was definitely the closest he had ever come to the goal. Yes. Both hands of the god Kepharra would enter into his possession before long. Once that happened, he would be in a position to perform the ultimate ritual. At that point, nothing, repeat nothing, would be able to stop him.

He felt the excitement course through his veins as thoughts of who he would become, and what he would be able to do, filled his mind. Even the King would fear him, and with good reason. Yes, he, Melenoc, High Priest of the god Kepharra would show the world what it was like to be really alive. But right now, what he needed the most was a cup of water. His thirst was becoming unbearable.

Using the hem of his robe he wiped his face clean as he prepared to get to his feet. Then, suddenly, his nostrils picked up the smell of smoke and it broke his train of thought. Was that really smoke? In a damp cave? That was odd!. Maybe the dryness from the thirst had reached his head and was beginning to play games with his senses. Carefully, he sniffed the air, realizing for the first time that it had become uncommonly dry. And yes, it was the smell of smoke! But what was causing it? Had some one lit a fire? But who? He was alone. He had made sure of that. Even his most trusted assistant, Caliph, had been sent 'to help with the preparations' for the feast of the sun. So where was the smoke coming from?

Then eventually he understood.

The swirling mass of bats exploded into a bright ball of orange flame, as the intensity of friction and heat, created by their unnaturally accelerating bodies, increased to an unbearable crescendo.

Suddenly the High Priest was in danger. The earth was trembling and pebbles and little rocks were beginning to jump off the wall. He jumped to his feet, screaming in pain as his clean-shaven head made brutal contact with the cave ceiling. The gods be damned! In the excitement he had forgotten that the cave ceiling was particularly low in these parts. He spun around, mentally berating himself for not having any water.

The burning creatures were suddenly everywhere and for a moment the huge, subterranean chamber was illuminated. The works of the great artist, Bezaleel, son of Ur, were lit up on the cave walls just as it happened during the burial rites of state officials. Just as it had been lit up so many years ago on that fateful night that he'd seen his father for the last time. But Melenoc did not have the time to look. When the time came, he would summon not only his father, but the others as well, from the darkness of afterlife, from whence they would walk anew, dedicated to a grand purpose.

Doubled over, and thirsting to death, he took off down the hall in the general direction of the stone corridor. The bats were pummeling and slapping into him from all sides. Then, one of the combusting creatures, as if guided by an unseen hand, unwittingly attached itself to the running man and ultimately his robe began to smoke. Hungry tongues of fire leaped in greedy anticipation at the thinness of his priestly fabric.

As he ran, Melenoc tried to stem the increasing tide of the flames, but it seemed in vain. No!! This was not possible! He could not die! Not now! Not after he'd heard those whispered words! Why was this happening? Had he done something wrong? Was Belial displeased that he had allowed his third eye to open for any other than himself? Or was it all a bad dream?

But the searing heat from the fire was real. The High Priest of Kepharra was being transformed into a torch. And the scream, when it finally came, matched the intensity of the heat that was slowly melting the flesh from his still running bones.

As he ran, Melenoc tried to stem the increasing tide of the flames, but it seemed in vain…

CHAPTER SIX

When the feast of the sun finally came to an end, General Abou Bakar rushed off to meet his son, Iroha. Together they walked off through the crowded streets of Itjawy, the capital city, making their way to the rendezvous with the Vizier.

Although most of the shops were closed on account of the ceremony, the streets were too crowded for horses or camels, so walking was the fastest option. As they walked in silence, Abou Bakar noted that most of the people on the streets had an air of unease about them, as if the day's event had left them worse off than they had been. The General knew that the King's late appearance would be interpreted, nation wide, as an evil omen. Tonight most families would gather around the fire of the evening meal with heavy hearts. Once again, their King had let them down. He had failed to reassure them that everything would be all right. In his speech, he had not even mentioned any of the pressing problems that were plaguing the people. Was that not irresponsible? No one expected the problems to disappear overnight. But it was crucially important for the people to know that their leaders were working very hard, under the sun and the moon, to fix the problems of the land, not worsening them by showing open disrespect for the gods as the King had done today.

How hard was it to reassure a people? Too hard? If the King could not do something as simple as that in a time of peace, how will he fare in a time of war?

"Do you see the big stone building that is fenced off at the end of the street?"

"Yes," his son answered.

"That's where we are going. When we get there, you will wait for me in the hallway while I go in to talk to the Vizier. There will be a few armed guards around, and if any of them should question you about our mission while I am inside, tell them anything but the truth. This news is boiling with heat, and it must be handled very, very carefully. You understand that don't you?" Iroha looked into his fathers eyes and nodded.

A few moments later, they were shown into the building by an armed guard.

"This way, sir," the guard said, walking down a seemingly endless corridor that was finished in white stone. He had been in here many times before, but it was protocol. He did as the man requested.

Half way down the corridor, the guard stopped and knocked on huge double doors that had been carved out of the finest *Bobinga*. They were decorated in detailed relief, depicting the profile of some high state official who must have occupied the building in the distant past.

"Someone will be here in a moment to lead you to the Vizier," the guard said. "But your body guard must wait here," he added, looking at Iroha.

"But of course," Abou Bakar agreed, nodding at his son. A moment later the huge double doors swung open and another guard appeared. Like the first, he was armed to the teeth. At least some people were ready for battle, the General thought, as he stepped through the doorway, into the huge hall that served as antechamber to the Vizier's workrooms.

"The door across the hall leads directly into the Vizier's office. He will see you in a few moments," the second guard said and disappeared into a narrow side opening.

Involuntarily the General began pacing up and down the tiled floor of the hall.

For the second time that day, Abou Bakar wondered if there was some truth to the rumor that the last King had been poisoned by his second wife, in order to facilitate the ascendance of her son to the throne of Kemet. The old King was said to have died in his sleep forty days before the ceremony of inheritance, which had been slated for the solstice of the sun.

By custom, he had been expected to 'whisper' the name of his successor to the council of Kingmakers. But by dying without the highly anticipated whisper, the crown had fallen on the head of Nehesy Aesare, the current King, who was Neferhotep's first son, born by the second wife, since the first wife had not had any children.

There had been other wives who had born plenty of children to the King. But by law, none of them could bypass the first son and ascend to the throne without the King's express wish. So Aesare had become King amidst rumors that he had not been anywhere near his father's thoughts as a possible successor.

"General?" Abou Bakar turned around. The door to the Vizier's workrooms had just been thrown open and there was a man standing there. An Aamu. That much was obvious from his features.

He was powerfully built, in his late thirties, and he carried himself with the air of one who was used to giving orders. Probably, a newly appointed personal assistant for the Vizier, the General reasoned. He had never seen the man before, of that he was sure. The livid scar that ran down the left side of his face was not something he would have forgotten.

"Yes," Abou Baker answered. "I am Abou Bakar, from the tribe of Abou Ramzi, Nomarch of the northern province, and General of the King's army in Avaris. I am here to see the Vizier in charge of border security and it is an emergency of the highest order."

"But of course my dear General. I know who you are. Your great reputation precedes you. Please, come with me." The man turned and marched back into the room. Abou Bakar walked in after him.

Once in the room the General noted that it had been transformed since his last visit. Somebody had covered the murals that King Zoser had commissioned hundreds of years ago for the walls of all public buildings. In their place were expensive wall length carpets that had been imported from the east. Even the carvings on the central pillars that were usually dedicated to the Kings of the past, had been scraped off, and polished to a smooth finish. The huge gold recliner that had occupied the center of the room with its matching table was nowhere to be seen. It had been replaced by dozens of carpets, cushions and pillows that had been arranged in a rough semi circle on the alabaster floor.

The only thing that did not seem to have changed was the huge desk, the high gilded ceiling, and the four, gold plated, life size statues of the gods, that were standing at the four corners of the room. Apart from the man who had led him in, the room was empty.

"So how can I be of service to you today, my dear General?" the man asked, turning around again to face Abou Bakar.

"By leading me to the Vizier" Abou Bakar said.

"You are talking to him," the man replied with a smile.

"You? You are the Vizier?"

"Yes," Abou Baker answered. "I am Abou Bakar, from the tribe of Abou Ramzi…

"Yes, I am. And my name is Cikatrix."

"And…and where is Itzo?"

"Itzo?" The man frowned. "I take it then that you have not heard, have you?" Abou Bakar's ignorance was apparent as the man continued. "Please, pardon me," he added, turning around once more and walking further into the room as he spoke.

"Two weeks ago, he and a few other men were implicated in a conspiracy that was directed against the throne. He was relieved of all duties. A very sad episode indeed, I assure you." The man frowned. "But enough of that. I hear that you are the bearer of vitally important news. What is this about, my dear General?"

For the first time in a very long time Abou Bakar was tongue-tied. He felt as if all of his blood had been drained from his veins. Itzo, involved in a conspiracy! He knew the man.

He'd known him for years. He was the closest thing to the father that the General had never known. So, what had happened? Had Itzo become too frustrated with the way things were going? That was feasible. Anyone who had served under King Neferhotep for as long as Itzo had done would be thoroughly frustrated with the way this new King was handling things. It was the only possible explanation that Abou Bakar could come up with. But what a time for that to happen!

The General found himself wondering if it was the hand of destiny, or if it was a convenient coincidence. He ran the events through his mind, trying to make some sense from the timing. All of a sudden, he was not sure if he should trust the newly minted Vizier in charge of the Kingdom's borders. What if the man was not who he was claiming to be? What if his loyalty was not to the Kingdom? Should he talk to the man? Why not? What were his own reasons for suspecting the man? Silently Abou reproached himself as he conceded that his own suspicion had been activated just by the man's *foreigner* look. "Go, slowly Abou Bakar," he told himself, "People are not evil or good because of their hair type." His mother used to say that a lot.

"The Kingdom is under attack," he finally said.

"What?" The expressions of surprise and shock that crossed the new Vizier's features were almost palpable. "Where did you acquire this information? Are you sure?"

"Yes, I am, and we do not have much time," he answered. "An army is marching from the north and it will be upon us any day now."

"For how long have you known about this, and why did no one alert me until now?" The man was visibly angry.

"I was in Avaris when I learned of the situation and it took me a few days to get here," Abou said. "I arrived last night, but the King was too busy to see me. So I came to you." And it took sixteen hours for you to see me, he almost added, but decided against it. This was not the time to be pointing out faults. If Salatis was going to be defeated, unity in the Kingdom was critical.

"And what did you learn about this army?" The new Vizier was now pacing around in a circle. He seemed to be deep in thought.

"It is said to be at least fifty thousand strong, it is well armed, it is marching under cover of darkness, and it is led by a very capable man. His name is Salatis."

"Salatis? The same Salatis?" Abou Bakar nodded

"Shouldn't he be an old weakling by now?"

"Not at all," Abou Bakar answered feeling the guilt of his failure of over twenty years ago. "This is a very tough fighting man whose skill is born of experience in warfare, and he must be given very serious considerations. Underestimating this man would be a terrible flaw in judgment."

"You seem to know the man very well, my dear General. Is that the case?" Abou Bakar was not sure if he detected a slight mocking tone to the Vizier's voice.

"Yes. I wrestled with him two decades ago in the battle of Avaris. I defeated his army but unfortunately he got away, a situation that I regret to this day."

"With good reason, don't you think?" the Vizier interjected. Abou Bakar felt the jab bite into him, but he did not take the bait. He was one of the few people within the Kingdom who really knew how dangerous Salatis was, and how important it was to act with speed and unity. He was not going to allow himself to be drawn into a verbal confrontation with this man.

"So now you know the urgency of my message. How soon can I see the King?" he demanded.

"Well, my dear General, I am sure that you could see him within the hour, but I am certain it would not be necessary. Coming to me was a very wise move. I shall inform the palace immediately, and I expect the army to be fully mobilized within the coming days."

With an effort, Abou Bakar masked his surprise. What if an immediate council of war was convened? Shouldn't he be there?

"With due respect to your decision, I am also the Nomarch of the northern province," the General pointed out. "And from experience, I think the King will call for an emergency meeting with the council of elders, and my presence may be required."

"Quite correct, quite correct, my dear General, but I think it is best for you to return immediately to Avaris. And I mean immediately. You must find a way to slow Salatis's advance. The King will surely understand if your presence were not a possibility, don't you think? After all, what's more important at this point than to stall the advancing army and give us a little time?"

As much as he did not like it, Abou Bakar could not argue with the logic. There was a small army that was permanently stationed in Avaris and its primary duty was to keep the desert trade routes of the north open and safe for the camel caravans, not to stop an advancing army like Salatis'. But at this moment that was of no import. He would do what needed to be done, and hopefully the effort would be effective.

So back to Avaris he must immediately return, -except for one little thing that needed to be taken care of right here in the capital. He saluted the Vizier, turned on his heels and marched out of the office.

Vizier Cikatrix watched him as he walked out. He had heard many stories about the General. But there was no time to dwell on them. A gentle cough interrupted the Vizier's thoughts and he spun around, his hand inches away from the hilt of a sword that was hanging from his waist.

"When did you get in here?" he whispered, hating the fact that he had been taken unawares.

"You are slow my friend. Too slow. You would be dead by now if that was my intention," the intruder whispered without moving.

He was a very slim man, almost to the point of emaciation, and he was standing next to the opposite wall. It was not obvious how he'd gotten into the room or for how long he'd been in it. It did not seem as if he was about to volunteer any information, either. His snake's eyes were focused on the Vizier. His hawk-like features gave nothing away.

"So you think that the holy one is just an old weakling?" His voice was a whisper.

"But of course not, my dear Hasim. I had to play the part. It was important."

"Important? To dishonor the one in whose hand your future lies? I am sure that he would understand if I were to relate this to him, don't you think?"

The Vizier went silent. He had a history with Salatis so the threat was not missed. He'd also heard stories of things that had happened to other people who had been 'disrespectful' to Salatis, stories of eyes that had been gouged out, tongues that had been cut off, and limbs that had been hacked off while the victims screamed themselves unconscious.

"Please Hasim. I swear upon the manhood between my dead father's legs. I meant no disrespect to the holy one," the Vizier said. "I am just a servant at his service and his wish is my pleasure."

"Is that so? Then why is the King awake?" Hasim's voice was a bare whisper.

The Vizier swallowed hard, barely concealing his nervousness. "How am I supposed to know that, Hasim. You yourself said a man would meet me and hand me a little pouch. I was to pour the contents into the King's cup of wine. That's what happened. I risked my neck and did as the Holy one asked. If the King is still awake, blame your shaman whose medecine is not strong enough!"

Hasim digested this information in silence. He did not like or trust this man. He felt that the man was lying but he could not be sure. It was known that royal babies, especially those with a chance of sitting on the throne, were fed very, very minute quantities of the most lethal roots, bark, and leaves. Some children fell ill, and a few even died, but most usually survived and were introduced to bigger doses of thesame substances as they got older. By the time they were adults most of them had deveveloped a high tolerance for poisons that would kill everyone else. It was protection against poisoning a King. "Salatis will not be happy about this," he said. "You can be sure that the matter will be investigated and the shaman will pay dearly. If he is found to have provided an unsuitable potion."

"If? But my dear Hasim," the Vizier implored, "who else could it be? Potions and doses are complex secret information known only to shamans and I am not one. My loyalty is with the holy one. Please, convey my greatest respects to him." He, bowed low holding out an outstretched palm. In it, was a little bag. Hasim stepped forward and scooped up the bag, raised it to his nose and sniffed.

"Hmm, Nubian gold."

Greedily he untangled the rope that secured the contents of the little pouch and peered into it. He grunted in satisfaction and the bag promptly disappeared. "Maybe the holy one will be passuaded that it is not your fault," he said with a wolfish smile, "especially if you take care of a little matter that he has had on his mind for a few days now."

A little matter? Another little matter? The Vizier recoiled inwardly, careful to keep his expression neutral. Hasim was like a mamba, -very treacherous. One never knew with him. He just hoped that the *little matter* on Salatis's mind was not as risky as the last one. He shuddered at the thought. If the King ever found out that the reason he had not been able to get up in time for the feast of the sun was because he had been drugged, everything would be over. Not even the fact that the Vizier had secretly replaced the potion that was intended to kill the King, with one that went no further than to cause *the sleep of near death,* would help.

Hasim stepped forward and scooped up the bag, raised it to his nose...

So instead of death the King had not been able to wake up from sleep on the day of the sun! His breathing had been normal but no amount of rousing would get him to open his eyes, to speak, or to sit up. It had thrown the royal palace into absolute disarray. The medicine men, shamans, and soothsayers had all been baffled. They had finally decided that for some reason the sun god was unhappy, and that the King's condition was a symptom of his anger.

"I am always at the holy one's service and I feel very honored that he has chosen me to serve him," the Vizier said. "I will do whatever he asks of me."

"Good," Hasim said, jumping up and catching hold of an overhanging bar. "Very good. I shall get back to you." He swung himself onto another bar, and then into the rafters and was gone.

Cursed be your mother! The Vizier swore in silent rage.

Cursed be the day you were born. And cursed be your whole blood line he almost spat out, for treating me like a coward and a cheap, common slave. Why? Have I not suffered enough at your hands? You will even take my life in a moment, if you realized that I see myself more as Kemetian than Aamu. Yes, I do. A Kemetian living within the bitter curse of discrimination and inequality, but a Kemetian all the same.

For a moment the Vizier felt his anger change directions and move from Hasim and his liege to the Kemetian Palace.

Most Kemetians, although more accepting, still insist on treating Aamu people as less than themselves. Yes, as less than themselves, almost as if the Aamu life in me was of lower quality and as such worth less than any other life on earth, the man thought. And what is their reason? The texture of my hair! The color of my eyes! It was a strange thing. And it affected every aspect of his life. Especially relationships. The one with King Aesare was a good example.

Aesare was the one individual who actually had the ability to bring discrimination to an end in the Kingdom. As young men growing up together, that is before he became King, Aesare had promised repeatedly that he would do just that, if he ever ascended to the throne. The scarred Vizier, who was not Vizier then had believed him, although he had also known that the chances of the young prince being chosen as a replacement for his father were slim. So slim, to the point where he had felt it necessary to intercede with secret sacrifices at the feet of his own ancestral gods. Without Aesare's knowledge, he had entreated these gods to allow for a King who would use the power of the throne to destroy division, discrimination, and inequality from the Kingdom of Kemet, so that he himself and those who looked like him could be treated fairly and equally. The gods had listened.

Upon the death of Neferhotep, Aesare had become King. But the greatest revelation thereafter was that the new King had begun to change his mind about a lot of things he had promised to do. The Scarred one had not believed it. Not at first. How dare he go back on his word?

He had confronted the new King, something that he could do and get away with only because of their close friendship. But his friend, who was now King, had just laughed.

"Common Cikatrix," Aesare had said, calling the scarred one by his first name, during one of their first meetings, after he became king. "Things are not that simple."

"What do you mean things are not that simple?" Cikatrix asked. "No one said it was going to be easy, but you on the other hand, have not even tried."

"Oh, but I have, and no one will stand behind me."

"You don't need anyone to stand behind you to make this happen Aesare. You are King."

"Yes, I am, but I cannot govern alone. I have to work with others, and if these others do not like what I am doing, it might cause a lot of problems that we do not need."

"But you gave your word, Aesare. You made this promise to me that if you ever became King you would extend equality to my people. And you can do it too, Aesare. You have the power. Think of all the good it would do. Think of how popular it would make you."

"Popular? With whom? The Kingmakers? The councils? The elders? You know as well as I do that these are the most powerful people in the Kingdom and they are also the most conservative. They are the ones who decide if a man is to be King, and for how long he will sit on the throne. And they are not so willing to let go of a status quo that holds and props them up high above everybody else. Its about control, money, and power. They will fight me if I should try anything that may alter this state of things. The most they will do, is allow me to talk about it as if something was being done, but in reality, they will kill me first before they see the change that you are asking of me."

With time, over several conversations with the King, Cikatrix finally began to wonder if he would ever get the King to help the Aamu immigrants in any meaningful way.

It had therefore become necessary to start looking elsewhere for the salvation that his people so desperately desired. Which was the only reason why he had found Salatis' proposal to be interesting enough to the point of accepting an invitation to attend a secret meeting that had been set up on behalf of the man, -Cikatrix's first meeting with Hasim. How he wished he had known what he had been getting into. But it was too late now. He was trapped. And getting out of it would require some very difficult decisions.

Cikatrix's first meeting with Hasim.

CHAPTER SEVEN

Cameroon, Central Africa

I was transfixed. As fantastic as Jean Pierre's story was, I knew that the man was speaking from the heart. I could see it in his eyes. How I wish I did not believe him. But I did. War was imminent! Almighty greed was about to marinate my whole country in blood. And all of a sudden I was about to be in the middle of an attempt to prevent it. It was madness! I was just a simple, poor cartoonist! What could I do? But then, what would I not do to prevent war? Of course I would help. This was my country! My whole family was living here. This was our home! What kind of man will stand by while beasts went about destroying his own farm? I would do whatever I could. How effective that would be, was a totally different matter.

"You can count on me," I said, knowing that I still had to check on the story. "But first, I need to hear the rest of what you have to say. I also want to meet and talk to your girlfriend. I must know everything about the plot. I need to know what you know. All of it!"

Jean Pierre let out a sigh of relief. "But of course I will tell you everything right away. Want another beer?" I shook my head in the negative "Do you play chess?" He asked.

"No I don't."

"You should take it up sometime. It is a game about baiting, strategy, and manipulation. At its best, a good player could make a move, which creates a domino effect that has the capacity to bait his opponent into unwittingly committing suicide. The key is that the opponent has to be caught off guard, so that by the time he realizes what is going on, it is too late. So he ends up becoming an ignorant participant in his own slaying. The French plot is along those lines." He coughed. "The good news is, such plots are relatively easy to derail if one has foreknowledge and acts in advance. Which is what we must do. But first, let me tell you about the whole plot."

"Ok," I said apprehensively. I could already see myself drawing an elaborate cartoon story about whatever information Jean Pierre was getting ready to divulge. He took another sip of water and glanced around furtively.

A man and a woman had come into the restaurant.We both watched them survey the almost empty room, select a table at the opposite end, and sit down with their backs to us. Nevertheless, Jean Pierre leaned closer, using both hands to shield his mouth.

"The U.S. secretary of state will be paying a visit to the English speaking provinces of Cameroon on Friday the tenth." His voice was a whisper and his lips were hardly moving.

"Yes, I know about that. It is in ten days."

"Yes, it is," he agreed. "She will be assassinated."

"Oh my God!"

"Yes. And her assassin will evaporate in the commotion that will be created by the shooting. But his abandoned weapon will be found," he paused. "It will be of Chinese make, and it will have the alleged killer's finger prints all over it."

"Really? And these fingerprints?"

"Will belong to a Cameroonian national. His name is Yao. Balthazar Yao."

"Balthazar Yao? The Balthazar Yao? Of the SCNC?" I was stunned. "Yao is planning to assassinate the U.S. secretary of state?"

Jean Pierre shook his head. "I did not say that," he whispered. "I said the weapon used in the crime will be found, and that it will have Yao's fingerprints on it. I never said he would be the gunman."

"This is crazy! With Yao in the middle of it, everything will be turned upside down."

"Which is precisely the point," he agreed.

In order to understand the S.C.N.C. (Southern Cameroon national congress), a little bit of Cameroonian history is necessary and I will make a summary of it.

When Africa was butchered in 1884, Germany acquired Cameroon. But in 1918, when the Germans lost WW I, Cameroon was seized from them by Britain and France, who divided the territory and offered it to themselves.

They proceeded to impose and enforce their respective cultures on the territories, in line with the colonial policy of *divide and rule*. This was so effective that the people in the English part of Cameroon began seeing themselves as essentially different from their brothers in the French occupied section and vice versa.

This division was so serious that in 1960, it was only the French occupied section of Cameroon that became independent, adopting the name '*La Republique du Cameroun*', while English speaking or Southern Cameroonians, were still fighting to be free.

At that point, for unknown reasons, the British decided that the only way that English speaking Cameroon would be allowed to achieve political sovereignty, was to merge into one of its already independent neighbors: French Cameroon also called *La Republique*, which is to the east, or Nigeria to the west.

English speaking Cameroonians protested vehemently against this option. They argued that it was necessary for the territory to become independent by itself first, before merging with any of its neighbors. That way, the territory would have the leverage and respect associated with *political independence*, which would be a critical factor in negotiating the terms of uniting with either *La Republique du Cameroun,* or Nigeria. The British refused.

So in 1961, in order to be free, a dependent English speaking Cameroon was forced to be absorbed into *La Republique du Cameroun*, which already had Ahmadou Ahidjo, a hand picked stooge, as its president.

From day one, English-speaking Cameroonians were treated as the junior partners in this two state federation. They were continually reminded that their freedom was *gifted* to them by *La republique*, who had the grace to allow them to 'board the ship of independence' which it had procured. This logic became the foundation upon which French-speaking Cameroonians justified their control, which they maintain to this day in the executive, the judiciary and the legislative branches of government, -powers that give them the ability to partition the national cake along unequal lines. Of course, all of this is greatly resented by English speaking Cameroonians, whose part of the country seems to be richer in natural resources. It was just a matter of time before the resentment transformed itself into a movement.

The movement goes by the name of S.C.N.C (Southern Cameroon National Congress) and within it is a militant faction that favors secession as a means of separating from the much hated, French sponsored dictatorship. At present, the man who is alleged to be the leader of the secessionist faction is Balthazar Yao, an individual who has given new meaning to the word 'enigma'.

If I recollect correctly, Balthazar Yao was born in 1965 into the household of the Bororo chief. Being an extremely intelligent child, he had graduated from high school in record time, and had gone on to Cambridge to read law on scholarship. But a few months into the program he had asked to change to philosophy. So he became a philosophy major. But that too, did not last.

At the end of the first year, he went home for the summer vacation and informed his parents that he planned not to go back to Cambridge. Instead, he was going to Mali. To study History at the first ever university to be established in the history of human civilization: The University of Timbuktu.

Against his father's wishes, he took off for Mali and spent the next half-decade, poring through ancient, dust covered manuscripts, that had been abandoned to themselves. At the end of his sojourn he returned home without any diploma or degree to show for his studies. But he was a changed man. His parents could tell that something had happened to their son. He showed scant interest in the things in which other young men of his age group were involved. He would lock himself up in his room and read all day. Books by, and about people like Patrice Lumumba, Kwame Nkrumah, Nelson Mandela, Felix Moumie, Mahatma Gandhi, Ernesto Che Guevara, Emiliano Zapata, George Washington, Pancho Villa, Sojourner truth, Mao tse tong, Martin Luther King, Karl Marx, Malcolm X, Rosa Parks, Marcus Garvey, Abraham Lincoln, Lech Walessa, Dubois...

Then, one day, he came out of his room and informed his parents that he was going on another journey, and that he would be leaving the next day. He did not give any reasons for the trip, he did not request any financial assistance, and he did not provide a destination.

He was gone for almost seven years, during which time his family could only wonder about his whereabouts and hope that he was all right. Some say he was in China, others say the Soviet Union, but no one seems to know for sure where the man was. When he returned home he shocked the Bororo Chiefdom by letting it be known that his place was no longer in the palace. Of course, he was not renouncing his assigned duty in service of the Bororo tribe. He just felt that this duty went far beyond the borders of Bororo land, to include all of the Country, and possibly the continent.

Then in '89' he made national news as the brains behind the biggest political rally in Cameroon since its independence. The sheer size and scope of the rally took everyone by surprise and suddenly every news organization in the country wanted to interview Yao. The only journalist, who got the opportunity, reported that 'there was something very lethal about the man'. It was a quote that would make more sense when Yao's name began appearing more frequently in the news, and usually in connection with the militant faction of the S.C.N.C.

Timbuktu.

"So, the French are planning to set Yao up as the assassin?"

"That's correct," Jean Pierre confirmed.

"But why?"

"Why? What do you think will happen after the shooting?" he demanded rhetorically. "Think for a moment. Every news network on the globe will be on the story: The U.S Secretary of state, a woman, a mother of three young children, has been shot and killed in Cameroon, by a Chinese sponsored Cameroonian rebel movement. It will be interpreted as an act of war and

Washington will be screaming for blood. International sympathy will be overwhelming but not as loud as the outrage. Cameroon will suddenly find itself in the spotlight and the pressure will be intense. Faced with this scenario, the Cameroonian government will do two things: first of all, the visit of the high-powered Chinese delegation will be called off. Immediately. You know, no one wants to be seen walking arm in arm with a man who may be implicated in a murder, especially if the victim is a US Secretary of State. Secondly, a media covered military operation will be launched. An armed battalion will be deployed into the rain forest to put an end to Yao's shenanigans. It will be a strong and convincing signal to Washington that the Cameroonian Government did not approve, and was not in any way, shape, or form, a participant in the conspiracy that took the Secretary's life. The army will head into the jungle with strict orders to find Yao's camp, destroy it, and bring back the man himself, dead or alive." He paused. "The only problem is that Yao will be ready for them. A few days before this, he will have entered into possession of enough weapons to give the Government forces a run for their money."

"And your government would have supplied Yao with these weapons, I take it?"

"Technically, no." Jean Pierre replied. "It would be more appropriate to say that the French government will orchestrate things in a way that would put Yao in a position to possess these weapons."

"Oh I see! Yao will have no idea about the benefactor's real identity. Correct?"

The French man confirmed with a nod. "The quality and quantity of the weapons will enable the rebel leader to deliver such a formidable blow on the Government forces that they will be forced to retreat. At about the same time, the mainstream media, probably led by RFI (Radio France International), will begin broadcasting that it has secret new information to the effect that, the Cameroonian rebel leader was planning a huge push, all the way to the capital city. As expected, this will cause a stampede within the Cameroonian government, and the President, in panic, will run to France for immediate military assistance.

The French government will have foreseen this, and will be ready to deliver the *Coup de grace*. Naturally, they will convey a willingness to assist their former-colony-in-crisis. But the assistance will come at a cost. An elaborate set of documents will be forwarded to the Cameroonian head of state for signature. Among many things, it will contain an article which will nullify any possibilities of an economic understanding with China, and make France the sole player in Cameroon for the next fifty to one hundred years."

"And what if for some strange reason, the Cameroonian head of state suddenly decides not to sign." I knew it was unlikely. The Cameroonian strong man was not of the same cloth as Gadhaffi or Mugabe. But it was the next logical question. Jean Pierre did not even hesitate with his answer.

"Yao's secret benefactor will suddenly furnish him with enough firepower to actually sack the government. By this time, Yao too, would have signed documents specifying and acknowledging the debt which will be owed to this mysterious military supporter, -to be paid once he ascended to the presidency. Nothing is personal." Jean paused again. "But if the Cameroonian head of state should choose to cooperate, then the rebel leader will suddenly find himself under severe firepower from a foreign air force with no visible emblems. His good benefactor will suddenly evaporate, his men will be routed, and all of their positions and troop movements will suddenly be known to the government forces." He finished with a knowing look. "So how soon can you get this story published? It has to be soon, really soon, like yesterday."

I thought about it for a moment. "It will be in the next issue that's coming out on Thursday, if I can pull it off."

"You have to," Jean Pierre whispered leaning back. "Once the story comes out, the whole operation will be suspended. First of all, the Secretary's visit will be cancelled, and the French will furnish a spirited denial of being involved. Just make sure that there is no doubt about the identity of the main players in the plot. And speaking of which, here is something that will help." Jean Pierre slid an envelope across the table to me. I picked it up and looked in. It contained the picture of a Caucasian male of about fifty years old. He was tough looking, and sporting a moustache that would have made Stalin envious. But what caught my attention were his eyes. Although he was smiling, they were cold.

"Who is he?" I asked.

"That is Yves Mammon, but he goes by several other names. He is the man who is charged with overseeing the whole operation. He is also my boss. My girlfriend took that picture at the Seme beach. He did not know that he was being photographed." I put the picture in my pocket and got up from the table. I had work to do, and time was of the essence.

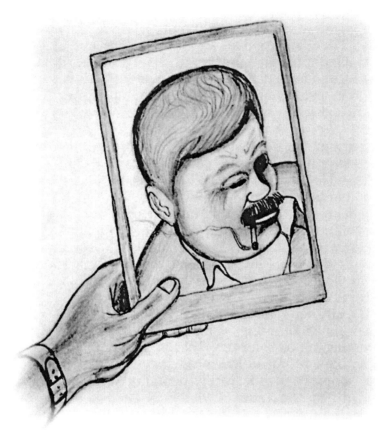

He was tough looking, and sporting a moustache that would have made Stalin envious.

CHAPTER EIGHT

Kingdom of Kemet, 1720 B.C

$\mathcal{A}$bou Bakar looked at his son and he felt himself swell with paternal pride. He was everything that a father could wish for. At the age of twenty-three Iroha had grown taller than his father and was as strong as a bull. He was the General's only child and had been born to him by S'sara, the only woman that he had ever loved, -a damsel from the Bororo tribe.

Even now, as he visited memories of her, he felt his heart contract. He'd known several women but to him, she would always be the most beautiful by far. And he still missed her after all these years. What a woman! He recalled their first meeting and as always, it brought a bittersweet feeling with it.

In those days, the Bororos, a tribe far beyond the southern border, had begun hijacking trade caravans from the distant forest Kingdoms, and it was becoming a problem.

Then one day, the King's ambassador to the Yoruba Kingdom, a land on the other side of the Sahara desert, had been taken hostage while traveling on a mission to the forest people. The Bororo had taken the man and were asking for a huge ransom. The King had turned to Abou Bakar.

It was one of the few missions that, to the General, had been fully successful. Nothing had been jinxed. Every detail had been executed exactly as planned.

He had attacked the village where the King's messenger was being held, and, as expected, the Bororos had been caught off guard. They had not imagined that a punitive force could come this far south into the forest, and on such a mission. In fact, it had never occurred to them that the Kemetian King would not allow himself to be disrespected. They had calculated that the Kingdom was so rich that the King would not think twice about paying the ransom. Other Kings had complied before, so they were not expecting anything different. And it had left them open to the surprise attack, which the General had implemented in the early hours of a rainy morning.

After they realized what was happening, the Bororo put up a

heroic fight. But it had been to no avail. In a bid to avoid unnecessary bloodshed, the Bororo chieftain sent one of his officials to negotiate surrender. And the official had been a woman.

In a surprise move, he had attacked the village...

She had been the most beautiful woman that the General had ever seen, a woman who carried herself with the grace of the desert breeze, walking, head held high, as if she were the queen of all the earth. Abou Bakar the general had been struck. No, he had been smitten. He had found himself deciding that the rescued man was too sick to travel, a perfect excuse for postponing his departure from the forest people. He and his men stayed in the village for a full month. During this time, he had found an excuse to see her everyday, usually to renegotiate or iron out some invisible clause in the terms of surrender.

At first, his advances had amused her, but as the days went by, she had realized that the man was deadly serious and he was not planning to give up on her. He was even writing poetry to her. She consulted her father on the matter and he gave her his permission. The General was a good man with a good heart, her father had said. Did he not treat them with respect? Had he not given the Bororo very lenient terms of surrender? If he did not have a wife already, then he was welcome to make himself her husband. That is, if she was willing to accept his hand.

Abou Bakar married S'sara in a traditional Bororo celebration that had lasted a whole week, and it had planted a seed of peace between the forest people and the Kemetian Kingdom. By the time Abou Bakar and his men set off for home, his bride was pregnant with their son whom she had insisted on naming 'Iroha', after her own father.

Now, as he walked towards Iroha, he could see so much of his mother in him, his proud stature, the dark copper of his skin, the beautiful almost effeminate lines of his face, his easy smile, details that reminded him of how much he had loved his wife. Or better still, how much he still missed her.

For the thousandth time he wondered why the gods had decided to take her away from him, -especially the circumstances that had surrounded her departure.

At the time, Iroha had just turned two and Salatis's raging rebellion had shut down the northern city of Avaris. When King Neferhotep had asked Abou Bakar to go and deal with the problem, the General had insisted that his new wife remain in the capital. She had not liked the decision but he had put his foot down. In his mind, that had not even been an option. The north would be too dangerous for a woman and a little boy. He had reasoned that it would be better for her and the boy to stay in the capital city where it was safer, until the situation in Avaris was stabilized. At which point he would come back for them.

When the fighting ended, he journeyed back to the capital where a festive delegation had been waiting for him outside the city gates of great Itjawy. He was led directly to the royal palace where high-ranking members of the government had gathered in a special feast to honor him. Everything had seemed fantastic except for one thing; his wife and son were nowhere to be seen. Had the King forgotten to invite them? That was very unlikely. So what was going on? Upon inquiring, the royal butler informed him that his wife and son had been sent for, but in the meantime, the King had requested that the General appear in front of the throne.

He was led down the wide aisle amidst thundering applause from the seated dignitaries, to stand before the Monarch. It was at that point that a strange thing happened. The King rose from his throne and stepped off the dais. He walked to where Abou Bakar was standing and in the presence of all the seated officials, he put his arms around the General in an embrace! And everyone held their breath.

"I am sorry," Nerferhotep whispered.

It was common knowledge, that, to come into any kind of physical contact with the King in public was a sure way to ask for death. Even the General had been baffled. Was this how the King was repaying him? By asking for his life? Was that what the oracle had decreed? That his name be honored for all times in this way? If that was the case, what could he do? Challenge the gods and the King? How would that help? He was just one man and he would accept his fate like the man that he was. All he would ask, was enough time to look once more into his wife's eyes, and say good-bye, both to her and their son.

Then, the King had stepped back, raised his left hand and touched him on the right shoulder with the royal scepter. Everyone breathed a sigh of relief. A touch on the left shoulder was the touch of death. But the right shoulder was reserved only for those in very high standing with the palace. It forgave all sins and crimes, including the sacrilege of coming in physical contact with the King's body.

"I am so sorry my son," the monarch repeated again. "So very sorry for what the gods have done."

Abou Bakar had looked into the King's eyes and instinctively known that S'sara, the woman he had married, the woman who had born him a child, was no more.

They had found her and her lady in waiting, burned beyond recognition by a fire that had consumed their home. His son had survived only because he'd been playing away from the house.

No one had been able to explain the source of the fire. Not the guards, not the servants, not the neighbors, not a single soul. Maybe, the desert winds had blown over a candle. Maybe, one of the cooks had forgotten to douse out the cooking fire. Maybe, a servant had mistakenly spilled oil on the blinds that covered their bedroom walls. Maybe, the gods had decided to punish him for a sin that he could not remember. Or, was it that he just happened to be a man whose best efforts were predestined to always bear seeds of bitterness?

His pain lasted for many moons. It was beyond anything he could have imagined, a pain that consumed his soul and transformed his spirit into an inferno of torture. A pain that banished the sleep from his eyes and filled them with tears of sorrow and helpless frustration, a pain that took away his appetite for food and replaced it with a seemingly unquenchable thirst for wine.

Why had he insisted that S'sara stay in the capital city? Would she not be alive today if he had allowed her to come with him to Avaris?

In his wine-sanctified grief, he had judged and condemned himself a thousand times, usually with imagined thoughts of her last moments flooding his mind. He would see her waking up to the smoke of the fire, coughing and choking as she struggled to breathe, tears filling her eyes, her lungs exploding in pain as she tried to get her bearing, making a desperate dash for the hallway, only to be pushed back by the angry flames, thinking of her son and the man she loved, screaming out his name and willing him to appear and save her, and finally realizing that she was going to die all by herself in a foreign land and far from her own people. These images would flash through his mind and bring tears to his eyes. Every time. And it had gone on and on and on, night after night, while his young son slept.

Then, one day he fell asleep just as the sun was rising and he had a very different vision. In it he had seen his wife in the after life. And she was looking radiantly beautiful, and bathed in a peaceful glow.

In the vision, she explained to him that the afterlife was, in fact, the real life, -eternal life. And life on earth was but a passing dream, a very short dream that lasted for only one night within the context of eternal existence where she now lived. Birth on earth, she told him, marked the beginning of this dream as one fell asleep in eternity, while death on the other hand was the process of waking up from that sleep.

So in her case, she had awakened from sleep to the realization that her life on earth, from birth to death, had been but a night's dream in eternity. Her life with the Bororo tribe, meeting and marrying him, having a son, dying in the fire, were all part of that dream. And though it had seemed to last for ever, it had really been quite short, - only one night's dream in eternal existence, -just like the dreams that people on earth had. While they happened, the dreamer would sometimes think that they were real. But in the morning it becomes obvious that it was just a dream that had lasted for just a few moments.

She had further explained that the people in the world where she now lived, -the eternal plane, were transported down to the earth in these dreams in order to experience these moments during which they were called upon to make character-formatting choices. What was most important while we experienced this dream, she added, was to honor God, to respect all the things he had made, to love our neighbors like ourselves, and to do unto other people as we would like them to do unto us. That, she told him, was the ultimate lesson that God wanted every person to learn, -a lesson that shattered pride and ego, and instilled humility and love into man, -a sinequannon for advancing into the realm of divine truth.

Then the vision ended, and Abou Bakar had awoken to a newfound understanding. His grief had evaporated and so had his thirst for wine. Once more, he had become a father, a father that his son had almost lost to grief. And he had made it up to the boy, taking him wherever he went, teaching him everything he knew, and making him into his best friend. Since then, they had been through a lot together, in times of war and in times of peace, and every moment had been a treasure.

Now as he walked towards Iroha, he marveled at how fast the boy had grown. He had become a man almost overnight. And it had happened right in front of his own eyes. He was sure that wherever she was, the boy's mother was proud of the man that he had turned out to be.

Iroha sensed his father's presence and turned around. He could tell from the General's walk that the meeting had not gone too well. His posture had been worried when he had gone in. Now he was tense. Almost as if he could smell something suspicious in the air.

"Lets go," the General said, leading the way out of the building. Iroha saluted and fell into step. The man was his father and he loved him with all of his soul. But he was also his General. And in public protocol had to be respected especially when the General was on mission for the Kingdom.

Once out of the building, the General turned to his son. His eyes were worried. "I want you to gather the men and prepare for a return trip to Avaris. We leave at midnight. Get fresh horses and supplies. Then wait for me under the baobab trees outside the north city gates. And keep out of sight," he whispered. "I think something is afoot."

"Shouldn't I come with you, father?" Iroha asked.

The General hesitated, taking in a very deep breath. The question was familiar in an uncomfortable way. "No my son. I will be all right. Just keep your eyes open and be ready to ride when we meet." Then father and son embraced, and the General turned on his heels and disappeared down the dark, crowded street.

As he walked, he noted that even though a few more shops and taverns had opened their doors, the atmosphere of celebration that had been expected in the streets on this day was half hearted. It was obvious that there was an invisible cloud hovering over the city. Just as he had predicted, rumors that the sun god was angry had spread like wild fire. Salatis would be thrilled if he were to find out that his army was marching on a Kingdom that was waiting to experience divine wrath, he thought bitterly.

He turned around the corner and realized that he was going the wrong way. Impatiently, he corrected his trajectory and quickened his pace. The King's prison was at the end of the next street and that was where he was going. The story about Itzo's demise was a little strange, and he intended to talk to the man himself; learn more about the conspiracy of which he was alleged to have been part.

He found the road that he was looking for and turned into it. It was dark, forlorn, and apart from the huge prison-house, which was still some distance away, there were no other buildings in sight. There were no people about, either.

About a thousand paces away, he could see the entrance of the building. It was clearly highlighted by several burning torches that served the purpose of a lighthouse to those like himself, who wished a nocturnal visit.

He'd been to this facility before, once to demand the release of one of his officers, a man who had been wrongfully implicated in a crime that had had nothing to do with him. And on another occasion, to deposit the arrested leader of a legendary Nubian gang, who had masterminded a failed plot to rob the King's treasury in Simbel. He vaguely remembered both visits, which had occurred during the day, so there had not been any burning torches as was the case now. Nonetheless, he recalled that this particular jail was reserved for those who were considered to be a serious threat to the smooth running of the Kingdom. And once in there, it was quite difficult for a man to

69

get out, and in most cases it required a pardon from the King himself, hence the name, *the Kings prison.*

He started down the road, squinting into the darkness to make out his way. If he remembered well, there were a few date palms around here and he did not want to collide into any of them.

Wait! Was that a movement? Were those footsteps?

From the corner of his eye, he picked out the silhouette of a running man about twenty paces to the right! The man was bent double, his weapon was drawn, and he was advancing rapidly towards the General.

"Who goes there?" he asked, raising his voice and bringing his left hand to rest on the hilt of his sword. "Identify yourself and state your business." Instead, the crouched figure picked up speed! It was an attack! Instinctively, the General pirouetted on his toes, spinning his whole body around in a quick graceful movement that culminated in a powerful flick of his right wrist. The tiny blade that was unleashed whistled angrily through the night air as it flew towards its mark. He did not wait to see the result. He had done this too many times to miss. Even in the dark.

He spun to his left, somersaulting once, knowing that a highly sharpened object had flown at high velocity through the space where his body had been a moment ago.

He came up on his left knee, swinging his drawn sword at the same time in a low, wide arc. He knew there was going to be a man there. There was. The weapon made contact, slicing clean through both knees and the man screamed in pain, shattering the silence of the night.

By the time the man's body hit the ground, Abou Bakar was up and running. He charged a third man, feinting to the left and deflecting the thrusting scimitar that would have severed his head from his body.

The man swung again barely missing the General, who parried with a horizontal double swing of his own. His attacker jumped back and tripped over the body of his fallen comrade. It was more of an opportunity than the seasoned General could ask for. He seized the opening and his blade took a hefty bite. Another scream. Right arm was completely severed from shoulder and in unreal slow motion it fell to the ground, fingers still tightly clasped in their intention, to the handle of the scimitar. The man screamed again, more from shock this time than pain. Desperately he clutched his right shoulder. The superfluous flow of blood was superfluous indeed. This one would die by the end of the next hour if the flow did not abate.

He charged a third man, feinting to the left and deflecting the thrusting scimitar...

Suddenly there was a spattering of footsteps somewhere to the left and the General spun around in anticipation. About thirty paces away, a fourth man was trying to get away and his running form was clearly outlined against the low moon. It was an unevenly paced run, and the runner, a heavyset man with short stumpy legs, was doing his obvious best to confuse whatever aim may be taken at him as he made his exit. The General took a deep breath, stretched himself to full height, raised his sword-carrying arm high above his head and took a backward right step. Then, with practiced ease, he threw, and the weapon executed the long flight, spinning through air, before burying itself into the running man's left thigh. The man cried out, lost his balance in full stride and crashed to the ground. Suddenly, it was all over, just as quickly as it had begun. Once again it was quiet on the lonely, dusty road.

The General straightened up, listening for any tell tale sounds. There were none. He flexed the muscles of his right arm as he walked to the fourth man. The man was lying on his back with his wounded leg propped up in an unnatural angle by the sword that was sticking through it. The General bent over the fallen man. He examined the man's wound and shook his head. It was not good but he would live.

"What is the name of the man who is asking for my blood?" he demanded. The man shook his head.

"I do not know his name."

"How interesting. I am certain you would not recognize him either if you saw him again, Correct?" The man was silent. "Listen my good man," the General continued, "The only reason you are still alive is because I choose not to kill you. And that is extremely generous, bearing in mind that your intention a moment ago was to take my life." He paused. "I think it is only fair that in exchange you tell me the name of the man who sent you. No?" The man did not reply. He was looking straight ahead as if there was some silent vision in the night air that was visible to his sight only.

Abou Bakar grabbed the handle of the sword and twisted it. The man screamed in pain, attempting to slither away. "I think you should tell me the name," the General insisted. "It will save you a lot of unnecessary pain." He reached for the sword handle again and the man's open mouth sucked in air in dreadful expectation.

"I do not know him," he gasped. "None of us have this information."

"I am sure you don't. Only problem is I don't believe you. Would you know any reason why that may be? Could it be because I think you are lying?" The man did not reply, and a moment later his tortured voice tore through the night air again as the blade in his leg was twisted once more. Then the silence and the heavy breathing.

"You see my friend, I am in a rather hard place at this time and you do not give me many choices, and as hard as it may be to believe, I do not like doing this to you at all. But I must know the name of he who sent you. It is imperative. Too much depends on it. Much more than you can probably imagine. You will give me his name or I shall keep my hand permanently on this sword handle until you do." The General grabbed the sword handle. With both hands this time.

The man's harsh breathing was almost loud. Potent fear was dripping from his voice.

"I am just a soldier," he moaned. "And I was just following orders," he added, licking his lips nervously. "Sealed orders."

"You are a soldier? Did you say sealed orders?" Abou Bakar could not believe his ears. "Are you sure?"

The man nodded. "Yes I am."

A *sealed order* was a term that was immediately recognizable within military circles. Usually, it was used in reference to the nature and dynamics involved in a particular category of instructions, –instructions that were so secret that the recipients could never discuss them or divulge their source, even after the mission had been completed. And not many people had the power to issue such an order.

Customarily, these instructions went to soldiers who had been apprehended in some high crime against the land, and were now in prison just waiting to die. Such men would cling even to the most fragile straw of hope. So, they would logically jump at any opportunity that smelled ever so faintly of another chance at this thing called life. Even if that chance came in the form of a dangerous mission or task that they had to complete in other to earn the required pardon.

Such men would never question the moral content of any mission they were lucky enough to be confided. In fact, most of them would pray and kill to be given a sealed order, irrespective of what it demanded. For them it came down to one thing: another chance at life. It was that simple.

The General also understood that with sealed orders things could easily become a double-edged sword. If the mission was not achieved, then those who had failed were usually better off dead because at that point the reserved option was fearful indeed. They would be tied up and taken to the banks of the Aur River, where they would be thrown alive to the sacred crocodiles whose hunger was said to be permanent. It was an alternative that ensured a desperate need to succeed, whatever the mission at hand happened to be. Even cowards became brave under such pressure. Who did not love to live?

"I was a good soldier once," the man said. "But I have been in prison for eleven years now. For a man with a wife and children that can be hard. This mission was my last hope."

Surprisingly, Abou Bakar found himself sympathizing with these men. He knew exactly how they felt. To be driven by the fear of death, or love for one's family, as the case may be, was something that he understood. He had come to believe that life was essentially a contest between love and fear, and that people, even great people who achieved superhuman feats, usually acted out of these two impulses.

He understood that wholly. From personal experience.

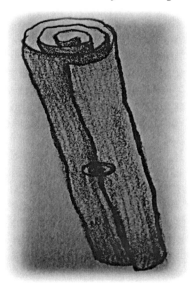

A sealed order...

CHAPTER NINE

*A*s the boy recalled, it had all started with the death of the man who had been the High Priest of Kepharra. It had been a very important death, mainly because the occupant of this office was entrusted with the sole duty of holding in safety, and guarding with his life, the sacred right hand of the god, Kepharra.

The story about the *Hands of Kepharra* was one that every child had heard at some point. It was a story that told of how one of the most treasured ornaments in the history of the Kingdom came to be.

The story told, that at the inception of the Kingdom, the council of one thousand shamans held a month long meeting, dedicated to placating the gods and incurring their blessings for the future. Crocodiles, pythons, and vultures, had been sacrificed in droves. It was said that the smoke from the offering had risen so high it had been visible from the ends of the earth.

Then, on the last day of the ceremony, as ten bull elephants were being prepared for the altar, the chief shaman had gone into an unexpected trance which had lasted until the last piece of elephant meat became charred. When he came back to himself, he claimed to have visited with the god Kepharra, whom he said, had asked for a very special ornament to be created in answer to the people's requests. It was to be an ornament that would ensure that the hands of the gods be always on the Kingdom, to guide and to bless it. It was to be made of the purest gold, and it was to be called the Hands of Kepharra.

Upon hearing this, the council had not wasted any time to execute the entreaty. Ten of the most skillful goldsmiths in all the land had been recruited. And then, guided by shamanic instructions, these goldsmiths had fashioned a necklace in the form of two separate, life-sized hands, with the fingers spread out to expose the palms. In the center of each palm were words whose meaning was based on deep esoteric knowledge. Rumor held that the words were supposed to have the power of magic, and had been written in the ancient arcane script of the spirits from the outer beyond.

The part of the story that the boy, like many others, had never heard, was that at the end of their work, the finished piece had been presented to the council of shamans, but in lieu of being paid, these shamans had pulled out their daggers and attacked the unsuspecting artists. They had been brutally murdered behind the locked doors of the shamanic temple. Their brains and hearts had been cut out while their bodies were still warm, ground into a poultice and mixed with the very first menstrual discharge from a virgin albino. With both hands steeped in this gory concoction, the virgin had been bound and buried alive, while the voices of one thousand shamans had chanted incantations that were calculated to infuse into, and imprison her spirit within the necklace. This was to ensure that she would always return to the earth in a never-ending cycle of reincarnation, to find and touch both hands of the necklace. It was said that as long as this cycle of reincarnation continued the potent energy within the artifact would be preserved as the foundation of a never-ending Kingdom.

By the end of these mystical orchestrations, the shamans were satisfied that the ornament had been transformed into an object that had the potential to manifest supernatural energy. If it was used correctly.

They created a new divine order and named it the priesthood of Kepharra. It was charged with the sacred duty of doing every thing in its power to guard the ornament. Shortly thereafter, the first High Priest, who was also the leader of the shamanic council, had been initiated into office.

At the initiation, both hands of the necklace had been placed around his neck. And that had lasted only up until the moment that the first King, called the scorpion, had taken office. At that point, as stipulated by the dictates of the Kepharra priesthood, the High Priest had transferred the golden left hand of the god to the chosen King, as a symbol of divine authority.

And it had been like that ever since. No King could sit on the throne without being in possession of Kepharra's left hand. And no one thereafter, High Priest or King, was ever allowed to bear both hands at the same time.

So, given the importance of the office, the passing of the High Priest could always be expected to have far reaching ramifications. For the boy, this particular passing-away had affected him in a way that he had never expected.

He'd known that his mother was fortunate to be employed as one of the caretakers of the temple who assisted in special ceremonies within the priesthood. It was an important responsibility and she had taken it seriously. The god Kepharra could be extremely demanding and even illogical sometimes.

She had striven to be at her best, to be available and to serve the order in all the ways that she was called to do, holding nothing back. Not even her body. Of course, no one ever had the courage to comment or even mention the coincidence of extreme physical resemblance that existed between the boy and the chief priest of the order. And so in general, life had been good. She had a house in which to stay, food for her son, and enough money to give him an education. But it was not to last.

One rainy night, a few days after he turned fifteen, there had been a knock on the door of their small house. From his mat on the floor, the boy had listened to the creaking of the door as it was opened. And then suddenly his mother had begun to scream. He'd jumped to his feet and rushed to the door, only to realize that her voice was now coming from outside. Out into the dark, rainy night, he ran, with his young heart beating wildly in his chest. What he had seen that night was a spectacle that would be forever imprinted on his mind.

In the torchlight, his mother was fighting off two men who were both draped in the white and black mourning garments of the Kepharra priesthood. Both of their faces had been painted with the ceremonial symbols of death: skulls in white paint. The men each had one of her arms and were dragging her away into the rain. At fifteen the boy had been old enough to understand what was going on. He bounded after them, screaming at the top of his voice and ignoring the plea in his mother's eyes when she saw him

"NO, my son. NOOOOO!" She screamed as he rushed forward. "GO BACK INSIDE!" But he ignored her and jumped on the first man, burying his dagger into his chest. The man let go of her arm, his eyes widening in unexpected shock as he fell backwards. His comrade had not waited to see anything more. He took off into the night leaving the boy alone with his sobbing mother.

"Oh, my son," she said through tears, "Please forgive me, for I have brought disaster upon your life." His heart had broken at the pain in her voice. "Now you must leave. Go quickly before they come back," she pleaded, running into the house. When she reappeared a few moments later she was holding a little bag that she had hastily put together for him.

"Here, take this. There is some food and all of our savings. Now go."

"No." He knew exactly what would happen if he left her behind.

What had transpired was that the High Priest of the god Kepharra had died that very evening in his sleep. In following with tradition, his body was embalmed in preparation for his journey into the next world, in conjunction with his most precious personal effects, since he would need them in the next life. Then, as it happened sometimes, the oracle had decided that it was necessary to honor this particular chief priest with one of his trusted servants.

And the boy's mother had been chosen by the shamanic oracle to be buried alive with the corpse of the defunct High Priest. The two men had been leading her away to be prepared for burial when he had attacked.

He did not regret it. He would do it again, every time, if the alternatives were the same. He would challenge anyone who required that his mother be buried alive. Against her wish.

So, the boy and his mother ran off together, hiding during the day and going under cover of darkness, heading for the sub-Saharan Kingdoms. It was far enough, he'd reasoned, and no one would recognize them there.

Unfortunately, his mother had taken ill a few days journey from the southern borders of the Kingdom. She had become exhausted, hungry, and thirsty. That had forced him to scout around and find a cave where she could rest and regain her strength, while he searched for water and something to eat. Which was where the border patrol found them, -dehydrated, weakened, and almost dead.

Since they had been picked up near the border, the patrol had taken them back to the office of Vizier Itzo, the man who had been in charge of overseeing border security.

Meanwhile, the story of the debacle spread like wild fire, creating waves of controversy as it was told and retold. Everyone had wanted to know what would happen to the young man who had intervened to defy the oracle. Was it not a sacrilege? Who was he to deny the High Priest a servant? What if the god Kepharra decided to take revenge on the whole Kingdom?

Clearly, something had to be done. And quickly. The council of a thousand shamans had convened in an emergency session. In a unanimous decision, they had asked for the ultimate penalty.

On the same night that the King was to sign the verdict into law, Vizier Itzo's mother, then one hundred and twenty years of age, paid her son a final visit. She spoke uninterrupted for the duration of the visit, and then she had passed away moments later, with a smile on her face.

Itzo had gone to see the King. Still grieving for his mother, he had spoken to the monarch in the same way that she had spoken to him, pleading with the King that the boy was just a child whose reaction could probably have been different if he had been older. What child would not stand up to defend his mother? Would Neferhotep himself not have defended his own mother under the same circumstances? What dam can hold back the love that a young child has for his mother? Should the boy not be given another chance? Was love not in accordance with the Kingdom's philosophy of *Maat*?

The King had been swayed, and at the risk of alienating the council of Shamans, a difficult compromise had been reached. It was decided that the boy should go out into the wilderness, hunt down a Nephilim lion, bring back its heart, its bile, and its fangs. These would be used in a special ritual that would placate the deity of the priesthood and soothe its anger back to sleep.

The boy had been given forty days to accomplish the task, with the understanding that, if for any reason he should fail to return within the stated time, his mother would die.

The unspoken truth was that no one expected him to succeed. Did the wise men not say that he who goes to hunt the lion could easily become food for the lion? And this particular lion was not just any lion. It was a *Nephilim!*, a terrible beast even to very seasoned hunters. They were known to grow to the size of a bull and many a hunter had lost their lives to such.

Armed with a bow, a quiver full of poisoned arrows, and three iron spears, the fifteen year old rode out into the wilderness, towards the savannahs of Cush, where the paw prints of the giant cat were known to be seen.

On the morning of the twenty-sixth day he came upon a brook. As he was bending down to satisfy his thirst he noticed something. Right next to his face, clearly imprinted on the soft clay by the stream was a huge paw print! The boy recognized it immediately. It was a lion's, and from its size it could only be a *nephilim*!

Immediately, he dropped on all fours and studied it more closely. It was about a day old. He felt the hair on his head standing on end, and suddenly the reality of the situation dawned on him. Here he was, a young man of fifteen rains, on a mission to hunt down one of the most feared predators that was known to man. Nervously, he glanced around. He seemed to be alone.

Quickly, he led his horse away from the stream, to a cave that he had found. It was about four miles away but it looked safe and uninhabited. The animal would stay there when it was time to execute the plan that was formulating in his mind.

He chose a narrow strip of land by the stream, where the clay was particularly soft, and he began digging. It was hard work and it took eight mornings. But it was the only way. He could not work during any other time of the day for fear of encountering the cat. They usually preferred evenings at the watering hole.

Finally, the hole was deep enough for a tall man to disappear into, while the length and the width corresponded to the height of the boy's own body. Then at the very base of one wall, he excavated more clay to create a little square recess, almost like a connecting chamber, except smaller. It was just big enough to hold his whole body if he folded himself up into a tight ball, with his chin on his knees.

On the ninth morning, he was finally ready. He stood up, stretched his mud-covered body, and surveyed his work. It looked as if it could work. It may save his mother and that was all that mattered.

At the center of the hole, he planted two of the three, long iron spears, with their poisoned tips pointing upwards. Then he said a silent prayer to 'The maker of all the world' before jumping into the hole. Once in, his vision became limited to the sky above. But he had anticipated that possibility and rolled in a rock on which he could stand to get his head out. That way, he could spy the surroundings without getting out of the hole. Then he had settled down to wait. He was as ready as he was ever going to be. It was time to confront his worst fears.

Late that afternoon, he'd raised his voice and began mimicking the cry of a deer in distress. It was a sound that violated the quiet of the wilderness and he knew that it would be heard for miles around.

An hour later he had attracted a deer herd, some impala, an ostrich and a dingo, all of which quickly disappeared upon realizing that the creature in the hole was not what it was claiming to be. But it was a sure sign that his mimicry was effective. If the lion were in the vicinity it would wander in at some point. A deer in distress was probably a hurt animal, and that made it an attractive option to a big cat. It was an easy meal that may not require much of a hunting effort.

Just before the sun disappeared behind the western horizon, he spied a flock of vultures flying in from the southeast. They were heading directly towards him and he watched them warily. He knew that vultures would sometimes follow a predator on the hunt, especially if they could see a prey in the predator's path, which was a guarantee for leftovers.

When the birds got to the airspace directly above the boy, they began to circle! That was a definite sign! Whatever they were following had led them to him. With his heart jumping in his chest, he raised his voice one last time and mimicked the cry of an animal in pain. Then, stepping on the stone he raised his head slowly above the rim of the hole and looked around. For a moment there was nothing to be seen. But just as he was about to get off the stone, the lion stepped into view. By the gods!

It was a *Nephilim*! And it was bigger than he had imagined possible. It looked a full head taller than a cow and it was indeed a fearful sight to behold. It sniffed the air, its ears erect, looking from side to side as it tried to pinpoint the exact position of the prey.

The boy felt his heart miss a beat. It was time to rise up and prove to himself that he had not journeyed this far into the wilderness for nothing. He swallowed hard and tried to reach for an arrow. But, surprise of surprises, his arm did not move. He gritted his teeth and willed his fingers to uncurl out of the tightly clenched, muddy fists. Nothing Happened. He was suddenly gripped by a paralyzing fear and his whole body began to tremble uncontrollably. His hands were shaking so badly that he could hardly hold on to the bow. Sweat was pouring down his face, blinding him momentarily. Again, he willed himself to move, but it was in vain. He tried even harder, grinding his teeth in insane desperation, but it was to no avail. He was transfixed in panic. And death was, literally, standing fifty paces away from him. He closed his eyes. This was the end.

Then he remembered his mother.

He thought of the mental torment, the sleepless nights and the imagined torture to which her spirit was being subjected at that very moment. He envisaged the emotional suffering that she would experience upon hearing that he had died. Or the sheer terror of knowing that she herself would be buried alive in a sarcophagus, -all because he had failed? No. NO! HE COULD NOT FAIL!

It looked a full head taller than a cow...

And a small door was opened in the boy's heart. A door through which all the love he felt for his mother flooded into his being. A love that flooded every inch of his spirit and banished the spirit of fear that had taken him hostage. Immediately, the trembling stopped and he opened his eyes. The huge lion had not moved. It was still scanning the area for its meal.

With surprising calmness, the boy retrieved a poisoned arrow from his quiver, fitted it onto the string of his bow, pulled the string taut, took aim, and let the arrow fly. It zipped through the air and buried itself into the beast's enormous neck. It let out a terrible roar, vibrating the earth and startling a flock of birds into sudden flight. There was no time to waste. Quickly he pulled out another arrow and sent it flying at the creature. Once again, the arrow found its mark, but this time, alas, the beast had seen the boy. With another earth shaking roar, more dreadful than the first, it charged.

With all the speed that his fifteen-year-old body could muster, the boy flew off the stone and wiggled himself into the tiny space that he had excavated along the bottom wall of the hole. At that same instant, the sky above him was darkened in a flurry of movement, and he was staring into the angry eyes of the *Nephilim*, its foul stench invading his nostrils and suffocating him with terror.

The creature's huge head was just a hand's breadth away from the boys face, and the look in its eyes was the most hideous thing that he had seen in all of his fifteen years. It emitted another fearful roar, as it struggled within the tight hole to inch forward and chew off the boy's head. Just a few more inches.

And the boy seized the opportunity, and stabbed and stabbed and stabbed at the *Nephilim's* face, while the beast roared and roared and roared. But it was all in vain, for the lion could not budge. The suction within the wet, muddy hole had taken the creature captive. In addition, both of the iron spears that the boy had planted at the centre of the hole had pierced right through the creature's massive body.

After what seemed like an eternity, the beast finally stopped struggling and lay still. The boy heaved a huge sigh of relief as tears welled up to his eyes. They rolled down his cheeks as he worked to get himself out of the tiny opening in the wall, into which he had been blocked by the lion's bulk.

Finally, he made an outlet that was big enough to squeeze through. Trembling, he crawled out of the little enclosure and clawed his way onto the warm carcass of the beast before jumping out. The giant lion lay dead, and the fifteen-year-old Abou Bakar could not believe that he had actually killed it. But he had. Yes, a river had flown uphill! The sun had come out at night! A worm had swallowed a goat! A mere boy of fifteen rains had taken down a *Nephilim*!

The General mused about the episode as he glanced at the colossal outline of the King's prison. Where had the strength come from? As he grew older, he had often wondered about that. Had he been victorious because of the love he'd felt for his mother? Or was it because he'd known how fearful the alternative was? And what was the driving motive behind these men who had recently tried to take his life? Fear? Love?

He looked up at the lit entrance of the prison house, hoping that he would find Itzo alive in his cell. The need to speak with the former Vizier was more urgent than ever. There was something to be learned from in there. Of that, he was now certain.

He turned his attention to the wounded assassin. He was still lying on his back with the sword sticking through his thigh. A dark, growing circle had since appeared on the ground beneath the sword wound. He had lost a lot of blood and he appeared much weaker.

On a personal level, Abou Bakar was getting really frustrated with the man. He seemed to prefer pain to giving up any information. Maybe, what he should do was go talk to the other men. Perhaps one of them was a coward who would not tolerate pain. The possibility was unlikely, but it was worth a try.

He squinted into the darkness, raising his right arm to block off the distant glare from the lit torches at the prison gate as he walked over to another of the wounded men. It was the man with no legs. The man had crawled to one of the coconut trees and was sitting up with his back propped up against the vertical stem.

"How are you doing?" The man did not reply. "I need to talk to you." The man stayed silent prompting the general to go down on one knee.

The man's head was much closer now but in the dark of night it took the General a moment to realize that he was not breathing. His eyes were open but he was dead. This was strange. Abou Bakar had been in too many wars, and from experience he knew that the man should not have died so quickly from the wounds. Of course he had lost blood, but not enough for such a quick death. Wait! What was that smell? He grabbed the man's lower jaw, forced open his mouth and peered in. The overpowering smell of lethal *Ngubenem* leaves confirmed his suspicion.

He found the other man and ascertained that he too was

dead from the same poison, -*Ngubenem* leaves! Quickly he ran back to the man he'd left alive. The man was still lying on the ground, the sword was still stuck into his thigh, but this time, his jaws were masticating, almost imperceptibly. He was chewing something!

The General grabbed the man by the head and pried open his mouth. The resistance was halfhearted. But it was too late. The man's eyes were already rolling in his head as life ebbed out of him. Suicide!

Feeling exhausted, Abou Bakar let go of the man and sat back on his haunches. The wide, night sky, directly above seemed within reach. He could almost touch it if he stretched his hand far enough. There was Orion wearing his belt as usual. And over there, was the North Star, god of travelers. Was the sun god up there as well?

For a moment the great man wondered what it all meant? What did the gods talk about? What did they care about? Did they really pay attention and intervene in human destiny? Were they aware of his predicament? Of the Kingdom and its problems? What about the invading army? Was it truly because the sun had been angered? Was he really going to punish the whole land, and was the punishment commensurate to the circumstances? There was going to be a war! Women would die. Children would die. Disease. Drought. Famine. What kind of parents would punish their children in such a way? Where was the love?

What did that say about the sun god? Did he care about anyone but himself? What kind of god was he? Was he a god who... Wait a moment! Was he a god? Or was he born of man's imagination? What about the other Kemetian gods? Were they false as well? Could they hear, or see, or talk, or fight, or do any of the other things that they were supposed to be able to do?

Closing his eyes Abou Bakar mouthed a silent prayer to *The maker of all things*. This was the one God that he had somehow found enough faith in whom to believe. Mostly, because not believing in anything divine did not make sense. How could it? If something as simple as a spear, or a hut, or even a garment, needed a maker, what about something as supremely complex as the eye through which we have sight? Or the ear that allows us to hear? Or even the earth. What about the heavens? Where did it all come from? Did someone make them? And if someone did, where did that someone come from? Did someone create Him too? Or was it a She?

It did not make sense. It never did. The finite mind of man did not seem to have the capacity to grasp the concept of divine infinity, he told himself. But did that mean the concept did not exist as a fundamental truth, simply because it could not be comprehended by a finite mind? Was truth therefore limited only to what was within the realm of man's understanding? What if man did not exist? Would everything that man could see, just disappear? Maybe it would, in the same way that a picture would disappear if one were to shut, or blind the eyes that were looking at it. But did that mean the picture that the eye could no longer see had ceased to exist? Would the sun, the moon, and the stars all go away simply because man was not here to see and admire them? Probably not. They would simply be out of sight. And their existence would become part of that truth which went beyond human perception. Like the one true God whose love and wisdom must have created everything.

In silence, the General directed his thoughts to the instances in the past when he had felt the need to pray to this God. Almost immediately, he felt his faith take a little leap. *The maker of all things* had answered him before. He hoped it would happen now. He needed wisdom, strength, guidance and protection, for his son, for himself, and for the Kingdom.

He turned his attention to the wounded assassin. He was still lying on his back with the sword sticking through his thigh...

With his prayer said, he grabbed the four hundred year old

sword handle, pulled out the weapon from the dead man's thigh, and cleaned the blade by plunging it into the sand. When he was satisfied that it was clean, he ran a finger along the cutting edge of the weapon to make sure that it was smooth and ridge free. It was. He returned the weapon into its scabbard and stood up.

He was about to walk off when a thought came to mind. Why not, he reasoned. He was right here, so he might as well. In the dark, it took about an hour of careful searching to go through all four corpses.

When he was almost about to give up, his fingers felt the edge of something that seemed to have been sewn into an inner garment. He tore open the fabric and extricated the object. It was a small scroll of light papyrus that was still warm from the heat of the man's body. Although it was too dark to read, he knew that it was the sealed order that was asking for his own head. He stuck the scroll into his tunic as he got to his feet. It was time to go talk to Vizier Itzo. Hopefully the man was still alive.

CHAPTER TEN

Cameroon, Central Africa.

1 finished the drawing and held it up for closer inspection. It was the last scene of an elaborate photo story that depicted everything Jean Pierre had told me. Satisfied, I slipped it into a cardboard file, which already held a detailed pen and ink portrait of Yves Mammon. I raised my shirt, stuck the edge of the flat file into my belt, and let the shirt drop over it.

Silently, I crossed the tiny room that was my home, and inspected my self in front of the piece of broken mirror that was hanging from the unpainted plank wall. The file was not visible. I picked up the last bottle of beer that had been sitting on my easel slash table, drained it in one go, put my shades on, and stepped out of the room.

It was a hot and humid morning as it can only be in Cameroon, and the little stony street on which I lived was as busy as it was ever going to get. There were people, especially women in very colorful dresses and wrappers, either going to, or coming from the Soppo market, which held every Wednesday. There were also children and men, carrying bundles or pushing carts that had been loaded with all kinds of fresh food, from fruits and vegetables to grains and tubers.

For a moment I was distracted by this colorful canvas in front of me, a scene that in some ways was a slice of the Africa with which I was so deeply in love, the Africa that seemed to be singing, smiling, and dancing, almost as if it was unaware of the daily toil that was famous for grinding the skin down to the bones. A few voices could be heard already, rising above the din, to advertise some ware that the seller had judged worthy of the effort.

And it all made my heart very sad, to think that the overwhelming greed in the world was defining such simpler ways of life as nothing more than a liability which could be disposed, if the people were deemed to be a hindrance to the smooth extraction of raw materials. It was a specimen of greed that was so ruthless it would not hesitate to destroy everything on this land, just to get its bloody fingers on the treasure.

...carts that had been loaded with all kinds of fresh food, from fruits and vegetables to grains and tubers...

I locked the door of my little room, noting with some surprise, that the neighbor's door to my right was open. That was peculiar. My neighbors, a family of four that had moved into that room a month ago, would usually be at their stall on market days, not here. With work as scarce as dog's tears, they were very dependent on the little money that the tomatoes from their garden brought in. And they would not miss a market day if they could help it.

"*I salute O,*" I shouted my greeting into the open door way. "*Na who dey house?*" There was no reply. Instead, the cheap, torn and threadbare blind moved and my neighbor's face came into view.

"Sango, is the morning good?" I enquired.

"She is dying," was all Sango said.

"She is dying?" I asked incredulously. Sango nodded, stepping aside to let me into the room.

It was approximately the same size as mine and stepping into it made me realize just how spoiled I was. Here was a family of four, sharing the same five meters by five meters space about which I would not stop complaining. There were all kinds of things everywhere, as can be expected. There was even a pot on the same bed on which the comatose woman was lying. And the two children, aged five and three, were standing around the bed, aware that something was terribly wrong, but not sure what, or how to fix it.

"Quick, Sango, there is a man down this street who owns a car."

"Yes I know him."

"Send a child to his house. We need to take her to the hospital right away"

Sango just shook his head. "We just came back from the hospital," he said. "The doctor asked us to leave."

"To leave?"

"Yes. There was nothing he could do."

"Nothing? Nothing as in 'she is too sick', or as in 'the cost of the remedy is too expensive?"

"She needs an expensive operation"

The words tore at my heart.

How many times had I heard that before? How many children, women and men needed to die before somebody took notice? For how long could we afford to keep on living in a world where money was more important than life? Where children were forced to watch parents die, because they were too poor to afford treatment? Just thinking about it, especially in light of the terrible corruption that was wasting everything away, made me really angry.

"Send the child to the neighbor's. Here is some money," I said, putting the money that Jean Pierre had given me on the table. "Hurry, take her back to the hospital. I will get whatever balance may be lacking."

Words cannot describe the expression of sheer gratitude and hope that came across the man's face. He could barely find the words to thank me. A moment later both children ran out of the room and sped down the street. They were going to the house of the man who owned a car, to ask him to come and carry their mother to the hospital.

By the time I got to the office, it was almost midday, and I was perspiring from the heat. The *office* as we called it, was an old building that had been constructed to serve the unique purpose of a home, which it still did. You see, the owner of the newspaper shared his home with the staff, -a sacrifice that was indicative of his fierce dedication to truth.

"Hey Abanda!" It was my friend and colleague, Opio. He was also a contributor, and one of the proofreaders of the paper.

"*O Boy na how noh?*" I inquired.

"*Massa no bi me this? Something dey again? How for you?*"

"*I dey dasso.*" I answered, walking up the stairs, and onto the balcony on which he was standing, and we shook hands. "Is Charlie here?" I asked.

Charlie was our busy editor in chief, and he had the authority in the office, to either kill or publish a story. He was a veteran journalist who had proven himself within the world of media. I knew that if I could get him to believe me it would make everything else easier.

"Yes. He just got here," Opio answered. "When you are done seeing him, come and join me out here, lets sit and enjoy the view," he added mischievously, eyeing a curvy derrière that seemed to be protesting the limited space within the mini skirt.

I walked into Charlie's tiny office, and he asked me to sit down. I did.

"What's going on?" Charlie asked. It meant 'good to see you and what can I do for you'. Without wasting time, I told him everything that I had learnt from Jean Pierre. When I was done, I pulled out the file of cartoons and lay them on his desk. Charlie sat back and for a full minute he did not say a word.

"I know you do not have any reason to sell me a lie," he finally said. "But what if it is not true?" he whispered leaning forward. "Can you comprehend the implications and possible complications that could arise?" He was looking at me with serious hooded eyes.

"And what if it is true?" I persisted

"That's not good enough," Charlie said, getting up and walking around the desk. "What you are asking me to do may lead to panic and tension. If there is not sufficient justification, it will be very bad all around. First, it may just give the government the excuse they so badly need to shut us down. And it will not end there. We will be branded as a paper of anarchists who are deserving of death. With some luck we may end up with no more than long jail terms." He paused. "Do you understand what that would mean? Not only are there thousands of Cameroonians who count on us for an objective view on issues, our families depend on what we do to survive." He paused again. "Now these are serious issues and I refuse to rock the boat on the basis of a story that I have not personally verified. I will have to meet your friend."

"He can't come here. I do not think he would risk being seen here."

"Then I will come to him. I will meet with him tonight at ten at a place of his choice. All I ask is that he be there with his pregnant girlfriend."

I thought about it for a moment. It was more than fair. "No cameras?"

"No cameras. But he must be willing to let me talk alone and at length with his girlfriend."

"Deal," I said, getting to my feet.

"Leave those here," Charlie said, indicating the file of cartoons. "It will be edited and readied in case the impossible becomes the possible. But I do not promise anything. You understand that, don't you?"

More than ever I wished I were wrong, that Jean Pierre was wrong, and that all of this would simply go away.

"Leave those here," Charlie said, indicating the file of cartoons...

CHAPTER ELEVEN

Kingdom of Kemet, 1720 B.C.

$\mathcal{T}$he Chief Warden of the King's prison in Itjawy was a little man whose life always had something to do with death, at least, much more so than the average person's. And this could be attributed, for the most part, to the nature of the man's job. Some poor prisoner was always dying, either from natural or unnatural causes, or sometimes a combination of both. Not that it was of any consequence. In truth, it did not really matter anymore how these men died, just so long as they did.

They were prisoners who had achieved a special status due to the gravity of their so-called crimes. They were the *prisoners of the King*, a title which ensured that the Chief Warden himself had to personally verify, confirm, and most importantly record every death when it happened. Not to do so would be asking for serious trouble because most of these men had enemies in very high places. Sometimes that was the only reason why they were in prison in the first place.

The Chief Warden knew this, but he also knew his own place. He was just a little man from a poor family who had somehow managed to rise up from the ranks through hard work, dedication to, and longevity of service. He had simply refused to let anyone tell him that he was too small to do anything. So, here he was as the Chief Warden of the Kings' own prison. He was the first of the little people in the Kingdom to rise as high as he had. Warden of the King's prison! Unbelievable! It was a highly coveted position that provided for extensive material benefits, and he had been appointed to it. What a joy that had been! The whole land had finally seen that little people were just as intelligent as everyone else.

Thus, with reasoned logic, the Warden saw himself as a pioneer in little people's rights. He saw himself as a man who must succeed at all costs in whatever he did, so the world could begin viewing his kind from a more respectful perspective. And being smaller, he had had to work much harder than every one else just to be noticed. But he had not minded. The gods had provided him with a massive brain, which allowed him to memorize all, or almost all, of the information that was so important to this job. Already people were talking of the dwarf who was a very efficient Chief Warden. And not just of any prison.

In his position mistakes were too costly to even be contemplated as an option. Could one imagine what would happen if the King, or some official, came to the realization that their person of interest, who was supposedly in prison, could not be accounted for? Phew! That would be a nightmare! It had happened just a few times in the past. The most recent incident had occurred seven years ago, where a man who had supposedly died in prison, had been seen riding with a band of foreign mercenaries who were pillaging the villages on the western frontier. It had led first to an uproar, and then to the Chief Warden being sent to the crocodiles. Actually, that was how the vacancy in the position of Chief Warden had been created in the first place. And the little man had been chosen to fill the position on that same day, stepping right into shoes that were still wet and warm with the former Warden's blood.

He cringed at the thought. What a way to go. Had the gods reserved such an end for him? All of a sudden it felt as if there was no air in the room. He could hardly breathe. Was it the ulcers or was it just worry? He jumped to his feet, hurried over to the doors and threw them open.

Instantly the relative quiet in the man's office was interrupted by noises that were plainly suggestive of communal chaos. More like violence to be precise. And it seemed to be emanating from somewhere within the labyrinthine bowels of the huge prison house.

But the violence was not what worried the man. He knew what it was all about, where it was happening, and why it was happening in the first place. He also knew that the situation was being properly managed, or as properly as one could hope to manage the violence that usually accompanied the delivery of a *sealed order*. It happened every time, without fail, and it was happening now. Especially with the rare phenomenon of two such orders being delivered at the same time, like last night. Something was definitely going on. Two sealed orders at the same time was almost unheard of.

The orders had been directed to the prisoners within this particular prison. And although the specific task or tasks were not yet known, twenty of the most hardened inmates, all former members of the King's army, had already come forward, wanting the mission very badly. And every one of them was prepared to fight with each other, injure each other, and kill each other off, just to prove to all concerned, that they, more than anyone else, was most meritorious of the mission. Eliminating all the other contestants in a ruthless combat had become the only proof undeniable that the last man standing had actually earned the right to the opportunity, on the basis of personal achievement.

Instinctively, the Warden picked up the scrolls of papyri that were lying on the desk in front of him. They were as yet unopened and the unbroken seal was testimony to that. Last night, when they had arrived, he had sent the word out to the prisoners and the news of this development had spread like wild fire.

He examined the scrolls more closely. What was the mission within? Who had asked for it? Was it in the name of justice? Would it serve the Kingdom, or was it for some egoistic, personal whim. Would lives be lost because of it? What a foolish question that last one was, he thought. Were lives not being lost at this very moment within the prison yard because of it? Was that not what all the shouting was about? The men who had elected for the mission were killing each other in a ringed fight while their fellow prisoners cheered on. And it would go on into the small hours of the morning, or until there was only one man left standing. That man would be handed the scrolls. Then, he would pick a team that would go with him to execute the mission. Success would mean immediate freedom.

Just then, there was a loud, drawn out shout that sent reverberating echoes all along the corridors of the huge prison. Some dramatic high point had been reached in the fight.

He replaced the scrolls on the table, said a little prayer, and stood up. It was time to go and check on the fight. To see if there were any corpses that needed to be processed. Grabbing a ring of keys, he stepped out of his office.

"Excuse me sir?" The Warden turned around. It was one of the guards who were constantly patrolling the corridors.

Why had he failed to notice the man? Were there any other people lurking around? It was not an absurd question to ask. It was too dark in here anyway. What if a prisoner escaped?

"First thing tomorrow I want the number of lit torches within the prison to be doubled," the Warden barked looking up at the guard.

"Yes sir," the guard answered bowing stiffly. "It will be

done as you wish," he added respectfully.

"Good, see to it," the Warden muttered as he turned around and walked off once more. There would be no more dark corners in this entire prison yard. If someone were planning a nocturnal get away, it had better be tonight. If not, then never. That was his job.

"Sir?" The voice intruded once more into his thoughts.

"WHAT!"

It was the same guard. PHEW! What did the man want? Couldn't he find something else to do? He had things to do tonight.

"There is a visitor here to see you," the guard said quietly.

A visitor? At this time? It was too late for that.

"Ask him to come in the morning," the Warden said turning away.

"Sir..." the guard hesitated, choosing his next words very carefully. It was obvious to him that, not only was the Warden becoming very impatient, the man had put on one of those many worry faces for which he was famous. "This visitor's name is Abou Bakar, of the tribe of Abou Ramzi."

The Warden stopped dead in his tracks. Suddenly his mouth went dry. Abou Bakar? The Abou Bakar? The same General who was also Nomarch of the northern province? Visiting the prison at this hour of the night? Cursed be the moon!

This could only mean trouble. What did the man want? Was he one of those high state officials who liked to check ever so often on an archenemy that he himself had thrown into prison? No, that could not be the reason. The Warden was intimately familiar with all the files in the King's prison, every name, case, date, death, and he had seen the General's name only once, but not in connection to such an arrangement. In fact, he knew the exact file in question, its shape, its location, its weight, everything. It was a tablet that had been carved out of a donkey's jawbone, and he could see it in his mind's eye, up on the shelf, on the opposite wall across from his desk.

Was there another file somewhere pertaining to the General? Or was it a scroll? He thought about it for a moment and concluded that it was very unlikely. So that left just one last possibility. Had it somehow been misplaced? Oh no! 'Misplaced', was a bad word right now, and he had better not be using it. Quickly he wetted his thumb on his tongue and stamped a print of it on his massive forehead. That should chase away any bad luck.

"First thing tomorrow I want the number of lit torches within the prison to be doubled..."

But still, had he lost a file?

Once again, he wetted his thumb and touched his forehead. What if he had somehow failed to account for one man, - the one man that the General may be coming to see? If that were the case then his ultimate nightmare was here. And it could only mean one thing; that he, the first little man who rose to any prominence in recent times, would be dead by morning.

"Show him in to my office," he told the guard. "I shall see him immediately." The voice was surprisingly steady for a man who was convinced that he was about to meet with either death's brother, or death himself.

The guard spun around smartly and marched down the torch-lit corridor, leaving the Warden once more by himself.

From the huge ring of keys, he selected one that was as long as his forearm, stuck it into the lock and reopened the door into his office. As he stepped into the room he wondered if this was the last time that he was doing so. Once again his thumb darted from his mouth to his forehead.

He glanced around the room, soaking in the details of the already familiar space. Would he miss the high ceilings? The walls that had been transformed into shelves, the stacks of papyri scrolls? The hundreds of fired clay tablets? What about the countless hours that he had spent on the stone floor committing these records to memory? Had it been worth it?

The sound of footsteps from the corridor outside indicated that the nocturnal visitor had arrived. The guard marched into the room and saluted stiffly.

"Sir, here to see you, General Abou Bakar, the Nomarch of the northern province." He bowed low, showing the General in.

"Welcome sir, welcome," the Warden said, taking a bow. "We are at your service and we are most honored to have you here," the Warden added. "We also know that you are a very busy man, and as such, we shall do everything in our power to assist you in the most timely manner."

"Thank you very much, my dear man," the General replied, taking in the disorder within the room. "I know that the job of a prison Warden is a difficult and hectic one. Especially here at the King's own prison where you are expected to hold and keep all these dangerously wicked characters without fail."

"Err yes, yes sir...no, yes," the Warden stammered in reply. He could not even think clearly. "Its...its hard sometimes but we are very happy and... and definitely most grateful to be of service, sir."

"It is greatly appreciated, I am sure," the General said with a small frown, wondering if something was wrong with the man? Was he always like this? What about the noisy uproar that was clearly discernible in the background? He had heard it first upon stepping through the gates into the prison and it had not stopped since then. Was it a prison riot? It sounded like it. "Are you well?" He asked the question looking directly into the Warden's eyes.

"Y...yes I am," the man answered.

"What about the rest of the prison? Is everything quiet?"

"Yes sir. "

"What about the uproar?"

"The exercise yard, sir," the Warden informed, holding up the sealed scrolls of papyri. "The prisoners are in the process of establishing, by way of a fight, who among themselves is most worthy of these documents."

"Oh I see. Sealed orders..."

"Yes sir."

"Do you get many of those?"

"Usually, about one every year," the Warden said. "Sometimes less. Except, for last night. We received both of these. A rare occurrence I should say."

"Hm!" Abou Bakar digested the information, wondering how many other prisons had received such orders. Had the same person issued them all? Men from a different prison facility had carried out the attempt on his own life. "And would you know their provenance?"

"I do not sir," he exhaled slowly. "I do not."

"Of course, you do not," the General agreed. "I can see that the scrolls are yet to be opened. Excuse my assumptions." He paused. "But tell me; do you think it has anything to do with the recent conspiracy against the throne?"

"Mmmmm?" The Warden's heart skipped several times. These ulcers were killing him. Why was the man asking him these questions? These were deep things, very deep things. Men like himself were not supposed to know about, hear about, or much less, talk about such things. "I am just a Warden, Sir."

"I know. I also know that you are not stupid, which is why you keep this job. I will understand if you do not feel inclined to speak on these matters. But it is of the gravest importance and you should know that, not only will you be well protected, honored, and rewarded, the whole nation will eventually learn of your great service. Think about it"

The whole nation? Great service? Honor? The Warden was now confused. What was going on? "In the mean time," the General continued, "I would like to have a conversation with Itzo, the former Vizier of border security. He is in here, is he not?"

The Warden breathed a deep sigh of relief. If that was the reason behind the General's visit, then things may not be so bad after all. He knew the man that the General was talking about. Nervously, he cleared his throat.

"Sir," he began, making his way around the little desk. "I

am your servant, I will always be your servant, and all I want to do is serve. Presently I am in a very difficult place. I have become Nsi, the proverbial fish for whom water became a fatal curse: living in it will lead to death. Living out of it will equally lead to death."

"What do you mean?" Abou asked, pretending to not understand the man. "Death is a subject that is heavy on the soul. Why do you speak its name?" The little man was now standing directly in front of the General. In response he held out an unfolded scroll that he had picked up from one of the walls. He was holding it out so the General could read.

...the prisoners are in the process of establishing, by way of a fight, who among themselves is most worthy of these documents..."

It was dated from about fifteen days ago, and it was a written confirmation from the King, stating that the Palace had found Vizier Itzo and a few other men guilty of treason. Further instructions were specific about the state of absolute isolation in which these prisoners were to be held.

The General looked at it and frowned. "Can you hold that a little closer to the light?" he asked, bending over the spread out scroll. "Yes, right there. Now look at the signature. It seems a little... er... different from the King's, don't you think?"

The Warden could have sworn that his heart had stopped. Urgently, he raised the scroll to a few inches from his nose, keeping it tilted towards the light. Yes, he could see it now! By the gods! Somebody other than the King himself had effectively signed the document, and he, the Warden, had been fooled!

"I think the document is fake," the General concluded, dipping into his tunic and pulling out the scroll that he'd taken from his would be assassin. He unrolled the piece of Papyrus and held it next to the one in the little man's hands. "This is the same signature," he said, "And it is not the King's hand either. You can see that, can't you?" The Warden's eyes were wide, frozen moons. The big head was unmoving, staring at both scrolls in total disbelief. How had he missed that? How? This was the end. He had let himself be tricked. What a shame! Now everyone will say that little people were not smart enough, and could not be trusted with serious responsibilities. What a disgrace he had become to his own people.

The pain that accompanied the lines of deep sadness on the man's face was not lost on the General. He felt his heart soften as the little man's body began shaking with sobs that threatened to break his very frame.

"...Now look at the signature. It seems a little... er... different from the King's, don't you think?"

"Listen." The General cleared his throat. "It was a grave mistake you made and it should not have happened. But right now things are not what they seem, and even as we speak," he paused, "a foreign army is marching on the Kingdom."

"What? A foreign army?" The Warden's tear stained face was incredulous. "From the south? The Ethiopians? The Bororo? Cushites?"

"None of the above. It is an army from the north, and that signature may be at the very centre of the plot. Your mistake may actually be a blessing from the gods themselves. We shall see." He paused again. "But first we must open the sealed orders and inspect the signatures. At this point we have to. And then I have to speak with Vizier Itzo."

CHAPTER TWELVE

T he Warden jumped to his feet, and skipped out of the door. "This way sir," he shouted, sprinting down the corridor with the huge ring of keys jangling down to his knees. "I will lead you to the man myself."

Good, the General thought, breaking into a jog. The little man was fast for his size and the prison complex was a maze of tunnels in which no one wanted to get lost, especially at night.

The Warden took a left turn and disappeared around the corner. "Be careful sir," Abou Bakar heard the man shout. "This passage has a low ceiling. Apart from that, it is excellent; probably the work of little people from long ago."

When the General got to the spot, he understood what the Warden meant. It was a somewhat smaller side corridor that had been painstakingly carved out of solid rock. Even in poor lighting the skill of the builders was more than obvious. All the walls had been chiseled and sanded down to an uncommon smoothness, except for the floor. It had been intentionally ridged to provide for footholds, since the tunnel was now assuming a gradient that was going deeper into the cold earth.

Several moments later, the General caught up with the Warden. The man had stopped in front of an ancient looking iron gate, and he was fumbling with his huge ring of keys. He found the one that was needed, slipped it into the lock, and the gate opened with a noisy protest.

"Would you like us to light up the torches, sir?" It was a new voice. The General turned towards it but it was too dark to see anything.

"No, that will not be necessary," the Warden, replied. "Lead us instead to Itzo's cell. The rest of your men can stay here."

"Yes sir, right away" the invisible guard answered, and the General heard a pair of light footsteps turn around and take off at a run. The Chief Warden, with his breathing audible, set off behind them. The General brought up the rear. After a series of long corridors and confusing turns, all going deeper into the earth, a distant light appeared at the end of the corridor. Soon thereafter, the outlined form of the leading guard became visible as he came to a halt in front of another heavy, iron Gate.

Beyond the gate was a torch-lit hall that had been equally

carved out of stone.

The forerunning guard moved to the side as the Warden came up to the gate. He fiddled with his jangling ring of keys, and the gate, just like the first ones, yielded with a loud protest.

The man had stopped in front of an ancient looking iron gate...

"Wait here," the Chief Warden said to the guard, who was now fully visible to Abou Bakar. "Let no one in..."

"...Let no one out," the guard completed.

"Good." The Warden stepped into the hall "This way sir," he said to the General. He was heading towards what appeared to be a line of cells that had been dug into the walls and barricaded in by heavy metal bars. "There are four other interconnected under ground halls like this one here. This particular one, which is the smallest, has twenty-five holds, and the convicted Vizier Itzo is in one of them. Here is the key to his cell." He was holding out an odd looking key.

"You will not regret this," Abou replied, reading the man's mind as he took the key. "And please stand where I can see you. I may need your assistance or have a question."

"You will be able to see me from here, sir," the Warden

said, settling down on his haunches. "Just raise your hand and I shall be there."

The first two cells were empty, while the next three each held men that the General could not recognize. Itzo was in the sixth cell. Although he had lost a lot of weight the General recognized the man immediately. He was sitting on the cold stone floor with his back to the wall and staring up at the ceiling. The expression on his face told the General that the indomitable spirit for which Itzo was known, was still very much alive.

Itzo had been born to peasant parents whose livelihood came from the sweat of their brow. And they had wanted nothing more than to see their children ascend from the toil of subsistence to a better lifestyle. From a very early age his mother would regularly say to him, "Itzo my son, when you grow up you will be a big and important official who would have the King's ear." And then she would smile and rub his head affectionately. On his twelfth birthday, his father took him to the home of a desert patrol officer to whom they always sent huge baskets of food at the end of every harvest season. The patrol officer had looked the boy over and then promised to talk to his chief. Itzo's father had been so grateful that he had gone home directly and slain the only animal that he owned, a cow, and sent all the meat back to the home of the patrol officer. Five moons later Itzo had gone on his first patrol.

By the time Neferhotep became King, Itzo had developed a solid reputation as one of the few patrol officers who had been over every inch of the Kingdom's borders. So his subsequent appointment as Vizier of border security was widely approved and supported, even by the old guard. But his true worth had come to light eleven years later, following a territorial claim that the Berbers had made on an eastern oasis that had been in the Kingdom's jurisdiction. It was a part of the Kingdom with which few people were familiar, so Itzo's maps had been vital. They had proven to the Berber delegation that the oasis they were concerned with, was actually different from the one in question. And an expensive war had been averted. Everybody had let out a sigh of relief, and Itzo's place as Vizier of border security and foremost cartographer in the land had been cemented.

Looking at Itzo now, Abou could not help wondering how wasteful it was to have a man with such knowledge spend even a day in jail on charges that had most likely, been fabricated.

"Itzo, Son of Mustapha, I see you," Abou Bakar greeted.

"What? You?" The older man was surprised. He scrambled to his feet and rushed to the front of the cell. "Is it really you? Abou? What are you doing here?"

"To see you, my friend," Abou Bakar answered, opening the lock on the thick Iron Gate.

"To see me?"

"Yes." He stepped into the room and both men embraced in silent greeting.

"Then you did not get my message. Did you?"

"Message? What message?"

"I sent you word just before I was arrested. Obviously, you did not get it, or you would not be here."

"What do you mean? Did the message have anything to do with the attacking army?"

"Attacking army?" The pain in the old man's voice was obvious. "Has it come to that already? Was nothing done? By the gods! What have we done?" The man hid his emaciated face behind both hands. "Where is the King?" he asked.

"I do not know the answer to that question."

"What? You do not know where the King is? Did you not say there was an attacking army?"

"I have tried very hard to meet the King without success," the General paused. "Irrespective of the fact that I was the bearer of very important news in connection to the invaders, I was not granted audience. It was rather odd, so I went to the office of the one man whom I knew could get me to see the King in an emergency, but you were not there. I was informed that you were now in prison due to a conspiracy against the throne, in which you had been implicated."

"Lies! All lies," the Vizier interjected hotly. "It was all put together by men who are probably taking over as we speak."

"I met a man today. A man with a livid scar running across his whole face."

"Cikatrix?"

"Yes. He was the one who informed me of your demise, so to speak. As things stand, I am not quite sure who is on our side or not. I feel ashamed that I suspected this man Cikatrix just because he is Aamu. Is he involved?"

"I am not sure but I will not be too surprised because the man belongs to a demographic that has been subjected to discriminatory inhumane treatment in the kingdom for too long," Itzo replied with his face strained in thought. He was pacing nervously around the room, his thin frame bowed forward with both hands behind him. "but I will tell you what I know. When I am done you can make up your own mind." He cleared his throat.

"Just a moment," Abou Bakar said, turning around to signal the Warden, who had been watching them all along. The man jumped to his feet and came over.

"How can I be of service, sir?"

"Send for some hot soup and flat bread. And warmer clothing for my friend here."

"Immediately sir," the Warden replied, and hurried away to dispatch instructions.

"He is a good man," Abou Bakar heard Itzo murmur. "He has a conscience that he fights with regularly. He is one of the many who are forced to serve a corrupt King."

"Corrupt King?" Abou Bakar's fears were coming true. "Is the King involved as well?"

"In a way, yes." The former Vizier looked up at the General. "He has failed the people at a time when they most need him. The man is a fool."

"Sshh!" Abou Bakar whispered, throwing a quick glance around the underground chamber. In all of his life, he had never heard anybody call a King a fool. It was not a wise thing to do.

"Is the King not supposed to be the father of the land?" the old man asked. "Does a father not take the time to listen to his children? Does this King listen to any advice? No, he does not. He is nothing like his father who was truly wise. How do I know? Because I tried several times! A case in point is the recent intelligence that I received from one of my patrols about the army to the north. When I brought it to his attention the man had just stared at me. I remember wondering if he was hearing my words or not. It was as if his soul had been inhabited by some foreign entity."

"What do you mean?"

"I do not know how to explain it, but it was peculiar. I have never seen anything like it."

"Did you have any concrete proof to the effect that this army was planning to march on the Kingdom?" the General asked.

"No, not at first because at the time this army was gathering too far to the north for any one to be certain about its intention." The man paused. "We all know that there is not one King in all the world who will not want to have possession of the Kingdom.

Our civilization is the greatest that the world has ever seen. It is a shining light in the darkness and people from distant lands are drawn to it. News of our success has traveled far and wide. Our advancement in the science of numbers, scribing on papyrus, medicinal potions, the knowledge of the body, architecture, and the paths that the waters of the sea and the winds follow, the heavens... all of these advancements are deeply coveted by foreign Kings, and some of them have become very jealous of late, especially of our trade in gold." The Vizier cleared his throat. "But to be sure I sent out a secret party of men, you know, to find out as much as they could about this army. None of the men came back. That was the first sign that something was wrong. My patrols always came back. At least one person could have survived. I concluded that they had been found out and executed. But that still left the question of why it had happened in the first place? What had given them away so easily? These were seasoned men who had been on several missions, so I could not understand it. The answer to this riddle became evident a short time later when another one of my patrols intercepted a secret message from this foreign army. Unfortunately, the bearer of the message killed himself before my men could get the name of the person for whom the message was meant. But it told me that there was a spy or spies amongst us, spies who were high enough in hierarchy to know about the missions that I sent out." He studied his feet for a moment. "So I went back to see the King. This time when I saw him, I was shocked beyond words. Not only did it feel as if he was possessed by something foreign, he was surrounded by an eerie group that was led by Cikatrix..."

"This is interesting. So does the new Vizier have something to do with it,..."

"I am not sure," he reflected. "There is infact a connection between Salatis and this 'Cikatrix. But it does not make much sense. Cikatrix is said to have gotten his scars from Salatis himself. He'd been tortured and left out in the desert to die. Fortunately he was found just in time, and by Aesare himself."

"He was found by the King himself?"

"Yes. Back when he was still a prince and his father Neferhotep was on the throne. That was twenty years ago, during the rebellions of Avaris. Remember that? Every one was so proud of you." Abou Bakar did not answer. Suddenly his mouth was dry. How could he not? He remembered Avaris all right, but not the event in Itzo's narrative. "By the time the young prince found him, Cikatrix had already been unconscious for a few days. He had also been badly cut up. The scar you see on his face is said to be one of the smaller ones. His whole body is covered with them," Itzo said. "The story goes that Salatis did that to him because his family had allegedly cooperated with our forces. Every single member had been hunted down and killed, his father, his mother, his sisters, his brothers, his cousins, even their friends...he was the only one who survived. Aesare took the wounded boy who was about the same age as himself, back to the palace. When King Neferhotep heard about it he'd been moved, like everyone else, by the story of the young Aamu orphan who had endured extreme hardship from Salatis because he had cooperated with our forces. Ever the politician, King Neferhotep had seized the situation as an opportunity to show the people that riches and favor were the rewards reserved for those whose loyalty lay with the Kingdom. He had publicly adopted the boy as his own and lovingly named him Cikatrix, meaning, 'scar of honor'. He'd also given him a luxurious apartment in the palace, where he has lived to this day. Prince Aesare is now King as we all know, and I hear that the two of them are still good friends who..."

Suddenly Itzo fell silent. His attention was focused beyond the General's shoulder. "Something is wrong," he added instead. "The Warden has returned, but there is something to his gait."

The little man was urgently limping towards them with a tray of food in his hands.

Abou Bakar turned around. "Yes," he agreed. "And I think he is not alone."

The Warden had crossed the hall, and was now putting the tray on the floor in order to open the door of the cell. At the other end of the hall, a small group of about eight or nine uniformed prison guards had appeared. The were standing shoulder to shoulder, weapons drawn, facing the tunnel and obviously getting ready to confront a foe that the men in the cell could not see as yet.

"Is everything quiet?" the General inquired.

"No sir, the quiet is gone."

"What is the problem?"

The reply was drowned out in a sudden cacophony of clashing metal that ended with a cry.

Abou Bakar closed his eyes and took a deep breath. He held the air in for a long moment, said a silent prayer, and exhaled very slowly. Then he opened his eyes, picked up the two wooden bowls of warm vegetable soup and handed one to Itzo.

"Drink, old friend," he whispered, "It may be the last meal we have for a long time." And with that, he raised the bowl to his mouth, tilted back his head, and emptied its contents.

Calmly he returned the bowl on the tray, stood up, loosed his sheathed, shorter sword and tossed it at Itzo, who had also emptied his bowl. The man caught the weapon in mid air, ready to do battle.

If the Warden saw the action, it was not obvious. Instead, he kicked the tray out of the way as Itzo stepped out of the prison cell, followed by the General.

If truly the Kingdom was under attack, then that was distressing. But the Warden also knew the law. It stipulated that in times of full-blown war, all prisoners were to be released. They were to be offered freedom with the condition of joining the army and defending the Kingdom. Every Chief Warden knew this.

Over the thousands of years that the Kingdom of Kemet had lived, it had had to fight for its life several times, always managing to survive even when the odds against them were so great that every one was dispirited. There was even an account of how, in one of the several wars that the Heka khasut had waged, the Kingdom had been saved by a former prisoner.

The Heka khasut had chased out the King and his army, and built their new capital in the southern lowlands of Simbel, only to be vigorously rinsed out ten rains later by an over flooded Aur. The flood had left the Heka Khasut confused and disoriented, a state of affaires of which the great Palankar Masopo, a man, not like many, had taken advantage. With just a few men, he had ridden for three days and nights, seized back the Kingdom and beheaded the Heka khasut leader. The move had taken the Heka khasut by surprise and thrown them into deeper disarray, forcing them to abandon everything and flee. Palankar had given chase, smiting hundreds of Heka khasut as they fled. The Kingdom had survived, nursed itself back to health and became once again the centre of learning and culture in the world. All because of the bravery and persistence that had been displayed by a former prisoner who was rumored to have had only one testicle. The story of Palankar Masopo was one that was well known.

"What is the problem?" Vizier Itzo demanded loudly as he led the way, rushing towards the guards.

"Who wants to know?" a very strong voice replied. Its

owner was barely visible due to the wall of guards who were blocking the way.

"I do," Itzo answered spiritedly, forcefully pushing the guards apart to make way for himself.

About ten steps away and facing the line of guards, was a bloodied, violent looking group of prisoners.

There were about twenty of them, all were Aamu, and all were armed to the teeth with spears, machetes, swords, knives, bows, axes and several other weapons that they could have taken only from prison guards. On the ground in front of them was the bleeding corpse of a guard.

"Who are you and what are your grievances?" Itzo asked again. "Please speak, so that they may be addressed."

"Call me *The Innocent Prisoner*," the leader of the pack answered cynically. He was a muscular, barrel-chested individual with a mop of dirty brown hair. His thick powerful arms went down almost to his knees.

"The Innocent Prisoner?" Itzo asked. "Is that what your father named you?"

"The name that my father gave me was lost to the sands of time while I was rotting in this place," the man sneered. "That apart, my men and I are not here to answer your questions, so can you please step out of our way? We have important business at hand."

"Important business indeed," Itzo replied, pointing towards the body of the dead guard. "And by whose authority is this business sanctioned?"

The man ignored him. "Chief Warden," he bellowed. "Where is the Chief Warden of this prison? Warden!"

"I have told you that the scrolls are fake," the little man said, emerging from behind one of the guards. His short sword was drawn. "Those signatures are not the King's."

"That is for me to say," The Innocent Prisoner hissed, taking a step forward. "You were not supposed to even open the scrolls," he added, glaring malevolently at the Warden. "Your duty is limited to holding them until a winner emerges from the fights. The law of the land is specific on that, is it not?"

"It is," the prisoners answered in unison.

"It also says," continued their leader, "that the winner of the fights must enter into possession of the sealed orders in question. And who is that winner?" he asked, cocking an ear with his left hand.

About ten steps away and facing the line of guards, was a bloodied, violent looking group of prisoners.

"YOU!" Came the deafening response from the men who were standing behind him.

"Good," he concluded. "Now give me the scrolls." He took a menacing step towards the Warden. "Is that not the custom? Or is this another one of your evil ploys to keep me and all who look like me in jail." He took another step forward. His men, weapons drawn, were close behind him.

"Give the scrolls to the man," Abou Bakar said, stepping forward past Itzo.

"And who are you?" the innocent prisoner asked defiantly. Abou Bakar ignored the question.

"Give the scrolls to the man," he repeated looking at the Warden. "He has won the fight and he merits their possession. Go on, give them to him. I shall be responsible for the decision. If it turns out to be of bad judgment, let me be held accountable and not the Warden," he added looking around. The little man stared at him for a long moment. Then, slowly, he lowered his sword, stuck his hand into his garments and pulled out two rolled scrolls. He threw them at The Innocent Prisoner. The man caught them in mid air.

"Who can read?" he asked.

"I can," a few voices answered. One was that of a prisoner.

"Let the prisoner read for us," the man decreed. "We trust him not to manipulate or pronounce different words other than the ones on the scroll."

"As you wish," the Warden replied. The inmate came forward, was handed the first scroll and he began to read from it.

"This is the word of the King. Sent out on the fifteenth day of the first month, in the year of Oso. Let it be entered, that I, Nehesy Aesare, King of all Kemet, send out an order, sealed by myself, and delivered by hand to the King's prison here in the capital city of Itjawy." The reader paused, took the second scroll and continued. "The said order, having been arrived at after due consideration and strict procedural justification of their guilt, I, Aesare, demand the heads of the following men for nothing less than the grievous crime of high treason. This is the word of the King and it goes forth with his power. To challenge it is to touch the King's own body with your hand." The prisoner proceeded to read out a list of about twenty names, which included Itzo's. Every name, except for the old Vizier's, was followed by a shout of protests from a cell in the hall. At the sound of his own name, the man instinctively raised up the sword that the General had loaned him.

"You? You are one of them?" The Innocent Prisoner jumped forward, sword arm going for the old man's throat. But Itzo was not about to be had so easily. Gracefully he stepped to the side and deflected the lunge. The innocent one growled in frustration and charged again.

"BREAK THEM UP!" The authority in the General's voice was unmistakable and it activated the guards who jumped into the foray of clashing metal and pulled the men apart.

Once out of harm's way, Itzo stopped struggling and let himself be pacified, contrary to The Innocent Prisoner whose reaction was immediate. Momentarily, the guards, who were trying to restrain him, were soon groaning and twisting on the cold stone floor in obvious pain.

"That is enough," Abou Bakar said.

"Enough?" the man asked, raising his sword and pointing it at the General. "Is that how you plan to keep me from becoming free?"

"No one is trying to keep you from becoming free."

"Then get out of the way because you are interfering with the job at hand." He took a step forward.

"You are free," the General said quietly.

"Free?" The cynicism was loud.

"Yes, free," the General paused. "I, Abou Bakar, from the tribe of Abou Ramzi, Nomarch of the northernmost province, and General of the Kings army in Avaris, I, give you my word, that the freedom I give to you and your men will be guaranteed by me in the presence of the King." For a moment there was complete silence in the hall.

"And how do I know that this is not some evil ploy to keep us here?" The Innocent Prisoner asked, interrupting the silence "Yes!" another prisoner chimed in. "How do we know that you are the man that you claim to be? By whose authority do you speak these lofty words? I should have your head at the end of my spear."

"I have given you my word," the General said, ignoring the threat.

"Your word?" The Innocent Prisoner interjected "Hahaaaa! What a laugh! And you expect us to believe that? You really do, don't you? Amazing! How many times has the King and his fine looking officials like yourself given us their word only to break them again? Can you count? Is that justice? Is that the best justice that the very civilized people of the great Kemetian civilization can achieve? Or did your enlightenment fail to reach the level of the conscience? Maybe so, because it would fully explain why I, and people who look like me, are always treated differently from everyone else." The man spat onto the floor in obvious disgust. "Do you have any idea what that feels like? To know that for mostly unjust reasons, people like myself make up nine tenths of all the prisoners in the Kingdom, although our total population in the land is less than one tenth? We Kemetians invented the science of numbers. Tell me, how does that add up? Is it because people of our complexion are simply born as thieves? Or that the lightness of our skin could be some mark of uncleanliness? Or maybe we are cursed by the gods with this hair type that will not stay in place, just so that the rest of the *civilized world* can readily identify us as the lesser race? Is that what it is?" The smile on the man's face did not belie the scorn in his voice which was dripping with bitter sarcasm.

"I can understand why you are angry and disappointed," Abou Bakar said taking a deep breath. "But there is more to it than that. And were I to say that you and yours have not been victimized just for looking different, it would be a lie because you have, and it is still going on although many will not accept it. That said..."

"So why should we trust you?" another prisoner interrupted

"Because it does not really matter at this point," the General answered. "The Kingdom is being attacked even as we speak."

"WHAT?" The surprise was uniform in both guards and prisoners alike.

"This is not true. Who would dare to risk the wrath of the greatest army on earth?" An older looking prisoner was now speaking. "This man must be lying," he said. "He and his men should get out of our way. We have the scrolls. Most of the names on the list are in this room, right here, right now. If we miss this chance, there might never be another one. Let us finish the mission. We would at least have earned the right to keep these scrolls," he implored. "They are the only real guarantee we have. If it turns out that the signature on the scroll is not the King's, then fine! At least we would be out of here. Out of this god-forsaken place. Think about it. Plus, I am sure that the King is not a fool. He must know that in jail prisoners would not find the kinds of tools and materials that are required to make high grade papyrus, ink, or even the royal seal. The royal wrath will run in the right direction, not towards us." The man concluded.

"Not if I tell the palace that you had been warned about the doubtful nature of the signatures," the General said, watching the men closely.

"Which is why you will die with the names on the list," another prisoner put in. "General or not, the palace will understand why you died." The man's bow was raised, and the poisoned arrow was aimed at the General. "Die," he shouted, stretching the bow.

What happened next may have been too fast for the eye to follow. But the result was not. The prison guard who was standing closest to the General screamed suddenly. Almost at the same time the archer began shaking, coughing, spluttering, choking, suffocating in spasms, then wilting, his bow falling away as his body collapsed to the floor. The General was down on one knee. One of his throwing knives was buried deep in the dead archer's throat.

"That could have been avoided," he said, sword drawn, "But you know it was my life or his. And I will always defend my life with all of my life, just as I expect every one else in this room to do. So if you have come to take mine, be ready to lay yours down," he added. "That said, I give you freedom once more with the authority bestowed upon me by the King. This is my last word and I have given it to you in honor. It is the best I can do under the circumstances. As of now, you and your men are free to walk away from here unchallenged. If that is your wish, let it be so. But if not, then I hope that as free men you will elect to join the King's mighty army and fight for the honor of the Kingdom," he finished, getting to his feet.

"Honor! Did you say honor?" It was The Innocent Prisoner once more. "Pray tell me, what kind of honor do you mean? Do you even understand the meaning of the word?" The General was watching the man in silence, weapon at the ready.

"Die," he shouted, stretching the bow.

"Anyway, whether you agree or not is not really important at this point," the man said, mimicking the General. "What I, and my men are saying, is that we believe you are part of the policies that have deliberately fostered an air of discrimination and subtle segregation, especially within the prisons. You have kept the light skinned away from the dark skinned, the Arabs away from the Hebrew, the Kemetians away from the Berbers, the Cushites away from the Aethiopians, teaching them to fear and hate each other's culture, to despise each other's religion, to perpetuate feuds, and to kill each other. Why?" the man asked. "So you can keep everyone distracted from the evils that you and your fine friends are perpetrating, right?" The voice had fallen to a sudden whisper. "Getting rich while the poor are busy fighting with each other. Divide and rule. Very clever, very clever indeed, and it has worked beautifully." He spat loudly on the stone floor. "Then today, you suddenly decide that we are all equals. You even offer us freedom without the required conditions having been met. Is it because you love us so much? I don't think so," he provided the answer. "I think it is because you are desperate. The Kingdom is under attack and you need help." He was smiling now. "The King and his fine officials like yourself need help. So, you come placating us with empty promises of freedom and false equality, forgetting that most of your policies are still calculated to segregate and victimize us." The man lowered his weapon. "I am sorry, but our answer to you is 'No'. We accept the freedom you offer but we refuse to join your army. We refuse to defend a status-quo that does not recognize us as equals."

And with that, the man raised his left hand. Two of his men picked up their fallen comrade, and then they began retreating into the dark corridor from whence they had come. The Innocent Prisoner was the last one in the hall. He gave a mock military salute, turned around, and disappeared after his men.

He gave a mock military salute, turned around, and disappeared after his men.

CHAPTER THIRTEEN

Cameroon, Central Africa.

$\mathcal{T}$he meeting between Charlie and Jean lasted all night. They met in an empty market stall in which Charlie had the opportunity to interview Jean at length. He asked the man a thousand questions, listened patiently to the answers, making notes in the process, challenging everything, searching, re-examining the details. After several hours, although not satisfied, he was sure that he had enough information to start something. Then it was the turn of Jean's pregnant girlfriend. He spoke to her for several hours as well, asking questions, and corroborating her answers with the responses he'd gotten from her boyfriend. By the end of it all, Charlie seemed convinced that publishing the story was the right way to go.

"But it would not be in the news section," he said. "It will be published as the winning entry for a fiction story competition. Of course that may change. Especially, if I can find concrete proof to back the story, because as it stands, I have not. But this way, the story will still be published, on the front page, with a catchy, controversial title that will not be missed. Now, if the story is true, those behind the plot will pause, and we may start noticing some new activity around here, which will be an indicator. But if the story is false, then it's just a harmless fiction story from a cartoonist, who chooses to use real people and real situations.

I went home hoping that the story would be published in the Thursday's edition if everything went smoothly.

It was almost mid night the next day, when we got the news that the press team had been picked up by the police. You see, our paper does not own a printing press. As such, every edition has to be taken to the city of Douala, which is an hour's drive away for printing. This was the job of the press team. The team had been on its way to the printing press, the report stated, when the members had been picked up and taken straight to jail. That meant the paper would not be coming out on Thursday morning as expected. Was it a coincidence? Jean Pierre did not think so. He insisted that Charlie must have made phone calls to ascertain the veracity of the controversial cartoon story. And that had let the cat out of the bag. It was a possibility, I agreed. Who would not, especially with such a story? But I also reminded him that rampant harassing, detaining, and torturing of journalists was common practice in the country. This was not the first time that members of the newspaper had been arrested without justification. The arrests may be just coincidental, I pointed out, hoping that I was right. Now all we could do was wait.

The team had been on its way to the printing press, the report stated, when the members had been picked up and taken straight to jail...

If, in the morning, our lawyers did not succeed in getting the press team, which had not been charged with any wrongdoing as yet, released, it would be an indication that Jean Pierre may be right. It would also suggest that the French secret service had much longer hands than I had thought possible. And that would mean the option of destroying the plot by exposing it through the press may have failed. Time was of the essence and it was running out. The US secretary of state would be here in a few days. It was becoming obvious to both Jean Pierre and myself that a different option had to be considered.

"We must find a way to meet Yao," Jean Pierre finally said. "He is the single most powerful factor in the whole plot. If we reach him in time, we can still undo the whole thing."

I knew that he was right. But there was a problem. I had heard enough about the rebel leader to realize that going into the rainforest to meet with him could possibly be the very last thing I did in this life. And at this point it was slowly becoming an option.

"First, lets wait," I insisted. "If our lawyers fail, then we may look at that as a viable alternative, yes?"

"*Bien sur.*"

---

*A*fter twenty four hours in a car, it took us another twenty-three hours of sweat drenched marching to get to the other big river. My calves and ankles were throbbing from the exertion, my shirt was stuck to my back, and I was thirsting badly for a beer when the waters of the river came into sight. The gently flowing currents were a welcome change after hours of dark jungle. Jean Pierre stopped at the edge of the forest, dropped his backpack to the ground and sat down on the root of a huge tree.

"This is the beginning of Yao's territory," I said, looking at a small hand-drawn map that he had procured from God knows where. "Once we cross the river, we shall be at his mercy. I hope that his men will not shoot us even before they hear what we have to say," I added, taking out my water bottle and unscrewing the cap. "He and his men have a reputation for shooting on sight," I informed unnecessarily. "Rub this on your body." I handed over a little tube of body paint. "And tie this around your head." It was the flag of the S.C.N.C. "Make sure that your hair is covered and that the colors are well exposed. From this point we can only go so far into Yao's territory before his men spot us. What will happen at that point, I cannot say, but we must avoid anything that would make us appear as threatening. Also remember to keep your hands exposed, so whoever spots us first will know that we have no weapons."

"And what will happen when they realize that I am not an African." Jean Pierre asked, swatting away at some flies. "Does that not make us even more suspicious?"

"It may, but I can assure you that you will be shot on sight, if you try approaching Yao's camp, looking as you do. Your best bet is to become as African as you can. By the time they realize that you are not black, we should be close enough to where they would know beyond any shadow of doubt that we are unarmed." Jean Pierre nodded to my logic as he began applying generous quantities of the dark body paint onto himself.

Of course, I could go into the camp by myself, and hope that Yao would believe me, even though I did not think it was likely. Anyone in their right mind would want to crosscheck the story as thoroughly as possible. If Yao decided to listen to me, the least I could do was to have Jean Pierre be available to corroborate the story. The rebel leader was said to be a lot of things, including being *very suspicious*. But no one could say that he was stupid.

When Jean Pierre was done darkening himself, he turned around slowly for me to inspect his handiwork.

"So do I look like a Bayangi?"

"Yes," I answered playing to his sense of humor. "You look like a councilor in my village."

"Wow! Now I am impressed. I wish I had a Camera to capture my unique Bayangi moment," he said with a smile.

"Oh, I am sure we will have all the time in the world to initiate you as a full fledged Bayangi. We just have to come out of this jungle alive," I said, picking up the backpack. I adjusted the straps around my shoulders, balanced the weight where I wanted it, and stepped out into the open.

"Down! Quick!" Jean Pierre said suddenly, pulling me down to the ground.

"Over there," he whispered, pointing down the river and handing me a pair of binoculars. I followed his cue and raised the device to my eyes. A small group of mounted men were fording the river about half a mile downstream. They were headed in the same direction as our selves, and they were all armed. Carefully I counted them, focusing on each face. There were five in all, and apart from Jean Pierre's boss, Yves Mammon, I did not recognize any of the other men who were all African.

"Your friend is here already," I told Jean Pierre, handing him the binoculars. He raised them to his eyes and focused.

"*Putain de merde!*" he swore. "Now we really have to hurry. But we must be very careful. This man is extremely dangerous and we cannot underestimate him. I think he is going to the same place as ourselves. We have to do everything to get there before he leaves Yao's camp. If we fail in that, then we would have truly failed. But until then, we can try."

I nodded, keeping my eyes on the line of men who were now swimming their mounts across the river. Slowly but surely, they were prodding and coaxing the frightened horses further into the fast flowing current, and from where we were, it was obvious that the animals were not happy about it. At that same instant, one of the horses, the last one on the line, was suddenly pulled below the surface, giving its rider barely enough time to jump at the nearby bank where some of his *compadres* quickly yanked him out of the water. Almost immediately, the water around the poor animal's last visible position came alive, as crocodile heads and tails butted and slapped at each other for a chance to get a good bite of horse meat.

"I bet that last man is taking a shit in his pants right now," Jean Pierre said. "That was close."

"Yes it was," I agreed, watching the men regroup themselves and disappear into the green foliage of the rain forest. With one horse less their progress will be slower.

"Lets go," I said, stepping out into the sun and setting off along the river. I knew a place a little way up stream, where the water would come up to my knees. One could cross the river there without fear of loosing a limb to ferocious amphibians. And that was where I planned to cross. A moment later, I heard Jean Pierre panting behind me.

Almost immediately, the water around the poor animal's last visible position came alive…

CHAPTER FOURTEEN

Kingdom of Kemet, 1720B.C.

*I*roha glanced at the eastern sky for what may have been the tenth time. It was now the beginning of the fourth watch, and he was getting worried.

His father was a man of his word and if he had failed to show up on time as promised, it definitely meant that something unexpected had delayed him. Of that, Iroha was sure. But by what?

His father knew that Emoon, the one woman that Iroha loved, lived in a little sandy village not too far from the capital city. If he had known that he would be gone for this long, he would have said something to the boy who usually lived too far to the north to have any meaningful time with her. Plus, with war almost certain, he needed to make sure that she would be safe. So, where was his father?

"I am going back into the city," he said, getting to his feet. Instantly, all of his father's men got up as well. They all knew what he meant. The General's delay was getting them worried as well.

"I am coming with you," one of them stated.

"By all means, please do," Iroha answered, knowing full well that it was the only way any of these men would allow him to go. They were all from his father's age group, had all served the General for at least two decades, and so they viewed him as if he were their son, too. He knew that they would not hesitate to tell him what to do if they felt that he was veering off onto a wrong course. He understood all of that: it was part of a time-honored custom that viewed the upbringing and guidance of a child as the responsibility of the whole community. Iroha did not mind. His own mother had not been there when he was growing up, so he had learned to appreciate the value of such communal parenting. That apart, he recalled a month long visit with his father to the land of Cerenea, where as a boy, he'd been shocked to find Cerenean parents more afraid of standing up to their own spoiled children for 'fear of alienating' them, to the point where they'd almost allowed a whole generation of youth to run amoc on wings of indiscipline. The pain, confusion and selfdoubt in the children's eyes had stayed with him.

"The rest of you will stay here with our food and the horses in case my father shows up," he said, loosening the cord that held his horse to the trunk of the baobab tree. "And if anything should happen to make you move from here, make sure to leave some signs for us, something that would guide us to your whereabouts should we return and not find you. Any questions?" He adjusted the saddle on his horse and mounted.

"No," the eldest of the three remaining men answered. "Just be careful."

"We will," he promised, riding away, followed by the man who had volunteered to be his companion and bodyguard.

Some moments later the northern gate of Itjawy came into view and the two men directed their horses towards it. Although it was still dark the city gate was crowded.

Iroha could see that they were mostly farmers and traders who had come to the city with their wares and goods. Today was the big market day of the month, and they all knew that it was usually a busy day that required an early start if one wanted to do well. There were even caravans with hundreds of loaded horses from...wait! Did he just think that? No, that was not possible! Iroha could hear his heart beating in his chest as he surveyed the caravans.

Slowly, he rode past the closest caravan, studying it closely, but it was still too dark to really see anything. What if he was wrong? He wished his father were here. He would know exactly what to do.

He prodded his horse past everyone, right up to the gates of the city. They were still closed, but he knew that there were guards on the other side. Always.

About ten paces from the gate, he stopped.

"Hail to the valiant and sleepless keepers of the north city gates. I salute you," he greeted with a loud voice.

"Hail to whomever you present yourself to be," came the sleepy, almost muted response.

"I am Iroha, son, body guard, and armor bearer to General Abou Bakar, the Nomarch of the Northern Province," Iroha replied. "And with me is my companion and bodyguard."

"And what is your business with us?" the voice asked.

"I have to get into the city."

"Into the city? But you must know, Son of Abou Bakar, that by law these gates can be opened only after the sun has shown its face."

"I do, but this is an emergency," he replied, glancing furtively behind him.

"An emergency?" It was from the young man's companion and bodyguard. The surprise in the whispered question was obvious. "What are you doing, Iroha? Trying to offer our necks to the King for breakfast?"

"Shshhh...I will explain in a moment," he whispered back, hoping that somehow he would be proven wrong.

"What kind of emergency would require us to let anyone into the city before the sun comes up?" It was the same voice from the other side of the wall.

"I cannot speak too loudly. It is something that the mouth should speak only into the ear. Even the wind must not be allowed to hear this. Too many lives may depend on it. You must let me in."

There was a moment of silence in which Iroha could sense the man on the other side of the gate, as he considered different options. Finally, he heard the sound of a sliding bolt and a tiny window on the huge gate was opened.

"What do you have that can prove your name?" asked the face that had appeared in the little window. "You could be anybody."

Iroha cantered his mount up to the gate and handed over something through the little window. It was a piece of parchment that bore the General's seal. "That is my father's," he volunteered, as the face disappeared from the window only to reappear a moment later.

"What else do you have?" the man asked.

Iroha hesitated for just a moment, and then, took off the signet ring that he always wore around the forefinger of his right hand. He handed it to the man who grunted, closed the little window and disappeared again. The bolt slid home.

"This has to be really serious," whispered his mounted companion who had also ridden up to the gate. "Your father would not be happy if this were some kind of doubtful intelligence."

"I think I am right," Iroha replied. "Even though I pray that the gods will prove me wrong."

The bodyguard stiffened. Those were serious words. Even from a young man.

"What do you mean?" he asked urgently.

"Look carefully at the biggest caravans," whispered Iroha. "Some of them are supposed to be loaded with silk from the east, right?"

"Right."

"Which means most of them are supposed to be coming from as far away as Persia, correct?"

"Yes," the bodyguard concurred, still wondering where the young man was going with this.

"And after selling what they carry, these caravans would be loaded once more with gold, ivory, salt, herbs, papyrus, and medicinal portions for a return journey, correct?" The man nodded as Iroha continued. "In my estimation, that is a very long distance, and any merchant who knows what trading is, will tell you that camels are best suited for such trips. First, they cost less to buy, carry heavier loads, and consume less water."

"By the gods!" the bodyguard whispered in shock. "The horses!"

"Yes, the horses," Iroha whispered. "Why do they have so many of them when they could have found that many camels for half the price. What kind of merchants are these? Or are they merchants at all?"

"This is an..."

The reopening of the little window interrupted the man's words and once more, the face appeared in it.

"The gate commander will let you in, but this had better be good," the face whispered. "Go east along the wall for about a thousand cubits and you will come upon a third clump of trees growing right next to the wall. Someone will be waiting for you there. But you must hurry."

Iroha prodded his horse away from the gate and rode off into the windy desert darkness, away from the caravans. Close on his heels was the other man. As the men rode off, it would have appeared to any one who was observing them that they were headed for some hamlet in the Kingdom's wilderness.

Once out of sight, both men circled around and headed in the opposite direction. Moments later, they came upon a clump of trees and Iroha descended from his horse. In the windy darkness, he could not see what kind of trees they were but he noted that the silhouette of a figure had stepped away from the shade of trees and was waving at them.

"There he is," Iroha whispered.

"I am to bring one of you with me," the man said over the

whistling wind. "Which one is it?"

Iroha turned to his companion.

"Go back and alert the other men about the situation," he said. "The sun will be up within the hour. Be ready."

The man nodded, took the reins of Iroha's horse and rode off.

Left to himself, the young man turned his full attention to the soldier who had come to lead him into the city.

"I shall have to take your weapons and blindfold you," the soldier said. "You do not have a quarrel with that, do you?"

"No, I do not," Iroha replied, handing over his sword and knives. The man wrapped everything in a piece of soft bark that he had brought with him in anticipation. Then he took out a piece of black cloth, shook it out in the wind, folded it several times lengthwise and tied it around Iroha's head, making sure that his eyes were covered.

When the man was done, he took Iroha's left hand, and began leading him away towards the darker shadows that were cast by the trees and the wall.

With his eyes blindfolded, Iroha walked as he felt himself directed. First, it was a curving flight of stairs, and he was in water up to his knees. That was followed by another flight of stairs, a left turn, a right turn, another left turn, and a long corridor, or so it felt. At one point he could have sworn that some one else had joined them, but he could not see so he was not sure. Then they were on the other side of the wall and someone was taking away the blindfold.

"What is this emergency that will not wait for the sun?" It was the commander of the north city gates and he did not sound too happy as he looked at Iroha. He was leaned back into a rattan chair, hands behind head, with both feet propped up on the table. He was not the only person in the small, almost bare, torch lit room, which served as the inner office of the north city gate.

Iroha glanced around the room for a moment, recognizing one of the faces that had spoken to him earlier through the little window. Every one in the room was quiet. They were all waiting for him to speak.

"Those caravans are not trade caravans," he said.

"What do you mean young man?" the gate commander demanded.

"Why do they have so many horses?" Iroha asked again. "If it were a genuine trade caravan from the distant east or north, should they not have camels instead?"

"I am still listening," the gate commander interrupted impatiently. "You have not yet said anything that is worthy of the time and attention that you have received so far."

Iroha hesitated.

"The Kingdom is under attack," he said.

"WHAT?" The gate commander bounded out of his seat. The lazy posture was gone and he was all tension "If this is some kind of joke, I swear upon my dead uncle's name..."

"It is not." Iroha said. "I am very serious. The Kingdom is under attack. That is the intelligence that my father brought in yesterday. And those caravans, in my opinion, are a disguised part of the invading army. We have to hurry."

"Hurry? To do what?"

"Barricade the gates," Iroha answered.

"Barricade the city gates? Have you taken leave of your senses, young man? Do you know what you are asking? If I do not open those gates with the sun, all those farmers and traders who are laden with goods and produce will not come in. That means the gate tax will not be collected. That means the farmers, whose food will go bad in the heat, will start a revolt that will carry the whole story right into the ears of the palace. Do you know what that means?" The man paused. "It means that the King will not be pleased," he added aggressively. The silence in the room was loud, as everyone in his own way processed this information, and attempted to translate the possible implications for themselves. "Do you still think that the Kingdom is under attack and that we should barricade the gates instead of opening them?" The question was a whispered threat.

"Yes, I do," Iroha replied as firmly as he could.

The disbelief in the gate commander's face and posture was almost comical. Except for the fact that it was not. Slowly he came around his table, peering into Iroha's eyes as if the young man had suddenly become some kind of impossible phenomenon.

"WHO ARE YOU?" The man screamed. "WHO ARE YOU?"

"I am Iroha, son of Abou Bakar."

"I know that," the man shouted in frustration, "But who are you? What do you want? What gives you the right to say such things? Do you think these are light matters? If you think you can get away with this, you are sorely mistaken. Today, you have stuck your whole head into a beehive and I shall prove it to you. Come with me," the commander ordered, marching out of the room. Iroha followed.

The man led him up a flight of stairs that came out on top of the huge city walls, almost above the gate. It was the first time that Iroha had been on the walls and for a moment he was taken in by the whole view. It was still very windy and the illuminated eastern sky from which the sun was about to burst, seemed to be wondering what to do with the thick, dark clouds. Within the city itself, apart from the first signs of the morning, like smoke from some early kitchen, there was little or no visible activity. The thousands of rooftops seemed to all be waiting for the sun. All in all, it lent an air of intense drama, almost as if the elements knew that the gods were coming together for some apocalyptic collision of intense proportions. And they, the elements, seemed to have been assigned the job of manifesting a fitting backdrop.

...the illuminated eastern sky from which the sun was about to burst, seemed to be wondering what to do with the thick, dark clouds...

Iroha lowered his eyes and peered at the distance. He could

barely see anything that was far off, but the crowd of waiting farmers and traders in front of the closed gate was clearly visible. It looked a little busier from up here. Everyone was preparing all the last minute details that were required for gaining entry into the city and its huge market.

"Are those the caravans?" the gate commander asked. Iroha nodded. "And which of them is your army," the commander went on, mockingly. And why have we not received any orders for immediate mobilization?" he asked. "It's been two full days since your father supposedly rode in with the news of war, as you claim."

"I don't fully understand, but..."

"But what?" the commander demanded turning towards the young man. "Look towards the east. What do you see?"

"I see that the morning is here and that the sun has already shown the beginning of its face..."

"Even though the north city gate is still locked. Do you think the King may be wondering why the trumpet from one of the four city gates has not yet been heard in the palace? Especially, if that gate is this one?" The man smiled. "Apart from that, are you aware that the passage in the ground through which you were taken is known only to a select handful of people in all the land? Now, for no good reason, you Iroha, know about it as well. The palace will not like that. Do you know what that means?" The man smiled again. "It means that your freedom is now in great peril." He paused and took a step closer to the young man. "Listen, I have a lot of respect for your father, but can you try to remember that you are not he?" he hissed with a sneer. "At least I hope you do when the King summons you to appear before him with an explanation for this delay." He turned away and strutted off.

"Let the north gates of mighty Itjawy be thrown open," he shouted, as he descended the last step into his office. Immediately there was a loud, long, drawn out trumpet blast, and very slowly, the gates began creaking as the pulley system that operated them was engaged.

The gate commander smiled. Another market day was here. It meant more money, especially with the obvious sizes of today's caravans. The amount of money to be collected as gate tax would more than double! So even if he kept a bigger than usual portion for himself, the treasury will not realize it, except for the men who worked at the gate with him. But they also took home a little something. He always made sure of that, for security. The crocodile may eat its own child, but would it dare to take a bite out of its own tail? The man chuckled to himself. Hopefully, he would die at this job from old age. Had the seer not told him that he would if he was careful? Now that he thought about it, he was sure that the hands of the gods were with him. Think about it! He'd been to see the diviner just yesterday, and the man himself had told him about everything in the future; the wealth he was supposed to make, the husbands that his daughters will find, a new and younger wife for himself, even the temptation that would come to derail him if he gave in to fear.

So, he had been warned. Imagine the disaster that would have occurred if he had not been expecting it, if he had not realized in time that the General's son was the messenger of temptation that the shaman had warned him about. What a tempter! He must be from *epkensu* himself! There was no doubt about it. The man wetted his thumb on his tongue and rubbed it on his forehead. "Bad luck be gone," he said silently to himself as he walked out into the early morning sun.

The scene that met his eyes could not have been better. The city gates were wide open and the first ten silk laden horses were being brought in. Behind these, was a long line of loaded animals that disappeared into the windy horizon. What a blessing! Of course the King would get his share in taxes, but still, the rest would be quite a sum. Was this not what the good life was about? Did that mean he was a bad person? But of course not! He was just doing what any good father would do to make sure that his offspring would not have to struggle. Was that such a bad thing? How much damage could he, as an individual, actually cause to the whole Kingdom? How much stone can the ant carry away from the mountain? Who would not seize such an opportunity? It was perfect. He could not wait to go back and see the shaman.

Satisfied with the way everything looked, the gate commander turned around and was about to head back into the Spartan comfort of the inner office when he noticed that the young man was still standing on top of the city walls.

Why had the guards not arrested him? Did they have to be instructed about the most obvious things?

"Guards! Arrest that man!" the gate commander bellowed, pointing up at Iroha. Immediately, several guards took off at a run, disappearing into the doorway of the little office through which they would access the top of the wall.

Standing on top of the city wall, Iroha heard the order and felt himself tense with indecision. He took a quick glance below and noticed that another of the horses was just stepping through the gates. It would be directly below him in a moment. This was his chance.

... the young man was still standing on top of the city walls...

CHAPTER FIFTEEN

With a loud cry Iroha jumped off the city wall and held his breath. His weapons had not been returned so he did not have any. But he could see his father's men, who had been watching him all along, positioning themselves below for the trouble that they saw coming.

He landed on the silk laden horse with a thud and a grunt. The frightened animal neighed, rearing up on two feet, attracting the shocked attention of a few merchants as the cargo of silk was displaced.

Beneath it was an armed man and his weapon, a short sword, missed Iroha's face by a hair's breath.

"LOCK THE GATES!" Iroha shouted.

"ATTAAAACK," Another voice screamed.

Both Iroha and the horseman crashed to the ground in a confused heap of silk, flailing arms and legs, as the frightened animal took off, galloping into the waking city.

"CLOSE THE GATES!" somebody shouted again, as one of the *merchants*, a stout fellow with a long beard, produced a little horn and sounded three sharp blasts. In response, several cargoes of silk went tumbling to the ground, revealing men, who were now sitting up on the horses that had been part of the trade caravan just moments ago.

"CLOSE THE GATES!" It was the gate commander this time. He had been jolted by the unfolding reality to spur on the guards who were strenuously involved in pushing the huge gates shut. But alas, the pulley system on which the task usually depended had not been serviced in a long time, as it should have been. It began to creak. Everyone, including the invaders, could hear the creaks, and they all knew what it meant.

"Order all horsemen to engage," Iroha shouted to the gate commander as he caught a sword thrown from one of his father's men, and quickly dispatched the man he had been grappling with. At that same moment, a group of mounted city guards appeared from around the corner and attacked the thick line of invading horsemen, who were intent on hacking, cutting, and butchering their way into the city.

"Every available man mount a horse and hold the gates,"

Iroha shouted. "And send messengers into the city, to the palace, to the council of elders, all the other city gates, and the house of the royal announcer," he told the gate commander. "About two dozen of these horsemen escaped into the city. Take some men and find them," he added, looking the man in the eye as he jumped onto a horse that one of his father's men had found for him.

"Thank you very much," he said to the man, before turning the animal around and galloping into the melee of guards, horsemen, spears, swords, knives, and clubs. It was obvious that both sides were straining in a deadly struggle to impose their will upon the creaking wooden structure that was the north city gates.

With a loud cry Iroha jumped off the city wall...

There was blood, there was pain, there were cries, shouts, and there was death. It was a contest of force that seemed to be so delicately balanced that it was just a matter of time before any one side capitulated, a chance that Iroha knew could not be taken. He knew exactly what his father would do.

"WATER!" he cried, and the order was repeated by several voices, carrying the instruction all the way to the appropriate quarters as the fighting intensified.

And then, just when it seemed as if the invaders were going to push their way in, a procession of three men was spied atop the city wall. They were slowly wheeling a huge cauldron of boiling water towards the gate. A shout of encouragement rose from the outnumbered city guards, as that invincible, elusive, and most precious sentiment, called hope, stole its way into their hearts.

"HOLD STRONG," Iroha shouted, mentally willing the men to redouble their effort.

But suddenly everything was in jeopardy. An arrow found one of the men on top of the wall. He fell off screaming, leaving the other two to manage the *scaldingly* hot vessel of water.

Slowly, the cauldron advanced. Then it was almost in place. But now, something more dreadful seemed to be happening. As if in a slow dream, the huge pot swayed dangerously. "Nooooo!" several guards cried, rushing to get out of the way as the two men on the wall struggled with the enormous vessel. But alas, its weight and the heat were just too much, and it began rocking, threatening to pour out its contents in the wrong direction!

It was at that moment that another man, bent double and running towards the cauldron, appeared on the wall. His appearance was heralded by another shout of hope from the embattled city guards.

The man, whose name later appeared in songs as Mohtoh, son of Elotinge, was a few steps from the cauldron when it actually began to tip over into the city. With a cry he lunged himself at it, secured a hold around the open rim, screaming in pain even as he used his full body weight to rebalance the object and force it to go in the opposite direction. He was dead by the time the contents came pouring over his head.

The boiling, steaming water came rushing down on the invaders, scalding and blinding both horses and riders, vanquishing them, killing several on the spot, and forcing a quick retreat. The tide of the struggle was turned and the gates began to close. After what seemed like an eternity a cry of victory went up into the air as the gates were forced shut, bolted, and barricaded.

It was a cry of victory, which, for Iroha, was soon followed by a dampening thought. Some of the people outside were Kemetian children, women, and men, and they had been left at the mercy of foreign soldiers. Not too far beyond them, in a little oasis village tucked in the sand dunes, lived Emoon, the woman that he hoped would be the mother of his children someday.

He hurried into the gate office which was now crowded with soldiers. A few of them had been wounded and were receiving care. At least something organized was going on, he noted.

He rushed across the little office and joined the line of soldiers, mostly archers, who were running up the stairs to the top of the wall. He came out into the turbulent morning air and immediately looked to see what was happening out side the city. Just as he feared, the invaders had taken everybody captive and were herding them into a camp that was being erected even as he looked.

"Somebody runs!" a voice on the wall shouted, interrupting his thoughts.

"Where?" Iroha asked?

"Over this way. Follow my hand."

Iroha slapped down the hand. "Do not point. It may alert the enemy and give the runner away." He squinted into the windy distance, at the direction the man had suggested. "I see him," he confirmed. "Over by the tail of the second dune. He must have seen the invaders for he is circling away to the south gate."

"He looks like he has been running for at least one week," an older soldier observed.

"Yes," another agreed, "From the way his right shoulder falls in rhythm with his left step, I would dare to say that he runs like Fada, the son of Lotin."

At the mention of the name, every man on the wall felt a little unease creep into his soul. Fada? The man was easily the best runner in the entire Kingdom. A legend whose skill in running could be compared only to *Nkwoh* the tiger himself, no more, no less. Does rumor not have it that he had been born with an extra pair of lungs? The man was a well-respected national treasure and there was no way around it. Had he not run from Mero to Mbalangi? How many people could run ceaselessly for seventeen days and night? And he'd arrived in the nick of time with information that had saved the whole Kingdom from peril. This had happened some years before, during the southern campaigns that Neferhotep had launched to punish the commercially disruptive Kings of the southern Kingdoms.

So, to say the least, news that Fada, son of Lotin, may possibly be the runner was unnerving because it raised another dampening question; who would risk such a treasure if the circumstances were not dire? Did the elders not say that serious news was hardly good?

Iroha felt the urgency of the moment rise a little bit. He did not have too much time. If he was going to find his sweetheart, now was the time to leave. Everyone was still distracted from the events of the morning. With a little luck, he could find his way through the secret passage and leave before any of his father's men realized that he was gone. He had decided that it was best that way. If he were alone he could travel faster, attract less attention, and be back with Emoon just before the evening meal.

He turned around and made his way back into the gate office. There were still some men about and they were all busy with the mobilization-orders that had been issued. None of them seemed to be paying any attention to him. He studied the little room, recreating the early morning scene in his mind. That was where he had been standing, facing the desk over there at which the gate commander had been sitting, he told himself. Which means he had been brought in from over that way, he concluded. Casually, he strolled down a corridor that led in the suggested direction. A series of confusing turns later, he was all by himself.

Yes, this felt like it. The stairs should be somewhere around here. Oh, there they were. He grabbed a lit torch that was hanging from the wall and disappeared down the dark flight of stairs. Suddenly he was below ground. He raised the burning torch, trying to make more sense of his immediate surroundings.

It looked as if he was in some kind of stone corridor that ran along the wall. He followed it for a moment, going deeper into the ground. It leveled off and then began climbing again. Then just when he thought he was lost, he felt a strong whiff of cold air coming from his right. He stopped and raised the torch even higher. The entrance to the side passage that he saw, had been deliberately designed to look like an outcropping of rock that one would instinctively seek to avoid And it had almost fooled him. He turned into it and a few moments later he was in water.

He waded across what may have been a stream. On the other side he came upon an almost vertical flight of stairs. He went up those and turned into another outcropping that ended in a dark grove of trees.

He was outside the city.

Silently, he advanced forward, pushing aside thick shrubs and leaves that were keeping out the sunlight. Then, very carefully, he inspected as much of the surroundings as he could see. There didn't seem to be any one around. He stepped into the open and began running along the wall, away from where he judged the foreign army was setting up camp.

A short time later he came upon a sand dune that was high enough to provide some cover, and he set off at a brisk pace, jogging along its base and heading towards the open desert. He would have to find a horse soon. On foot it would take much longer to get to the little oasis settlement that was his destination.

It was where Emoon lived with her family and they had lived there for generations. Her ancestors had dug the well that had made the place into an oasis, providing them a livelihood that was based on watering the thirsty caravans that were going to, or coming from distant places.

As he hurried forward, his thoughts took him back to the day they had met. He had been on mission for his father and had ridden into the lonesome settlement, tired and thirsty, only to find that he could not get any water. The place had been taken hostage by a gang of three rascals who lived in the desert and made a living from intimidating and robbing the most vulnerable. His arrival at that particular time had been purely by chance but it had changed everything.

He had confronted the men who had been no match for a trained fighting soldier like himself. Two of them had died in the altercation, and the last one had fled off into the desert, never to be heard from again.

The Patriarch of the very small family whose honor he had just defended, was so grateful that he had replenished all of Iroha's supplies at no cost. The man had also pledged the same free service to the young man if he should ever choose to call in the future. But what had impressed Iroha the most was the man's daughter, Emoon, as she climbed out of the dry well from where she, her mother, and her sister had been hiding. And that had been it for him. He had fallen in love with the beautiful girl and something inside had told him there and then, that this was the one woman in the world with whom he wanted to spend all of his days. Suddenly, the world seemed to have filled up with beautiful details that he had somehow failed to notice before; the intricate patterns on a common leaf, the gold in the color of sand, the smooth fur on his horse, or even just the miraculous fact of being alive. He was in love.

Right now, as he walked, he prayed that Emoon and her family had not come to any harm. He prayed that she was safe and that he would find her as soon as possible. Unconsciously, he broke into a run, ignoring the heat from the sun or the fact that he may tire himself out even though he still had a distance to go. Several hours later, he was still running.

The smoke that was lazily rising into the air was the first sign that all was not well in the settlement.

It was still about five miles away, and he tried not to look at it as he forced his tired body to run even faster. Panting and perspiring, he finally came atop the last sand dune, from where he could see the settlement.

By the gods!

It had been razed to the ground and the smoldering embers were all that was left of the place!

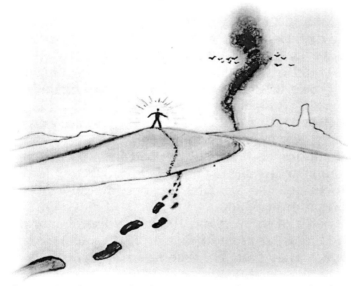

The smoke that was lazily rising into the air was the first sign that all was not well in the settlement...

Blinded by tears, Iroha stumbled into the desiccated homestead, not quite believing what he was seeing, searching desperately, pulling up whatever he could find, an ash laden plate here, a broken ceramic jar there, a smoking piece of wood, a stone ornament; moving on all fours, calling her name, over and over, getting burned but not giving up, until finally he collapsed in exhaustion by the well which had been wickedly filled up with sand.

---

*C*ikatrix, the newly appointed Vizier for border security, smiled bitterly, pulling the hood lower over his scarred face as he nudged the horse further down the dark, narrow backstreet. The animal acquiesced, albeit reluctantly, almost as if it could sense the unease with which its rider was going to this particular meeting.

It was a meeting that Hasim had called. And when Hasim called, Cikatrix did not have a choice. Nervously, he adjusted the dagger that was strapped to his thigh. With any luck, he would not need it. With Hasim, one could never be sure. Meeting him always carried a serious element of risk.

A few moments later, he dismounted onto the dark street, secured the horse, and walked to a low wooden door. Glancing around to make sure that no one was watching, he knocked twice in rapid succession, and then once. Immediately, the door was opened from inside and he stepped in.

He was in a mid sized, dust covered, cobwebbed room, that could have been a tavern at one time. There were a few wooden tables and chairs, most of them falling apart from disuse. A single candle was burning on a window ledge but its dim light left much of the room in shadows. Apart from several closed windows Cikatrix did not see any other exit. Trust Hasim to choose a location like this.

"Are you alone?" The voice was unmistakable.

"Yes I am," Cikatrix answered, spinning to squint into the shadows from where the voice was emanating. "I made sure of that."

"Oh, you did?" Hasim asked. He was standing with his feet slightly apart, arms hanging loosely by his side, almost relaxed. Cikatrix was not fooled. This was Hasim.

"Yes, I did."

"And why is that?" Hasim asked with quiet sarcasm. "Why did you bother?"

Cikatrix swallowed hard, licking his lips and choosing his words with the utmost care.

"Because, to be followed to a meeting with you may jeopardize or even compromise the very important mission at hand."

"Oh, could it?" A different element had crept into the voice, making it even more cynical. "Is that why the General is still breathing?"

"Um...um..."

"Shut up."

"Please Hasim," Cikatrix pleaded, "Please. This man is not like many. He is a very hard one. Of course, we shall eventually get him, but..."

"Eventually?" Hasim interrupted. "I don't like that word. In fact I don't even know what it means in this context. Do you?" The whisper did not mask the anger in the voice, and the Vizier broke out in cold sweat.

"Please Hasim. Give me until tomorrow night. I swear, I will have the man."

Hasim did not respond. After what seemed like an eternity he took a single step forward, allowing the light to fall on his skull-like features.

"Look at my eyes and know that I am serious. You have until tomorrow night," he said with a smile, sheathing a dagger that the Vizier had failed to notice until then. "After that, you will have only yourself to blame," he added, taking a backward step into the shadows.

"I will not fail," Cikatrix answered, breathing a huge sigh of relief. "I will not fail. I give you my word."

Silence

He squinted into the dark shadows. After a moment he realized that he was alone. Hasim was gone.

The Vizier took in a deep breath and exhaled slowly. There was no doubt in his mind about what would happen to him if the General did not die on time. Not that he had anything against the man. It was purely about self preservation.

Having him followed, in the hopes that an opportunity may arise, was not working. Abou Bakar was not the kind of man to leave himself open to surprises like that. To take his life, a man had to walk up in the light of day, state the purpose, pull out a weapon and attack. 'Head on' was the only way it was going to happen at this point.

He let himself out of the room, retrieved his horse, mounted and set off down the dark and empty street. As he rode away, he could have sworn that the feeling of Hasim's eyes on his back was real.

Damn the man, Cikatrix thought with impotent rage. Who did Hasim think he was? Wait! I will show them! My time is coming. Hasim and his *Holy master* could think that he, Cikatrix, was just a stupid errand boy. Which was good too. Did the elders not say, that when it came to one's enemies, it was sometimes better to be underestimated than overestimated?

As he rode away, he could have sworn that the feeling of Hasim's eyes on his back was real...

CHAPTER SIXTEEN

Cameroon, Central Africa.

Charlie, more than anyone else, except maybe for the owner of the newspaper, knew how precarious the situation really was. And he was not liking it. He was a man who had made many personal sacrifices just to be a truth-guided journalist. Working with the newspaper was not going to make him a rich man anytime soon, which he knew, but he was happy. At least, with this paper, he could indulge in objective journalism. Even though it was always at a risk.

It was more of a cause than a career. Luckily, the paper was mostly staffed by men and women whose passion for journalism went deeper than the skin; some of them, like Charlie, had been with the paper from its infancy, from those days when the paper was said to have been running on air and water, if such a thing was possible. But the newspaper had managed a dogged survival.

Now, just when it looked as if things were beginning to settle down, here was this absurdity of a story that was threatening to shake things up. And the whole thing could possibly be a fallacy. But what if the story turned out to be true? Would a decision not to publish it sit well on the conscience of history?

He had decided to publish the story and it would have been out by now, that is, if the police had not picked up the press team. But they had, and it had thrown some mud into the milk. In this line of work that was expected to happen every so often. He, himself, had been picked up, detained, and even subjected to hair-raising violence. But this case was different. A lot more could be at stake, which was why he was keeping the situation under very close scrutiny.

So far, it was looking as if the current detention of the press team was political, a probability with very disturbing implications and it had prompted Charlie to start looking at the Frenchman's story even more closely, playing and replaying it in his mind, asking more questions and considering impossible possibilities. The more he looked, the more the story gained the appearance of an unlikely truth.

He glanced at his watch while bringing the Toyota DX to a crawl, allowing the vehicle to navigate a particularly unfriendly group of pot holes, sputtering and coughing, sinking into the almost watery mud. How he wished he did not have to do this. But he had to and he did not have much time.

Following the notes he had made from interviewing Jean Pierre the French man, a big consignment of weapons had been quietly brought into the country very recently. It had been passed off, as *military grade construction material,* meant for renovation and expansion work at the French military base in Limbe.

With that information he had made more phone calls, gone to the Port authorities, asked questions about the shipments, determined the dates of entry, read the reports on the volume and weight of material in question. And then he had made even more calls.

It had not been easy to get a pass into the military base, but he had done it, mostly by calling in a few big favors. So here he was, four hours later, on his way to visit the base as part of a research project for a book on 'The long friendship and military cooperation that exists between the French and the Cameroonian Governments.'

He shifted gears, and sent the car bouncing up a little hill. A minute later, he caught sight of the first waves of the Atlantic, just as the Toyota drove past a huge metal sign, in bold letters, telling all, that this was a French military facility, and that access was automatically denied until specified to the contrary.

Wow, what nerve, Charlie thought. You come to my country, you kill the men, you rape the women, you pillage the land, and as if that is not enough, you grab prime coastal real estate, parcels of land which are some of the most expensive in the whole country, and on these you build your military base. Is there nothing wrong with that picture? I wonder what you would think, Charlie mused with a sardonic smile, if the Cameroonian government wanted a military base in The French Riviera as a symbol of the great and endearing friendship that exists between our two nations. You would laugh your head off and die from laughter before that happens, right? Yet you will not hesitate to kill me if I should ask you to dismantle your base in my country, yes? I pray for your sakes that karma is not real...

He looked at his watch again. Not really to check the time, just out of tension. He wanted the visit to be done with as quickly as possible. He did not trust these French soldiers. They always looked at you with a smirk, as if they were better than you, as if they would not hesitate to kill you if ordered. And he had no doubt they would.

Two hundred meters away, rising from the mud, coiled barbed wire was glinting in the sun right next to a ferocious looking sentry post, both in obvious agreement with the metal sign. Not too far beyond that, becoming more visible as he got nearer, were more signs of a military installation.

By the time Charlie pulled up in front of the gate, two men, both French, in military uniform, carrying rock steady weapons, had stepped out of the guardhouse and onto the dirt road.

"*Que voulez vous?*" One of the men asked.

"I am the journalist-slash-writer." Charlie said, leaning out of the window
and holding out his ID card. The man took it, stared at it in aggressive silence, then at Charlie's face, then back at the card. When he was satisfied, he nodded at his comrade who had just finished a third tour of duty around the little, muddy Toyota. The comrade walked back into the sentry guardhouse and momentarily, the gates began swinging open.

He shifted gears, and sent the car bouncing up a little hill.

"*Tout droit*", the soldier said, handing back Charlie's ID. He took it, dropped it on the passenger seat, stepped on the clutch, shifted into first gear and drove into the base.

"*I* am as sure as I will ever be." Charlie said, speaking into the cell phone. "Especially under the circumstances."

He was standing on a street corner, right next to the little Toyota, which had been parked in front of several roadside newspaper kiosks. The person on the other end of the line was Opio, a staffer at the office.

It was only eight in the morning, yet the day was already underway. All the little, tightly crammed stalls that were always overflowing with cheap, colorful Chinese displays, were already open. Even the foot traffic of mostly eye-shoppers was increasing in volume by the minute. Although it was relatively early, Charlie was already getting some not-too-subtle indicators that it was going to be a very hot one. He could even feel his T-shirt beginning to stick to his back.

He pulled out a clean, neatly folded handkerchief, and dabbed off the first beads of sweat that were starting to form on his forehead. Phew! It was hot. A perfect day for the beach. But he knew that was a just a dream. He had work to do.

"And when are you coming back?"

"I am almost done. I just have one more stop and that should be it. I expect to be back at my desk sometime soon."

"Good, because F.W. wants to see you ASAP."

"Then arrange a meeting for four p.m. I should be there by then."

F.W. was referencing the proprietor of the newspaper. It was how he was called around the office. And when he called, everyone listened.

"Done," Opio said.

"Good man," Charlie said, cupping his hands around the cell phone to keep out the loud and noisy drone of a sputtering diesel engine that seemed intent on smoking everything out as it went by.

"And please don't forget to get me a copy of *The Economist*," Opio said. "I will give you the money when you get here."

All the little, tightly crammed stalls that were always overflowing with cheap, colorful Chinese displays, were already open...

After putting away the cell phone, Charlie walked up to the nearest kiosk, picked up a copy of *The Economist* and one of *The Times*. "I also want a *Newsweek*," he said.

"Will that be all for you today?" asked the seller, a teenaged boy, as he reached into a box to fish out a copy of *News week*.

"Yes," Charlie confirmed, handing over some money and taking the magazine. On its cover was a photo-shopped picture of an African map, wrapped in several foreign flags, with

Chinese colors dominating the rest. Beneath the picture, in bold letters, was the question, -'A new Africa'?

"That is one interesting story," the boy said, noticing what Charlie was reading.

"Is it?" Charlie murmured distractedly as he turned a page.

"Oh yeah, it has to be. We have sold an uncommonly high number of those," the boy volunteered with a smile.

"And is that good for business or what?"

"Of course it is," the boy replied, disappearing into the back of the small stall to get a plastic bag. "I wonder what about the story makes it so important."

I bet you do, Charlie thought, as he walked back to the Toyota. It was still very common to find people who did not yet grasp the possible implications of Chinese progress in Africa. And even when they did, their understanding would usually be rather superficial and almost certainly un-researched. Apart from that, the degree of Chinese presence on the continent was a relatively new occurrence, which was still generating more questions than answers. It was partly because of such questions that he himself had come out to the town of Limbe. And the trip seemed to have paid off.

Three whole hours had been spent within the French base, mostly in interviews. He had spoken with the base commander, a jolly good fellow who seemed more willing to talk about women than anything else. Charlie had indulged the man, trading war stories from his high school days when he himself had been something of a player.

And it had worked. The Base Commander had been laughing so hard that when Charlie asked to see the important construction work that was supposedly ongoing, the man had not even hesitated. He had gotten a jeep and personally chauffeured the journalist across the sleepy looking military base, to the work site.

The work site, if it could be called that, was nothing but an empty parcel of land that was located next to two, huge, barn-like buildings.

"Over there, is where ze vork is going on." the Commander said, with a pronounced French accent that reminded the journalist of a trip he had taken to Nantes.

"I see," Charlie agreed, not certain if he was missing something. "And ve expect to *commencer*...sorry, commence painting sometime early next veek. It should be the last phase of the *projet*."

"I see," Charlie agreed again, not quite sure what to say. To be sure, there was a lone bulldozer, two wheelbarrows, and a few other odds and ends, but nothing that was suggestive of convincing on-going construction work. All the people he could see around the base, all speaking French, and mostly in military fatigues, were all involved in something else. There was even a group of guys drinking beers and messing around with a soccer ball. But no one was working.

"Well," Charlie began carefully. "We were of the impression that the work in question would be much more ...er... substantial..."

"Us too. It was only vhen the materials arrive that ve realize is mistake. First, the shipment was just one tenth of the originally expected size. That has slow us down and very much reduce the scope of vork that ve do. Ve vere suppose to start building a small war games field. One on vhich our two armies could carry out joint exercise. Oooh, those are fun," the commander said excitedly. "I even bring a girl once. Yes, I did, and she saw the power of France, oh yes she did," he said proudly.

To be sure, there was a lone bulldozer, two wheelbarrows, and a few other odds and ends, but nothing that was suggestive of convincing on-going construction work...

"So what did you do after realizing that the whole shipment had not arrived?" It was a risky question. Charlie knew this, but he had to ask. And boy, was the answer a surprise.

"Procedure," the commander said, "I call Pari, and they tell me to worry no more about it. Is mistake," they say. "Happen all the time. Some fool back home need to take accounting." He explained with a laugh.

Maybe not, Charlie thought, as he sent his car speeding down the single lane highway. Maybe that was the original plan; put together a consignment of mostly weapons, mixed in with some construction material, falsely label it as *military grade construction material*, get it into the country, and then divert the whole thing. Which would explain why the base had not received the whole shipment even though it had entered the country, a fact that Charlie had verified. There were papers to prove it.

So where was ninety percent of the shipment? And more importantly, what was the content? Construction material? Weapons?

CHAPTER SEVENTEEN

Kingdom of Kemet, 1720 B.C.

$\mathcal{T}$ he man squinted, barely seeing the people in the street as he threw more leaves into his mouth, chewing all the time, and seeking a better visual interpretation of his surroundings. The leaves were helping with the pain, even though they left him lightheaded. Without them he would not have been able to be on his feet with the condition of his body. But he was a man on a mission that could not wait.

Transferring his staff to the left hand, while shielding his burnt out eyes with a heavily robed right arm, he got up from the stone on which he'd been resting, and set off once more. Although he could not see, he could feel everything, from the animals, the children, the women, and finally, the men. Even the panic, and that was key, the panic. He wished he could see more. It would be the only true measure of how things were really going. Of course, he was excited about this new ability to feel things, but eyes were eyes...

Some time later he got to the bottom of a little hill and stopped. Was that the dome on the palace? He was not sure but the feel of the golden glow, not more than a blur to his damaged sight, felt very much like it.

He took another sip of water from the goatskin waterbag that was hidden under the fabric of his thick robe.

Carefully, he adjusted his clothing to better disguise the bag before putting a few more leaves into his mouth as he started limping forward again. This time, there was a little more urgency to the whole bundle of man, water, and robes, as he squinted blindly in a vain effort to see. He wished he did not have to chew so many leaves. He was beginning to feel somewhat disoriented. And today of all days was not the day to not be fully present. A foggy mind could complicate things.

He quickened his pace, biting his lower lip in frustration and willing his almost burnt out eyes to see more than they could. It was frustrating. So much was going on, and he, the one man who was making it all happen, the one man who truly understood the totality of the whole picture, with its various possible implications, could not even see.

"Hey old man. What do you have that we can take?" The half blind man stiffened. It was an adolescent voice and it sounded like trouble. He gritted his teeth in determination and took another step forward. They were probably just children and he could not allow them to get in the way. Nothing could get in the way of the mission at this point. Nothing would be allowed to.

"Watch your mouth, young one," the blind man threatened. "Or I shall have you whipped in front of your parents for insolence."

"Ha-ha! Is that right" another young voice mocked. "Yes, Mister wise-adult-who-insists-on-being-listened-to. Is that the solution that was arrived at as a result of not listening to us?" The bitter sarcasm in the voice was surprising for one so young.

"We have always listened to you," the blind man said, licking his lips nervously.

"No you have not." Another one cut in. "You have just pretended to."

"That is not true," the man argued.

"Is it not? So why is the shameless child eater still among us even though he is hateful to children?"

"Who?"

"Evil Molek," spat another young voice. "Is he still among our gods because you have listened to us so carefully and learned that it is what we need?"

"I, ...listen...these are tough times and your concerns are very obviously genuine..."

"Shut up."

The blind man fell silent. This was getting dangerous. These children sounded really angry and who knows what a young angry mind will do next. He felt like another sip but he held himself in check. Now was not the time. If these children suspected that he was carrying this much water under his garments, he would be done for. He was sure that they would probably find it amusing to pour the water over his head, or some such stupid joke, which for him, would be lethal. He could not even contemplate the option. He had to handle this situation very carefully.

"What do you have that we can take?" The question was repeated angrily. "We don't have time to waste. The city is wrapped in the wrath of the sun god, and people like you, with your old, greedy, and corrupt ways, are about to die. So just hand it over and avoid the whipping. It is time for the young and the poor to become rich," the voice laughed. "Even if it is for a day only."

"I am not rich," the blind man answered, doing his best to now play the part of a poor, helpless, and blind beggar.

"You are lying," one of the voices said, walking around him. "Look at your sandals. They may be dirty but they are not cheap. Are you one of the powerful and corrupt state officials who never believed that a day of reckoning would come? Well it is here today. What happened to your fine retinue of chariots and guards? Were they too panicked by news of war to care about you?" This was getting dangerous indeed. A few people were beginning to throw curious glances at him as the children began to chant, slowly circling around. This was not going well.

"I have a gift for you boys," the half blind man said suddenly, a playful quality creeping into his voice.

"I have a real gift," he repeated, sticking his hands into the folds of his robe. For a moment, the children faltered in their chant and he pressed on, sensing an advantage. "I will wager some of you have seen these before, although none of you have ever touched or owned one. I have several," he laughed, bringing out both hands from underneath the heavy folds of his mysterious robe. "Here is your chance."

"Gold?" The voices whispered in awed disbelief. "GOLD!" This time the word was a choroused shout, and several people stopped just as the man tossed the contents of both his hands high into the air.

The confusion was immediate. As the coins spun in the air, catching and reflecting the light, attracting and distracting everyone, inspiring un-lived dreams, the street joined the children in a frenzied hunt for gold coins. During which time both the blind man and the war were totally forgotten.

He scuttled off into an alley, biting his lip and ignoring the pain that shot up his legs.

The alley led him to another busy, confused street, with more people reeling from the news of war. Without wasting time he melted into the throng of moving bodies.

The quality of pavement on the street was now different. Under foot, it felt too smooth to be anywhere else than the long chariot path that led to the gates of the palace. It was close now.

He quickened his pace, this time managing to ignore the feeling that someone, or more precisely, something, seemed to be watching him. What was it? The effect of chewing the leaves? Perhaps. Belial? Hopefully not. The thought of having such an easily angered spirit over his shoulder was not very reassuring, but it was too late for that now. Best to look at the benefits, he told himself. He took a deep breath and began pronouncing a protective spell upon himself as he continued the painful limp, all the way to the beautifully decorated palace gates.

"Is he still among our gods because you have listened to us so carefully and learned that it is what we need?"

"What do you want?" It was a very rough voice.
"Is this the King's palace?"

"Yes it is, and what is your business?"

The hooded figure did not reply. Instead he stuck out the strangest hand that the palace guard had ever seen. It was a human hand but that was where the resemblance ended.

The hand looked as if it had been very badly burned in some very recent fire. It was apparent to the naked eye that the skin had peeled off, leaving the hand looking more like a boiled, blistered and gnarled lobster. Slowly the fisted fingers uncurled to reveal a single object in the open palm. It was a gold signet ring that had been adorned with many kinds of precious stones.

The guard's eyes widened in surprise and he leaned forward and examined the ring. It was real! Gingerly, he picked it up, wondering who this man could be. The voice sounded familiar. Even the ring looked familiar. But right now he could not be sure. In the meantime, the authority embodied in the ring was sufficient to open the gate for the man. That was the law.

He pulled back the bolt on the little iron door and pushed it open. The hooded figure stepped through the side gate. At last he was in the palace of the King.

"Lead me to the King," he said.

"Right away, sir," the guard replied, signaling another man to come over. "Take this man to the King's secretary," he said, handing over the signet ring as well.

The guard who had just been summoned, turned and acknowledged the hooded figure with a bow. "This way, sir."

The blind man walked into the palace grounds, reveling in the familiar feeling of the place. He knew that this palace had been constructed about two thousand years ago according to a plan that King Seth himself had conceived.

It had been built in concentric circles, with the palace nursery occupying the very center of the circle. This nursery, which was under constant watch, was followed by the next concentric circle, which also happened to be the most spacious. It housed the vast quarters of the royal family, -the homes of the princes, the princesses, their spouses, uncles, aunts, cousins, and nephews. Within it, were also found the King's set of very private suites, which were totally cut off from the rest of the royal household. These two concentric circles were securely fenced off and separated once again from everything else in the palace.

Next came the third concentric circle. It contained the apartments of the numerous body and palace guards who were directly answerable to the hierarchy of the palace.

After that was the next circle which contained the homes of the scribes, the cooks, butlers, midwives, chemists, doctors, mathematicians, artists, and any other palace workers, whose skill or talent was deemed important enough to warrant a place there.

This was followed by the fifth circle. It had all the banquet halls, conference halls and the head quarters of all the different offices that were scattered in different parts of the Kingdom, both far and near. It was the outermost concentric circle, and it was separated from the general public by fences and gates through which no one could go without specific authority.

The whole palace, which was huge by any standard, had been designed with sumptuous pavilions, paved courtyards, luxuriant gardens, fountains, pools, and everything had been finished in alabaster and blue tile.

"This way sir," the guard said, leading the half blind man across an open, colonnaded terrace, decorated with colorful tropical plants that were hanging from cleverly hidden ropes. Yes, it was a very beautiful palace. No one could deny that, the blind man thought. He could sense the care, effort, design, and sweat that had been poured into the structure. But did the beauty compensate for the fact that not one room had been allocated to the High Priesthood? Not a single room! Did they think they would get away with it forever? Ha! What a laugh!

"The Secretary of the King will see you right away sir. But you must wait here," the guard informed him, before bowing and walking away to some other palatial duty.

A moment later, another guard showed up and led the half blind man through another little maze of beautiful rooms, halls, corridors, and finally into a large, sparsely furnished, but busy room.

The Secretary scrutinized the hooded figure, carefully checking his signet ring one more time.

"Do you have any weapons?" he asked the blind man.

The man dug into the folds of his robes and produced a short, sharp, and very decorated blade. Several embedded precious stones around its handle caught the light and glinted for a moment as he held out the weapon.

"You will go with these men," the Secretary announced, carefully taking up the knife and laying it in a tray next to the signet ring. "When you get to the King's presence you must be very respectful. Always bow your head when he is speaking. Never look into his face. And please, remember, you must be invited to speak before you open your mouth. These are the laws of the land. To disrespect them is to invite wrath. May you go in peace into the great one's presence."

As if the guards had rehearsed this, they centralized the limping, hooded figure, and marched him down the hall to see the King.

...they centralized the limping, hooded figure, and marched him down the hall to see the King...

CHAPTER EIGHTTEEN

Ridissi, son of Ngoma, royal announcer to the King's court and member of several councils was heart broken. Never in his life did he believe that he would live to see this day. The 'overwhelmingness' of it all made it even more difficult to find words that could express the intensity of the insanity.

The word was that this meeting had been called, following the suggestion of a powerful Shaman whose spirit had sensed that a lot of good was going to come from it. Which explained why almost every council member had shown up. They all realized that a lot was at stake.

The meeting had been announced as 'private', implying that the councilors were not to talk about it openly, since crucial, in-house secrets were expected to be part of the agenda. It was also calculated to prepare the councilors for the much bigger meeting with the King later in the day, at which all the different councils, the councils of war, Generals, The Chief Priests, and any other Kingdom official, would be present.

So, now more than ever, the councilors needed a cool head even though loud arguments had already erupted all over the room. Ridissi could not believe his eyes, or his ears, as he watched and listened in shocked silence. Could they not see that the very soul of the Kingdom was at stake?

The meeting had begun disruptively enough with loud complaints from a councilman who could not understand why troops had not yet been sent to protect the vineyards outside the city. Several others had concurred, with one in particular suggesting that the list should not be limited to vineyards.

"What about the hundreds of homes that have been constructed all along the Aur river?" the man asked. "Were they not part of the Kingdom's wealth, just like the shrines, libraries, the temples, monuments, and the statues of the gods? Should these not be part of the proposed statement to the King?" Several others nodded in agreement, even as another man jumped to his feet.

"This is treason!" he shouted, waving his short arms agitatedly. "It is treason I tell you! This King's ineptitude to protect the officials and wealth of the land, especially in a time of war, amounts to high treason. Am I wrong?" he asked, followed by several choruses of 'Yeses' and 'Nos'.

"Anyway," the man continued, "I think it is, and we should consider the possibility of initiating judicial action aimed at ejecting our exceptionally inept King out of the highest seat in the land."

"Watch the words that come out of your mouth, councilor." It was a man from the same clan as the ruling King. "We have had worse Kings and we have let them rule. If you want to eject a King from the throne today simply because your own fears have blinded you, you better shut your mouth."

"Or else what?" the first man retorted, stretching himself to full height.

"Or else you may regret the night in which your stupid father put you into your mother's stomach," answered the other fellow, a man whose intense love affaire with wine was very well known.

"You dare to insult my father? You, whose wife has to depend on others for everything? Maybe you want to tell us instead why your sons look more like your male servants than yourself."

"WHAT?" screamed the other man. "How dare you! If someone does not shut this fool up, I will tear his tongue out of his mouth."

"After I have butchered open and exposed the shit in your big stomach, you mean?"

This was madness, Ridissi thought, as he watched in disbelief. Total madness. The panic from the streets was consuming the councilors and it was threatening to undermine the whole purpose of the meeting. "Enough of this madness," Ridissi shouted. "Have we become children? Is this all we are good for? Because if it is, then we should really be ashamed of ourselves."

"Ashamed?" one of the councilmen asked. "Because we are concerned about our homes and farms on the banks of the river? Did we not work hard for these things? Or have you lost your head as well?"

"But my dear councilor," Ridissi began, hoping to restore some semblance of order and purpose.

"NOOO! Sit down," another man interrupted rudely. "You have nothing to say. This is not the King's court. Shut your mouth!"

"Shut my mouth?"

"Yes."

"That is no way to be speaking in a time when..."

"Just shut up," the man interrupted again.

"Really?"

"Yes, really."

"I see. And what if I don't?"

"Then I will shut it for you."

"Oh, I see. And how do you plan to do that O mighty Asombo?" Ridissi asked, getting to his feet and addressing the man. "With your six chariots and five mansions? Or is it going to be with the thirty thousand head of cattle that you stole in the south during Neferhotep's campaign against the Aethiopes?"

Suddenly there was total silence in the room, and for the first time since the meeting began, everybody was focused on what one man was saying. "I want to know," Ridissi continued, "Because all I have heard so far is a group of children who are more concerned about the state of their toys and the other surplus trappings that come from a dishonest life in power, at a time when that should not be priority. Is this all we are good for?"

"Who are you to talk down to us?" It was an older, overweight councilman with a few chins, and he was fuming. "Do you think you are better than the rest of us?"

"I do not and I never said I was," Ridissi answered as calmly as he could. "All I am saying is that after acquiring ten elegant chariots, you did not need an eleventh one that was covered in pure gold. Nor him, and him, or him over there," he added, pointing to an outraged councilor. "He owns so many houses, many have wondered if his middle name in the dialect means 'to own a house'."

"I see you, O most holy one who lives in great poverty without bread or water," the last man, one of the most powerful councilors in all the land, replied mockingly. "We all know that you are the purest of us all," he added, to derisive laughter. "Pray, tell us, what pure concepts will you include into our statement, to help illuminate our fool of a King?"

Ridissi studied the room around him.

"I am not innocent or different from you," he said. "Because just like you, I have amassed great personal wealth at the expense of the people and the public services that keep our Kingdom well and strong. Perhaps, my crime against the Kingdom is the most damning among all of us."

Now every one was really curious.

"As the first royal announcer to the King, you all know that I am the man who is in charge of the town criers in all the Kingdom. My scribes write down all the news that these town criers recite to the people as they walk along the streets." He paused. "Do you know how often I have had to alter the information that was going out? Do you know how many times the palace insisted that I do this?" There was total silence. "You do not because it is too many to count. And you know why? So we can *maintain and safeguard the peace, order, independence and sovereignty of the Kingdom*, or some such lofty excuse," he answered cynically. "So, my point is not that I am innocent, or that you are guilty. It is that our corrupt and decadent lifestyles have shredded the godly moral principles and spiritual fabric that holds our society together."

"Godly moral principle?" Another councilor snorted. "Why do we choose to burden ourselves with these gods and their so-called principles when all they do is give orders, anyway. Are we not intelligent enough to direct ourselves?"

"Of course we are, and we have, which in my opinion, explains how we got into this situation in the first place." Ridissi surveyed the room. "I think that this recent push for atheism is partly because we would rather not have any one, or anything, prick our consciences in any significant way, as we arbitrarily decide for ourselves what is right or wrong, or even that nothing is right or wrong, anymore. This is a dangerous path my friends, because it eventually translates into an everything-is-acceptable existence, which is suicidal to all societies, unfortunately." Ridissi coughed again and surprisingly no one interrupted the pause. "Granted, many of the gods and their doctrines are abusive, downright stupid, and most of their priests and representatives have become merchants of fear who seek, more than anything else, to control their flock for exploitative reasons. But that is not what I am talking about when I refer to godly moral principle. I mean the one true God who must be worshipped in truth and in spirit. Not religion. I mean the God who calls upon us to love our neighbors like ourselves and to treat other people as we would like them to treat us? Is that such a terribly bad idea? I don't think so. In fact, I believe that nearly all the current problems in the land arose because we have lost our compassion for others and care only about ourselves."

"Are you joking?"

"No. I am serious. Think about it. Corruption, which is a very self-serving vice, was the biggest influence behind the decisions that have left us weak, and vulnerable, decisions that can never look integrity in the eye, because deep down, we know that they are selfish, and that they are never calculated to serve the greater good as they should." Ridissi paused, to catch his breath. "No nation, Kingdom, or civilization, can last for long without integrity."

"You have talked enough about the nature of the problem." This time it was the chief councilor, a surprisingly tall, thin, and very stooped fellow who looked a hundred, although he was only sixty. "What do you suggest as a solution?"

"I suggest that we humble ourselves, that we correct our ways, that we start seeking the face of God in sincerity, and most importantly, that we go back to living in respect, honor, and genuine love."

"Is that supposed to magically solve our problems?" It was another man.

"Not magically," Ridissi answered overlooking the cynicism. "But it is a good place to start because it will give us hope and empower our collective faith. With enough faith, everything becomes possible."

"Really?"

"Yes."

"Well, I disagree," another fellow said, standing up and stepping out into the aisle. "First of all, I do not think that having *your god* in my life is what is best for me. Secondly, I do not see what my personal beliefs and actions as an individual have to do with the so called, *failing health* of our Kingdom."

"Everything," answered Ridissi.

The man swore irritably. "Is this fellow serious? Are you saying that I am responsible for all of this?" he asked, waving short pudgy arms in the air in an effort to depict the confusion and chaos in the land.

"Yes, I am." Ridissi answered calmly, looking the man in the eye. "All of us, including you, have contributed to this predicament. Some more than others, but we are all guilty and I will tell you why." He walked to the centre of the room and took a drink from one of several carafes of water that had been provided. "Societies are like the sea, made up of countless tiny water droplets which come together to form an incredibly huge body of water. Now, for purposes of communication, let us refer to each droplet as a unit, which is the same as saying that the seas are made up of many, tiny, uncountable units. In the case of society, the difference is that people are these units. That said, I would like to point out, and this is extremely important, that the health of any society is dependent upon its collective moral value, and that this collective moral value is in turn, dependent upon the state of each unit. So, lots of fear possessed units for example, will logically equal a fear ridden society, just as fearless units will naturally translate into a courageous people. Now, we know that a godly spirit lives in truth and love and will always seek to encourage and empower others, a process which, if successful will always seek to replicate itself, leading to a permanently increasing number of empowered and strengthened units." Ridissi surveyed the faces around him. "It is unfortunately very far from where we are because our Kingdom is full of weakened, disempowered units, born from years and years of egoistic, self serving policies that have engendered poverty, distrust, suspicion, fear and hopelessness. How then can we expect these same collection of units to stand up, transform itself into a strengthened body and successfully fight off the present threat when we ourselves have been instrumental in sapping their faith and beating down their spirit? Do the wise ones not agree that a well fed spirit is happier, carries more hope, and will do much better in any kind of battle? Conversely when the spirit is starved, like ours is, then the Will suffers, and when one's Will is weak, everything becomes much harder to do, and taking the short cut becomes the norm. Consequently, it becomes easier to fail at whatever task one is facing because short cuts can be good, but they have a way of fixing the problem without actually fixing the problem. Which is why I implore you all, my friends and brothers, to see reason and return to the power of truth and love. We have to stop lying to ourselves and to the people because lies are ultimately self destructive, especially when they are repeated so often that the liars themselves begin to believe their own words. Look, for example, at our policies that thrive on militarism. We have allowed ourselves to buy into the lie that huge military build ups are necessary as a deterrence to war, when in reality it has pushed us down a path of fear and constant foreign aggression. How does this make us safer? What is the rational? Would there be more stabbings if nobody owned a knife? What kind of logic is that? The truth is that these wars are launched as a means to enrich powerful interest groups while needlessly sacrificing and traumatizing our youth, depleting our economy, rendering us vulnerable, and rerouting much needed resources away from home. And whose fault is that? All of us! Why? Because we are so willing to shut out integrity in order to preserve a status quo that benefits us, a small ruling class, at the detriment of the rest. This sort of lies telling needs to change, and we can start by agreeing to honestly tell the King, that as it stands, the Kingdom's defenses are a far cry from what they are supposed to be..."

"And why in the name of the gods should we take such a dangerous approach?" Another councilor interrupted, as if he could not believe the foolishness in Ridissi's words.

"For truth and love," Ridissi answered. "It is the only thing that will strengthen and set us free at this point. Yes, the King will be angry, but it is what we must do."

"Must?"

"Yes. Must", the announcer insisted. "At what point will our love for this land overpower personal greed?" There was no answer "Well, if the answer to that question is 'never', then surely it is time for us to fade into the dust bin of history." Ridissi finished and sat down.

Not a word could be heard in the room. Hopefully everyone had something to seriously think about, he thought. Now was not the time to be playing around. The meeting in the King's pavilion would be starting in a few hours. He hoped that there was enough time to arrive at an objective statement that would be read to the King, a statement that would inject some reality about the true gravity of the situation, even at the cost of exposing fear-ridden corruption. How successful can a hunter be if he sets out to the elephant's house to hunt down the beast, when he is unaware, and no one has told him that the elephant is nothing like the rat?

Already, he felt better. There was hope. The councilmen will do the right thing. He was sure of it. Better late than never. This was really exciting. It was like the old days all over again; when honor and truth and duty were sacred, when life had more meaning, when people had more respect for each other and when men had fought for worthy causes.

Where were the scribes, he wondered impatiently, craning his neck to look around, as the stooped chief councilor, with a look of total unbelief on his face, walked to the rostrum. It was time to announce and adopt a decision. But where were the scribes? Oh, there they were!

Ridissi could see two scribes in their white uniforms, whispering excitedly together as they readied various materials on a low stone table in preparation for scribing.

What Ridissi failed to see was the councilor, who had slowly made his way next to him. Without warning the man stuck his dagger into the royal announcer's back, pushing the long, curved blade, all the way into the unsuspecting man's heart, before forcefully pulling out the weapon. Ridissi screamed in pain. Then, slowly, in disbelief, he sank to the floor, first to his knees, and then to his back, with arms held wide as if his choking throat was somehow imploring the prophesied son of God to shine a light on the lies that were now taking his life. He was dying with the sad knowledge that the corruption in the Kingdom had bitten so deeply, eaten so much, and grown so fat, that it may not even be able to sit up in an attempt to save itself.

The room was quiet as the bloody councilor walked to the centre of the floor, and turned to address every one. "Great councilors and elders," the man began, pointing his bloody dagger at the chief councilor, who quickly departed from the rostrum and retreated to his seat, looking like a dog with its tail between its legs. "There lies Ridissi, a friend and a good man." The councilor took a moment to wipe the blade clean on his garments. "A very good man who wanted nothing but the best for the Kingdom. Can we deny, that even though he may have committed a few crimes in his career, he was not still a good man? No, we cannot, and to say otherwise would be an insult to the gods themselves who have blessed us all so abundantly!" The man surveyed the poorly lit room. "It would be more appropriate to say that he was a good man whose sense of goodness had become a danger to the security and well being of the Kingdom itself, a danger to men like you and me, men whose experience and judgment would be necessary for the survival of the Kingdom, especially in a time of turbulence like this. Tell me, what would be gained at this time if a witch-hunt were to begin instead? Would it not distract from the purpose of fighting off an army, which in my soldier's opinion, is not that formidable?" he asked. "I think Ridissi's overestimation of the invaders could be compared to the reasoning of the proverbial Nkwendong: a man who used the cover of darkness to steal his neighbor's goat. Upon looking up and seeing a stormy, lightening streaked night sky, he judged that a very heavy rain was about to fall. So he led the animal to the back of his house where he butchered it, roasted some of the meat, ate to his fill before curling up to sleep. When he got up the next morning, it was to the noise of an angry crowd that was led by his neighbor.

They had gathered behind his house and were threatening to burn the place down.

"Tell me, what would be gained at this time if a witch-hunt were to begin instead?"

Nkwendong, the goat thief," the bloody councilor postulated, "had miscalculated. He had overestimated the stormy weather, thus the heavy rains he had expected had not come and the goat's blood had been left unwashed for all to see on the stone altar where the illegally procured beast had lost its life." The councilor cleared his throat. "What if Ridissi were wrong?" he asked. "Or, maybe he was just making things look bad in order to stampede us into a particular reaction. You heard the man yourself. He had become a master at manipulating information for alternate purposes. Why he wanted to get all of us killed, I am not yet sure." The councilor licked his lips. "What I would like to be certain of, is that we all leave from here with a perfect understanding of what has transpired here today. What does that mean, you may ask? I then put the question to you: Did you perceive my valiant display of patriotism? Even though to an unpracticed eye, it may have appeared like murder?"

"Brilliant, very brilliant indeed," someone said.

"Thank you, thank you," the blood stained, double chinned councilor smiled, turning to acknowledge the new voice that had proved enlightened enough to understand his rarefied insights. But a feeling of slight unease went through him and his smile died off. The man who had just spoken was not a councilor. He was not even dressed like one. Where had he come from? How did he get in here? Was this not a secret meeting?

"And who are you?" Several voices asked at the same time as more people noticed the man.

Hasim, also known as the shadow, ignored all of them. "It is indeed brilliant that you all realize the necessity of true leadership," he said, walking further into the room. "I also, am happy that you realize it is something which may sometimes require painful decisions that could even appear as criminal."

"Who are you? Where did you come from? How did you get in here?" Several voices questioned. "GUARDS!" Somebody call the guards," a councilor shouted. "GUARDS!"

But there were no guards. All twenty-five of them were dead and most had not even seen their attackers, or even had time to react in any meaningful way. They had all met swift deaths at the hands of the stealthily quiet group of assassins who had come with the man Hasim. He whistled, and very silently, almost like whiffs of smoke, his men began filing into the room, emerging from the shadowy corners that had kept them concealed from the distracted crowd. The bewilderment of the councilors was total. And for a moment everyone was too stupefied to make a move.

Hasim raised his left hand, and the doors of the hall were locked, bolted, and quickly barricaded. Then he pulled out an evil looking scimitar that seemed to be gleaming with thirst. His men did the same. This was obviously too ominous an omen, and the councilors, most of them overweight, started screaming in frenzied panic. Hasim smiled. They could scream all they wanted. This was a secret meeting that had been held in a hall that was located below ground, and no amount of screaming would be heard outside.

"Spare no one," he whispered to the men by his side. Then jumping forward, he sliced through the nearest exposed head, spilling fatty cranial contents onto the tiled stone floor. He felt the blood coursing through his veins as he bashed in another head, gleefully licking into his mouth, a sliver of human something that landed sloppily across his lower lip.

"Kill them all," he shouted.

...jumping forward, he sliced through the nearest exposed head...

$\mathcal{T}$ he limping, burned, blind man, in the hooded robe, finally stood in front of the throne of the King of the Kingdom of kemet.

For a long time he had waited impatiently for this moment.

In that time, he had imagined the moment to the smallest detail, standing right here on this same spot, in this same hall, with every one sitting and watching the proceedings. He had even factored in the war, the uncertainty and fear in the room, and most importantly, Caliph, his personal assistant.

For a moment there was a little confusion as the announcer suddenly realized that he did not know who the hooded man was. He leaned over to another man and said something. The man hurried off and promptly returned with a tray that contained the signet ring and jeweled dagger that had been taken from the robed figure. The tray was placed in front of the announcer who looked at it with trepidation.

The initials and crest on the ring, he recognized. But why was the man himself suddenly covered from head to foot? Why did he seem a little heavier? Not quite sure what to make of it, the announcer cleared his throat. "Melenoc, son of Andala," he announced. "High priest and keeper of the golden right hand of the god Kepharra." The hall went quiet. The implications of Melenoc's titles were not missed. But was this the man? Why was he dressed in a hooded robe? Where had he come from looking like this? Why had he missed the ceremony of the sun? Was that not one of the reasons why the Kingdom had been cursed?

"Speak now, high priest, or be forever quiet in the presence of the King," the announcer broke the silence.

Melenoc bowed, straightened up, pulled back the hood and exposed his burned head. A murmur rose in the hall at the sight of his roasted features.

"Yes, I am Melenoc, or the rest of what is left of me, your highness," he said, in a shaky voice. "Not only is the signet ring genuine, but Caliph, my trusted assistant of twenty years, whom you all know, is here as well." He turned toward Caliph who bowed immediately towards the throne at the mention of his name. "I am sure that he would be more than capable of telling if I were an impostor."

"Speak." The announcer said, looking at Caliph, who took a low bow and nervously cleared his throat.

"Upon my honor, I declare that I have assisted Melenoc, son of Andala, High Priest of Kephara, for many years, and I swear that this is his voice. I would recognize it in my sleep." Caliph said, silently praying for the hundredth time, that the god Kephara would find him worthy enough of life to thwart the intentions of death. The man was convinced that the events of

170

the past two days had come from death's own hand, especially the unexpected disappearance of the High Priest.

Initially, his mind had rejected the realization that Melenoc was not present for the feast of the sun. But the High Priest's seat, which had remained unoccupied all through the ceremony, had forced Caliph to accept what he was seeing. The King, when he had arrived six hours late, had wanted to know why Melenoc's seat was empty. Being the next in hierarchy within the priesthood, and not knowing the whereabouts of the High Priest, had seemed to irritate the monarch, further transforming Caliph into a nervous wreck.

Then, he'd learned that a foreign army had camped outside the walls of Itjawy. This had pushed the man into a state of panic. The implications of an invasion had not been lost on him. Being the assistant High Priest, he was well aware of the law, which stipulated that in the case of an invasion, the priesthood was to temporarily hold both hands of the god until the danger to the Kingdom was past. It was usually very tricky business and no chief priest ever looked forward to it. In fact, most of them hoped to never have to exercise this prerogative during their tenure in office. Was it an easy thing to walk up to the lion and ask for its mane? Do the elders not say that the heart which covets what the King loves is a heart that hungers for death? This situation was like a scalding plate of food. Even a very famished man had to proceed with extreme caution.

Much against his wish, Caliph had penetrated into the secret underground chamber beneath the temple of the Kepharra priesthood, and retrieved the sacred right hand from the stone altar on which it always lay in undisturbed solitude. He had wrapped it up in a piece of soft clothing, borrowed the absent High Priest's chariot and headed for the palace, hoping to honorably execute the fearsome duty that the god Kepharra had seen fit to throw upon his lap.

The apparent confusion at the palace had only exacerbated Caliph's anxiety. So he had been understandably relieved when the hooded figure had walked up to him and addressed him by name. He had recognized Melenoc's voice immediately. Stumbling with relief, he'd handed over the wrapped up golden right hand as if it was too hot to hold. With Melenoc now present, the duty of asking for the other hand from the King was not on Caliph's shoulders anymore.

Upon contact with the albeit wrapped up right hand, the High Priest had sensed the pain in his own body reduce by almost half. Yes, it was happening and it would only get better. Especially after he gained possession of the other hand, and he will. He just had to be steadfast. That was key.

Now, he peered at Caliph, sensing the man's doubts and questions, but mentally willing him to not speak. This was not the time. The assistant High Priest acquiesced. He believed that Melenoc was wise.

Melenoc took a step forward, bowing low. "I greatly apologize to you, O great King of Kemet, for appearing like this and dishonoring your most honorable eyes. But I wanted you to see for yourself what the man Salatis has done to me."

About twenty paces away, richly attired, and comfortably seated in a high throne of solid gold, the obese King managed to lean forward in surprise as everyone held his breath. A flurry of advisers were rushing to his side, flooding him with intelligence on Salatis.

Melenoc smiled inwardly. The mention of the name had caused the desired effect. It was strange how quickly people reacted to fear. Even love, which was much stronger, would hardly elucidate such a rapid response. And he knew that.

"My lord," he continued, "I had gone into the desert to meditate on a particular dream that had come to me in my sleep. A dream in which the great Aur River had gone dry, all the pyramids had disappeared, and the sand grains of the desert had been transformed into men who were rising to wipe the Kingdom off the surface of the earth. It was while delving into the meaning of this vision that Salatis' men found me. They took me to his camp, deeper in the desert, where I was tied to a pole and suspended over a hot fire. Thus was I reduced to the burned creature that you now see," he lied. "My lord, as you can tell, I am in pain, but it pains me even more to be the bearer of this news. Salatis let me live only so that I could bring it to you. But what can I do? Should I lie to my own King because the news is bad? Should I not talk about Salatis's vast army that I saw with my own eyes?"

At this another murmur went up in the room, but Melenoc ignored it. "Yes, my King, it is a vast army indeed, bigger and more deadlier than anything we have ever had to face in the history of the Kingdom. I would estimate it at one hundred thousand"

"ONE HUNDRED THOUSAND?" It was the announcer. "Has the High Priest taken leave of his senses? Who in the entire world can raise such an army? Surely this must be an exaggeration!"

"You can choose not to believe me at the peril of the Kingdom," Melenoc answered. "But ask yourself; what can I possibly gain from such a story?"

The King raised his hand and one of the men hovering at the side of the throne came closer. He whispered something into the man's ear. Immediately the man ran across the carpeted platform and whispered something in turn into the announcer's ear.

"The King now calls upon the knowledge of one who should know something about this situation," the announcer said, "May the great, important, and newly appointed Vizier in charge of the Kingdom's borders, please come forward?"

At these words, every head in the hall turned to look at Cikatrix. With all eyes on him, he got up from his seat, bowed low, and approached the throne. "My Lord and my King, I am sorry to say that we do not yet have all the information pertaining to this situation, but I can assure the great King of Kemet that, even as we speak, all of my men are out and about on a furious intelligence-gathering mission. While this is ongoing I recommend that we stay alert because Salatis is a very determined, ruthless, and cunning individual," he finished with a bow.

"We would like to have some definite information on the situation by tomorrow night," the King said very softly "See to it."

"Yes, my Lord," Cikatrix answered with another bow. Then he turned around and marched back to his front row seat.

Presently the King heaved his massive bulk, barely leaned over, and said something. Immediately, all the men stopped talking and turned toward the hall. A man left the small group, went over to the announcer and handed him a papyrus scroll.

The announcer took the scroll, stood up, cleared his throat, and began to read from it. It was a royal edict, authorizing the treasury to meet whatever needs the Generals might have in their need to defend the city. "...And let it be so," the announcer concluded.

From his seat Cikatrix watched the line of Generals as they got up, bowed to the throne, and marched out of the room. They would not be needed anymore for this particular meeting. They had a war on their hands, and their armies had to be readied. As the men marched out of the hall, Melenoc, who had not yet moved, took a few steps toward the throne, bowed as low as he could, and waited in silence. Finally, the announcer motioned for him to speak. He thanked the man and took another step forward. But before he could speak, another guard rushed into the hall through a small side door, went directly to the announcer and spoke to him. Immediately the man held up his hand silencing Melenoc, who resorted once again to wait in silence in front of the busy throne. He was unperturbed. No matter how long it took or whatever the delays may be, he was going to do what he was going to do. Quietly, he threw a few more leaves into his mouth and began to chew.

The announcer stood up and proceeded to vocalize the latest piece of news. He announced that Fada, son of Lotin, the legendary runner and bearer of news, had arrived exhausted at the eastern gates of the city just in time to hand over a bloody scroll, before collapsing into the arms of Anubis. An arrowhead had been found buried in his left chest area.

The King raised his scepter and the bloodied scroll was rushed to him on a gold plate. Once by his side, another officer picked it up, unrolled it and whisper-read the contents into the King's ear.

Melenoc watched the King contemplate the information for just a second before raising the scepter hand again. The scroll was taken to the announcer, who stood up and began to read from it.

What the announcer read from the scroll was music to Melenoc's ears. It could not be better. It was a message from the north, which confirmed the fact that the rest of Salatis's army was on its way to the capital city of Itjawy. The destruction and pain that this army was causing on its march was succinctly delineated. There was no information as to how the King's northern armies had fared.

At the end of the reading a loud murmur rose in the hall, as everyone suddenly wanted to speak at the same time. The King held up his hand and the hall fell silent. It seemed as if for the first time since the crisis began, the true gravity of the situation had just dawned on the people. The tension in the hall was palpable.

Fada, son of Lotin, the legendary runner and bearer of news, had arrived exhausted at the eastern gates of the city...

Melenoc smiled under his hood. They were beginning to understand. Even Caliph, his assistant, was shaken. He could sense an increase in the man's heartbeat as they both waited in silence. There could be no more delays.

He was right. A few moments later a single sheet of papyrus was dispatched from the throne to the announcer, who stood up once more and began to pronounce the grave declaration. With all eyes on the throne, the King slowly stood up and beckoned to Melenoc. Yes! This was it!

With his heart fluttering in excitement, Melenoc took out the right hand of Kepharra, unwrapped it and held it up for all to see as he approached the throne. The object was proof undeniable that the Kepharra priesthood had the authority to ask for and to hold the other hand, until the council of elders could prove that the very soul of the Kingdom was not in danger anymore.

Still on his feet, the King lifted the gold scepter and pointed it at the High Priest. In accordance with tradition, Melenoc got down on his knees and bowed, touching the floor with his forehead before getting up again. As he did so a guard who was carrying a gold tray approached him. Lying in the center of the tray was the glittering left hand of Kepharra. This was what he had come to get. It was what he had been born for.

He took an exciting step forward, reaching out his right hand. The guard bowed low, all the while holding the tray up and out toward the High Priest.

"Wait! Stop!"

Melenoc froze, angry bile rising to his throat. It was Caliph. How dare he? How dare he interrupt such an important procedure?

"Yes?" the announcer queried with a puzzled look on his face. Every one in the room seemed at odds with the interruption. Even the King had bothered to lean slightly forward. Was the man crazy? Did he not know that others had lost their heads for such interruptions?

"Oh don't mind him, my lord," Melenoc reassured quickly, mentally willing Caliph to close his mouth as he took another step forward, reaching again for the glittering artifact on the tray. "He is concerned about some minor and unimportant custom within the priesthood."

"Unimportant?" Caliph asked, jumping forward, not sure that he was hearing right. Was the High Priest falling into a deeper sickness than the one for which his body was now covered up? The man's pain was probably making him delirious and robbing him of wisdom! He could not let this happen. Quickly he grabbed the whole tray away from the unsuspecting guard, who was on the verge of handing the artifact to Melenoc. Immediately several guards rushed forward to surround the tray bearer, the High Priest and his god-fearing assistant who was now holding the hand that had come off of the King's bosom. The announcer had jumped to his feet.

"What you have in your hands is older than all of your

known ancestors put together," the announcer spoke gently, pronouncing each word with care. "Almost as old as the Kingdom itself, and it is known to rest, permanently, on the King in times of peace. The King would like to know what this show of disrespect is about," he added.

Nervous, shaking, and suddenly sweating, Caliph approached the throne and bowed with the tray still in his hands. This was it. He had just crossed a line into a very dangerous place and he knew it. But somewhere deep down, he felt as if he was doing the right thing even if it was about to cost him his own life. The exhausted High Priest, whose suffering and subsequent fatigue he himself had underestimated, will be grateful for this later.

"My Lord and King," he said, " When I think of what I have just done, I wonder if I have lost my head. But what else can your servant do when a law upon which the Kingdom's foundation was set, seemed about to be unintentionally desecrated? Does the law not say that no one man is ever to enter into possession of both of Kepharra's hands? Is the King, who is by far the wisest and most worthy of us all, allowed to carry both hands on his bosom? No! Even the King himself cannot be allowed to carry such weight. So why should the High Priest, who is under the King, want to do something that the King himself is not allowed to do? Has he forgotten that it would amount to a sacrilege? Has he forgotten that it is for this same reason that the law calls for both high and assistant High Priest to call upon the King for this important transaction? I do not think that the good High Priest has forgotten all this. I believe that he is ill, exhausted, and in too much delirious pain to remember, for I know him well and he is a good man who will never allow anything that belongs to the King to be desecrated. And neither would I, which is why I interrupted the very honorable and illustrious presence of our great King and ruler of Kemet," Caliph finished, bowed very low and waited with his heart thumping in his chest.

The King conferred with a few heads, and then turned to Melenoc. For the first time he raised his voice.

"Is this true what I hear, son of Andala? Do you now think that you are mightier than I?"

For a moment Melenoc hesitated. It was obvious that Caliph was not going to stand by and watch him do what he had come to do. That was something that could not be helped. He had known that the man could possibly oppose him, but he had not suspected that Caliph would have the courage to risk it in front of the King.

"Son of Andala, is this true?" It was the King again, and although his voice was neutral, almost soft, the threat was obvious. Under the robe, Melenoc felt himself begin to shake in anger. He had spent a whole lifetime of planning to get to this point, and he was so close. There was nothing he would have liked to do more at that moment than to put his hands around Caliph's neck and just squeeze. But wait, a King was talking to him, he reminded himself. Now was not a time for weaknesses. He had to be calm.

"How can it be true, my lord?" He asked in the most solemn voice that he could summon. "Is the great King and ruler of Kemet not the greatest dancer in the world? Will he not give Salatis a lesson in dancing before this day is over? Where are the servants?" he shouted suddenly. "Clear the hall and prepare the floors," he said with an expansive gesture. "Salatis the Aamu is already in the city to challenge our own dear King in a dance duel," he stated, breaking into loud laughter and dashing forward towards the throne with open arms, obviously determined to give the King a loving embrace. He did not get far. He was seized by several guards who quickly took away the golden right hand.

As he was carried from the hall, Melenoc's ears were flooded with all kinds of sympathetic comments; Poor High Priest! Could anyone blame him for losing his mind? Just look at what Salatis has done to him!

They could believe whatever they wanted to believe about him, he thought. It was not important. For now he would agree to be a mad man, just to avoid the King's wrath. It was also time to implement a different strategy, one that would devastate any possible resistance to his ultimate intention.

He was seized by several guards...

As quietly as possible he sucked on the goatskin bag, wishing for the thousandth time that the pain had not required him to chew so many leaves. He was feeling so lightheaded that for a moment he actually wanted to laugh. Which just pushed his carefully concealed temper to above boiling point. Would today's meeting have gone differently if he had not been so light headed? Very gently, almost carefully, the temper took control of the man, but his exhausted frame was not a match for the guards who seemed to barely notice any change as they led him away.

…the announcer…

CHAPTER NINETEEN

*I*tzo hurried down the hallway, doing his best to keep up with the General. The guards and officers, recognizing both men, quickly showed them through, rightly suspecting that they had come to the Palace for this emergency meeting that every one knew was actually a council of war.

The two men marched through the last checkpoint, and passed through the huge double doors that opened into the King's pavilion. It was a hall that Abou Bakar had been in before, mostly for feasts and other light hearted, social functions. He had never seen it used for an emergency council of war. He recalled that Neferhotep, the King before this one, who also loved to have a good time, had added this particular pavilion to the palace. He had insisted on very high, artfully decorated walls, wide arches and gilded, gold adorned ceilings.

Directly ahead, the red carpet rolled on, all the way to the base of the alabaster platform on which the throne was sitting. It was a beautiful room, which in his opinion, was better suited for its original, lighthearted purpose. Not for a council of war.

As Abou Bakar marched towards the throne, he wondered where Iroha was. He himself had been greatly delayed within the King's prison, where the riot had turned out to be more extensive and damaging than he had imagined.

But of greater concern, was the fact that the capital city had been attacked that same morning, proving that even he had underestimated Salatis. Instinctively, his thoughts went into another prayer but he never had the time to finish it. The announcer, who was on a separate platform, lower than the King's of course, had been informed about Abou baker's arrival, and he began loudly presenting the man, reciting the many achievements and exploits that had made the General into a legend in his own lifetime.

Cringing from the praise singing, Abou Bakar bowed low, noting at the same that his appearance had prompted some nervous movement on the platform by the throne. He could see a man whispering something into the King's ear, while pointing at Itzo, who was standing by the General's side.

"What does this mean, General?" the announcer asked, suddenly recognizing the former Vizier of border security.

"Why is this traitor among us?" Already, guards were advancing menacingly, weapons at the ready.

Abou Bakar raised his left hand and summoned the bearer of the golden tray, a gesture that stopped the guards in their tracks. It meant that there was an explanation for everything, an explanation that was worthy of the King's immediate attention.

The tray bearer rushed forward and the General bowed, placing three scrolls of papyri into the tray, one on top of the other. The tray bearer spun around and sped off to the announcer who picked up the scrolls and stood up. But before he could begin to read, Cikatrix, who had been sitting in the front row, suddenly jumped to his feet, surprising every one, and darted down the aisle, toward the door. Before any one in the audience could react, the man had reached an outside balcony and jumped off of it, disappearing from view. The silence in the hall was almost loud.

"What is the meaning of this, Abou Bakar, of the clan of Abou Ramzi?" It was the King, and he was not looking very pleased.

"My Lord and my King," the General said, stepping forward with another bow. "Itzo, whom you put in prison, was supposed to be dead by now, just like myself." The King leaned forward, not sure if he had heard right. Dead? He himself had put Itzo in jail, yes, but he had not asked for the man's head. Not yet. The case against him was still being investigated. And concerning the General, that was preposterous. The man was the main reason why he, himself, was still hopeful about this whole situation. Even his own father, Neferhotep, had greatly relied on this man. And someone, probably Cikatrix, judging by the way he'd just exited, had wanted him dead? What a fool Cikatrix was! The man was incorrigible. He was always up to something stupid. For a moment the King let himself wonder what would happen if the man disappeared for good. It was the first time that the King had considered the option, and the answer came up as a question: Would he, himself, Nehesy Aesare, King and ruler of Kemet, be able to live on easily without help of the very special medicine that was in Cikatrix's possession? Maybe not, but he, Nehesy Aesare, was getting tired of forgiving the man.

Before any one in the audience could react, the man had reached an outside balcony and jumped off of it...

"Was he the author of the scrolls?" The King asked, gesturing at Cikatrix's empty seat.

"I am afraid he may have been, my Lord," Abou Bakar answered. "I was not sure before, but the man's flight confirms my worst suspicions. On our way here, Itzo and I stopped at the royal warehouse, and the clerk to whom we showed these scrolls recognized and identified them as from a different and much more recent batch of papyrus. He said that their color was slightly different because the paper makers had over exposed the papyrus to too much heat as it was being made into paper, something that does happen every once in a while. This clerk, who is a trusted man," Abou Bakar went on, "also informed us that instead of dumping this quality of papyrus, which is still good, though not for royal use, it is given to the different offices in the capital on a revolving basis. The batch to which these belong had been delivered to the man Cikatrix." Abou Bakar finished, looking up respectfully at the throne.

At that moment, the shocked silence in the room was broken by a faint and hauntingly painful recital, floating in from outside the palace. It was a town crier's voice, in the singsong tradition of news bearers, and it was lamenting the death of several councilors who had been found murdered in cold blood. Everyone in the room stiffened.

With great difficulty the King stood up, obliging everyone else to follow suit. He cleared his throat and began to speak. Scribes could be seen writing furiously, recording for posterity on this third day of Anu, the words of Nehesy Aesare, King and Lord of Kemet.

"Sons, daughters, and children of our great Kingdom. At this time our intelligence suggests that the bulk of our enemy's army is not here yet, so we can still send word to our friends and allies but we must act in speed." The King paused again. "In the meantime, let the right hand of kephara be returned to the priesthood. These are my words and let it be so."

Immediately the golden right hand was taken out of the tray and handed to Caliph, while the left one was carried back to the throne. Then very gingerly, the King sat down again, signaling the end of the meeting. A group of ten well built men rushed forward with two gold plated bars which they slipped into specially designed holds on the sides of the throne, gently lifted it off the floor and marched down the carpeted aisle towards the double doors. For now the hand will remain with the throne.

CHAPTER TWENTY

Cameroon, Central Africa.

$\mathcal{T}$he meeting started badly. First, because the fat man did not like that he had been kept waiting. But he had and for over an hour. As if he did not have anything better to do with his time. Plus, he found it disrespectful.

Very noisily, he cleared his throat, forcing the man who had been speaking to pause.

"Thank you, the fat man said, obviously determined to not let the speaker finish. "I agree that such an investigation is dangerous, but to not do anything about it makes it even more so," he added. "What if he finds something? I mean, the man is a journalist, *pour l'amour de Dieu.*"

"Yes he is," the other agreed reluctantly, "but that is not enough reason to warrant action."

"Is it not?"

"No, it is not," the man insisted. "First of all, I think that you are overestimating this man, and secondly, Yves Mammon is the only one who can make that decision. Not you, not me, and not him," the man finished, pointing a bony finger all around the small dark, cigarette smoke filled room.

"I beg to disagree." It was the fat man again.

"You do?" This time there was surprise to the other man's voice, almost as if he had not expected any one to still be disagreeing.

"Yes, I do," the fat man said, surveying all the other faces around the table. "I disagree, firstly, because I happen to think that the boss, if he were reachable, which he is not on account of his trip into the rainforest, would agree with me that something has to be done about the *Journalist*. It is simple common sense. Eliminate the danger before it becomes unmanageable. And believe me, the more time we waste, the worse the situation will get." And he left it at that. He was a fairly good judge of character and he knew how the others were thinking. Already he could pick up some barely discernible fidgeting from the oldest of the three men, -the same one who was insisting that they wait until Yves Mammon could be reached and consulted on the decision.

"What if something goes wrong?" he asked. "None of us

will survive the scandal. Surely, you can see that, Can't you?"

The fat man did not even hesitate. The phone call earlier had been crystal clear. He was expected to rise above everything in assisting *Monsieur* Yves Mammon. And that was what he was going to do. Even if it meant killing a nosy Cameroonian journalist whose digging was threatening to compromise the whole operation.

"Something is already going wrong," he stated, "and if you guys don't listen to me, there will be hell to pay."

"May be, maybe not," the other man said looking around the little table and blowing away cigar smoke. "But, if you insist on going ahead with your plans, I would like for the record to show that I was opposed to it."

"The record? What is this? A parliamentary session? *Putain!*"

"Ok, that's it." It was the only man in the room who had not said anything yet. "Let's put it to a vote," he said, raising his left hand. "I say we take care of the problem".

"I say we take care of the problem," the fat man repeated, putting up his hand as well.

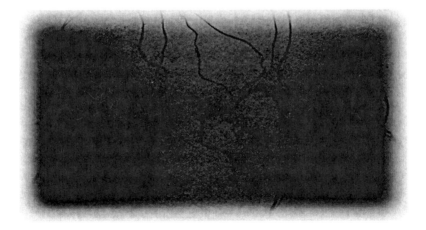

I beg to disagree…

Charlie emptied the contents of the *33export* bottle into the glass, pushed the bottle away and raised the glass to his mouth. It was his first drink of the week and he was proud of himself. His wife, sweet woman that she was, was letting him know in very subtle ways that she was happy with his decision to cut down. Not that she had complained. She understood that Charlie's life as a journalist involved a lot of meetings with contacts, and mostly at bars. Plus, he was a man. What do you want? This was Cameroon. Men hung out at bars.

"I give you new glass or you dey fine with da one?" The barman had sidled over, holding a fresh bottle of *33export*, and naturally expecting another sale.

"*Ma own don do*", Charlie said, shaking his head and getting to his feet. "You drink. On me."

"*Kai Walai!*" the barman exclaimed in happiness, breaking out into a celebratory dance. "*God dey up, today na ma lucky day! Who wan try?*" Raising the bottle high, he popped the cover with exaggerated style and alacrity. Then, with uncommon exactitude and steadiness of hand, he poured out onto the cracking cement floor a carefully measured out tenth of a droplet, over which loud and overflowing blessings were pronounced. "*Ma brotha, make papa God keep you O. Make E hand guide and protect you all time. Make man no get you bad mimba, and make die e hand taya when e try for hold ya shirt.*" With that, the barman raised the bottle to his mouth while the few, mostly jovial and tipsy customers chorused a loud 'amen'. Why not? Was free beer not a good thing? *Abeg leave man!*

Charlie just smiled. It was Cameroon. How he loved this country,...the people, the simple ways, the easy camaraderie,...Another beer would have been good, but he had to leave. He had come here to meet somebody, an individual, who, because of his job would know every transaction pertaining to the French shipment, that is, for the period of time that it had spent at the port. He was hoping that the man would know the identity of whoever had picked up the rest of it, since they were no records to be found. But the man was now an hour late.

Impatiently, Charlie glanced at his watch. Again. Had the man changed his mind? He hoped not. Maybe something unexpected had caused a delay in an area without cell phone reception. Or maybe...maybe what, he asked himself.

Well, he knew where the man lived, and he could go there. He would give it another hour and if nothing happened, then he would try the man's house. He paid his bill, stepped out of the bar, walked to his car, got in, sat down and pulled out a folded copy of The Economist.

Fifty minutes later, the man still had not shown up, so Charlie pulled out his cell phone and made a call to the seaport.

"He did not come in today," said the girl at the other end.

"Oh he did not?" Charlie was not sure what to make of it. This was Cameroon. Sometimes people could not make it to work. But those people would be answering their cell phones if they had one. He had spoken to the man late last night, and they had set up a meet, so he had expected the man to be here.

"Maybe he is not well," Charlie said to the girl.

"Maybe," the girl said at the other end. "If he doesn't come in tomorrow, then we will look into those possibilities. Have a nice day, sir." The girl hung up.

One hour later Charlie pulled over to the side of a little stony, yet somewhat leveled out street, parked the car and got out. The man lived in one of the few remaining Cameroonian middle-class neighborhoods, a place where life was just slightly better than at the very bottom. Here, at least all the houses had more than two bedrooms, water and electricity, even though the supply could never be guaranteed.

Charlie locked the car, dropped the keys into his pocket and walked up the street. Although hibiscus hedges blocked out much of the man's house, he could see parts of it. It had been built from concrete bricks and then roofed with cheap sheets of silver zinc that had once caught and reflected the light with a blinding glare. Now it was more orange than silver, from rust. Like all the other houses, it badly needed a paint job. Next to the house was a little corner store, probably operated by a neighbor. Right in front of it, a group of girls were involved in a loud game of 'Seezoh'.

He walked past the store and turned into the yard of the man's house. Quietly, he went up the stairs, onto the verandah, and knocked on the door. There was no answer. He knocked again, this time louder.

"Any one home? *Na hu dey house eh?*" Quiet. He tried the doorknob but the door was locked. Glancing quickly at the street to make sure that no one was watching, he stepped off the verandah and went around the side of the house to the back. It looked pretty much like the front, except for the fact that it was totally hedged in, had fewer windows, and one smaller door. Wrapping a handkerchief around the doorhandle, Charlie tried it. It was open.

He stepped into the house and found himself in a small, tidied room, with a made up sleeping bed on one side and a cooking stove on the other. Up against the wall was a neat row of jars, pots and other utensils that had been carefully lined up on a make shift counter.

Silently, he moved forward, stepping over a cheap rug to open a connecting door at the other side of the small room. It led into the living room of the house. And Charlie halted in his tracks. The room was just as neat as the other, except for a trailing line of dark red stains. He bent closer and examined the line. Blood! It was leading into the only other bedroom in the house. He followed it.

The other bedroom was equally small, had a bed, a side table, a chair, and even a small closet. It was obviously the master bedroom, and the master of the house was in it. On the bed. On his back. And he was not breathing! *Yes, Garri don high pass water!*

Very carefully, with heart racing, Charlie backed out of the room, made his way into the living room, and out the small back door through which he had gained entrance. This was no place to be. No sir, it was not.

Once outside, he retraced his steps around the house and then exited the front yard onto the street. The game of *seezoh* had picked up speed, and none of the children seemed to be paying any attention to Charlie as he walked to his car and got into it.

The man was actually dead! Murdered!

Had he been dead for long? Who did him in? Did it have anything to do with the investigation? Although he would have very much liked to think that it did not, somewhere deep, down in his soul, Charlie knew, without knowing how he knew, that the man's death was somehow connected to the shipment.

Now what? Where did this latest development leave him? As the primary suspect? He broke out in cold sweat. Had he touched anything in the man's house? Fingerprints? He wished he had a drink!

As the Toyota sped along the two-lane highway, Charlie ran the sequence of events over and over in his mind. Trying to make sense of everything, shifting and moving parts and pieces of the whole story as if it were a jigsaw puzzle, and the whole time feeling as if the answers were all around him, close yet invisible. The only thing he could see were the endless rows of palm and rubber trees that were on both sides of the road.

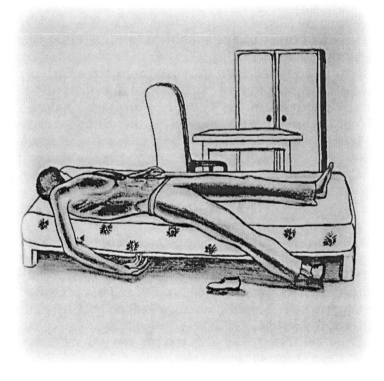

On his back. And he was not breathing!

It was probably because of all these thoughts that he failed to spot the other car when he should have. It was a black 96 Golf with heavily tinted windows. And he turned to look at it only because, instead of overtaking quickly as a car from behind would do on a single lane highway, the Golf accelerated to Charlie's speed, and just stayed there.

There were two people in the car. He could tell from their body types that one was male and the other female. The man was driving, and the woman had the gun. Both wore masks.

The sight of the gun was enough to activate the journalist's reflexes. Several shots rang out, with glass exploding, as Charlie slammed on the brakes, throwing off the Golf, which was seeking to glue itself onto the Toyota. The car quickly slowed down as well, only to be surprised by a sudden burst of speed from the Toyota.

The Golf wasted no time in getting to the chase. Frantically Charlie spun the wheel, steering into the middle of the road in multiple S bends as he attempted to keep the other car from coming abreast. Another shot rang out. And then another one, and more glass exploded.

With engines screaming, the cars raced down the narrow highway. And then very slowly, the black car began gaining on Charlie until it was almost abreast once more. How he wished he had a gun. Desperately, he sent the Toyota slamming into the side of the Golf, forcing it into a tailspin that ended against a high shoulder. But the Golf was far from over. Its turbo engine could be heard screaming defiantly as it drove off the bushy shoulder and back onto the road. It took no time to eat up the Toyota's lead. Charlie glanced at the rearview and swore as yet another shot rang out. The black car was coming up. It would be driving abreast in a moment. Charlie spun the wheel again, driving into the car, trying once more to force it off the road.

It did not happen. The Golf took the hit, engine screaming, and stayed on the narrow highway. More shots. The sound of clashing metal, the smell of rubber, as eight tires negotiated a tight bend, which was meant for much slower speeds.

Then, without warning, happening too fast for the distracted journalist to follow, there was a sudden blur and a loud crash as the golf ran head on, into a red minivan that had appeared on the bend, coming from the opposite direction, and not expecting anything in its path.

Charlie just drove on. He had been shot several times and the bleeding was heavy.

By the time he drove into an area with cell phone reception, his vision was already blurred. Somehow, he succeeded to pull up and park the car without an incident. Painfully, he retrieved his cell phone, dialed a number, and waited for the tone signaling that it was ringing at the other end.

CHAPTER TWENTY-ONE

Kingdom of Kemet, 1720 B.C.

$\mathcal{T}$he Queen mother pulled the veil lower, totally obscuring her face as she hurried along the beautiful hallway. This was a private visit happening within the palace, which explained why she was accompanied by only ten ladies in waiting.

As usual, guards and servants were falling all over themselves to acknowledge her as she and her little train sped by. She ignored them all. Her son was the one who was always falling prey to flattery, not she. If he were not King, would anyone care about her opinions? Would they even look at her? Or would she become one of the many women who just lived in the palace?

She could swear that since the beginning of the siege there was a slight edge of silent hostility from the guards and even some servants. The attitude seemed to be growing with the days, in tandem with the devastating effects of the whole situation. Survival was challenging all the loyalties around her. These people were like rats that were beginning to wonder if the ship had the stamina that it would take to ride the storm and not go under. Rats that were beginning to cast fearful glances overboard in the hope of spying another vessel. So why should she not ignore them?

Instead, she focused on what she was going to tell her son.

He was the King, yes, but he was her son first. She knew that there were those, especially of the old guard, who were particularly unhappy about how close she was to her son. They felt it weakened his ability to make independent decisions. Maybe true, but so what? Was a man going to stop being a child to his own mother simply because he had become a King? Where would that King be if that mother had not existed first? Did they have the slightest idea what she had had to do to get the throne for her son? Or did they think it had just happened? Of course they did! What a laugh! Nehesy Aesare, the King and ruler of kemet had come out of her own body, he owed his throne to her, and she was not about to let that go to waste.

She turned a corner and came up on the gilded double doors that led into her son's private quarters, so private that not even the royal harem was allowed access.

The guards, who were standing on both sides of the door jumped to attention, wondering what to do. The King had been specific about the fact that he was not to be disturbed.

The Queen mother sensed their indecision as she came to a halt and threw off the veil from her face. The look in her eyes said it all, dissolving any resolve that the guards may have had. The times were shaky, that was obvious to them, but did that mean one should create a new enemy in the Queen mother? Who knew what tomorrow would bring?

One of the guards threw open the doors and disappeared inside, running to warn the King that his own mother had chosen to disrespect his wish with a surprise visit.

She breezed into the room just as the King was waving away the man who had just spoken into his ear. She gave the man a malevolent look and he quickly ran out. When she heard the door close, she turned her full attention to the King.

He was sitting on a wide chair and doing one of his most favorite things, -eating. The table in front of him was covered with trays that were loaded with all kinds of foods, and as usual he was cramming as much of it into his mouth as he could.

Apart from the royal food taster, there was only one other person in the room, -Cikatrix. He was seated at the other end of the table.

"Mother," the King spoke with difficulty, "Is everything quiet?"

She ignored the question, turning instead to her ladies in waiting.

"Wait outside," she said to all of them. Without a word, they obeyed. Even the royal food taster stepped out of the room.

If it were up to the Queen mother, no one would ever see her son like this. "Can you excuse us?" she said, turning towards Cikatrix. Instead of getting up and leaving the room as she had expected, he stayed put, looking instead to the King who shook his head.

"No, mother, he can stay and finish his food. You can also sit down and tell me what you have to say."

She forced a smile. Her assessment of the situation was correct and the irony of it was not lost on her. She herself had asked the King to appoint Cikatrix to the post of *Vizier in charge of the Kingdom's borders*. And she had not done it because she liked the man. The only reason she had eventually asked Aesare to make him Vizier was because the High Priest had specifically requested for it to be done. So, for Cikatrix to now become openly disrespectful because he thought her son would protect him was unacceptable. Plus, he was beginning to wield undue influence over her son and no one seemed to know why. But the whole situation had not really bothered the Queen mother until she realized that the King was making more and more decisions without consulting her. Apart from that, he seemed to have changed overnight. It was as if some foreign entity had actually possessed his body. The Queen mother recalled an episode a month earlier, where she had not even been able to get the King to focus and listen to what she had to say.

So, she had rallied her formidable influence at court and launched a very secret investigation into the matter. It had yielded some surprising results.

One of the maids who were charged with cleaning the King's quarters had been secretly replaced with one of the Queen mother's 'girls'. The Queen mother had instructed the girl to hide in the King's rooms for the duration of one night. The girl had hidden in a huge ceramic vase from which she could hear and see everything. Towards midnight, she saw the King walk into the big room accompanied by Cikatrix. No servants, no guards, nobody, just the two of them. They sat down, clearing a space on one of the royal tables, and Cikatrix took out a pipe-like device, put a little rock into it, and handed it to the King, who took it with a smile. Then Cikatrix picked up one of the burning candles from the table and held the flame directly under the bronze instrument. The heat caused whatever he had put into it to start sizzling, giving up some smoke that the King slowly inhaled, coughing, almost choking, but successfully holding down the smoke. Then shakily, with teary eyes he handed over the device to Cikatrix who filled it up again. Both men indulged repeatedly, while carrying on a conversation that the girl did not fully grasp. All she could tell was that Cikatrix was pressing the King to do something for *his people*, something to do with writing and publishing a new law. But the King had successfully held off by offering even sweeter promises. Then sometime around the third watch, stumbling and wobbling, Cikatrix hid the pipe, wiped off all traces of their smoking, and poured out some essential oils to camouflage the smell. Then he walked to the door to let in a party of people who quickly turned everything into an orgy.

The spy had watched everything from inside the vase,

risking her life to the point of being vomited upon by a drunken partier, who could not have known that there was someone in the vase.

Now, as she stared at her son, the Queen mother could see that for the first time since he had become King, he was willing to not only challenge, but to fight with her as well. He would do anything to protect this new habit that was actually stealing his soul and leaving an empty shell in its place, a process that would eventually endanger everything she had fought for. Which she could not allow, so it was a problem. And she would solve it in her own way. Even if the priest disagreed. In fact, the way she planned to go about it, he would hear of it only after the solution had already been achieved. It was alright if he lost his temper then.

"Nehesy," she addressed her son as she began to pace around the table, gesticulating as she spoke, and doing her best to ignore the other man. "What is this supposed to mean? Can I not have a private audience with my own son? Who is this man whom you allow to not only disrespect me, but yourself and consequently the whole Kingdom? Have you forgotten what it means to be King? Or is it that you have forgotten how you came to be sitting on the throne?" From the corner of her eye she saw Cikatrix stiffen.

"Mother!" The King leaned forward threateningly. "I forbid you to say another word!" He was panting, the fear and hatred on his face, a study of contrast.

"Or else what?" The Queen mother asked with a smile. "Will you arrest me and have me beheaded as you should have done with him?" She was pointing at Cikatrix, who seemed to have found some courage in the King's presence and was staring back at her, unflinchingly. "Is that what the great Nehesy is planning to do? And what excuse will you give the people? That you had to kill your own mother in order to prevent her from speaking up against a dog that was causing the King to be disrespected?"

"You are exaggerating, mother. No one in the whole Kingdom will dare disrespect me."

"Really? What do you think the people are saying to themselves?" The King was silent. "That the King is so loving and forgiving for not having the will to do what is right? I wish that were the case, but unfortunately it is not. Instead, they are beginning to think that the King is weak." She paused. "A weak King, especially one who did not ascend to the throne on merit, is not feared. Is it not a matter of time before one of your so called friends stands up to challenge your legitimacy?" she asked, looking pointedly at Cikatrix who was trying, without much success, to hide his surprise.

"MOTHER!" The King was on his feet and he was bristling with rage. "I shall have your head for this."

"No you shall not," she answered back, turning once again to Cikatrix. "Leave the room. I must consult with my son. Alone." she said, bowing mockingly to him. He hesitated, not sure what to do. Furtively he glanced at the King but the monarch looked away. Quietly, with his features cast in sandstone Cikatrix stood up and hurried out of the room. The Queen mother turned to her son.

"Now he knows too much," she said, with a small smile. "What are you going to do about it?" she whispered the question. "Are you going to let him live? Can you risk it?" The King was quiet. "CAN YOU TRUST HIM?" she screamed.

The King sat down, turning away in resignation. Inwardly, the Queen mother laughed. She had known all along that she would win. She always did.

"Mother, I really, really, hate you," the King said with venom, food particles flying out of his mouth.

"No you don't, you just think you do," the Queen mother replied. "I am your mother and everything that I have done has been done for you. I gave you everything. Everything. Remember that!"

"Yes, mother, you gave me everything. You made sure that I won, no matter the cost." The King paused to swallow. "Success was the goal, whether merited or not, and so here I am today as King. Mother, do you think it has anything to do with why I am so inefficient? Why do you expect me to run when you have never been able to let me learn to walk by myself?"

"It is a lot of weight you have on your shoulders, and most men will die from the exhaustion of it," she flattered. "But I am here to help you. I will always help you."

"Always? And what will I do when you are no more? Tell me that! What shall I do then, mother?"

The Queen mother turned away to hide a smile.

He would not understand. Later, perhaps, but not now. Right now she still had a few things to do. Cikatrix had to be dealt with. After that, she would go and see Melenoc. Some urgent things had to be discussed with the High Priest.

"I gave u everything. Everything. Remember that!"

CHAPTER TWENTY-TWO

*W*hen Salatis was told that only twenty of his disguised, advance guards had gained entrance into the city of Itjawy, he lost his temper and beheaded the bearer of the news. This was a very, very, carefully thought out plan that was not supposed to have failed.

When he learned that this had happened because the man he had put in charge of the operation used horses instead of camels, his temper quickly transformed into the famous rage that had earned him the nick name, 'Devil'. Two more bodies succumbed to his sword as the rage took control of him like a foreign entity with a mind of its own.

He rushed out of the tent screaming in agony and running off into the desert night. No one dared to follow. All of his commanders were well aware of this madness that he had, and it was understood that he was rushing off into the wilderness to be alone, to avoid hurting anybody else. Eventually he would calm down. It had happened many times before. Sometimes he would be gone for hours, only to return again, mutilated, limping, bleeding, but calm and calculating once more. Which was exactly what happened.

He limped back into camp and summoned his chief commander into his tent. With only twenty of his men in the city, new plans had to be made. Quickly.

Although he was confident that he had enough manpower and resources to eventually take down the city, he also knew that it would now require more time than he had anticipated. He had already sent word to the front lines, asking the commander to begin an effective siege while waiting for the bulk of the army to arrive. He understood that with sieges, the key was not so much the city wall as it was the moral fiber of the people. With the city of Itjawy he did not expect too much resistance because he was well aware of how deeply corrupt the very affluent culture had become. Salatis knew that Corruption had never been friends with Courage.

By the time he himself arrived at the frontlines, the siege was underway. He had taken immediate command of things and began the implementation of a strategy that was calculated to additionally soften, weaken, and finally break the moral of the city dwellers. His men had located all the wells and oases around the city and filled them with sand. Just as a beginning.

Then, the next six days had been used to effectively raze all farmland to the ground, disrupting and destroying vital irrigation systems on which farming depended.

For the next six days archers had rained thousands of arrows into the city causing untold pain.

The next six days had seen huge earthen jars that had been filled with bees being catapulted into the city.

This was followed by six days in which chunks of smelly, infected, rotted meat from ten thousand camels had been loaded into more earthenware and catapulted over the walls. While the rotted meat was being catapulted into the city, another part of his army arrived with the rest of the heavy equipment.

It had cost him a lot in time, manpower, and other resources. But everything was here now and that was all he cared about. Even now as he watched for signs in the night sky, Salatis could hear his men unloading the huge rocks that from now on, would go on the catapults. Tomorrow at first light they would be used to shock and awe the city dwellers. For the first time, they would know the true might of Salatis. He would open their eyes and they would see how hopeless the fate of the city actually was.

Victory was close now, very close, but he still had to remind himself to be patient. Impatience usually led to anger, and anger was the brother of mistakes. He had made too many of those and he was determined not to lose any more time in that way.

He took another sip of the hot tea that he was using to stay warm, put out the pipe, and was turning to head back to his tent when he heard footsteps.

"The catapults are all loaded, ready, and in place, my lord," a man reported.

"How many?"

"All thirty, my lord."

"Good. Go back, change the guard, and report back to me in the middle of the fourth watch."

"As you wish my lord," the man said, bowing to Salatis's turned back.

$\mathcal{A}$s the eastern sky was lightening, Salatis was ending a meeting in his tent with his commanders. He had outlined the day's plans, specifying the order in which he wanted things to proceed. The men had all listened carefully, asking questions here and there, clearing up all doubts, and polishing off all the details. After about three hours of thorough examination he was finally satisfied. There would be no mistakes here today. *No horses would be used in place of camels.*

"Anymore questions?" he asked. There were none. He got to his feet and the men followed him out into the cold morning air.

The sight that met his eyes filled him with so much joy that he almost smiled. It was a dream that had finally come true. Here was his army, one of the biggest that any man had ever put together. And it was ready to go. He had done it. It had taken twenty years but it had been worth it.

The surrounding plain for as far as the eye could see was dotted with small fires that his men had lit in order to stay warm. Directly ahead he could see the catapults. They had been loaded with the huge rocks that had been brought in on rafts along the river. Further away, outlined against the eastern sky, was the prize itself, the great city of Itjawy, Capital of Kemet, centre of trade, learning, and the eye of the civilized world.

The sun would be coming up in about an hour. The time was now. As he led his commanders in a file through the camp, all those who recognized him in the firelight prostrated in respect, and the message quickly spread that Salatis himself had arrived the frontlines and he was going to direct the attack of the day. Success was close. In the soldier's minds, the specter of gold, silver, women, and all the booty that they had been promised was coming true.

When Salatis got to the line of loaded catapults, he stopped. These machines never seized to amaze him. He reached out and gently caressed the closest one. Gathered around him, his commanders, looking overwhelmed by the historical significance of the moment, were standing in awed respect.

"Let the work of the gods begin," Salatis whispered, raising his sharp scimitar and bringing it down with precision. There was a loud *whoosh* as the taut ropes that held down the loaded weight were severed. A rock that had required thirty men to lift was catapulted into the early morning air. It was tossed high into the sky, looping slowly, before beginning a rapid descent towards a city that was still asleep.

By the time the rock landed, there was another one in the air. Teams of men, working feverishly, were taking turns to operate and reload all the catapults as they discharged their terrible weapons.

Presently a loud wailing broke out from within the city and Salatis, who could hear it from his camp, almost smiled. Yes, justice was finally coming to repay the evil people of Kemet for all the pain that they had inflicted upon his family, and his people.

"May these cries of pain flow like sweet music to the very gates of anubis." Salatis whispered.

By the time the rock landed in the city, there was another one in the air...

Cikatrix, known to most people as *The Scarred One*, was feeling very, very scarred, by the fact that, now, he had to hide like a common thief. And in the sewage tunnels under the ground! What a stench. But this was now his reality.

How he wished things could have been different. But they were not. He had tried everything in his power to influence the new King in a way that would ensure positive change for the Aamu people. Not only had he failed, but he had also managed to attract the terrible wrath of the King's Mother. He wondered what she would think if she realized that Salatis had wanted her son dead and that were it not for Cikatrix the King would be no more.

He stepped off the block of carved stone and began making his way, slowly, along the tunnel. He was determined to survive and he had a plan. First, he would see the King. It was risky but worth it, he thought. It may possibly be the last time that he did. He suspected that deep in his heart Aesare did not want him dead. The problem was the King's mother. Cikatrix was certain that, if given the right motivation and or pressure, Aesare could stand up to his mother. Who knows? Another meeting with the King might be what was needed. Aesare could decide, for friendship's sake, to stand and fight for what they had together.

If at the end of the meeting Aesare had not changed his mind, then he would implement the second part of his plan; going to see Salatis. Survival was worthy of that, at least, he consoled himself. For a split second he wondered what his father would say now, looking at his son's fate.

It was ironic that Salatis, the man who had almost killed him, may be the same person who was going to save him from death, while Aesare, his friend, savior, lover and King of Kemet, was going to let him die, even though he could prevent it.

...and began making his way slowly along the tunnel...

CHAPTER TWENTY-THREE

*H*asim dug his fingernails into the tiny, shallow space between the bricks and hoisted himself upwards by another painful inch.

Very carefully, he extended a thin, sinewy leg, seeking with his toes until they felt a shallow lip on the wall. Gingerly, very gingerly, he transferred some of his weight to the leg, taking great care to avoid any sudden and or unnecessary movement. Even his breathing had to be carefully regulated. He was like a fly on the wall, the ground was at least twenty-five cubits below, and any mistake at this point would be fatal.

Breathing very gently he angled his head, looking upward, and searching for another hold on the almost smooth wall. Some moments later he spotted what appeared to be a little recess, only big enough for a finger, not too far above his head. This was it. If he could reach it, then the window ledge would be accessible.

He stretched out his right hand, but it still proved too short. What to do? What to do? For the thousandth time he cursed Cikatrix under his breath. If the son-of-a-mangy-dog had not failed in taking Abou Bakar's life, he himself would never have found the need to scale this wall in order to get the job done. He would deal with the man later.

He tried reaching out once more, but again his fully outstretched arm was not quite long enough. For the first time he was forced to acknowledge that the situation was critical. His own life could even be in the balance. He had to think. Fast. His hold onto the wall was at best, very fragile. Even a gust of wind could blow him off. And he could not climb back down.

With sweat dripping down his face, he gauged the distance that separated his fingertips from the recess, closed his eyes and visualized the space in his mind's eyes. It was less than the width of his palm, not a great distance to be sure, but at this height? He took a deep breath, whispered a silent prayer and lunged himself upward, knowing that failure would mean a headlong plunge to the ground below. It was a move that very few people would dare to attempt, but only a creature of immense and formidable talent like Hasim could even expect to succeed.

His right, middle finger found the tiny recess in the wall, and he hooked it in, just as his whole body began swinging dangerously in a little arc. Instinctively, he kicked out, putting unbelievable strain on the finger, widening the swing, and forcing his right leg to go all the way to the window ledge. With lightning speed, he wrapped a foot over the ledge as the bone of his strained and bleeding middle finger snapped, losing its hold onto the wall. And he was hanging from the window ledge by his feet. A few moments later he was in the house.

He stretched out his right hand, but it proved too short...

Focusing through the pain from the finger, he looked around, realizing that the window had led him into the General's empty sleeping quarters. It was a big, sparsely furnished room, with little or no pretense of luxury. Apart from the centrally located double bed and single low table, there was no other furniture. On the table was a basket of fruit, right next to a carafe of wine. This should work, he thought to himself as he tiptoed over the many hand drawn maps that were strewn all over the floor. At the table, he picked up the carafe, sniffed at its opening and nodded in satisfaction. Then, carefully protecting his hurting finger, he dipped into his garments, produced a tiny pouch, untied it with some difficulty, and poured the contents into the wine.

He was barely done when he heard footsteps outside the door. He scuttled across the room, climbed out through the window, and hoisted himself onto the roof of the building, just as the door was thrown open and General Abou Bakar walked in.

The tension in the General's posture was obvious as he marched into the room and picked up one of the several maps that were lying on the floor, next to the table. For a long moment, he scrutinized the map, furrowing his brows in thought as he considered the possible shortcomings that could arise with the plan. As bad as it looked, he was convinced that it was the best option that was available under the circumstances.

Salatis's siege had obviously been well thought out, and it was wreaking untold havoc on the city. It was doubtful if the city could hold out for much longer. Only one storehouse of grain was left, and that was not much. Everything else in the city had been rationed out, eaten, and more deaths from famine were being reported everyday.

But the worst part of it all, were the huge rocks that had started falling from the sky. They were causing too much damage for it to go on. Seriously, something had to be done. A decision had to be forced.

He dropped the map on the table, picked up the carafe of wine and raised it to his mouth.

The catapulted boulder slammed into the building, smashing through walls, throwing the General off of his feet and knocking the carafe of wine out of his hands. He landed on his back and rolled over just as a huge piece of carved rock came down where his body had been the moment before. Then everything was quiet.

"Sir, are you alright?" asked the first of his two aids who rushed into the room.

"I think I am." The General replied, getting to his feet and dusting himself. "See what you can salvage," he instructed, looking around the destroyed room. "Especially the maps. I may need them for the meeting," he added, as he stepped out.

Now, more than ever, he hoped the King would be convinced to authorize the plan.

---

*B*y the time Abou Bakar got to the palace almost everyone was there. They were seated in a smaller hall and waiting for the King. He walked in, saluted a few people, and found a seat for himself.

A short time later, everyone stood up as the King was quietly carried in. He was preceded by guards and followed by a small retinue of officials. Very gently the throne was deposited on the raised wooden platform at the end of the room.

The meeting began with a greeting from the announcer who went straight to the business of the day. He explained that the King had been invited here today by General Abou Bakar so that the royal ears could listen and either give approval or disapproval to any new, and even extreme ideas that may prove effective against the unsustainable onslaught from the foreign army.

At that point, the King reached up and took the royal crown off from his head. It was an indication that anyone could speak up without prior permission from the announcer. Immediately, the various state officials and Generals began volunteering what they thought were feasible solutions to the crisis. All kinds of ideas were brought to the table, even ones that Abou Bakar would not have imagined possible. One man, an adviser who was well known for his appetite, went so far as to suggest cannibalism. He shamefacedly argued that there were enough babies and elderly people in the capital to sustain strong adults like himself who were actually the ones who would be required to fix the problem. "Why not? Did it sound too crazy? Were these not crazy times," he asked?

"These are very crazy times, no doubt," Abou Bakar said, when it was his time to speak. "But I do not think any kind of craziness should cause us to become animals! And at the expense of our own children? Is it because they are babies who are too young to speak up for themselves that we would presume to dispose of them in this way, just for our own convenience?" he asked. "Are the elderly useless as well just because they are now old and weak? Have we forgotten that they harbor the most experience, and as such good advice? For us to be considering such an option, in my opinion, amounts to cowardice and it will not help us." He paused, feeling suddenly weak and nauseated. "But enough of that," he added, wondering why his body was suddenly feeling strange. Was it the wine? But he'd barely tasted it. Then as suddenly as the feeling had come upon him, it departed and once more his head was clear. "The reason I called this meeting is because I wish to ask the King for permission to open the gates and take the fight to Salatis."

Everyone held his breath.

"Why not?" the General continued, "First of all, he would not expect us to make such a move. Secondly, why should we sit and wait for death? Does anyone here doubt Salatis's determination to break into this city? Does any one here think that if he should succeed he would spare our lives?" The room was quiet. "I don't think so," the General answered his own question. "I know the man very well, and I think that we have to make a move now before it is too late. What are we waiting for? Our allies? What if they do not come to our aid?" He looked around the room. "We are hungry already. Let us attack Salatis now, before we are too weak to stand."

"Too weak to stand?" It was the child eater. "What is this fear mongering? Are you hoping to find your boy alive in Salatis's camp? Is that why you want to endanger us all? Because it is not Salatis that you want to go and confront out there, is it? You had an opportunity to kill the man twenty years ago, and you failed. What can you possibly hope to accomplish today when he has a huge army with him and..."

Everyone began speaking at the same time and the meeting quickly degenerated into a verbal fight, which the General watched in silence. As hurtful as the man's accusation was, there was truth to the words. Were his hopes misplaced? Did he really believe that there was a chance of attacking and defeating Salatis' army? Or was it just about his son? How he wished he had let Iroha to come with him to the King's prison house. Was the boy alive? What would his mother think in the afterlife? She herself may still be alive today if only he had listened to her wish to accompany him to Avaris twenty years ago.

Finally the King raised his hand and the hubbub died down.

"Many words have been spoken here today," the King said. "While many of them were driven by fear, it was all from the heart and I thank you all for that." He paused. "From today's meeting I have made two decisions: the first one is that Abou Bakar is to be called 'General of Generals'. He is to take charge of all the Kingdom's armies and all other Generals must answer to him. That said, I also grant him permission to open the gates of the city and prosecute the war into Salatis' camp, and let it be so," the King added. "The second decision I have arrived at today is to make Abou Bakar temporary keeper of Kepharra's left hand."

"NOOO!" It was the Queen mother and she was marching into the hall, with her full train of ladies following just behind.

"And let it be so," the King finished.

"NO!"

"Yes, mother!"

"How can you do something like this?"

"Why not, dearest mother?" the King asked, mockingly. "Am I not King?" he smiled sourly. "Would you like me to make you the keeper of Kepharra's hand? Would you like that mother?" Gently, the King stuck a pudgy arm under his robes and pulled out the left hand of Kepharra, ultimate symbol of kingly authority. He summoned the tray bearer and placed the shiny necklace on the golden tray. Immediately the tray bearer turned around and advanced to the edge of the platform where he came to a halt. The room was in total silence.

The Queen mother, who had advanced to the platform, came to stop directly in the path of the tray bearer.

The silence in the room became deafening. Could she risk defying her son in such a public place? Was she going to reach out and pick up the golden hand? Even in a time of war, the consequences would be terrible. She took another step forward, smiling coldly at the tray bearer who could not dare to look into her face. Then, abruptly, she turned around and marched out of the room. "You will regret this day, O King," she said as she walked out, not caring that her back was to the throne. "I swear by my womb from whence you came, that you will sorely regret this day," she screamed, as she rushed out of the hall with her train of ladies.

After the doors of the hall had been shut, Abou Bakar

walked forward to the tray bearer and bowed deeply. With both hands, he picked up the golden hand of the god. This new responsibility had taken him by total surprise but it was alright. He knew exactly the man to whom to entrust this treasure. The little man would find a good place in the huge prison house in which to hide the hand. There was none better equipped for it. He stood up, suddenly feeling weak and nauseous once again. That was strange. It was not like him. Did he eat something that he should not have? Once more the moment did not last.

She took another step forward, smiling coldly at the tray bearer who could not dare to look into her face ...

As the King was carried out of the room, the monarch turned and looked directly into Abou Bakar's eyes, envying the man for his strength, wishing for the thousandth time that he himself had never become King. If only his mother had listened. If only she had just listened to him. But no! How could she, when it had never been about him? He could see that clearly now. But it was too late. What could he do? Abandon the throne? He wished it were that easy. Do the King makers not say that to abandon a throne can be much more dangerous than to seize it? Will the vacuum not lead to a power struggle for which he would be blamed? And will the new King feel secure enough with the former King still living? Was that not trouble he would be asking for? Just thinking about everything was making him hungry.

   ... wishing for the thousandth time that he had never become King...

CHAPTER TWENTY-FOUR

$\mathcal{T}$he apartment in which Melenoc was being kept was within the fourth concentric ring in the King's palace. It had been decided that it was a good idea to keep the 'ailing' High Priest in the palace where the King's own medicine men would keep an eye on him. And they were doing their best in this regard even though the High Priest did not seem to be getting better. None of their theories could explain what seemed to be happening with the man.

And Melenoc preferred to keep it that way. Was it not easier to rant for an hour everyday while they were visiting? If he should reclaim his sanity, would he be able to face ridicule from a city that had defanged a High Priest? Where would he dare to show his face? Only one thing counted now; the hands of Kepharra. Had it not been for Caliph, he would be in totally different circumstances right now. But no, the man had had to open his mouth when he should have kept it shut. Damn the man!

Angrily, the High Priest swept off an array of decorative alabaster pots that were sitting on a low windowpane. They crashed to the ground, breaking into countless tiny pieces. He stomped on them, jumping up and down, cutting and hurting himself, not caring, bleeding, screaming, and eventually becoming too exhausted to stand. Breathing hard, he leaned against the wall and took a long drink from the goatskin bag.

Then, someone knocked on the door, a sure sign that he had a visitor. Quickly, he limped into the other room and hid behind a curtain from where he could see them enter into the apartment. Seeing the visitor would decide the quantity and quality of mental instability that he would display.

He saw the door open and two figures stepped into the room. Both of them were women and they both halted in their tracks at the sight of broken pottery. Presently, one of the women whispered something, and the other deposited the basket of fruit that she had been carrying onto the floor and backed out of the room. The other woman locked the door, turned around and walked further into the room, throwing aside the veil that had hidden her face.

It was the Queen mother. Melenoc smiled to himself. He

stepped from behind the curtain as she walked, hesitantly, into the inner room.

"Welcome amongst us, woman," he greeted.

"Thank you, High Priest," the Queen mother answered. "Is your health returning?"

"As the spirits wish. I see you are worried. What is the news? Is everything not going as we have purposed it?"

The Queen mother shook her head, going straight to the point. "Is everything really under control? This foreign army, is it truly within your power?" she asked. "Will Salatis listen when you ask him to stop? How will you do that?"

"How will I do that?" The High Priest limped forward until he was standing just an inch away from her. "Are you beginning to doubt me now?" He whispered. "Is that what this is about? Doubt?" The man paused, turning around and walking away. "Did I not make a promise to you that if you do as I say, Neferhotep, your late husband, would be replaced by your own son? Did I not say that a foreign army would march into the Kingdom at this time and that the scarred one will be blamed for it? Did your brother not get the contract to supply all the spears, knives, and shields that the army may need, just as I promised? And did your cousin not supply all the horses? When have I said something that did not come to pass?" he asked, turning away from her. "I know it has taken much longer, and there has been more destruction and death than I had anticipated, but so what?" he asked. "Is that not life? Things don't always go as planned. But we cannot let that get in our way and you know that. Look at me," he continued. "Do you think I planned to get myself burned and partially blinded? No! I did not! Is it stopping me? No, never! And I should hope that everytime you look at me, you see my resolve and steadfastness in this quest upon which our destinies have embarked."

The Queen mother took a deep breath as conflicting emotions raced through her head, her mind, and her body.

"Every time I look at you, I see my lover, and my true King," she said. "I see the man who promised to take the throne for us, the man who told me that the gods had given him the ancient secret of life, -the same secret which some parchments claim was lost in a great garden called Eden. And I believe you, my King." She paused. "But I also see a man who may have been blinded by pride, and subsequently may have become over confident, a man who does not yet know that the newest threat to his throne is a truly formidable opponent whose reputation speaks for itself." She stopped for effect. "Abou Bakar has just been made the keeper of Kepharra's left hand," she added quietly. Melenoc froze.

"So, does my lover understand why I am worried? The hand is not within my reach anymore because my son gave it away today. I tried to stop him, but I was alone," she added resignedly.

Neferhotep...

"I need to be by myself," Melenoc said in a hoarse whisper. "Please leave me," he added with difficulty. "And send immediate word to the pilgrim who is staying at my house to come and see me. He goes by the name of Hasim."

The Queen mother did not argue. She knew the man well enough to not press any further. He would think about the situation and he would have a solution by her next visit. He always did.

Once more by himself, the High Priest began moaning and limping around the room, his pain more in his head than in his body. Had the spirit departed from him? He stopped for a moment and recited the first paragraph of the prophecy in the secret tongue. Immediately he felt the vibrations. See, Belial was still with him!

So, what was the problem? Why were things going the wrong way? Why was he almost blind? Why had Salatis's disguised guards been discovered before they could enter the city? Why had he not let Caliph receive the left hand from the King, even though he himself had had the right one in his own hands? Getting it later from the man would not have presented any real obstacles. So, why had he not thought about that? Maybe because he had become light headed from chewing too many leaves. But why had he needed the leaves in the first place? Was it not because of the pain? So why had he been burned? WHY? He wanted to scream, to hurt himself, but all he could do was take another sip of water.

Now, the situation was even more complex. Not unmanageable, just more difficult. And difficult tasks called for difficult solutions.

---

*H*asim, also called The Shadow, took a last look around, before stepping out into the open. Keeping his movements to a minimum he began sliding down the sand dune, away from the wall. This was one of the most important missions that he had ever been confided. And it could save his life. Finally, he had something that Salatis wanted badly, something with which he could use to placate the man's anger, that is, if Salatis should learn that Abou Bakar was still alive.

This last month had not been easy. Hasim had had to manage with fewer men than he had been promised. Out of three hundred, only the first twenty-five horsemen had actually gained entrance into the city. And some of them had been hunted down and killed. Luckily, he had been able to lead the rest to a secure hiding place beneath the High Priest's house, from where they had operated, albeit with limited success.

They had caused some damage within the city, beginning with the slaughter of fifty councilors, in a secret meeting that he had learned of from the High Priest. They had also gone out at night, spying for a chance to open any of the city gates, but it had been in vain. Some of his men had been killed in one attempt, and the rest had been very, very fortunate to get away. From that point on, pressure had increased and movement within the city had become limited.

Thus, when the High Priest had asked to see him, he had not known what to expect. He was aware that the man had an understanding with Salatis, but that was all he knew.

He had gotten into the Palace with a signet ring that had been provided by the Queen mother and he had met the High Priest who had given him precise directions on how to find the secret passage in the walls of the city. He had not believed it at first. But here he was, out of the city and headed for Salatis's camp, which was visible from the sea of campfires that seemed to extend around the city.

He was almost certain that the holy one would not kill him, -at least not right away. Salatis would need him alive if he were to lead his soldiers back to the hidden passage. Which was good enough, Hasim thought. He was already rich beyond his wildest dreams. He had buried several caches of gold and silver in different spots out in the wilderness. He would leave the Kingdom at the first opportunity. Living in a Kingdom where Salatis was King did not sound like a very good idea to him. He had worked for the man long enough, and contrary to what some might think, he, Hasim, son of Hakim, swift shadow of Anubis, feared blade of the desert, and bringer of silent death, was planning to die of old age.

$\mathcal{M}$elenoc let the body of the last guard drop to the ground before pulling it into the darker shadows, away from the moonlight. Wiping the blade on the man's clothing, he glanced around, making sure that no one was watching him. No one was. The priesthood had strict rules that forbade anyone, apart from the guards, to be on the premises when official business was not in session.

The temple of Kephara had been built during the reign of Khufu and was one of the oldest buildings in the city, a fact that aggravated Melenoc's nerves. He was tired of the constant disrespect that was always on display against the priesthood, like this ancient, crumbling mausoleum. What was wrong with a newer building? Could the palace not see that Kepharra's deity and biggest symbol of royal authority was in need of a new house? What gall!

Listening intently for any footsteps, he advanced further into the outer hall of the building. A few torches were lit, throwing slivers of flickering light on murals that portrayed the god Kephara, exercising various aspects of divine duty. He walked past them, up to the one wall that carried a giant etching of Kephara's hands.

He came to a halt before the depiction of the left hand, feeling frustration at the fact that it was now in Abou Bakar's possession. What a damned fool the King was! Sometimes he regretted putting him on the throne. But what alternatives had he had? It had been the only way to assure a powerful alliance with the woman who was now Queen mother. Without her, a lot might not have been done. In fact, she was the one who had arranged for he himself to be smuggled out of the palace this particular night.

Once out on the streets, the mayhem that had greeted his very poor vision had felt like some special treat for which his burned body was yearning. The broken, charred, smoking houses, thousands of destitute people bedded for the night on mats or whatever they could find, was reassuring. Hungry, crying babies, frustrated mothers, fatigued men, looking dejected and demoralized, was to him, a source of great hope..

Feeling better, he'd limped off into the night, headed for the home of the assistant High Priest. Caliph had been delighted to hear that it was the High Priest himself, feeling better enough to pay him a visit. He had gotten out of bed, anxious to see his master, and enquire about the state of things at the palace. He had not known that it was his death that had come calling. So the High Priest had found it quite easy to distract the man and take his life.

In the darkened room he squinted at the mural of the left hand, barely seeing the lines that ran across the palm. He swore under his breath. The last time he'd been in this building, he had had all of his sight.

In silence, he made his way into the inner sanctum. All the torches were burning. Even the candles on the altar of sacrifice were lit, throwing light on the purple and blue curtains that were hanging from the ceiling. The gold vessels used for special ceremonies were laid out in preparation for spiritual consultation. It was as it should be. Caliph had kept everything in order, irrespective of the war. What a reliable assistant High Priest the man had been. Too reliable for his own good.

Melenoc walked to the altar and leaned against it. He ran his fingers along the chiseled edges until his forefinger found the secret ridge. The location of the ridge was such a secret that only two people could know about it at any one time. And now only one did.

He applied pressure to the spot, and presently the whole altar block began to move, sliding backwards to reveal a descending stairway. Melenoc descended the stairs which led him into a small underground chamber. At the centre of the chamber was another altar. This one was made of yellow gold, and it also bore burning candles, incense, and ceremonial vessels containing essential oils. Above the altar, hanging from invisible threads, and catching the candlelight, was the right hand of Kepharra.

Melenoc advanced toward the golden right hand, mouthing words from which none alive but himself, could make any sense.

Abruptly, a light wind blew through the room. Ah yes! He could feel the energy that was emanating from the hand. Gently, his hands closed around the gold object, and for a long moment everything stood still. Wordlessly, he caressed the golden hand as if it was the first time he was seeing it. It was not, of course. It was just the first time that he was claiming it as personal property, and it felt good.

With great care, Melenoc unhooked the clasp, raised the necklace and placed it around his burned neck. The necklace had finally come home. He rearranged his robe, careful to cover the shiny hand as he made his way out of the temple.

Melenoc advanced toward the golden right hand...

Cikatrix tiptoed to the end of the stone corridor and stopped. He cocked his ear and listened for any tell tale signs that some one else might be around, watching him, or waiting to spring upon him. Nothing. It was quiet.

With one hand trailing against the cold stonewall, he walked on, taking care to be as quiet as he could. The Queen mother's girls, who were probably hunting for him even now, were known to have the ability of gliding noiselessly, especially at night, or in dark places.

About a hundred cubits ahead, barely discernible in the poor light, was the little door that opened directly into Aesare's private rooms. On the other side, it had been cleverly disguised as a functional fireplace through which a monarch could escape if he had to. It was a passage that had to be known only by the King but Aesare had let Cikatrix in on the secret, as a means to facilitate their secret meetings. It was an effective way of avoiding the uproar that would ensue if anyone were to find out that he and the King were intimately involved.

Cikatrix got to the end of the tunnel and leaned his head against the cold, dry stone of the door, listening for any signs of what may be happening on the other side. Sometimes Aesare would not be by himself. At times there would be a party of merry makers with him in one of the adjacent suits. They would be drinking and eating, among other things, until everything degenerated to an orgy, at which the pipe would be proudly passed around until everyone had had his fill.

Initially, when the King had introduced the pipe as his 'very special medicine', no one had questioned him or showed too much interest, although it had been automatically understood that it could never be talked about, just like everything else that happened within the King's rooms. But before long, they were all trying it out and finding that the 'medicine' was not *so bad*.

Cikatrix plastered his ear against the door and listened again. Nothing. Maybe he was in luck. He slid his hand along the bottom edge of the door until he found the relatively loose block of stone. He applied pressure, pushing with both hands, until the door began swinging open, allowing a shaft of light to spill into the dark passage. When the door had opened wide enough to admit his body, he stepped through the opening, pushed it closed, turned around and walked quickly and quietly through a series of large, comfortable resting rooms, and then down a wide, beautiful corridor that was the gateway into the Kings bedroom suite. He tiptoed into the suite, drinking in the lushness of Kemetian royal decoration.

The King was not in bed with his pipe as Cikatrix had expected. Hmm, he mused with a small smile. There was only one other place that Aesare could be at this time. He stepped out of the suite into the corridor. No one. He made a left, followed by another left, and then a right. By the time he stepped into the private dining hall, he could hear the King's noisy chewing as he chomped down on a piece of domesticated fowl meat.

The King was seated at the end of a long table that was

covered with trays and trays of food. As usual, he was working methodically through the closest piles.

"What do you want?" he asked, looking up with a tired expression on his very fleshy face.

"Is that the first thing you can find to say to me, after what happened with your mother?"

The King swallowed. "I am actually very kind to let you come in here and you know that, so do not be disrespectful."

"Disrespectful? Aesare, can you, for one moment, imagine what it must be like to be me? Have you ever, in your whole existence, had to live in a sewer because you were running for your life? I am begging you to save my life, something that you can easily do and you talk of disrespect?" Cikatrix paused. "For all these years I have pleaded with you to make new, enforceable laws that would end discrimination, and for some reason you have denied to do this. As you are well aware, my people constitute a minority that is constantly profiled, harassed, and victimized. Do you think I feel respected by your indifference?"

The King did not answer. He tossed another piece of meat into his mouth and picked up a gold carafe of wine.

"What do you want?" he asked, looking up with a tired expression on his very fleshy face...

"Now it has come down to my own life." Cikatrix added. "And you are willing to let me die..."

"And I should, too." The King cut in, taking another bite, his eyes on the other man.

"Really?"

"Yes, really. And why not? Can you give me any reason why I should let you live?" Aesare asked. "If you were King, would you let a subject like yourself live?"

"Aesare! I am not just a subject! Surely I must mean more to you than that. I am the only person who really cares about you, and you know it. Not even your dear mother, who also happens to want me dead, cares about you, or what you really want, and you know that as well."

"I do?"

"Yes, you do."

"And what about you, who claim to care? Do you really?"

"Aesare, You know that I love you and..."

"You do? Is that why you are so loyal?"

"With all due respect, I do not think you have anything to teach me about loyalty, Aesare. Especially since we both know that your sense of loyalty was groomed by your mother."

"Shut up."

"I am just saying that..."

"Shut up!" And Cikatrix fell silent "The fact that you and I have been close does not give you the right to take me for granted as you have done. And leave my mother's name out of this."

"I am sorry Aesare, but your mother has everything to do with what is going on. Is she not the reason I have to hide like a bat? Is it not because of her that you are powerless? Is she not the one who dislikes the Aamu? I am almost certain that she is opposed to any meaningful race reforms," he paused. "Why does she hate us so?"

"She does not hate you"

"She does not?"

"No, she does not."

"So why does she oppose you whenever you bring up the fact that the Aamu living conditions in the Kingdom need improvements? Must we always dwell in slums? Is her opposition to my people not a betrayal to her own values, considering that she is supposed to care so much as you claim?"

"A betrayal? Don't be dramatic! She is not the one who betrayed the Kingdom to Salatis."

Cikatrix froze for a moment. "I know you think that's what I did Aesare but you are wrong," he said.

"You have been meeting with the man."

"Yes I have, but..."

"You met with our enemies in secret! How could you?"

"He asked me the same thing. *How could you go to the Kemetians, to live in sin like them*? But Salatis promised to end discrimination and extend equality to my people." Cikatrix defended feeling foolish.

"Really? And you believed him? After what he did to you and your family? Is it not obvious to you that the man considers you to be a kemetian and not an Aamu? He does not trust you."

"Maybe if both you and Salatis can stop looking at me as either an Aamu or a Kemetian, and just see a person, it would clarify things and help you treat me and my kind with more dignity and..."

"Will it change the fact that you betrayed your Kingdom?"

"There you go again. But I did not."

"How do I know that you did not? Is his army not here?"

"He had already smuggled a lot of his men into the country by the time I became Vizier. And I did not give him any information that he did not already have. Had I provided the maps that he was asking of me, or had I shown him any of the secret passages, or had I been willing to kill you, then one would call it betrayal."

"You are lying."

"It is true." Cikatrix insisted wondering if the King would ever believe him even though he was telling the truth.

"I don't believe you."

"Of course you don't, but the only reason I met with Salatis was because I did not seem to have any alternatives. That said, I did not betray the Kingdom, Aesare."

The King went on as if he'd not heard "You betrayed the land as if your personal plight were so desperate as to triumph over your sense of honor? Are your struggles, whatever they may be, be more important than the fate of a whole Kingdom? C'mon, Cikatrix, it cannot be that bad. The Aamu people are not weaklings who must always complain and whine about a situation that in truth is not bad at all. What are you complaining about? Look around you. You are living in the most advanced and richest civilization that has ever existed. Look at the quality of life that the Aamu have found in the Kingdom. Owning land to farm or build on. Many Aamu are successfully pursuing careers in trade, many more like yourself have been appointed to very influential positions in the country. And every one knows to give them equal respect as they would to other Kemetians. It is not like the old days when things were really bad, so I suggest you stop claiming that the *bahama* grass has suddenly become an *iroko* tree, because I am getting really tired of it."

"Which makes my point..."

"Which is?"

"That you have no idea whatsoever how it feels to be a victim of discrimination, which is why you can be so dismissive and nonchalant about it. If you had been in my shoes your tone would be different. If you were the father whose little daughter came home crying because she had been bullied or insulted due to her hair type or culture, you would be speaking differently."

"Interesting, interesting," the King mused. "You are not suggesting that I am somehow enabling discrimination against you and your people, are you?"

"Well, you are being indifferent to it. What does that say about you?"

"What does that say about me? I mean,... you and I are, ... or, ... were lovers. Does that not at least tell you that on a personal level I, Aesare have nothing against Aamu people?"

"So why is it so hard to dignify them with state laws, as you do every other group in the land?"

"We have been through this before and I don't want to talk about it. If I did not like your kind would I allow you to be intimate with me?"

"Really? For how long have men been sleeping with women? Since the dawn of time, right? For how long have those same men been treating those same women as second-class citizens? Since the dawn of time, correct? Proof of association does not disprove anything I just said."

The King snorted impatiently. "Listen, I am hoping that you did not come in here to argue with me. Take your chance now while you have it and leave the Kingdom before my mother finds you. It is the best I can do and you should be grateful under the circumstances. These are my terms: I will let you go, if you will swear an oath upon your dead family's honor that you will never seek to cause harm to the Kingdom. If you agree, I shall send you off, escorted and well provided for, all the way across the Sahara Sea of sand, to a prosperous rainforest nation of your choosing, where you can stay until things cool off."

"Is that right? And what's there to cool off? If I were your mother's son, would she be so adamant to take my life? Have worse things not been done around here?" The King took another bite, totally ignoring the jab. "And what if I refuse?" Cikatrix asked, even as he wondered what his options were.

"Then you will have only yourself to blame." The King answered.

"Then allow me to go north instead."

"No. I feel that if you go north, it will be easier for you to change your mind and make your way back here, where Salatis will be more than willing to work with you. See, it is a chance I cannot take with you any more. Or anybody else in similar circumstances." The King paused. "So what is your answer?" His voice was cold.

For a moment, Cikatrix was aghast. Obviously, he should not have come here. He should have gone directly to Salatis. He took a deep breath. Be calm, he told himself. There were no guards in the suite but they were always a call away.

"Yes?" The King asked with ice in his voice, not once interrupting the eating. He was hoping that Cikatrix would be sensible enough to take the proffered option. Who knows, maybe someday in the future, when the war had been won and his mother and her friends were no more, he, himself, would be able to rule with enough freedom to actually make the Kingdom free and equal for all. Then he would send for Cikatrix, who would come back to the Palace, in a land where people were respected and loved, irrespective of their orientation, race or culture.

It was a good ideal to aspire to, but for now it was not possible and the King knew it. He did not yet have the power that it would take to fight the entrenched conservative power base that benefited economically from maintaining the status quo. He also knew that he would be dead in a moment if he refused to do as they asked, and his own mother, who was one of them, did not have the power to protect him, although she believed otherwise.

"Aesare, I cannot go on exile to the south. The curse of the mosquito will mean a quick death. You have to save me."

"That is the best I can do at this time. Our mother will not listen to anyone on this issue. Not even me. I will not have your blood on my hands."

"But you already do, Aesare. You already do because you are the one who made the choice to become this weakling who cannot lift a finger if his mother does not hold his hand..."

"Shut up!" the King hissed through a mouthful of food.

"...Just like you made the choice to let her prostitute the Kingdom..."

"I said shut up!" the King repeated with a cough.

"Where will it end? Do you think it will? How will that happen when you choose to remain a coward? You see, Aesare, that's one thing of which you cannot accuse me. I might not be a General in your army, my methods of operation can be questionable and lacking in your newest favorite quality, loyalty, but I am not a coward. Call me a traitor, but I am proud that all of my 'treachery' was for equality, -a cause that is nobler than allowing one's own mother to kill one's own father, so that one could seat on the throne."

"GU...GUA...GUARDS!" The King chocked on the words and broke out in a coughing fit. Suddenly, there was the sound of running feet and shouting from the corridor.

"Good-bye my lovely coward King," Cikatrix said, turning to give the King a last look as he prepared to make a hasty exit. Aesare's obese body was heaving and writhing as he struggled for air, choking on a morsel that must have gone down the wrong path.

Instinctively, Cikatrix rushed forward, forgetting all plans for escape, and slammed both of his hands on the Monarchs huge back, repeating the procedure over and over, hoping to dislodge whatever food particle that may be blocking the air in his chest pipes. But the King, still seated, continued writhing, eyes bulging, with veins rippling on his forehead as he struggled for air.

The King was still gasping, and grunting, as the guards, with much roughness, delivering blows and kicks, seized Cikatrix and pulled him away from the Monarch. As he was pulled away, Cikatrix himself could not believe that he had sacrificed his only chance of escape to try and save the King, a man who was not willing to do the same for him.

Suddenly his whole life flashed before him in an unreal time sequence; scenes where the most pivotal decisions had been made, decisions that had somehow led to this end. For a moment he saw himself as a boy of ten living in Avaris with his parents and family as respected members of the Aamu community. He saw the yearly feasts that the community used to have, the fun games, and the debates. Then he saw his 'uncle'. The one everybody was afraid of. The same one who was rumored to murder Kemetians and bury them in the desert for sport. Cikatrix remembered the bitter arguments that his parents would have with this 'uncle', a man who disagreed with the fact that his *cousin* was leading his family to ignore Aamu culture and fully adopt Kemetian ways. "They don't even like us," He would thunder, "and you are trying to become like them? Is that the reason for the change?"

"But this is our home now, we are are now Kemetian."

"NO, YOU ARE NOT. THEY WILL NEVER SEE YOU AS THEY SEE THEMSELVES!"

"But my children were born here. They are full blooded Kemetians. Even you can see that."

"And why do *they* not?"

"Some of them do..."

"Pffffff!"

Then, came the revolts, led by this same 'uncle' who by now had gone underground and reborn himself as the mysterious 'Salatis'.And that, for the most part, was what Cikatrix remembered of that life. His new life had begun with him waking up in the palace, badly cut up and swathed in bandages. He'd been told that 'the man Salatis' was responsible. He was said to have also killed the rest of Cikatrix's family *"for cooperating with Kemetian soldiers during the revolts."*

The pain had seen the beginning of many questions. Was he really Aamu as Salatis maintained or was he Kemetian as his father had argued? What did it mean to be Kemetian? What did it mean to be Aamu? Personally, he'd always felt more Kemetian than Aamu. Plus, his own father had always wished, for his family to be fully accepted as Kemetians. The man had even died because of it. "Well, Papa here I come to join you." Cikatrix thought bitterly as he was taken away. "I did my best to intergrate our people but I failed. In my efforts, it is possible that I may have crossed a few lines that I should not have crossed. Please forgive me and smile upon me when we meet."

Once in the palace, Melenoc sensed that something had changed. He was not sure what it was, but he could feel it in the air. Wondering what it could be, he limped down a dark passage, where one of the Queen mother's girls was waiting to lead him through a confusing set of secret pathways hidden under the huge palace.

Finally, he was in the apartment that had been assigned to him. He pushed open the door and stepped into the front room. Sobs were coming from the inner room, and even before he saw her, Melenoc knew it was the Queen mother. She was kneeling on the floor and her whole body was rocking from side to side.

When she raised her tear stricken face and saw him, she got to her feet, a different look coming across her features.

"My son is dead," she said.

Melenoc was silent for just a moment as he considered the implication of this development for the mission.

"When did he die?" he asked.

"Not too long ago. He was murdered. Strangled. And the killer was caught in the act. He claims that he was trying to save the King who was supposed to be choking on a particle of food."

"Really!" The High Priest asked. "Do I know the man?" The Queen mother ignored the question.

"His brother may be a little young, but we have had younger Kings before," she stated. "And your word carries more weight in these matters than most. You are Melenoc, Chief High Priest of the god Kepharra, supreme head of a thousand shamans and most powerful Kingmaker in all of Kemet. You must act before it becomes known that my eldest son is dead. We have the surprise factor on our side. If you summon an emergency meeting of elders and Kingmakers, you can get a new King on the throne before the sun comes up. Everyone will assume that Aesare's death was punishment for disrespecting the sun. Everyone will see that the gods themselves have miraculously healed you yourself, and no one will dare challenge your choice of King. The people will understand. After all, these are not normal times."

"Careful now, mother of Kings," Melenoc said gently. "True, these are not normal times, but has that made anything easier? What will the other sons of Neferhotep say? I cannot even be sure that the other Kingmakers will vote along the same lines as myself, if I should propose your younger son for the throne. I cannot guarantee success..."

"That is not good enough anymore, Melenoc," The Queen mother interrupted. "Surely, you can see that, can't you?" She wiped away an imaginary tear. "The King is dead, and his brother is ready to wear his shoes. You are the most powerful Kingmaker in all the land and you must make that happen." The fear and desperation in her voice was obvious. Wealth without power was unbearable and she would do everything to uphold her status quo as Queen mother.

"But, my love," he ventured, taking a step forward, hoping to reason with her. "Your pain hurts my heart and my unseen tears do weep for you. I wish that I could reverse death, bring the King back to life and make you merry once again. But I am not a god."

"Is everything lost then? Are you saying that my son has died for nothing?" she demanded. "Are you saying that the whole Kingdom had to be put through all of this for nothing? No, Melenoc! I refuse to lose everything because of you."

"Lose everything? Because of me?"

"Yes! It is all because of you! If I had not listened to you, my husband would be alive. If I had not listened to you, Salatis's army would not be here. If I had not listened to you, perhaps my son would still be alive." She paused. "But I did, and look what happened. He is dead, even though you said it would never come to this. The Kingdom is almost overrun, even though you said it would never come to this. It is too much to sacrifice and still lose everything. But it does not have to end like this. If you do this one thing, just think of how beneficial it will be for everyone. Even Abou Bakar will have no choice but to bring in the hand, for use on coronation day. You will have killed several birds with one stone. Think about it."

Melenoc had to admit that her argument was making sense. She always had a sharp mind. "I see the truth in your words. All I am saying is that it will be tricky."

"I know it will be difficult but you can do it. You have the weight of a thousand Shamans behind you."

"Maybe..."

"You should," she said. "It is the best option under the circumstances. With my other son on the throne, we would at least maintain control of the palace."

"Maybe so," he chided gently. "Is Aesare's body secure?"

"I arranged for it to be kept a secret, but it is just a matter of time before someone starts wondering why the King is not up with the sun."

"That is good enough," Melenoc said. "I think I have a plan that will make everything right again."

"You do?"

"Yes, but it is risky. Very risky and I will need all the help you can give," he said thinking of how truly risky the new strategy was. Any mistakes would be fatal.

"I am ready. What do you want of me?"

The High Priest thought about it for a moment, hesitating as he weighed different options. This was indeed risky and it had to be handled with utmost skill.

"On second thought, I think I should do it myself. It might require a little more time, but at least I am certain that..."

"No, Melenoc," interrupted the Queen mother. "Do not be afraid to let me help you. After all, this is about my younger son. What will I not do to make everything successful! Let's not waste anymore time. You know you can trust me."

"Yes, I do, but not when you are under so much pressure. You have just lost a son, you have been crying, and I can see from the look in your eyes that if you don't get rest soon, your head will start hurting," Melenoc said, referring to the bouts of headaches from which the Queen mother was known to suffer.

"But you are my physician," she said, with a small smile, "And your potions have always helped. Give me something that is preventive. Surely you can do that, yes? You know we don't have much time, and this cannot fail. Please...Please Melenoc."

"Alright, alright, Melenoc murmured, knowing that she would not give up until she had her way. She was very stubborn like that, especially when her interests were at stake. "Where is your other son as we speak?"

"In bed."

"Good." He paused. "Hopefully, this will help. Chew it," he added, holding out one of his balled up medicinal potions. "It will prevent any head throbbing, it will take away your worries, but most importantly it will clear your head and re energize you."

By the time she realized that the little ball was deadly, it was too late.

After her body stopped moving, Melenoc stepped back and surveyed his handiwork. Well, at least, he had properly handled a potentially explosive situation. The death of the King had not been something he could have foreseen, -at least not at this point. And the Queen mother asking for her other son to be crowned had sounded dangerously stupid. And turning her down would have meant trouble. She was not the kind of woman that one wanted to make into an enemy.

He bent over and closed her dead, unseeing eyes. She was the one person without whom nothing could have been possible. So in a way it was a painful moment for him. But what could he do? Was she more important than the mission?

He stepped out of the apartment, locking and securing the door behind him. The palace was no longer a safe place to be. There were too many important and undiscovered corpses here. The bodies would be discovered at about the same time and the confusion would be total. Everyone would know who was responsible, but that was all right at this point. The High Priest expected Salatis's army to be in the city by then. Everything was still going according to plan.

He took a sip of water, planning in his head how best to handle the meeting with Salatis.

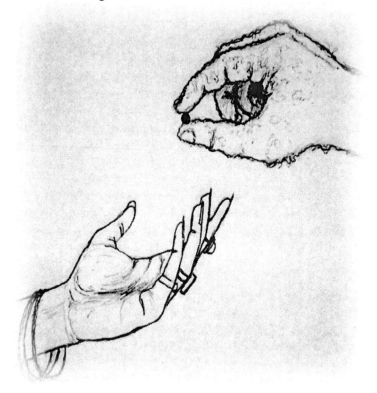

Hopefully, this will help. Chew it," he added, holding out one of his balled up medicinal potions...

CHAPTER TWENTY-FIVE

$\mathcal{A}$s he rode towards the north city gates, Vizier Itzo's thoughts were dominated by the realization that this day could mark the end. And he was afraid. Not the kind of fear that a man may feel if you told him that the King may soon be asking for his head, or that his fatal ailment did not have a cure, or that he was going to die. It was much more than that. It had little or nothing to do with his personal chances of survival. He had lived a full life, traveled the world, fought many wars, and he was not as young as he used to be. So, that was not the issue. What he was afraid of was the possibility that the end of the Kingdom was in sight, that a civilization that had existed for thousands of years was about to end. That all the knowledge that had been collected over the years and associated with the name of the Kingdom, was about to be wiped off the face of the earth, once and for all. The magnitude of such a disaster was overwhelming.

He had mentioned these fears to Abou Bakar but the General had had very little to say, short of voicing his own regrets about the King's refusal to attack Salatis up until now when it was almost too late. If the man was having other doubts, he had kept them to himself. And Itzo had totally understood. He knew that the burden on the General's shoulders was colossal indeed. Plus, the man was in pain about his only son, and there was no one to console him. Instead he was expected to lead, to console, and to encourage the men who were fighting to keep this city from the claws of the invaders.

When the north gate came into view, he slowed his horse down to a canter, noting that the bulk of the army had already gathered here as Abou Bakar had asked. There were men of all ages, some as young as twelve and others as old as a eighty. There was even a spear-clutching ninety nine year old who argued that he had come to die on a battle field where he stood a chance of taking along one invader in the process. Everyone was armed, hungry, and as ready as they would ever be under the circumstances. Everyone knew that this was going to be the greatest fight of their lives.

Itzo took his place along the line of mounted horsemen, bowing gravely in salutation to the souls to his right and left.

Obviously, it was not the time for small talk. These men were asking themselves the most fundamental questions about existence. Most of them were wondering why the sun god had chosen to punish them in this way, why it had fallen to them to defend the city at this time, or, if it was even the will of the gods for the defense to be effective.

Itzo's thoughts were interrupted by a loud, cheering shout. Surprised by the sudden air of courage, he stood up on his stirrups to see what it was about. It was General Abou Bakar himself, in full military regalia, mounted, and coming to lead his army.

It was General Abou Bakar himself...

At the sight, Itzo felt his eyes water as memories of their first meeting flooded his mind, -the young, emaciated and alienated youth, who had already been counted as dead. Who would have known that a day would come when the fate of the Kingdom would rest in his hands?

"Long live the General," several voices chanted, as Abou Bakar slowed his mount to a walk. "Long live the conqueror of Salatis," others shouted.

Abou Bakar raised his hand, and everyone fell silent. A silence that made the moments longer. A silence in which every heart hoped, prayed, and waited.

The General spoke. "Tonight, my friends, is a very special night. It is a night like no other. It is a night in which fathers will fight next to their sons, and boys will rise to take the lives of grown men." A shout of encouragement went up into the night. "For many a day we have watched Salatis sit outside our city and take away our freedoms. For many a day, we have watched him destroy our homes and streets, watching, waiting, and hoping that the man would somehow come to his senses and leave us alone. But that is not what he wants to do, is it? No, it is not," he answered the question for himself. "He has set his heart to our total destruction. Already he has caused us much suffering, sickness, and death. Even now as I speak, several among us are starving. Yes, many are hungry and some may even be afraid," he paused. "But is hunger and fear reason enough for a man to give up?"

"NOOO!" came the chorus.

"Is suffering and pain a good enough reason for a man to willingly choose death by refusing to fight?"

"NOOO!"

"Yes, I too, say 'no'," Abou Bakar paused. "I say 'no' because if, peradventure, Salatis should get into the city, he would use us to make an example that would put fear in the hearts of all the surrounding Kingdoms that may think of opposing him. He will kill and burn everything that can be killed and burned. Therefore, my brothers, let us forget that we are hungry and let us forget that we are afraid. Let us forget that Salatis has a hundred and fifty thousand men while we are just thirty three thousand. Let us forget that our friends may not get here in time to help us, that is, if they choose to come at all. Let us forget all these things that put fear into our hearts. Instead, let us choose to remember the faces of our children and our wives for whom we fight. Let us remember our loved ones who suffer or have lost their lives because of this dog from the north. Let every man know in his heart that victory is ours if we are willing to reach up and take it."

"YEEES!"

"So tonight, we fight with everything in our souls. We fight with the cunning of the snake and the courage of the lion. We stand to tell that dog from the north that our hunger for life is stronger than any fear that his army brings, that our thirst for freedom is more powerful than any army he may throw at us, that our families are worth more to us than our own lives, and that, we , the people of Itjawy will never ever bow our necks to his sword. DEATH TO SALATIS!" the General shouted.

"DEATH TO SALATIS!" chorused thirty three thousand voices.

"DEATH TO SALATIS!" the General shouted again.

"DEATH TO SALATIS!" the army answered.

"Let the gates of mighty Itjawy be thrown open."

There was a great shout as the northern gates of the city were opened. Very quickly, men began riding out.

"Prepare to charge," Abou Bakar announced, noting that opening the gate had taken the enemy by surprise. All of a sudden there was a flurry of movement in Salatis's camp as his men realized that they were actually being attacked. They had been expecting a surrender party.

"ATTAAACK," Abou Bakar screamed, leading the charge towards Salatis's fire lit camp. And what a charge it was. Horses, camels, donkeys, men, boys, all as one, bearing towards the enemy in a do or die move that was actually their only chance of surviving. Even the ninety nine year old took down a man before he himself was ruthlessly taken.

But at about the same time, something else happened. Something that the General had never anticipated: A few thousand Salatis soldiers, whom Hasim had successfully led back into the city through the secret tunnel, suddenly exposed themselves, and attacked the rear of Abou Bakar's advancing army.

Immediate word was sent to the General, who quickly put another commander in charge of the advancing assault before turning around to gallop back towards the struggling city.

As he rode into the city, the General realized how desperate things really were. Fighting had broken out everywhere. Fires were sprouting wherever he looked.

With brutal efficiency, he dispatched a figure that came screaming at him, taking the man's sword and throwing it into another's stomach. A third, a fourth, a fifth, sixth, seventh, an eighth, and even a ninth man died from his hand, in rapid succession, but more men kept coming. For the first time since the war began, Abou Bakar felt apprehension. Salatis' army was like the sand of the sea. Maybe it was bigger than he had imagined.

"Let the women and the children be moved to the King's Prison," he instructed, mentally reminding himself to find some time soon to consult with his own mother. Immediately a man ran off to relay the order. "And put the Warden of the prison in charge," he shouted after the man.

The fighting waxed stronger for all of that night and the following morning, ultimately delaying the evacuation of the women and the children. And the soldiers, too hungry, too exhausted and too outnumbered, began feeling that everything was about to be lost. Even the General's loud exhortations were being delivered with obvious strain.

Then, late in the afternoon of that next day the pressure became unbearable and everything was suddenly in even greater peril. Some of Salatis' men succeeded in breaking through the last line of defense. Abou Bakar felt his heart contract as the fear-filled screams of women reached his ears.

"NOOOOOOOOOOO!" he screamed, charging into a group of advancing men, and killing several immediately. But even he was too outnumbered, and slowly, ever so slowly, the man's strength began to fail.

"Oh, maker of all things," he prayed, bashing in a head. "Even as I die, I beg of you O God, to grant me this one request." He slashed off a sword arm. "Please, manifest some divine miracle and save the lives of these innocent women and children?" He severed a head from a body. "If this one thing you shall do for me, I shall lay down my sword and dedicate the rest of whatever life I may have to you..."

There was a sudden shout and Abou Bakar turned around to see a line of four horsemen, charging at him in a coordinated attack. The first rider died from Abou's thrown sword while the second succumbed to the very last of his throwing knives. A third man collided into him, dislodging him from his mount. He rolled into the dust, trying to get his bearing as another man swung. He ducked, grabbed the arm, pulled the man off his frightened horse and slammed him onto a rock. The man screamed as his back snapped. Panting, Abou Bakar spun around to face the fourth horseman who was already upon him.

But a sudden and unexpected wave of nausea flooded his

senses, attacked his focus, slowed down his momentum, and left him open and vulnerable.

The man's swinging sword arm was already too close for Abou to move out of trajectory. He shouted, expecting to feel the impact of sharpened metal even as a strange feeling of weakness washed over him.

But the horseman froze at the very last instant. His fingers went limp, letting go of the weapon, which fell harmlessly to the ground. The dazed looked that appeared on the face, stayed the same as the man fell. A sword was sticking through his stomach.

"General, we salute you," greeted the Innocent Prisoner. "You may not be the best of brothers, but you are still our brothers, and this country belongs to us as well. " He added, as one of his men dismounted and helped the exhausted General onto his feet.

"Thank you," Abou Bakar said, fighting off emotions that threatened to choke his throat. The innocent prisoner had returned just in the nick of time with a party of two hundred.

Wordlessly, the General took off his signet ring and threw it at the man, who caught it. "It is nothing, but let it stand against me and my name if I should ever forget the honor of your heart," he said, grateful that the feeling of nausea had passed.

On that day in Itjawy was much valor shown and the sons of the Kingdom did valiantly in battle, even as they fought with hungry stomachs.

All in all they did smite with the edge of the sword, one hundred fifty thousand of Salatis's hosts, destroying chariots, and setting catapults, tents, and elephants, on fire. The women and children were successfully evacuated to the safety of the King's Prison. And then, finally, the rest of the invaders began throwing down their swords and running for cover. It was a sweet picture and it was accompanied by a long awaited shout of victory from the dwindled Kemetian army.

But alas, the little band of fatigued, wounded, and greatly handicapped men looked up with disbelieving eyes, to the realization that all of the men that they had fought and killed had been but a portion of Salatis's army. The other portion had appeared on the plain and was advancing on a sea of rapidly moving horse drawn chariots, leaving a whirlwind of dust in its wake.

"Quick!" Abou Bakar shouted at his commanders "Get a fresh batch of horses from the kingdom's stables. Divide the archers into two groups and position them behind those dunes," he instructed pointing to his left. "Every foot soldier will stay with me to help create a distraction from our mounted cavalry, which will circle the advancing attackers. Upon my signal, the archers will unleash the first phase of our defense. And make every arrow count! While they are dealing with the confusion of an unexpected rain of arrows, I will lead the infantry up against them. But everything is contingent upon our mounted cavalry, which would have circled, and will attack the enemy from behind. It is the key to our success. if we coordinate ourselves efficiently and move with speed, I am certain that victory..."

"Excuse me, sir."

Abou Bakar turned to face a cavalry commander.

"Yes Mozez, what is it ?"

"There are no horses."

"WHAT?"

"There are no more horses," the man repeated.

"But how can that be? The records indicate that we are supposed to have a reserve of two hundred horses in the Kingdom's stables. Are you sure about this?"

"Yes sir."

"Go and check again."

"There are no horses, sir."

For a moment the General was silent as his tired mind struggled to process the implications of the latest revelation. Some high state official had probably made the decision to keep for himself resources that should have been used to procure two hundred extra horses. And now the whole Kingdom was about to pay the price. Without the horses, the small, battered army did not stand a chance. In that moment Abou Bakar could not help wondering if the gods had played a part to thwart his final efforts in this battle, or if it was all from the hand of man? Or was it that all his actions were cursed?

Salatis's chariots were getting closer and Abou's men were waiting for a final decision from him. He knew that they were ready to die by his side. But he'd been in too many battles to miss the fact that any attempt to confront the advancing attack without a calvary would amount to suicide. Did he have a right to ask them to lay down their lives for nothing?

"Everyman must carry as much food as possible. Load up every available cart. We shall not need water. Follow the women and children. To the King's Prison we must go. Hurry!"

...*advancing on a sea of rapidly moving horse drawn chariots, leaving a whirlwind of dust in its wake.*

CHAPTER TWENTY-SIX

$\mathcal{M}$elenoc still could not believe what his half blind eyes had been telling him for the past few days. Was this a bad dream? By what miracle had thirty three thousand, weak, demoralized and hungry men managed to wipe out an army of one hundred and fifty thousand?

"Are you a fool?" he asked, turning around to look at Salatis. "Was your father soft in the head?"

"Shut up," Salatis screamed, standing up from the throne. "Or I shall pull your tongue out of your mouth. Do you forget who you are talking to?" Both men were alone in one of the many banquet halls of the palace, which by chance had been left almost intact. "I am Salatis, King of all the world."

"Are you now?" Melenoc asked mockingly. "So tell me great King of all the world, where is the symbol of your authority? Where is the one thing that will let everyone across the land know that the hand of the god is upon you? Where is the proof that you, Salatis, were chosen by the sun to replace Aesare?" Melenoc asked, turning his back to the throne.

"Who needs a symbol? Don't I have you and all the shamans? What are you waiting for? Begin preparations for a coronation ceremony that shall be the talk of the cities."

Melenoc shook his head in frustration. "You do not understand, do you?" He took a quick sip of water. "What I am saying is that if you do not have the hand of Kepharra to wear around your neck on coronation day, you will never be accepted by the people as the divinely appointed King. This is a tradition that is thousands of years old, and not to respect it is to ask for severe pain and rejection from the hands of the gods, whose instrument you are. Did you not hear that Aesare's death was punishment for disrespecting the sun?"

Abruptly Salatis sat down, licking his lips nervously. "So where is this hand?" he asked.

"It is with the remnant of rats who are holed up in the King's Prison. You must get it."

"Get it? How? Have we not tried our hardest these past ten days? One can only go so far in there. The place was hewn out of solid rock."

"YOU MUST GET IT!" Melenoc screamed, almost

choking on his own rage.

"HOW?" Salatis screamed back, "I have told you that the place is a fort and my commanders tell me that the man who is defending it is very capable"

"Nobody denies that Abou Bakar is formidable, but he is just a man, not a god."

"What? Abou Bakar? Is Abou Bakar still breathing?" Salatis skipped from the throne and rushed out of the room. "HASIM!!" He bellowed, "WHERE IS HASIM?" Men were hurrying to get out of his way as he advanced, dagger drawn. "WHERE IS HASIM?"

"YOU MUST GET IT!" Melenoc screamed, almost choking on his own rage.

$\mathcal{T}$he King's Prison house in the city of Itjawy was so full it was almost bursting. There were people everywhere, men, women, children, and some animals that were being saved for meat. The Chief Warden had furnished maps of the whole building, including some rare ones that showed an extensive network of tunnels and chambers that even the General had not known about. All available supplies had been located and hauled down. Everyone had been directed down the tunnels and into the underground chambers, which were huge. Then, employing a special, ancient knowledge that was almost lost to the world, the little man had directed a group of men, using thousands of stones, huge and small, tar, special gum, clay, stone dust, and fire, to effectively seal off the mouth of the tunnel network. Everyone had been carefully counted, communal duties were delegated, sleeping quarters apportioned, and group leaders designated.

With the total number of survivors known, the Chief Warden confirmed to Abou Bakar that the amount of grain available would last for a total of thirty-seven days. "Forty, if we are lucky." He added. "We have all the ground water we need and Salatis does not have access to our supply, so that will not be a problem. After the food runs out, it will take another week or two before the first people start to die of hunger, but the hunger will be severe after that."

"What alternatives do we have?" Abou Bakar asked. "Anyone?" They were in a small room that had probably served as a holding cell, and a meeting was going on. In the room with the General was the Warden, the Innocent Prisoner, one of his men, and a prison guard.

"If Salatis should eventually succeed to break in, we will not be able to hide in the tunnels for long." It was the Innocent Prisoner. "Eventually they will find us."

"Not if we start digging now," the Warden said.

"Digging?" Abou asked. "Do we have what it takes? This is solid rock."

"Yes, it is," the Warden answered excitedly. "I know how it is done. My people are the best tunnel diggers that the world has ever known. It will be very hard work, partly because we don't have all the tools that we may need. But what we lack in tools we have in manpower. Plus, is it not better than to sit everyday and wait for death?"

It was decided that work should commence immediately, and naturally, the Warden was put in charge of the tunnel project. The man divided everybody into groups. The idea was that teams would take turns digging while the others rested, slept, ate, or did whatever else they had to do. In this way, the digging would be continuous and the most speed would be attained. Speed was the key.

From the maps, the Warden estimated that if everything went well, it would take about seventy days or so for the tunnel to reach the city walls. It was good time. In fact it was very good time, but it was not good enough. The food would be gone by then, and if people started dying, with no burial place to dispose of the bodies, a plague may be the next thing. Already, it was a challenge to have acceptable hygiene within the underground community. It seemed as if the only solution was not a solution at all. But it was the only available option, -to do the impossible and advance the tunnel at a rate of eleven cubits a day. If, somehow, they could manage that, which was doubtful, then there was a small chance that some people may escape.

And so, guarded with a certain determination that could only come out of desperation, the people went to work. Either they were going to do it, or they were going to die.

Either they were going to do it, or they were going to die.

CHAPTER TWENTY-SEVEN

Los Angeles, California.

By the time Selena found 0134316, Wilshire, it had started to drizzle. Not that she minded. In her opinion, the city of Los Angeles never got enough rain anyway. Plus, it would leave everything so much cleaner.

All of a sudden, people were hurrying to get off of the street as if rain was some kind of newly designed poison. She had always wondered what that was all about. Rumors of chemical trails, perhaps?

Deeply, she inhaled the smell of wet earth that was rising from the ground as the raindrops made contact with the fine coat of dust that had accumulated over the long, dry, summer. For some reason, it resurrected memories of a distant life in another part of the world.

Almost automatically she pushed the memories away. They always led to the same place, –the nightmares, the curse, the accidents, and the deaths. Now was not the time. She needed to collect her thoughts, to be focused on the now, not on a painful past.

She pulled the collar of her coat over her ears as she paused to survey the building across the street. It was an old, Spanish affair with huge windows and erected in mortar and bricks probably at the turn of the last century. From its look, she guessed that it had probably been a church or a library at some point. Today it was a lecture hall with a maximum capacity of seven hundred and eleven, and it was full.

Using her left hand to hold down her long black hair against a sudden gust of wind, she glanced both ways, first left, then right, and then left again, before quickly darting across the wet street. She ran up the short stairway that led to the main entrance and pushed open the tall double doors into the foyer.

Sitting pat in the center of the room, was an ancient looking front desk that had obviously been positioned to undermine the free flow of foot traffic into the hallway. Behind the desk was a spectacled senior citizen who was doing his best to explain to the line of people in front of him that the place was full and that there were no more seats, but that, if they did not mind, they may stand at the back of the hall.

As Selena walked up, he raised his head from the several lists of names that were scattered on the desk in front him, adjusted his glasses and proceeded in a slow monotone, to repeat what he had just told the man before her.

"I am Selena Soltera," she introduced, "And I am... "

"Oh, Miss Soltera!" he exclaimed excitedly, getting to his feet. "I know who you are." He grabbed her hand and pumped it with surprising energy for a senior citizen. "What an honor!" he beamed. Out of nowhere, an equally elderly lady materialized.

"Follow me please," she said, smiling at Selena. She led the way down a side corridor with a little door at the end. On it was a sign that read 'Do not enter'. She pushed it open and showed Selena into a small square room with another door to the side. The only furniture was a small corner table and a chair. "That door leads directly onto the stage. We should be ready in ten minutes. I will let you know with three knocks on the door. On my cue, just step through it and there will be a detachable microphone waiting for you. In the mean time I will get you a cup of hot chocolate and a hair dryer. And Miss Soltera," she paused. "I want you to know that we are really happy to have you speak here today. You are like a breath of fresh air, and may God give you strength."

"Oh thank you so much... um"

"Emma," the woman completed with a smile, as she stepped out of the small room and closed the door behind her.

For a moment Selena felt a rush of emotion overwhelm her. Emma had spoken to her soul. The one thing she needed more than anything else was strength. Not only did she need strength to deal with the memories and nightmares of her past, there were also the waves of controversy that had become the trademark of her speeches. As controversial as they were said to be, she believed all the things she spoke and wrote about. Not that she was claiming to be right, or that every one else who did not agree was wrong. She felt it was necessary for people to hear, and then to decide for themselves.

What she did not believe in, was for those who disagreed to represent their differences by means of violence. And she wasn't referring to the groups that would gather at the entrance of her events, with signs and placards that left little doubt as to what they thought of her. Some of them would even come in and sit down with these signs raised high for all to see. And it was okay, so long as they were not blocking someone else. Was that not what democracy was all about?

The cause of concern was the threat that had been made to her. It was the first of its kind, and she was not quite sure how to deal with it at this point. It was the reason she had decided to park her rental a block away. That way, she reasoned, if somebody did not agree with what she had to say, they would find it harder to locate her car and vandalize it as it had happened the week before.

She had spoken at the city community college, walked off the stage to a standing ovation, but the feeling of accomplishment had quickly vanished the minute she'd seen her car. She shuddered at the memory of what the Chevy volt had looked like at first glance. It had been thrashed almost beyond recognition and a typed note had been carefully affixed onto the bashed in windscreen! And how she had loved that car! Averaging nine hundred miles between fill ups, three hundred fifty miles on a single charge, was roomy, had a great sound system...

When the cops showed up ten minutes later they had tried to write it off as a case of juvenile delinquency. After all, it was a college campus. But tried as they had, not a single, foreign fingerprint had been found. Not on the car and not on the note. Who ever was behind it had either had a little time to plan, or they had just happened to have a manual typewriter with them.

Selena's thoughts were interrupted by three soft knocks on the door. It was time. She took in a deep breath and walked out onto the bright lights of the stage amidst applause. Apparently, she had just been introduced and the audience was obviously impressed. Out of habit she tapped the tip of the microphone lightly to ensure that it was live. It was.

"Ladies and gentlemen," Selena began. "The Bible tells us that two thousand years ago when the taxmen came after Jesus, he understood that if he did not pay his taxes, the government could use it as an excuse to obstruct his important work. So what did he do? He instructed one of his apostles to attend to the matter. He did not compromise himself. And I am sure that he would not be happy with the way his church has compromised itself today by accepting to shut up and look the other way in return for tax breaks."

Selena paused and took a quick drink of water from the bottle that someone, probably Emma, had thoughtfully placed by the microphone stand. "I believe that this is the day when we must all stand up to the church and ask our churchmen to pay taxes on the money that we give them. And by that, I mean all the money that we give them. Or no money at all! We must let the church know that we are serious. If churchmen around the world cannot speak up on all issues, political or otherwise, then there is no mediator between the people and the government. We need a church that can copy the example of archbishop Desmond Tutu and draw a powerful moral line in the sand." She paused again. "Granted, the church must never ever have the power to enforce its views as laws, since that could be dangerous, and it would amount to a violation of *the separation of church and state*. But it must have the capacity to speak up on all issues because, equally dangerous, is a church that has had whole sections of its tongue cut off. In Hitler's Germany, apart from a few people like Dietrich Boenhoffer, the loud silence of ecclesiastic leadership in response to the holocaust should be enough reason to make everyone think. Who knows what would have happened if the church leaders in Germany had taken a united stand against Hitler? Especially, when we realize that the church was probably the only group with the moral stamina to confront Nazism and yet did not. Remember that these church leaders had the support of millions of Germans behind them, good German people who would have stood up, and who, in my opinion, could have easily chosen God over Hitler, that is, if the church had given them that option." She surveyed the room. "Today, in most of our societies the church is equally silent on a growing number of issues that are deemed *political*, and this, in my opinion, is unacceptable..."

Somewhere in the back row, a blond woman that Selena could not see, and had never met, was sitting with her eyes closed and her head slightly tilted to the side. She was listening to the speech with rapt attention. As usual, she did not agree with everything Selena had to say. Some of it, yes. But not everything. And for the blond woman, it just made the waiting more interesting. She called herself Semon, and she was waiting for orders that would authorize her to 'engage' the speaker.

She had been following Selena for some months now, a period during which the speaker had been put under a discreet, twenty-four hour radar, that kept Semon on the know about anything and everything that was worth knowing about her. Today was three months to the day since the surveillance had started, and Selena was not aware of the fact that she was being tailed. Semon had made sure of that. The client had severely underscored the importance of keeping everything a secret. "The subject must never find out that she is being followed," he had croaked several times.

For what she was getting paid, the requirement was nothing. And for ninety three days everything had gone smoothly. Then Selena's car had been wrecked. She could tell that Selena had become tense since the incident. She was getting into the habit of throwing furtive glances over her shoulder, almost as if she expected to find someone following her. Just thinking about it made Semon very, very angry. She had gone to such great lengths to make sure that everything stayed quiet, and she was definitely not willing to let the boat be rocked because some little prick was being a stalker and tripping over everything in the process.

She glanced at the picture of the men behind the act and wrinkled her nose in disgust. It had taken four days and four nights of solid footwork to find them. But eventually it had paid off, thanks to the picture. It was a picture that had been taken by one of the women who worked for her. The woman, Aisha, had arrived at the crime scene just as the men were signing off on their work. And as always her camera had been handy.

A few of the pictures showed both men, in masks, swinging huge baseball bats at the chassis of the Chevy. But the one that gave them away was the shot that showed them riding off on a Harley with an impressively flashy paint job. The bike had been the clincher. Anyone who had seen it once had recognized it from the picture.

When Semon got up to leave, Selena was wrapping up her talk, and just a few people noticed the blond woman as she quietly walked out of the hall. She liked it that way.

When she stepped out of the building it was already dark, and although it had stopped raining, she promptly produced a small umbrella and raised it above her head. She did not like rain. Never had, and probably never would.

She walked briskly down the stairs onto the wet sidewalk. A gray, nondescript ford Taurus materialized and pulled over next to her. She opened the door, slid in, and the car pulled off from the curb, expertly avoiding a homeless looking, cart-pushing character, who was swathed in layer upon layer of dirty looking garments.

The woman behind the wheel was Aisha. Semon was certain that it was not her real name, but so what? In this business real names were not very popular and she understood that. What was most important was the fact that the woman was efficient. She was the one who had taken the picture of the men as they rode off on the Harley -which was the kind of thing that Semon appreciated.

As the car sped off, she made a mental note to slip in an extra five thou into Aisha's weekly. A woman who produced results on the job was always worth it. Plus, loyalty had never been a cheap commodity. Especially in the black market.

"Were they here today?" Semon asked, referring to the two men.

"Yes." Aisha replied without taking her eyes off the road. "They left another note on her windshield." She handed Semon a little white envelope. The single sheet of paper in the envelope had been neatly folded in half. Semon took it out and unfolded it.

...She was the one who had taken the picture of the men as they rode off on the Harley.

The message had been manually typewritten:

'Once upon a time, there was a canary that would not stop singing. It just kept on going and it soon became a problem. So one day, a neighbor, who, for a long time had been asking the canary to stop, decided to pay the bird a visit. While he was visiting, an accident occurred. The bird's neck was broken and it died.'

Semon rolled the note into a little ball and tossed it out the window. Using a pencil that was lying on the dash, she scribbled something on the empty envelope and handed it to Aisha. The woman glanced at it and nodded.

It was an address in the part of the city that was generally referred to as 'East L A'. The trail of the fancy bike had led them to it. Aisha visualized the neighborhood as she formulated a mental road map that would take them there. It was an area with which she was pretty familiar. She had grown up on those streets. But now, it seemed like such a long time ago.

Back then life had felt empty, but it had become really sad when it dawned on her that the world out there as per the television, which was on all the time, did not think she was as beautiful as other little girls because of her complexion. Was it why her parents had abandoned her?

Then one day, her uncle in the army, who had been living in a far away country, had come home. He'd brought a camera with him. The pictures that he'd taken of her were so...so beautiful that Aisha had had to be convinced that she was the one in the photographs. It was the beginning of her love affaire with photography. Now she wouldn't go anywhere without a camera. It was her baby, her passion. And if everything went well, she soon would have enough money to start an upscale photography and modeling business. She already had a name; Zebra world.

She downshifted gears, glanced at the rearview and executed a perfect U turn. The time on the dashboard said a quarter to eight.

As she sent the car surging in the opposite direction, Aisha could tell that something serious was about to happen. She was not exactly certain what it was, but she'd been in this business long enough to see the signs in the air. Some kind of shit was going down. Semon had that look in her eyes. It was a look that the other woman had seen before and it usually meant only one thing; death was going to have a conversation with some puny aspect of life. And in the world in which these women lived, death always triumphed. It was nothing personal, just a matter of self-preservation.

"We should be there in twenty minutes," Aisha said, as she merged the speeding vehicle into the flow of traffic that was heading east on the 10 freeway. "Would you like me to call Max?"

Semon shook her head in the negative, barely suppressing her irritation. Why did women always think that a man had to be there for a job to get done properly?

"Max would not be needed." There was an unfathomable quality to her voice.

She downshifted gears, glanced at the rearview and executed a perfect U turn.

Marcus 'fuckin' Franken could not believe the speed with which his luck had changed. It was fucking amazing. In fact, it was phenomenal, whatever the word meant. Two weeks ago he had been just another homeless bum on the look out for the next drink. And then clap! Just like that, everything had changed. Feeling foolish, he pinched himself one more time. It was definitely not a dream. It better fuckin not be!

He raised the open bottle of scotch to his lips and took another long swig. Then, lowering the bottle, he belched loudly, wiped his mouth with the back of his left hand and fished out a crumpled pack of cigarettes from his dirty shirt pocket. Gingerly, he opened the pack, selected a stick and jammed it between his colorful teeth. Yeah, this was the life. It was exactly how he had imagined it. How he had always wanted it to be.

Marcus had been born on the street to a mother that he could barely remember, and from a very early age he had learned to steal just to stay alive. By the time he was twenty his life had become a series of short trips into and out of jail, mostly for petty crime. Then on his thirtieth birthday he had been busted for burglary, and a judge had decided it was time for him to learn a lesson. He had sentenced Marcus to nine years in a maximum-security facility.

Those nine years had been the most miserable in his entire life. He had experienced, depression, fear, sexual abuse, and most of all, blood curdling racial violence that had scarred him in ways that he never would have imagined possible. And many a night he had lain awake in his cell, wondering why any government would tolerate such a segregated prison system that served more like a factory for the mass promotion of racism.

Upon release, he had walked out, determined never to go back. But re-integrating into society had turned out to be much more difficult than he had imagined. No one had been willing to give him a job, and he did not have any experience or education that was worth mentioning. Neither did he have any friends or family to support and help him through the transition. So he soon found himself where he had started out; pinching whatever he could find.

But even this familiar trade had evolved into a more complex and potentially dangerous exercise. While he'd been locked away, technology had grown in leaps and bounds and every fucking store now had a thousand fucking surveillance cameras installed. Being a good shoplifter was not good enough anymore. Even a *master trader* like himself had to become almost invisible just to eat. What a life! For how long could a man live with the fucking threat of fucking jail, hanging over his fucking head like the fucking sword of Damocles?

It was at that point that Paulie 'the small' Spinelli had shown up again. He remembered Paulie from the old days as this scrawny, little, beggarly street urchin, who had never had enough to eat. Every once in a while, when things were good, Marcus would toss the kid a few coins. "You look like you fuckin need it," he'd always say as he walked by.

Then he'd gone to jail and lost track of the kid. So seeing him again a decade later had been a bit of a surprise.

Paulie had shown up dressed flashy, sporting a false mustache, and looking every bit the successful small time thief who fancied himself a *Don*. And he had offered Marcus a job.

Initially, Marcus had thought it would be in the ongoing thieving scheme that Paulie was rumored to have set up for himself at the airport, where he worked as a part time security officer for the luggage department. But the job had been of a different nature.

"I need someone to help me follow this bitch around. It seems she has a big mouth, and there is a man who is willing to pay, quite handsomely I would say, for us to follow her."

"That's it?"

"Yup. At some point, he might 'indicate for us to engage' her..."

"Engage her?"

"Those are the very words he used, and he explained it to mean, 'throwing a scare into her'. Scare her into shutting up is what it is. Easy as cake. No risks, no stress, no bullshit."

Paulie had concluded by surprising Marcus with an advance sum that had bulged his eyeballs out of their sockets. Marcus had needed the money so badly that asking more questions had been out of the question. "For old times sake Mr. Franken," he had said with a little smile. "Plus you look like you *fuckin* need it." He'd added, getting a huge kick out of mimicking Marcus.

Need it? What an understatement, the pick pocket mused. Especially on the same day that the food stamp office had found another excuse to kick him off.

With the money, Marcus had gotten this little apartment on the east side of town, furnished it, and then procured some toys that he had been able to have only in his dreams. He was now the proud owner of a used Harley with a custom paint job that would make the devil fucking proud. He'd gotten some new clothes, a watch, a laptop that he didn't know how to use yet, hell, he even owned a fucking Iphone. And you know what? Women were actually beginning to look at him! How crazy was that? Huh? How truly crazy was that? So if there was anyone out there in the wide fucking world who thought that he, Marcus Franken, did not have a fucking reason to celebrate, they could go fuck 'em selves.

He leaned forward and touched the remote control that was lying on the cheap, low, glass table and the used flat screen came alive. Earl Morgan, the Blues legend, was on, and his silky baritone filled the small apartment.

...Yeah when the going gets good
It gets so good, so good, so good...

Drunkenly, Marcus lurched to his feet. This song was definitely about him. He forced his body to take a few unsteady dance steps. But he only succeeded in dislodging the cigarette that was hanging from his lips. Instinctively, he reached out to catch it but he was too slow and it disappeared between the cushions of the old leather couch. Bloddy fuckin cigarette! He reached once more into his shirt pocket, retrieved the pack, pulled out another stick, and stuck it into his mouth. Now, where the fuck was that fucking lighter? It had been here just a moment ago. Shit! Why was he always losing fucking lighters? He could swear it had been lying on the fucking table right in front of him.

Unsteadily, he reached down to move aside the copy of playboy that was spread open on the low table. Instead, his shaking hand knocked over the open bottle of scotch.

"Fuck!" he swore under his breath as it went tumbling over and sloshing its amber contents onto the dirty, threadbare rug. He wanted that drink in his stomach, not on the bloody fucking carpet. Damn!

As fast as he could, he grabbed the bottle by its neck but it was too late. It was almost empty. He cursed again and tossed it away in disgust. With some difficulty he straightened up and lurched into the tiny kitchen.

A moment later he found what he was looking for, -another bottle to replace the empty one. Impatiently, he unscrewed the cap and raised the bottle to his mouth. Good thing he had had the foresight to get a whole case. He took a long drink, smacked his lips in contentment and staggered back into the living room.

"Sit your ass down."

For a moment Marcus Franken was not certain if he was seeing right, or if the blond woman was just a drunken visual illusion.

"What?"

"I said, sit your drunk ass down," the woman repeated.

"Listen bitch," Marcus drawled, "this is my fucking apartment, ok? And you better watch your fucking mouth." He smiled drunkenly. "Now if you want a drink and a good fucking time, I am most certainly the guy."

In response, Semon raised her arm. For the first time Marcus saw that she was holding a silenced automatic. Without a word she pointed the weapon at him. Abruptly, he sat down, noticing as well that the .45 he'd left on the table was not there anymore. She had it in her other hand.

Resignedly, he leaned back into the sofa, slowly coming to terms with the fact that for the second time in two weeks, without any warning, his luck had changed.

"Turn that off," Semon said, emptying the rounds in Marcus's .45 onto the floor. With a trembling forefinger, Marcus leaned forward, touched the remote, and the TV screen went dark. The only noise in the little apartment was from the street traffic, four stories below.

"What other weapons do you have?" Semon asked, as she wiped her prints off of the .45 pistol.

"That's it."

"Really?" Without warning, she brought down the stem of the gun and there was a loud 'phluck' as cartilage gave way to gunmetal. Marcus screamed, instinctively raising his hands to protect his broken, bloodied, nose. Semon swung the weapon again, connecting with his left wrist and Marcus howled in pain.

"I swear," he moaned. "You can search the whole fucking apartment. Just don't fucking hit me!" His swelling face was contorted in pain.

"Who is your friend?"

"Friend?"

Whack! And the man cried out once more.

"Don't play dumb with me," Semon said, placing a picture on the table in front of him. Marcus looked at the picture and almost choked. It was a photo of Paulie and himself riding away on the Harley!

In response, Semon raised her arm…

Oh God! What had he gotten himself into? Should he try to lie? What if she did not believe him? No, he did not want any more pain. Plus, this was all Paulie's fucking fault anyway. He was the one who had sworn that there was no danger whatsoever to the job. So, fuck him.

For the first time since he came out of prison, Marcus found himself missing his life as a broke and homeless shoplifter. "His name is Paulie," he moaned.

"And I assume you have a number for him. Is that correct?"

"Yes," he answered miserably.

"Good. Call him."

"Now?"

"No, next year, you little bitch," Semon snarled. "And you better listen to me very carefully." She leaned forward menacingly. "You are going to call Paulie right now and you are going to do exactly as I say. One mistake," she paused, "you will have only yourself to blame. Is that clear?" Marcus nodded. "Good. Now make the call. Tell him that the woman whose car you smashed is here with you. You cannot explain how she found your address, but tell him that she is here with a purse full of hundred dollar stacks. Tell him that you suspect she wants to buy you guys off of her tail, so he needs to come over right away and figure out the situation since you have had one too many drinks. If he doubts you and wants to hear her voice you will hand me the phone. Is there any part of this that you do not understand?" Marcus shook his head in the negative.

"Good. And remember, it is your only chance. You will not get another one."

Three minutes later Marcus got off the phone. "He is on his way," he said, looking at Semon. "He should be here in fifteen minutes."

Semon did not say anything. She had been standing close enough to overhear the whole conversation. Instead, she took a step backwards and cocked the raised weapon. The look of shocked surprise that appeared on Marcus Franken's face was his last expression.

A perfectly round hole suddenly appeared on his forehead. By the time his body hit the carpet he was dead.

Somewhere in the small apartment, a cat that Semon had not noticed before began meowing miserably.

$\mathcal{P}$aulie 'The Small' Spinelli, adjusted the collar of his new silk shirt, flecked off an invisible speck before turning around to face the mirror. Yes, it was a good shirt, and even though the color was a little off he was not worried. He was Paulie and everyone knew that he was flamboyant. If that did not give him the right to a slightly off, but elegant color, then nothing should.

He adjusted the already perfect looking knot of his blood red tie, smacked in satisfaction at himself, and danced off to the little bar at the corner of the room. Even the shoes had surpassed his expectations. They were expensive and they were stolen, - like almost everything else he owned. So what? Was he not worth it? He was Paulie, and he felt almost as good as he looked. He just wished that the meeting today could have been relocated away from the church. He had not been in a church building in a long time and just thinking about it made him nervous.

He poured a stiff drink, threw back his head and emptied the contents of the glass in one gulp. He refilled the glass immediately and drank that down as well. That felt much better. In a few months the priest would be dead, he thought, and he would be totally free. Maybe, he would have to go into hiding for a little bit, or even leave the country. The Bahamas, south East Asia, South America or even Africa. It did not matter, especially if he had money. So, for now, he had to do what he had to do to get the funds, even if that meant going into a hated church building for a meeting.

He adjusted his tie yet again and dusted off another invisible spec from the shiny, faux silk. He was ready.

It was the third meeting with the man and he had not even seen his face yet, a fact that did not bother Paulie at this point. Why should it? Plus, there was time. He just hoped that he was meeting the man's expectations in keeping Selena in a state of fright because the money was really good.

After receiving the first paid installment, he had been truly surprised. But alarm bells had also gone off. For a man who was always on the look out for the next opportunity, seeing that much cash had put his brain into overdrive. Something was definitely up. Something that was big and important enough to have warranted the eventual death of Marcus Franken. His sniffing nose was saying that it represented the opportunity to the bigger money that he'd been searching for.

For a moment he shuddered at the memory of Franken's death, mostly thinking of how close he himself had come to walking into the trap at Marcus's apartment. To be sure, he was sorry that the man was dead. He missed hearing him speak with the word 'fuckin' inserted twice into every sentence. But hey, it was a dangerous life and Marcus had not been a child. He must have known that making that kind of money must surely come with some risks. And sometimes things did not always go as planned. That was life. Some people got screwed. He himself would be dead today, had it not been for Marcus's cat.

He whistled and the animal appeared from behind a sofa

and sidled over. He stooped, picked it up, and began stroking it very gently. It had belonged to Marcus but it was now his. It had probably always been meant to be his, -to guide and keep him safe so that he could eventually take care of the priest. Which was why the animal had warned him. He smiled. It all made sense.

On that fateful night, after Marcus had called, Paulie had hurried over to the man's apartment, intent on meeting with the lady who was supposed to be waiting there with cash and some kind of business proposal. Upon arrival, he had taken the lift to the fourth floor and was standing in front of Marcus's door, arm raised to knock, when the cat, covered in wet blood, had suddenly appeared around the corner looking like a dream from hell. Paulie had hesitated just long enough to realize that the blood was not the cat's. He had not waited to find out whose it was, either. The fact that the blood covered animal belonged to the man he had come to see was sufficient reason to be alarmed. He had picked up the bloody creature and left immediately. So, news that a man, later identified as Marcus Franken, had been found dead in his fourth floor apartment had not been a total surprise. The report also called for anyone with information to come forward. Luckily, no one had associated him with the death so far, and Paulie wanted it to stay like that.

Not only were the cops nosing around, now he knew for a fact that somebody wanted him dead as well. He did not know who it was, but he was certain that it had something to do with the Selena woman. Was it her? Had she killed Marcus? How did she find him? He had to be more careful.

He took the car keys that were lying on the polished wooden stand, picked up the pet carrier and exited the small, though stylishly furnished apartment.

One hour later he drove into the little seaside town of Ventura, turned into Main Street and parked on the corner of Oak and Main. He locked the car, took the cat, and walked off down the street, ignoring both window shoppers and shops as he headed towards what was probably the oldest landmark in the downtown area.

He turned into the Catholic Mission compound and walked up the short flight of stairs that led to the huge double doors of the old church. It was not locked. Apprehensively, he walked into the building, stopping for a moment to let his eyes adjust to the reduced lighting that was coming from the candles on the altar.

The interior of the church was exactly as he expected it to be; empty rows of wooden seats on either side of a wide aisle that led directly to the rostrum. The larger than life murals, stained glass windows, and statues depicting the stations of the cross, were reminiscent of a childhood that he would rather forget; a life of abuse in the hands of priests who were supposedly supervising the children in the orphanage where he had been raised. He felt the bitterness rising to the back of his throat and for a moment he almost gagged.

Promptly, he suppressed the memories by counting his steps backwards from one hundred. The sixty-seventh step led into the little, dark, confession booth. There was a bench within it. He sat down and placed the pet carrier on the floor.

"You are late," came the familiar voice from the other side of the screen. By ninety-three seconds, Paulie acquiesced silently, glancing at the expensive, though illegally procured Rolex that was gracing his left wrist. "I am sorry, traffic on the 101 freeway. It will not happen again."

"I appreciate that," the voice said. "But it will not be necessary. This meeting signals the end of the assignment."

The end? Paulie was momentarily thrown off. He'd not seen this coming. What had happened? Something must have, because his horoscope had been clear about the fact that the new opportunity would eventually become the doorway through which he might find relief. So why was the man terminating the job? It must be a mistake.

"There is a brown envelope taped under the last seat on the right as you go out of the church," the voice added. "It contains the balance of what you are owed."

Paulie hesitated for a second. "What about... my partner?"

"You mean the dead one?"

Oh shit! The man knew about Marcus. "Er... yes, I ... er ... think his next of kin should ...er benefit from his...work"

"I see," the voice croaked. "And I am sure that you were named in his will as the trustee, right?"

"Er... not really... just that..."

"Have a nice day Mr. Spinelli."

Damn! He had taken this job under an alias. How did the voice find his name? That was not good. Especially with the way things were going. This situation definitely needed some serious rethinking.

Hurriedly, he picked up the pet carrier, and stepped out of the dark cubicle. His thoughts were suddenly interrupted by the display of Catholic paraphernalia; statues, pictures, candles...

Immediately, images of his childhood came crashing once more into his thoughts and he almost panicked. Damn! Will this never end? Silently he began counting in odd numbers, one, three, five, seven, nine, eleven... but it was not helping. The faces of the priests just refused to go away.

The interior of the church was exactly as he expected it to be...

Frantically he fished out a little transparent ziplock bag from his jacket pocket, retrieved something from it and threw it into his mouth. Hmm, that felt better. Even the face of the one priest he was going to kill suddenly took on a Christ-like apparition. Paulie smiled. He was not fooled. The man deserved to die and he would kill him when the time was right. If the church was still bent on protecting vermin like him at the cost of innocent children who eventually became mentally screwed up adults, then someone had to take the law into their own hands.

Feeling better, he walked down the aisle. He got to the last seat before the door, bent low and retrieved the bulky brown envelope that had been taped underneath. Without bothering to check its contents he stuffed it into his pocket and stepped out into the bright sunshine with a big sigh of relief.

As he got into his car, he failed to notice the blond woman who pulled up in a Ford Taurus, parked and locked it, before walking down Main Street. Even if he had noticed her, it would not have mattered because Paulie had never seen Semon before.

Semon, on the other hand, noticed the flashily dressed man in the off color silk shirt who drove off in a decked out SUV, not because she recognized him, but because she had made it a habit to always take the time and look around. In her line of work it was a necessity and it had saved her life a few times. She, certainly, would have recognized Paulie as the second man on the bike if he had not had a mask on in the picture that Aisha had taken. But, as it was, she did not, although the *pimped out* car vaguely reminded her of the Harley Davidson. She crossed the busy street and set off towards the old church building.

"Can I get a dollar please?" It was a beggar on the corner. She ignored him, getting off the sidewalk and ascending the short flight of stairs that led her to the double doors and into the empty church.

Once in the confession booth she sat down and waited. A full minute later it was still quiet and the voice had not croaked. Noisily, she cleared her throat, more to remind him that she was here now and waiting for him to speak. There was no sound, not even the slurpy noises of him drinking water, that she had come to expect. She cleared her throat again. "Are you here sir?" It was quiet.

She got to her feet and stepped out of the booth. Going around it, she threw open the little door that led into the opposing chamber. There was no one in it. She was about to let the door blinds fall back into place, when her roving eyes spotted a big brown envelope. It was leaning against the foot of the stool upon which her mysterious employer should have been sitting. She scooped up the envelope, opened it and took a quick peek. As usual, it was stuffed with wads of fifty-dollar bills. She smiled, closed the envelope and stuck it under her jacket.

Somewhere in the envelope would be a neatly folded, fingerprint-free sheet of paper, with typed out instructions specifying the next location for a meet. Her employer preferred to keep his identity to himself, which did not bother her as long as she was paid what she asked, and on time.

This was supposed to have been their fourth meeting and she had never seen his face. She was not even sure if the croaky voice was real. But that was his business. He was not asking her to kill Selena. At least, not yet.

She crossed the street, opened her car, got in, backed out and drove up Main Street. On California, she made a right, followed by a left on Thompson, and almost immediately the on ramp for the 101-freeway South was right there. She got onto it, shifted gears and stepped on the accelerator.

As the gray Ford Taurus merged with the south flowing traffic, the beggar who had been sitting on the sidewalk got up, and made his way to a white, nondescript van, that had been parked on the street, directly across from the church. He got into the car, backed out, drove up Main street, made a right on California, a left on Thompson and drove on to the on ramp for the 101 south. Once on the freeway, the man glanced at the tiny radar screen on the dashboard and began to whistle. It was amazing what technology had achieved. The Ford Taurus was represented by a red, blinking dot, which was moving fast along a solid green line. He could follow this car all day while staying out of sight. It made everything so much easier. The man whistled another stanza to the song. It was a song that was so old, there was no one alive, apart from himself, who knew the words. But that was understandable. He was different. The fact that he had prosthetics in place of lower legs was just one example. He was exceedingly grateful for them nonetheless. The idea had come to him from watching a South African runner, on stilts, sprint his way to victory in the Olympic games. Granted, it had taken some time for him to get used to them, but they had made a huge difference. It made it a little better whenever his thoughts wandered to all the years that he had been at other people's mercy, because he could not walk. Now, all he had to worry about was his very poor vision and the weakening heart.

He changed lanes to let a faster sports car fly by. Most people were in a big hurry. He could understand that. Man's time on earth was too short and it was a pity. Personally, he believed that life was never meant to be mortal, and that a long time ago people used to live for hundreds of years. Even the bible recognized this truth.

He changed lanes again to follow the Ford Taurus that was exiting on Sunset Avenue. Twenty-five minutes later, it led him to a huge parking lot that catered to what looked like an auditorium. He waited in the van until the blond woman disappeared into the building before stepping out. Gathering his flowing, floor length robes, he followed her. She led him into a smallish, circular auditorium that was filling up fast. This must be it. Selena was speaking here tonight. He felt his old heart skip a beat and begin to race, shooting pangs of pain across his chest, and throbbing almost too loud to bear. This was a special moment indeed. He listened to all her recorded speeches, but this would be the very first time that he would listen to her in person, since Paraguay.

He went directly to the last available front row seat, sat down, adjusted his robes to conceal his metallic legs, before settling down to wait for the speaker to come onto the empty stage.

A few minutes later, a man walked onto the stage, tapped the microphone that was standing behind the podium with the tip of his forefinger, cleared his throat, and introduced Selena.

"...And now I have the honor to give you Miss Selena Soltera," he concluded the introduction to loud applause, as Selena stepped onto the stage

The minute she walked onto the stage, Selena felt as if there was something odd in the air. The 'energy' in the room had an almost palpable tingle to it, but she could not be sure.

"Ladies and gentlemen, good evening and welcome," she began, immediately noticing a man in flowing robes, clutching two bottles of water, on the front row. "My name is Selena, and I want to talk to you today about our culture of getting high."

CHAPTER TWENTY EIGHT

$\mathcal{A}$s she talked, a part of her mind kept wandering off into the same daydream of thought that had begun plaguing her upon first noticing the man. He was the only one in the row whose feet were totally covered on account of his flowing robes.

With a little effort she shut out the distracting line of thought and brought her full attention to bear on her audience and on what she was saying. "Most of you would agree with me that we spend huge amounts of time and energy trying to run away from ourselves," She said. "Personally, I believe that it is a big reason behind the frivolous use of chemical substances, to which most of us, unfortunately, have fallen prey at one time or another. But what concerns me, is the role that some pharmaceutical companies are playing to foster this scenario just to make a buck. And I am not saying that these companies have not, or are not being helpful, because they are. But to some of them, no human condition is natural anymore. All of life has become a problem that needs to be treated with some kind of pill. Even conditions that are purely psychological are often diagnosed as complex chemical imbalances that require a One-a-day pill. Patients are even exhorted to ask their doctor about so and so pill. This intense marketing of prescription chemicals, combined with a wide use of destructive illegal substances, is slowly transforming us into a society of drug addicts. These days we even have drive-through pick ups for these chemicals just like the fast food joints." She paused again. "What does it say about us? What does it say about the manufacturers of these pills? What kind of business is it that can only experience a boom at the detriment of its clientele? What would we think of a coffin maker who prays to God for a boom in his business? Where will it end? Even normal, active children are called hyperactive and put on *calmers* that just prep them for the big time. How long before we end up with governments where most top officials need to get high first thing in the morning before attending to the important duty of leadership? What kinds of decisions will they make? What kinds of decisions can come from a bunch of drugged minds? How will those decisions affect us?" She scanned a sheaf of papers that were sitting on the microphone stand. "In my opinion, we can go only for so long before errors in judgment become obvious in the decision making process. I think this will contribute to the political, economic, and socio-cultural breakdown of institutions upon which our societies depend. At that point, even the pharmaceutical industry itself will be struggling for breath." She smiled sadly. "Reminds me of the classic parasite that greedily sucks the life out of its host while refusing to think about the possible implications for itself if the host should die."

There was a sudden hiss, or was that laughter, and it was coming from the front row, from the man in the robes whose presence was being such a distraction. It seemed as if he was emanating some kind of energy. Was she the only one who was aware of him in this way? Quickly, she glanced at her watch, even as she regretted the gesture. But she wanted this hour to be over. She was already experiencing the onset of a headache. Or was it just the feeling of apprehension that was growing in the pit of her stomach?

Just then there was a cough behind her and she almost jumped out of her skin. She turned to find the sound technician standing there.

"Sorry about the sound," he sputtered apologetically.

The sound? Oh, the sound. She had not even realized that the sound system had failed. But it had and she was suddenly grateful for it. More than anything else she wanted to leave, to get away from the robed figure, and the glitch in the sound system was the perfect excuse. Nervously, she reached down and grabbed her handbag.

"Please, my dear lady," a voice croaked, "would you be so kind as to sign an autograph for me?"

She did not have to look to see who it was. Clutching her bag, she practically ran off the stage, leaving a trail of flying papers behind her.

As she disappeared backstage, her ears picked up a distinct hiss. Or was it a chuckle? The man was laughing at her! He was laughing as if he could see into her thoughts, as if he was aware of the effect of his presence upon her!

Selena scanned the newspaper without much interest. She'd found it on the table after getting a Tall Americano. She liked Starbucks. She found the coffeeshop environment to be one of the last friendly public places in the country where community was still being created, almost like a village square in times past. In fact, the atmosphere of simple camaraderie reminded her a lot of a small village square. She liked to come here in the mornings, sit, get a coffee, sip on it and engage in small talk or read the paper. But tonight, after her talk, she had needed the coffee rather badly. For some reason the permanently thirsty man in the front row seat had freaked her out. Who was he?

She put the paper down, picked up her purse, went up to the bar, refilled her coffeecup for almost nothing, before walking out of the shop. Ten minutes later, feeling more relaxed, she pushed open the door into her apartment, stepped in, closed and locked the door behind her, before realizing that she was not alone. A man was standing in the centre of her living room and he was looking directly at her. She could hear her heart thumping rapidly in her chest.

"What do you want?" she whispered, almost droping her coffee. "Who are you?" She was almost in a panic.

"Police officer Richards," the man said. "David Richards." He was holding out a badge.

"How did you get in here?" she asked, breathing easier but keeping her eyes on his face. "Why are you not in uniform?"

The man took an impatient breath. "Firstly, I got in here through the front door which was conveniently open, and secondly I am not in uniform because I did not want to give away the fact that a police officer had been to see you."

"I am not so sure that I understand all of what you are saying, but I assume this has to do with my vandalized car and the note that was found on it, correct?" she asked.

"Correct," the man affirmed. "But more than that, we now have reason to believe that there is a person of interest who may be following you."

Selena felt a chill go up her spine. She was not imagining it after all. This was real! She collapsed into the closest chair, not quite sure what to make of this new development. The police officer took the seat that was directly across from her.

"It may just be a bored individual who is taking things too far but we do not want to take any chances, if you know what I mean," he said. "It is rare but in the past, cases like this have turned out to be much more than was previously thought."

Great, this was all she needed.

"Do you have any enemies of which you are aware?" Asked the man.

"Would that include people who disagree with my speeches?"

"No, just people who may have a more specific reason to dislike you."

"Not that I am aware of."

The man studied her for a moment. "Have you recieved more threats since your car was wrecked?"

"No."

"Is there anything odd, or out of place, that you think I should know?"

She took a deep breath. Odd? Out of place? Was that not the story of her life? Where would she start? How many women were still virgins at thirty-five? Was that not odd? Why was it that every man that had shown a passing interest in her had ended in a fatal or disabling accident? What would the officer think if she told him that her life was cursed? Wouldn't he think that she was a mental case? Probably so. This was not the twelfth century. What of the man whose presence on the front row had distracted her so badly during her last presentation? Should she bring that up? How could she be certain that it was not just her own illusions? What if she were actually crazy? The thought scared her. But what if that were the case? Would she be committed into some kind of program? Probably so. First her name would make a round of all the news stations, she would be ridiculed and laughed at, then her driver's license would be revoked, and then other punishments would follow, until she ended up in a sanatorium. She could not allow that.

"No, not really." She finally said.

"Not really?"

"What I meant to say is 'No."

"Are you sure?"

"Yes I am," she answered quickly.

"O.K. Here is my card," he said, handing her a slip of paper. "That number will reach me at all times of the day or night. If you notice anything do not hesitate to call me. Do you have any questions?" She shook her head in the negative.

The man put the notebook back into his pocket and walked to the door. Once in the street he pulled out a tiny cell phone and dialed a number.

"Good evening sir," he greeted. "I am just calling to report that everything is stable."

"Good," The line went dead.

$\mathcal{P}$aulie was baffled. He could not understand what was going on, although he was certain that something was. It was more of a hunch than anything else and he needed hard facts.

After the meeting in the church at which the job had been terminated, he had decided to continue the surveillance on Selena. On his own. It was a risk that he had judged was worth it. With such a strong smell of big money in the air surely there was some to be made, and that was exactly what he planned to do.

So he had followed Selena everyday, even sleeping a few times in his car, outside her apartment. Now he knew everything about her; what she wore, her hobbies, the fact that she was very health-conscious, went to *Gold's Gym,* avoided GMO foods, shopping only from *Wholefoods* and *TraderJoe's*, and also the surprising fact that he was not the only one who was following her. There was a woman as well, and he had seen her a couple of times. This had intrigued him even more. What was it about Selena Soltera that made her so valuable to so many different people? Was it something she was hiding in her apartment? He had thought about it for a few days before deciding to break into her place.

He had searched the place from top to bottom, careful to not leave his prints on anything. And at the end of the search, which did not yield anything, he planted a few carefully hidden cameras in the apartment, one in the living room, one in the bedroom, another in the guest room, and a last one on the outside deck. The installations had made everything much easier. Now, he could park his car a block away and see everything happening in the apartment. And it had not required that much to set everything up. A customized laptop, a wireless router, and a few other gadgets that he had picked up from the local radio shack, was all that he had needed. Plus the SUV, which had been stolen in Canada and driven across the border just for the job.

He preferred to use an SUV as opposed to a van because vans, in his opinion, were just too classic, making them suspicious and therefore easy to spot. Granted, a van had more space but that was not an issue. The advancement in digital technology meant equipment was not as bulky as it would have been just a decade ago. He had folded down the back seat of the SUV into a flat bed and that had provided enough room to set everything up. Sure, it was a little cramped, but it attracted less attention, which to him was of greater importance. With the tinted windows, the SUV was just another Sport Utility Vehicle that was parked on the street.

Now, he could park his car a block away and see everything happening in the apartment...

He touched a key on the tiny laptop, and the view from Selena's bedroom camera appeared on the screen. Calmly, he watched the woman as she dressed herself. First the underwear, everything from *Victoria's secret*, then the skirt, the blouse, jewelry, little or no make up, perfume, shoes, A *Gucci* handbag, and then she walked out of view.

He touched another key on the laptop, and the view from the living room camera jumped onto the screen, but she was not in it. She must have walked into the bathroom, where he remembered seeing a wall sized mirror. That must be it. She was making sure that everything looked perfect on her beautiful body. Yes, she was quite beautiful, he thought. She could be any of the women who frequently graced the covers of the many fashion magazines. But, as usual, he was not attracted. Women did not do it for him. As far as he could remember, they had never done it for him. Except, maybe for one, but that was so long ago it probably did not matter. It was the girl with whom he had escaped from the orphanage. Although not much older than himself, she had understood the anger and confusion that he felt, at a time when he'd desperately been in need of someone on whom he could unburden the thoughts that kept him up at night while the other street kids slept.

Then, one morning, he went over to the street corner where she would usually hang out and found the area cordoned off. Cops and yellow tape everywhere. So much blood on the ground it had made him sick. She had slashed open both of her wrists. The memories that she carried, bottled within, had finally erupted to the surface and the avalanche had overwhelmed her. He, on the other hand, hung on. God had let him live on so he could bring justice to *that* devil-in-a-cassock who had specialized in abusing little children.

Selena walked back into view for a split second and then disappeared again. Paulie switched to the living room view and zoomed in. There she was, picking up some papers from the table as she prepared to step out of her apartment.

He turned off the laptop, jumped into the driver seat of the SUV and started the engine. She was giving another talk tonight, and even though he knew the location, he preferred to wait and follow her there. That way he'd be sure that he had not missed anything.

Presently he saw her car come around the corner and drive past him. It was followed a few moments later by the grey ford Taurus with Aisha behind the wheel. He engaged gears, stepped on the accelerator, and pulled away from the curb.

Cameroon, Central Africa.

*B*althazar Yao glanced at his watch, shifted himself into a much more comfortable position, and raised the binoculars to his eyes. He was lying on his stomach on the top of a small hill that allowed him to see the surrounding forests for miles.

He scanned the view, searching for any telltale signs. There were none as of yet, just the forest. He inhaled deeply, breathing in the dense, tropical essence of the atmosphere.

The beauty of the rain forest never ceased to amaze him. The huge trees, with all their leaves and fruits, the shrubs, the flowers, the grass, the animals, the birds, the insects, the streams, the rivers and all the forest noises. It was just amazing! And it had been here for thousands of years. But today, wanton exploiters who were protected by a very corrupt, very greedy, and very blackmailed government, were destroying it. All because of money!

That would end soon, though. He would put an end to it. That was his mission. It was his calling. Was a prophecy not spoken over him at birth? Was he not the descendant of ancient warriors who had migrated all the way from the Kingdoms of the North? Had the necklace not fallen on his lap?

Instinctively, he put his hand under his shirt and fingered the necklace that he had worn for almost all of his life. It had been given to him in a very secret ceremony on the day that he'd turned eleven. It was made of pure gold and had been fashioned in the shape of an open left hand. Gently, he traced the fine inscription that had been carefully engraved on the smooth surface. No one knew what it meant. He assumed that it was in some ancient script that had been lost to time.

As a young boy, he would make up stories in his head about the necklace, fantastic tales about all the different adventures that the object had experienced, stories that went beyond its known history. As an adult, there were days that he would wonder about the necklace's true history. Who had created it? Had it been for a beautiful woman? How old was it?

Yao remembered that one thousand days prior to his own eleventh birthday, his grand uncle on his father's side had begun a program of daily recitations with him. He would fetch Yao just before sunrise and take him to a secluded clearing in the forest where they would spend the whole morning recounting and memorizing, line by line, a particular story in Bororo history. It was a recitation of three thousand and fifty words which took him exactly one hundred days to master. By the end of the rainy season, he could recite the whole thing backwards in his sleep. But that was just the beginning, because he was expected to keep on with the recitations everyday for as long as he lived.

On the night of his eleventh birthday, he'd been summoned into his grandfather's room. Yao recalled the episode clearly. At first, he'd thought the old man, who had been sick for some time, had finally passed away. But once in the room, he found that it had not been a ceremony of last respects. The old man, who was the boy's biggest hero, as well as the leading oral historian to the Bororo chiefdom, was lying on his deathbed. On his chest was a necklace that the boy had never seen or heard of. Also present, was the village shaman, as well as two distinguished elders.

"My son," his grandfather spoke with difficulty. "You have been chosen to carry a weight that must never be talked about, a weight that is in fact a very great honor. To show yourself worthy of it you must recite to us, without a single mistake, the story of how this 'great honor' came to be with us."

Then, using a staff, the shaman prodded Yao into the center of a circle that had been drawn with white chalk at the foot of the sick man's bed, and the boy delved into the recitation:

"...then Abou Bakar passed it to Yalim who was incharge of the Kings Prison. And Yalim carried it for four years. This was during the time of the Great Migration that took the people southwards across the great desert. When Yalim died, Ankah was chosen to carry it. Ankah begat Saala and Saala begat Okum. When Saala became full of years he transferred it to Okum. Okum carried it for twenty and three years, up to the time that the people decided to settle in the land of the Hausas. When Okum was thirty and two rains old, he begat Sunu whose mother was Jemea of Bali. Sunu lived to a ripe old age, and before he died he passed it to the youngest of his twenty- eight sons whose name was Sama the touareg. Sama did not bear any sons, so he transferred it to his only daughter whose name was Manka'a. When Manka'a had twins her name was changed to Ma'anyi, which means 'mother of twins'. This was during the time of the Great Drought. When Ma'anyi's first son became a man she transferred it to him..."

And so the recitation went. It was a recitation about his ancestors, proud warriors from an ancient Kingdom that had lasted for thousands of years, a Kingdom that had been involved in many, many wars; most of them victorious, a few not so much. And sometimes the defeats had led to pain, suffering, death and even migrations. It had been on one such migration, the narration held, that the sacred object had been carried southwards across the great desert and into the rainforest. There, the people, protected by the curse of the mosquito, -a lethal fever that had forced their pursuers to retreat, had settled down to a new beginning.

In the safety of the rain forest, it had been passed down from generation to generation, until it had entered into the hands of Yao's great grandpa, who had handed it to his son, Yao's grandfather, who was now dying.

Yao recited the story over and over for his audience without a single mistake. At the end of the tenth recitation, the shaman seemed satisfied and called for a stop. Then Yao's head was shaved and the cut hair set ablaze within the circle of chalk. With smoke rising into the room, the shaman unclasped the hand shaped necklace from around the old man's neck and placed it on Yao. Then he was sworn into an oath of absolute secrecy. He was never to talk about the ceremony, he was never to mention the object, he was never to allow another eye to see the hand and most importantly, he was never to allow the sun's rays to fall upon it. It was to be worn under his garments. To breach any of these stipulations would invite the curse of the whole tribe. He would die violently and his body would be left to the hyenas.

He glanced at his watch again and looked at the sky. From the top of the little hill, he could see the warm colours of the distant horizon as the orange orb sank deeper into the earth. The sounds in the forest all around were begining to change as well, adapting as life took a nocturnal turn. In about an hour it would be dark, which was okay too. Light or no light, he would do what he had come to do.

He shifted his attention to the dirt road that was snaking around the base of the hill about two hundred meters away, following its winding path with his eyes until he got to the stream. It was a small, shallow stream, which was why he had chosen it in the first place. And the bridge, if it could be called that, was less than twenty meters in length. It was made of a huge tree trunk that had been split lengthwise down the center. Both pieces, arranged next to each other, sawed sides facing up, had been used to span the stream. The finishing touch consisted of several pieces of flat plank that had been bolted down across both surfaces to provide traction. It was a good bridge for what Yao had in mind. As he surveyed it in the dying light, he knew it was the right place. The dense forest that came down to the banks of the stream, provided cover for his men, who were down there.

He was lying on his stomach on the top of a small hill that allowed him to see the surrounding forests for miles...

He focused the binoculars again and scanned the distance. What was that noise? There it was again. The drone of car engines! He zoomed the binoculars into the distance.

In the failing light, they could not be seen with the naked eye, but the powerful binoculars brought them into view as they came around a corner; a convoy of three trucks,... no four!, traveling without lights and heading in his direction. They should be at the bridge in ten minutes.

He grabbed the rifle that was lying next to him and began slithering downhill. Half way down, he stopped and whistled softly. Two men materialized out of the bushes and joined him. Both were carrying sniper rifles. Just like the one he had, they were equipped with telescopic sights. They were not the best quality, but they were all he could afford. For now. He was doing everything in his power to obtain superior weapons. Which was the main reason behind today's action.

He raised the binoculars to his eyes one more time. The trucks were much closer. In a few minutes their contents would belong to him. They were transporting some 'heavy material' that he found useful. Maybe he would have chosen differently if he were buying. But hey, it was free for the taking, so why not? His meeting with the European businessmen was in a few days. That was more promising. The man had mentioned some very top-of-the-line rifles that Yao could not wait to get. Once they were in his possession, everyone would have no choice but to start taking him seriously. He could not wait. In the meantime, he had to be satisfied with whatever the trucks were carrying.

"There are four trucks," he said. "I will take the first one. You, take the second," he said to one of the men, "And you, the third. If we all score, it will make everything so much easier for our brothers down there." The men nodded as they took their positions, one to his right, and the other to his left.

The convoy was almost at the bridge now. Yao raised his rifle into firing position and the other men followed suit. He adjusted the telescope, brought the first truck into focus, and centralized the driver's head between the crosshairs.

The truck was now on the bridge. It drove slowly across it, got to the other side, and pulled over. The second truck did the same, followed by the third. And now it was the turn of the fourth truck. Yao waited until it was almost over the bridge.

"One," he counted audibly. The first driver's head was still centered within the crosshairs of his telescopic weapon.

"Two," the men joined in unison. They had rehearsed this.

"Three," it was the last count to make sure that everyone was in rhythm.

The fourth count was the combined sound of three shots ringing out as one. Somebody shouted, and the quiet forest dusk was transformed into the chaos of automatic rifle fire.

Yao's men, who were positioned on the opposite bank of the stream, were in full assault. The soldiers with the convoy reacted with military precision. Men in uniform were jumping off the immobile trucks, returning the fire that was coming from the riverbank as they sought to reposition themselves and repulse the ambush. The fourth truck, whose driver was still alive, began a reverse maneuver. It did not last. The amount of firepower that was emanating from the opposite bank soon convinced him that it was a bad Idea. Instead, he pulled out of the line and accelerated forward, carving a path in the roadside bushes as he made his way around the first three immobile trucks.

"Stop that truck!" Yao shouted, sprinting down the hill, his men in hot pursuit. If the truck succeeded in getting away from the bridge, it would have no problem getting to the base of the hill within a few minutes. And he planned to be there if that turned out to be the case. The trucks and their contents belonged to him now. Anyone who stood in the way of that would die.

He adjusted the telescope, brought the first truck into focus, and centralized the driver's head between the crosshairs...

Yao's camp was so well hidden that if his men had not found us we would never have located it. Jean Pierre's map had turned out to be good, but not that good. So we had just concentrated on following the trail that had been left behind by Yves's mounted party. And that had gone well for the first six or so hours. Then everything had changed.

First of all, the sun had gone down behind the horizon, but the mounted party had not stopped. So, although we were exhausted and being continuously tortured by mosquitoes and other starving bugs, we could not stop. Getting lost was not an option. With one flashlight remaining, we had kept on.

Towards the early hours of the morning, we walked into the ambush. Neither of us saw the men before it was too late. Suddenly, we were on the ground and I was doing everything to protect my head from the violent onslaught.

"We have a message for Yao," I managed to shout above the noisy rain of blows and kicks. But no one seemed to care. The beating just went on, and on, for what seemed like an eternity.

My bruised and swollen head was aching badly, and Jean Pierre was limping strangely as we were marched into the camp. It looked exactly as one would expect such a camp to look. It was tucked against the base of a hill, it was well shielded from the air by a cover of huge trees, and it was mostly made up of quickly constructed huts and tents that could be torn down in a minute. The shade provided by the trees made the camp almost dark, until one's sight adjusted to the softer lighting.

There were dangerous, tough looking, well armed men all around. A few people were roasting a well spiced, ram sized animal over an open fire, one man was playing softly on a stringed instrument, while others were just patrolling the camp. There were no women. The whole picture reminded me of a coiled spring.

"Take him to the cages," a gruff voice said. It belonged to the head of the patrol that had found us.

"No! We have to see Yao now," I said frantically.

"Shut up," the man said, bringing down the butt of his rifle into my ribs. I howled in pain as he repeated the action, forcing me to the ground. "Yao will see you when he is ready to see you. Until then I suggest you close your mouth and make yourself as unobtrusive as possible," he added, turning away.

"If you do not take me to see Yao right this minute," I panted, on all fours, spitting out blood, "I can assure you that you will regret it. Especially after he realizes that what we have to tell him has everything to do with the meeting that he is having at this very moment with the white man." The man spun around.

"Do you not know what it means to shut up?" he snarled, ramming the butt of the rifle once more into my body. The pain seared through me like a hot blade. The man took another step forward and landed a solid kick to my ribs, breaking at least one. The pain was like fire. He was about to kick me again, when another voice interrupted him.

"Stop," the voice said. "What do you know about the white man?"

"Enough to put all of Yao's army into my debt," I said painfully, spitting out more blood.

The man, a huge, very dark individual, considered me for a moment. "Take him and follow me," he whispered. I was picked up and dragged after him as he turned around and marched off.

The meeting between Yao and Yves de Mammon was in full stride when I was brought in. It was taking place in a tent that had been erected using several dark green tarpaulins attached to the base of the little cliff. The tent had been centrally located in the camp, and was well guarded by several of Yao's men who inspected me suspiciously, even as they stepped aside to let us in.

Once in the tent, my artist's eyes took in the whole picture at a glance. There were five men in the tent and Yves Mammon, Jean's boss, was one of them. He was looking uncomfortably hot in a jacket and hat that was ridiculous to behold in the heart of the rainforest. He had donned a pair of shades that kept his expression hidden.

Yao was also in the tent and I recognized him immediately. He looked older than his picture on the cover of *Jeune Afrique* a few years ago, but he still looked lethal. He had also grown a *Savimbi*, which kept much of his lower face covered, lending him an air of mystery, but failing to disguise the ball of energy that was lurking just beneath the surface. I did not recognize any of the other men.

They were all seated around a thick and wide cross section of a tree trunk that had been mounted on three big rocks to form a table. The seats themselves were pieces of smaller tree trunks that had been covered with layers of dried, thatched grass. All the men were focused on a pair of Chinese made type 56 high velocity assault rifles that had been mounted on display stands, on the centre of the make shift table. Both looked brand new, and even to me who knew little or nothing about guns, they appeared formidable.

For a moment, there was a lull in the intensity of the conversation as the man who brought me into the tent went up to Yao and whispered something into his ear. I could feel everyone's eyes on me, taking in the blood, the cuts, and my swollen face. Yao turned towards me.

"First of all, I would like to apologize to you for the obvious maltreatment you experienced at the hands of my men. They can be overzealous at times," he said, getting to his feet and bowing to me. Every one else in the tent was silent. "But as a journalist, you must know that my army is made up mostly of individuals who have seen and experienced a lot of grief at the hands of the political status quo," he added, walking slowly towards me. I held my breath.

As a journalist?

How did the man know that I worked for a newspaper? How could that be? I felt a coldness steal into my soul.

"Most of these men have serious anger issues which can spill over sometimes," he continued. "Did you know that anger is the single biggest reason why my army keeps growing?" he chuckled, bending forward to examine my swollen eye. "I wish I had the means and the time to provide you with the medical care that you require. But I am not a doctor. I am just a very busy man, as you can see." He turned around and strolled off. "And I, a man who does not like to wonder, is forced to wonder what you may have to say that cannot wait, to the point where you insist on interrupting me and my companions." He sat down again and looked up at me. "Yes?"

"Sir, with all due respect, I stand here to accuse the man you call your companion, of not being who he claims to be," I said. "He is a French secret service agent whose sole purpose here is to frame you for murder. His goal is to get your fingerprints, which he will if you touch any of these guns and then let him take them back without wiping them clean."

"Really?" Yves asked with a mocking, almost bored smile.

"Yes, and you, sir," I continued speaking to Yao, "will later learn about the assassination of the US Secretary of State by the same weapon which has your prints... "

"I must insist on proof of these accusations." Yves interrupted, reaching forward very deliberately, grinding out his cigarette and picking up the closer of the two rifles. Out of the corner of my eye, I noticed that Yao had not moved. Nor did he speak. He just sat there, with both hands out of sight, staring straight ahead with a little smile on his lower lip.

"For what is worse than to dishonor a man," Yves asked, getting to his feet, raising the weapon, and pointing it at me. His smile was gone and there were beads of shiny sweat on his forehead. "These weapons are what I say they are, and these two are samples of the thousands that Yao will be getting from me in a little while. I have already offered one of these to him as a gift of good faith. But I must keep one to protect my men and myself in case some wild beast should chance upon us during our return journey. But now you dishonor my gift, and you throw suspicion upon my intention and my business."

"Speak," Yao whispered, looking at me. "Because around here justice's middle name is 'Swift'."

"My friend has more information," I said, knowing that it did not amount to proof per se, but Jean's corroboration of the story would cast enough suspicion on Yves intention, which was all we needed.

Yao gave a barely perceptible nod and thesame man who had brought me into the tent pushed open the flap and stepped out. Apart from my own heartbeat, I could not hear anything. This was it.

The flap of the tent was pushed aside and Jean Pierre stepped in. By himself. He had taken a bath and the transformation was total. Not only was he dressed in a suit identical to Yves's, he had dark shades on as well. He ignored me as he walked to the table and sat down. Suddenly I realized that even his limp was gone.

"Jean Pierre," I said, walking forward, "will you tell these gentlemen what you know about Yves?"

Jean Pierre cleared his throat. "First of all, my name is not Jean Pierre and..." I did not wait to hear the rest.

With the last of my energy, I darted forward and rammed my shoulder into Yves's stomach. The rifle flew out of his hands as everybody around the table, except for Yao, jumped to their feet. But I was faster. The other rifle was already in my hands and I was raising it up, when something fell on the back of my head. The last thing I knew before everything went black was that Yao was the one who just hit me even though I had not seen him move.

---

*W*hen I came to myself, I was still in the tent. I was lying exactly where I had fallen, my head was throbbing and it was totally dark. I had been out for some hours, I thought. I tried to move, but the gesture alone sent pangs of pain through my body. Where was Jean Pierre? Had he left with Yves? Why was I still alive?

Finally, I sat up, realizing as I did so that there was a collar around my ankle that was linked to a heavy chain. I peered into the darkness and tried to make out the shapes, but it was to no avail. It was too dark to see anything.

"You are awake." I recognized the voice immediately.

"I am," I answered, turning to squint towards the direction it was coming from. But I couldn't make anything out. "Can you light a candle or a lamp?"

"A candle? What makes you think that we can afford such luxuries around here?" Yao asked. "And even if we could, why are you so sure that you are worthy of one?"

I did not answer

"Imagine for a second, what would happen if life on earth was to become like this tent," Yao said. "Where everything was invisible, where no man, woman, or child, could be seen, only heard. Think about it for a moment. No forms, no shapes, No bodies,... just breath and voices. Think of the difference it would make, not just in trimming down egos, but also in pointing us in the direction of the things that really matter." He paused. "People would not be so caught up with how they looked, what they needed to eat, or wear, or drive. Physical needs and insecurities would disappear overnight, and with them the fears, illusions, and perceptions of the ego which is at the heart of materialism. It would release a huge wave of spiritual consciousness that would wash over humanity, awakening souls, liberating them from the trap of time, and tuning them into the awareness of the present, or *the now* as Eckhart Tolle rightly calls it. Imagine what a great thing that would be? Pride will be exposed for what it is, the manifestations of the ego would disappear, and greed would automatically become nonexistent. Without greed, there wouldn't be imperialism, colonialism, neo colonialism or even war..."

"War?" I asked. "If you love peace so much, why are you preparing for war?"

"Because sometimes you have to fight for peace," he answered, "And those against whom we fight, will not stop stealing until there is nothing left to steal, at which point everyone would either be dead or dying of hunger and sickness anyway."

"Maybe so, but there is another way to fight..." I began,

"And you think I was born cradling a weapon in my arms? You don't think I have thought about that? Why do you think I choose to fight? Because I like killing people?" He laughed softly. "Because the system is designed to not work, that's why. Those at the top will do anything and everything to stop any and all meaningful reform. The status quo suits them just fine; they can stay in power forever, and they can rob state coffers with impunity while hard working citizens suffer and die very preventable deaths." There was a pause. "Have you ever had a loved one die from something that could have been prevented, if corruption had not been so rampant?"

"Yes, corruption is rampant," I agreed, opting to skip his question "But why are you fighting evil with evil? And why is your fight targeting the government only? Surely a man with your charisma could achieve so much more by building an army of teachers that would eventually flood the nation with knowledge of virtue, truth, justice and awareness, -qualities that in themselves would annihilate everything that you fight against. Remember what the scriptures say about creation? God did not bother to speak to the darkness even though it was there. He could easily have said, 'Darkness be gone,' but instead he said, 'Let there be light.' I think you should do the same. Stop focusing on the problem and start being the solution. Which I think, is what Gandhi meant when he said that we should be the change that we would like to see in the world, or something to that effect?"

There was a quite chuckle.

"I love your naive idealism..."

"Naive idealism? You'd still call it that after men like Gandhi, Cesar Chavez, and Martin Luther King have proven otherwise? You must truly love killing people."

"Quite persuasive I must say," Yao continued, as if I had not said anything new. "But for how long could we teach truth in a dictatorship like ours before some politician with too much power starts feeling threatened? And what if this politician should decide to do something about it? Do you think the justice system would come to our rescue if the masses do not? I don't think so," the words floated out of the darkness. "You know why?"

I sensed it was another rhetorical question and I was right.

"Corruption," the answer came again. "It is a terrible monster, and the surest way of killing it is by cutting off its head. And that head to us is the present government."

"And after you have cut off this head, what then?" I asked.

"We shall have the opportunity to start anew. First we shall suspend all foreign aid..."

"Suspend foreign aid?" I asked. "How would you rebuild the country from the devastation of a war that you would have helped to start?"

"Not with foreign aid," he answered. "Because, what is usually called *foreign aid* is in fact debt that is calculated to permanently enslave the recipient and empower the new international corporate ruling class."

"I don't believe you."

"You don't? Have you ever been to any of the so called 'first world countries?"

"No."

"Well, if you had, you would have noticed that a similar debt based relationship exists between credit card companies and their clients. The ultimate intention of these companies is to indebt hard working people in a way that would transform them into permanent or long term interest-generating machines. The same holds true for foreign aid donors like the World Bank, the IMF, or the WTO, who actually encourage corruption and inefficiency in so called third world countries that are rich in natural resources."

"Are you sure about this?" My journalist instincts had kicked in and I was treating this like an interview.

"Yes, I am." Yao's voice was firm.

"But why?"

"To weaken these countries and render them more dependent, or, shall we say, more 'controllable'. A good example is the HIPC that was initiated in 1996. It encourages these countries, which are already struggling in the first place, to increase their debts to unsustainable levels as a prerequisite for receiving aid. Apart from that, the creditors will often specify the ways in which the money must be used, with the result that genuinely good economic policies are shelved, in favor of ones that fix things without actually fixing anything. It is economic Nazism. Just like telling a sick person that you will provide medication for him only on the condition that he gets sicker. And when you do get around to providing the medication, instead of what the sick person really needs, you give him a *one a day* pill that will keep him barely breathing, and thus, even more dependent on you. So at the end of the day, these so called aid programs were never intended for use in ways that would empower the borrower to the point of economic independence."

"I can't believe that."

"Of course you can't," Yao mused. "You probably have to hear it from someone else to believe it. You should read Noam Chomsky. He is arguably the most respected intellectual of our age. Even those who dislike him agree that he usually knows what he is talking about. And if you find him too intellectual, there is a very good documentary based on a book by a fellow named John Perkins. It is called *Confessions of an Economic Hitman*. If that does not raise questions in your mind about the relationship between first and third world economies, then nothing will."

"Maybe it will, that is, if I ever get to watch it, which seems like a rather slim possibility right now. Apart from that how do I know you are not just telling a story?"

"A story?" Yao chuckled again. "Your reaction can be expected," he said. "You are not the only one who thinks like that. And I would agree with you if you could manage to give me the name of a single bank, any bank in the world, that would love to empower its clients to the point where the client would never have to borrow. Ever again."

I thought about it for a moment, but once again I was silent.

"So you see, believing me or not believing me is not important. The facts stand up for themselves; banking is what it is. We need bankers and they need us, but nearly all bankers have just one loyalty; money. As such we cannot trust them. Like governments, they must be strictly regulated, - especially international bankers. Failure to do so would allow them to grow into these huge and uncontrollable monsters that do not know how to stop themselves." Yao coughed in the dark. A moment later I heard him spit. "International bankers who operate in Africa are a good example. They are said to be even more ruthless in their quest to compromise the sovereignty and wealth of the continent."

"But how does that help the lender? Aren't they losing

money with all these debts that cannot be repaid?" I asked.

"No, never! They get paid by extracting all kinds of raw materials from these borrower nations, raw materials that are actually much more valuable than the loans for which they are taken."

"But how can the predicament of Africa be the fault of these lenders, when African leaders are the ones who choose to play along?" I was not ready to give up.

"I never said it was the fault of the lenders," Yao said. "All I am saying is that it is time for Africa to officially acknowledge the fact that the overall intention of these lenders has never been good. I fully recognize that most of the blame for this situation lies with our so-called leaders. Most of them are weak, spineless, *blackmailable* and will never dream of making the sacrifices that it takes to stand up. The future of our countries will continue to be mortgaged for as long as these individuals are in-charge. So we must fight. We have to fight because it is only after these corrupt regimes have been deposed that we can even consider raising an army of teachers, like you say, to teach truth to our children."

"What about electing a new government?"

"Is that a serious question?" There was an almost imperceptible trace of anger to Yao's voice. "On what continent do you live? When was the last time that free and fair elections were held in this country? Why do you think it is possible for the same person to successfully stay in power for over a quarter of a century even though elections are held regularly? How can one hope to win when the opponent in an election is also the referee? You are not that naive, are you?"

I did not have anything to say to that. I knew that the continent was noted for political leaders who had been in power for longer than I had been alive. Electoral fraud was the name of the game. "And what if you succeed to chase out the present government? What then?" I pressed on. "For how long can you maintain an ideal state of things before human nature expresses corruption once again? Forty years? A hundred? What after that? Another self-righteous warrior like your self, who thinks it's his divine right to plunge the country into war in order to save it? At what point shall we start teaching our children that violence is not the way to get to peace, because, more often than not, violence begets violence?"

"Are you blaming me for the violence in the world?"

"You and everybody like you," I said, surprised at my

anger. "You are in such a big hurry to start a war, even though the average citizen will not support you. What does that say about you?"

"Don't you call me a war monger!" Yao's voice had risen an octave.

"Or else what?" I was almost too angry to care.

"Or else I may be forced to remind you that the only reason why you are still alive is because I bargained for your life."

"Oh, you did?" I was not impressed.

"Yes, I did," he answered. "And it is not because I am in love with you, either. I just happen to need the attention that you, alive, and held captive by me, would generate. Your newspaper will make a big deal about it. It will carry the story for as long as I have you. Especially, if you send them a cartoon every month," he chuckled. "Eventually, some major international network will get the story, and our cause will start getting some attention. "

"I don't think I am worth that much to anybody," I said. "Plus, the guys back at the office will figure out that attention is what you want, and they are not cowards. They will not give it to you. What will you do then, huh? Become Joseph Kony and commence a program of child mutilation just to catch international attention and direct it to your so called cause?"

"Hopefully, we will not resort to 'Konyesque' tactics in order to inform the world of our plight. I believe your presence should be sufficient."

Suddenly, he struck a match and the sulfur flared for a moment, lighting up the dark tent.

Yao was the only other person in the tent, and he was naked down to his waist. As he stretched an arm to light a shortened candle, I noticed he had a very interesting looking necklace around his neck. It was formed in the shape of a left hand, and looked like it had been fashioned out of either copper or gold. In the darkness, it was hard to tell.

"Believe me, no paper will resist the story," he said with a smile. "Especially when your fingerprints are found on the weapon that takes away the life of the US Secretary of State." He chuckled again. "Here's a pen and some paper. Maybe your first cartoon could be an attempt to vindicate yourself, especially as everyone will soon figure out that the plan to which she succumbed was intimately known to you long before her visit. The world should at least hear why you think you are not the, hallucinating trigger man, don't you think?"

"But why should I expose my own plan in a cartoon even before I execute it?"

"Because you are crazy. Which perfectly fits the profile of the classic unaided, looney, partly deluded assassin who is trying to rid the world of evil." He did not stop laughing as he slipped into a jacket, buttoned it down and stepped out of the tent.

As he stretched a muscled arm to light a shortened candle, I noticed that he had a very interesting looking necklace around his neck...

CHAPTER TWENTY-NINE

My conversation with Yao left me shaken, confused, and totally numb. How did I get here? Who was Jean Pierre, and why had he betrayed me? What day was this? All these questions without answers. Had the US Secretary of State been assassinated? Had my prints been found on the murder weapon? Was my name and picture making a tour of the networks as the suspected assassin? Will any one ever believe that I had not been the finger behind the trigger? Would I even survive to tell my story? My life was over. I was beginning to understand how powerful political figures like JFK, and probably lots more had been shot by *that unaided, crazy dude,* because, somehow, I had ended up wearing his shoes.

It was getting harder to think about it while maintaining the grueling pace of the march. We had been marching all day, and my body, which had not had any food, or a chance to recuperate from the beating, was screaming in protest.

The circumstances that led Yao to break camp and move his army further into the jungle was not known to me, but I suspected that it was strategic in nature. He was not one to move his whole army for the fun of it. Either something was going on, or something was getting ready to go on. No one was saying anything and I was not about to ask. One did not ask too many questions around here.

The wounds and cuts that had been inflicted upon me during my 'welcome ceremony' were getting infected, swollen, and beginning to smell. There was nothing I could do about it. I ground my teeth and kept moving, even refusing to acknowledge the pebble in my left shoe. It was clear to me that any attempt to catch my breath or empty out my shoe would invite someone's wrath. I had had enough of rifle butts, and, come to think of it, the pebble in the shoe was not that bad. Instead, I mouthed a silent prayer, begging for a rest stop, while I did my best to keep up with the brutal pace of the march.

Twenty hours later, we were still going.

I was so exhausted that I was becoming convinced that the right thing to do would be to let myself slide to the ground and just deal with the consequences, -most probably, another beating. Surprisingly, that did not sound so bad now compared to the pain that was shooting up my legs and back. Who knows, maybe a good beating would help to black everything out. Forever. Did that make me suicidal? Did it matter? The reality was that on a tiny planet in one of the universe's infinite number of galaxies, a man had come to the end of his physical strength.

I staggered, but somehow stayed on my feet, willing myself to move, to take another step. Desperately, I searched my mind for some unknown iota of encouragement that I knew I did not possess. It was hard for me to believe that my pleading prayer for a rest stop had gone unanswered.

I staggered again, and this time my body came to a halt. I could not come up with another step. The man behind me swore.

"Move," he sneered menacingly. I tried, but the effort proved insufficient. "Move," he repeated, cursing aloud. I sensed the kick, even before the leg made contact with my back, sending me flying into grateful oblivion.

"Rest stop!" I heard the order called from far ahead as my tired body hit the ground. And I just lay there, on my back, in pain, in chains, thirsty, hungry, and breathing harshly through my mouth.

"Sit up!" I opened my eyes. It was one of Yao's men. He was holding out a calabash of something, probably water, I thought. But I was too exhausted to move, so the man placed the calabash by my chained ankles and walked off. After what seemed like an eternity, I managed to roll over and drag the calabash of water to my parched lips. Water had never tasted so good and I drank for a long time. Between sips, I glanced around, trying to get a better idea of where we were. It was hopeless. I could see only the foliage of big forest trees that were blocking out the light. Yao's men were all around, already impatient for the next orders from the rebel leader.

I, on the other hand, wanted nothing less than a parmenent stop so I could go to sleep. Maybe I can make it happen, I thought, allowing myself a cynical smile. Was God not on my side? Had I not prayed to him for a rest break? And had he not granted my wish twenty hours later? Had he not? How had he known that I had exactly twenty hours of marching in me? How had he known that? How had he known that it was better to leave me to suffer for twenty hours? How?

I could feel the bitter bile rising to my mouth. Anyway, God, I thought, it is time for you to stop being a figment of my imagination. You see, I have come to the end of my strength, and being God, you must know this. You must know that if I am asked to march any more today, I shall surely die. My wounds are seriously infected, I have a headache, my body feels very light in a strange kind of way, and my temperature is rising quickly. So, with everything that I have, in the furthest reaches of my soul, I ask you to make this rest stop a long one. Or do I need to make it into a declaration for this to be manifested? Surely that should work, no? Does the book of Job not say that if a man declares something it will be established onto him? Do the prophets not teach that our thoughts, intentions and words will create our reality? So therefore, God, I believe and declare that this rest stop is a long one, and it is established unto me...

"Break out and build camp," a new order came down the line, interrupting my words. "We shall stay here for some time. Stay close to camp and always within sight of a comrade."

Oh God! Thank you, thank you God. Thank you. Tears flooded my eyes, washing away my cynism and I just let my bladder go. A moment later, I was dreaming.

When I woke, my whole body was aching, and I had been chained to a big tree. It was dark again, but it felt like I had been sleeping for just a moment. Painfully, I peered around. In the moonlight, I could barely see the silhouette of Yao's hurriedly built camp around me. It was on an easily defended hillside and I could make out many tents among the trees. Apart from the sentries, there were only a few people up, and most of them were gathered around a small fire. The rest of the camp was asleep. From where I was, I could not see Yao's tent, but I knew it would not be too far.

My stomach growled, reminding me that I had not eaten in some days. I reached over and brought the calabash of water to my mouth. Slowly I drank some more, listening at the same time to more abdominal growls that refused to be pacified by an aquatic diet.

I looked around again, wondering if there was anything I could eat. I could not tell in the dark if there were any fruit to these trees, or if they were even fruit bearing trees at all. I had to get food. Somehow. I knew that no one would give me anything to eat. Not yet, anyway. I had read a well researched, *Jeune Afrique* article about Yao which held that he kept his prisoners by starving them to a point where they would not have the energy to even dream of escaping.

Slowly, I began crawling on the dew sodden grass, inching and feeling my way around, looking for whatever could be eaten. I had almost covered all of the territory that the chain would allow, when I noticed that a man had appeared in the shadows between the tents to my left, and he seemed to be wandering towards me. Silently, I prayed for the man to be a sentry on watch, and not some commander whose sleep had been disturbed by my clinking chains. Another beating would be the last straw. I stopped all movement and lay very still. The man got to where I was, stopped, and sat down right next to my head. Then he reached out and stuck something into the lock that held my chains. It fell open.

"Can you get to your feet?"

"You?" I recognized the voice immediately

"Shhh," Jean Pierre said. He had painted himself a dark chocolate. He had also covered his hair with a kneaded wool cap and in the poor light he looked convincing as one of Yao's men.

For a moment I did not know what to think. Jean Pierre the French man had come back. Could I trust him? Was this another ploy? But what options did I have, anyway?

"I can get up if you help me," I whispered, glancing furtively around. "I am in pain."

"Here, drink this," he whispered back. Suddenly my nose picked up the pungent smell of some potent alcoholic brew. Jean Pierre was holding out a flat shiny flask. Hastily, I seized it and poured the burning contents down my throat. I did not stop drinking until the flask was empty. The burning warmth was like healing magic, spreading from my stomach, seeping into my aching muscles, soothing, numbing, and transforming everything into a dreamy reality with which I could suddenly cope. "There is a huge rock at the bottom of this slope. You cannot miss it. Meet me there in five minutes." I nodded.

As casually as possible, he got to his feet and strolled off. Once he was out of sight, I made sure no one was watching me before crawling as quickly and as quietly as I could to the edge of the dark camp. No one shouted. Then I was on my knees, then on my feet, doubled over, half running and half limping.

When I found the rock, Jean Pierre was already there, waiting. We set off immediately into the dark jungle. Guided by the light of the moon and using the stars as a compass, we set a northeastern trajectory. A half hour later we came upon a little brook, where we quenched our thirsts, filled a water bottle that Jean Pierre had produced before setting off again. There was still no sign of pursuit, but I knew that the thought was at the back of both our minds.

"We have nine hours of darkness before the sun comes up," said Jean Pierre when he finally spoke. "If no one misses you before then, that would be a good head start."

"Or maybe Yao might decide that I am not that important anymore," I replied, breathing hard as we struggled up a muddy hillside.

"He may, but I doubt it," Jean Pierre answered. "At this point you are central to his plans, and I don't think he would let you off so easily."

"Central to his plans?" I asked. "How did I get to be so central to his plans? Can you tell me that? Or maybe you want to tell me instead how you've played me all along."

"Listen, I am sorry..."

"You are sorry?" I demanded. "You lied to me about everything from your motives, to the nature of your relationship with Yves Mammon with whom you were working from the beginning. He knew about me, and he knew about our trip. He was the one who told Yao's men to expect us, which explains why I was the only one who was beaten when we arrived at his camp. Then, when I needed you to testify about your own story, you betrayed me. Are you aware that anything could have happened to me?"

Jean Pierre climbed over a huge tree root, turned around to help me, but I was too angry to let him. "What else did you lie to me about?" I asked, brushing his hand away "That is, apart from your name."

"My real name is Jean. Not Jean Pierre. Jean Paul. I am Jean Paul le Sage", he said, looking directly into my eyes. "And I am sorry that I lied to you about a few things, but it was necessary."

"Necessary?"

"Yes, necessary. Would you have come, or let me come along if you had known that I was working with Yves? Would you have agreed to come here knowing that Yao would take you prisoner? I don't think so. And even if, by some happenstance you had, it was a chance I was not willing to take. For that, I am sorry, but I also knew that Yao would want you alive for a while. So, to my understanding, you were not in, shall we say, immediate fatal danger."

"Is that right?" I could feel my temper rising "What if you had gotten lost in the jungle as you returned to Yao's camp, which seems to be moving all the time! What if a crocodile had attacked you on your return trip, or one of Yao's men had recognized you once in the camp, or..."

"Apart from the camp which moved, forcing me to track it

down deeper into the forest, none of those things happened," Jean cut in, "You are here and you are alive."

"And I am supposed to be grateful that you saved my life?" I asked, spitting in disgust. "What about the fact that if you had not jeopardized my life in the first place, there would not have arisen a need to save it? Did you think about that?" I demanded, pushing him out of my way and forging ahead into the dark forest.

"Look here Abanda..."

"Don't you Abanda me!" Now I was angry. "Do you know what the word means? Roughly it means 'brother', and you my friend, cannot call me by that anymore. You know why? Because a deer would never send its own brother into the lion's den.

"Come on Abanda...,"

I lost my temper. I cannot fully remember what happened or how it happened, but Jean Pierre and I were suddenly rolling and grappling all over the ground, punching, tearing, biting, and kicking.

"Who are you?" I screamed, applying pressure to the headlock in which I had secured his head. In response, I felt his sharp teeth digging into my arm and I let go. A thundering fist exploded into the side of my head, stunning me for a moment.

"My name is Jean Paul and my father was monsieur Le Sage," he huffed, circling warily.

"What about Yves," I asked, feinting to the left. He fell for it and my right leg shot out connecting with his abdomen. He went down. "Is he also the son of Mammon?" I landed another one to his ribs.

"No, he is not," Jean answered from the ground with a scissor kick to my swollen ankles. I stumbled and collided into a trunk. "He was the son of Mammon but now he is dead," Jean panted, getting to his feet. "I killed him..."

"Liar." I kicked out. My foot connected with his right knee and he came crashing down beside me. Quickly, I landed a flurry of punches to his exposed head, drawing blood, but regretting the fact that I was too weak to cause any real damage.

"I also took away the rifle that had your finger prints," Jean huffed, pushing me off, rolling away and coming up on one knee.

"How do I know that you are not lying?"

"Two things," Jean said. "First of all, I have the rifle hidden a little way ahead and you can see it when we get there.

Secondly, you will have the opportunity to fish out Yves's corpse from where I hid it. Maybe you would like to perform a post mortem, *oui*?"

"And why did you kill him?"

Jean coughed and spat out some thick blood filled phlegm.

"I will tell you," he said breathing hard, "But first we need a little peace around here. I am getting too old to be fighting and talking at the same time." I did not bother to reply. I was breathing too hard to speak.

"It goes back a little ways," he said. "A century ago, the British realized that one of the best covers for English spies in other countries was the Royal Geographic Society. It was very successful, so France was more than willing to borrow a page from this book. The French teams were instructed to scout out and list all mineral deposits in French colonies. They were also expected to hide all findings from the locals and report all progress to Paris." Jean spat out again. "Yves went along with this plan, but only up to a certain point. For Cameroon, he had kept two separate lists, one for Paris, and one for himself. And they were both different. Yves's list, which he always had on him, was the accurate one, with maps, landmarks, measurements, and all the necessary details that pinpointed important mineral deposits. It even listed the precise location of a small diamond field..."

"Is that the source of your money?"

"Indirectly, yes. Yves had made a few trips to this field, so when I searched his place and found a small bag of rough, uncut stones, I decided to get the list. I felt that in the wrong hands, it would fan the flames of a war that would be tempered only by greed. Most imperialist nations, with that list in their hands, would manufacture all kinds of excuses to put boots on the ground. It has happened before. The strategic location of this country, coupled with the quality and quantity of mineral deposits, would be considered well worth the effort, and blood will flow for money. And I could not discuss it with Yves. First of all, I did not expect him to understand, and secondly, I did not want my opinion on the matter, known in Paris. The only way to handle it, I decided, was to have him in a remote location, with the maps, where I could bring up the issue, and force things to a showdown. This trip seemed perfect. I knew that he would bring a map to the meeting in Yao's camp as a way of impressing his own importance upon the rebel leader..."

"My name is Jean Paul and my father was monsieur Le Sage," he huffed, circling warily...

" And to be invited, you had to bring me."

"Yes," Jean answered, looking at me. "Yves instructed me to follow him into Yao's camp, with you, where we would be expected."

"What about the story of the US Secretary of State, the Chinese, the impending war...?"

"All of that is true..."

"And your relationship with Yves, you guys were actually partners before you turned on him, right?"

"It was not like that..."

"Of course it was not," I retorted sarcastically.

"Sure, he and I had an understanding and we were working together. I saw it as my opportunity to quietly make a fortune and start a new life full of dreams that had almost been forgotten."

"So what happened?"

"Yves had other plans. He decided to actually go ahead and orchestrate a regime change without a green light from France. He had become friends with Yao, and he wanted nothing more than to have the man as president. He even showed me copies of contracts that he was drawing up, contracts that would grant him extensive mining rights all over the country once Yao got on top. That was where I changed my mind. I was willing to make money, but causing a bloody regime change just to do it, in my mind, was crossing the line. After I met my girlfriend I began thinking of getting out. By the time she was three months pregnant I was actively planning an opposition."

"Wasn't Yves worried that the French government would come after him? After all, Paris has invested a lot of time into the current regime. They would like to tweak it. Not break it."

"That's true, but Yves had calculated that by the time Paris figured out what was going on, it would be too late. By then Yao would be inches away from the presidency."

"And where would Yves hide after that? In this country?"

"Probably, Yes. At least, for some time. Not only would he have Yao's new government behind him, he'd collected enough dirt on the French government to hold them in check. His focus was on the money. He believed that destiny had put him here, at this time, for that reason. He saw himself as the remnant of a great generation that had the balls to venture out into the wild world and defy the elements in order to seize and plunder the moment. And Yao, as president, would make all of that possible for him. Yao was the key." Jean Pierre coughed. "So he decided that he needed another man to be set up as the fall guy in the Secretary of State's undoing, someone that was not part of Yao's army, someone that Yao himself would later be able to give up to the international community as the true culprit behind the assassination. Without that, Yves reasoned that Yao would remain on the list of wanted terrorists, a fact that could complicate things for him and his partners, especially with the Americans."

"So you decided that I was the perfect fall guy?"

"Not me. Yves. He picked you out and then instructed me to engage you in a self incriminating cartoon story, which I did."

"Did you think about the damage to my character if the cartoon story got public?"

"Yes, very much so. Apart from that, my girlfriend would have my balls if anything happened to you. I had calculated that Yves would leave for Yao's camp before myself, which he did, giving me ample time to prevent the cartoon story from being published by arranging for the press team to be picked up. And like I said, I was certain that Yao was not going to want to shoot you, because it would not be in his best interests. At least, not with the way he and Yves had it planned out."

I digested this, feeling revulsion. "And you could not discuss any of this with me?"

"You would not have understood..."

"Not have understood?" Classic, I thought, giving him a dirty look. "Really? And why is that? Because I'm too stupid? What makes you think you are smarter than anyone else?"

"You know that's not what I meant. I use the word 'understand' in the context of 'accepting' and 'becoming flexible about another person's position and beliefs'. I was not implying any doubts on your ability to grasp the idea or the concept," Jean said looking at me. "You didn't have to play the race card," he added sourly.

"Oh, is that what that was? The race card?"

"Of course, and you know it too."

"Come on Jean, are you telling me that it is not possible for me, or anyone who looks like me, to point out that your attitude comes across as superior, without it being racial?" I asked. " Do you remember the second time we met? You swore that you were telling me everything! Remember that? But you were lying. All of your actions suggest that you know what's best for me. By not consulting me on a plan in which my own life would be on the line, portrays me as disposable and you as superior. And by claiming that everything was under control is definitely playing God. Are you saying that I would not have noticed, or even mentioned this superior god-playing-attitude of yours if you had not been Caucasian?"

"No, I am saying that it is too easy for everyone else to accuse white people of acting superior. I am saying that these accusations are almost always given subtle, racial undertones that only poison the atmosphere, worsen racial suspicion, and render communication more difficult."

"I agree, but why is that? Why is there so much mistrust between the races? Do you think it is because, from the colonial days, imperialist western governments have always maltreated and discriminated against local people, 'for their own good'? We all know what happened in the Middle East, Asia, Australia, Africa, and the Americas, where indigenous people were subjected to racism white supremacy and humiliating discrimination. And it is still going on today! Which makes me think it is the main reason why there is so much racial suspicion in the world. Granted, a lot of progress has been made, but there is still a lot that needs to be done, especially when we think about the fact that there exist powerful, mostly conservative forces, that are fighting to maintain the racist status quo, particularly in Europe."

"Particularly in Europe? What do you mean?"

"Just that. There is much more racism in Europe than in America."

"Really? Are you sure that this is not your bias against the French?"

"Oh come off it! I don't need bias to prove that French foreign policy is shit. Not only do former French colonies have the worst economies in all of Africa, but there is certainly more racism in Europe than in the United States, which, by the way, has elected a black man to the white house. Even as we speak, it is common to find overt displays of raci-nazism in Europe. In fact, the racism in Europe even has a choir, made up of soccer fans whose deep seated insecurity and cowardly sense of self has gotten them frothing at the mouth at the possibility of belonging to a Hitler-youth type movement. And sadly enough, most Europeans carry on, insisting that 'things are not that bad'. It is shameful."

"What about the discrimination that exists against blacks in Latin America, North Africa, The middle east, India and China? Is that also the work of Caucasians?" Jean challenged.

"No, it is not," I answered, "but the nature of the discrimination is the same; directed against darker skin; an attitude that gained global prevalence only with the establishment and propagation of the transatlantic slave trade."

"And what of Zimbabwe and present day South Africa, where white minorities are being discriminated against?" Jean interjected. "I know it's a reaction but is that not racism just because it is against white folk? What do you say to that?"

"I say that it is racism, I say that it is very sad, and I seriously condemn any injustices that have been, and are being heaped on white people in these countries, but lets not forget how it started."

"Agreed, but it is still a shame that it is not being talked about as much." Jean added.

"I agree."

For a long moment we were both silent, mutually realizing that the long tentacles of racist suspicion had followed us all the way into the rainforest, and was being a poison even now.

"Something needs to be done differently."

"Yes, and the media has an extremely huge role to play in it. They have to start framing things differently."

"Yes, I..."

The shots rang out, taking us by surprise and galvanizing both of us into action.

"Quick. Over this way," I said sliding down the muddy hillside."

"Can you see anyone?" Jean asked, coming down behind me. Differences or not, we were going to need each other to get out alive, that much was obvious.

"Over to the left, by those trees." But more gunfire drowned out my answer, and all I could do was dive for cover. "Over there by the trees," I repeated, shouting into Jean's ear.

"But it doesn't seem to be directed at us."

"Maybe not, but I am not standing up to find out." I said, sliding away. He followed as even more gunfire erupted in the darkness. I noticed that it was not coming from the last position. Obviously, someone else was here, not just Yao's men. The night was coming alive with action and we seemed to be sandwiched right in the middle of things. It looked like the French government had already missed Jean and Yves, and pressure had been put on the Cameroon government to rescue the two French 'hikers' from Yao's claws. It was the only plausible reason that was coming to mind.

"We have to get out of here," I said. "I am not so sure that the government forces will have an easy time with this." He nodded in agreement and began slithering away.

I set off after him, staying as low as was possible. A few minutes later the ground began rising, and before I knew it we were some way up a cliff face, with the forest below.

"Luckily, the moon is staying behind those clouds," Jean said, disappearing behind a rocky outcrop some distance above my head. "We are sufficiently out of the danger from gunfire and we can afford to take our time with this cliff," his voice came floating down.

And then it started to rain. First, it was just a mist, and then a drizzle. The first actual rain drops came when we were more than half way up the cliff.

"Maybe choosing to scale this cliff was the mistake," I said, reaching for a rocky hold above my head.

"Just follow my path and everything will be alright. I have been up and down a few cliffs in my time and this one is ok, believe me. Just stay focused and take your time."

At that same instant the ledge on which my weight was resting, gave way. Instinctively I shouted in fear, clawing onto the rock face as my body swung out of balance. Oh God! The strain of my weight on my arms was just too much as I struggled to hold on. Then the tip of my searching toes felt what seemed like a little platform. Slowly I breathed out, gingerly bringing my weight to rest on the invisible platform and reducing the strain on my arms.

Then the platform gave way as well.

Several rocks were dislodged from the cliff face, and they went crashing into the forest below and I suddenly found myself in mid air. Jean's arm, which had miraculously found a hold on my shirt collar, was the only thing keeping me from falling with the rocks.

"Quick, do something," he whispered harshly. The strain of my whole weight was audible. I tried to angle my head in order to gauge how vulnerable his hold was, but it proved impossible. Instead I assumed the *vitruvian position*, spreading out my arms and legs as far to the sides as was possible. After what seemed like a lifetime, my left hand felt something, probably a thick vine, or a root. I grabbed it.

"Let go," I croaked and Jean did. I could hear him breathing harshly above my head. "I think I found a tree that will probably take us to the top of the cliff. But we have to climb it separately because I am not sure how deep the roots go, or how strong the tree itself is."

"Okay Abanda. You go first." I did not argue.

By the time I made it to the top of the cliff it was raining very hard, and from the sounds of it, the fighting down below had become more intense. My ears could pick up the chatterring from heavy artillery fire.

"Looks like Yao and his men are getting much more than they bargained for," Jean said as we climbed over the edge.

"Are they now?" Yao's disembodied voice asked, surprising both of us. "I would think that you and your friend are in a worse predicament, don't you think? Especially, since it is now obvious that we are not on the same side." For a moment the moon showed its face and Yao's outline became visible for a second before everything went dark again.

He was standing about ten paces away from the cliff edge and there were about three or four men with him. It was too dark to be sure.

"Maybe you are right," I heard Jean say as I quietly lowered myself to the ground and began creeping away. "But then again, you could be wrong and wouldn't that be a shame? Think of

what would happen if you mistook your best friends for your
enemies," Jean added.

"You are good with words," Yao chuckled, "but that is all
they are, empty words."

"And how empty are they, would you say? Like the four
military trucks that drove straight into your ambush a few days
ago? Who do you think tipped you off? Think of what your men
would be doing right now if you had not taken those trucks. If
you kill me now as you are obviously contemplating, who will
be the source of your next tip? Your grandmother? If you know
what is good for you, you will send some of your men to escort
us out of this jungle and back to civilization."

Yao laughed. "So, you knew about the convoy, so what?"
he asked. "That just means you may know too much, that's all.
And by the way, what do you think we should do about that?"

Before Jean could reply, there was a flash of lightning,
which illuminated the cliff edge scene for another quick second.
For the first time Yao noticed that I was not standing by Jean's
side anymore.

"DAMN!" he swore jumping forward. "THE
JOURNALIST! GET HIM! GET HIM!" I heard Yao screaming
frantically and his men reacted with several gunshots. Just then
there was another flash of lightening and I saw Jean stagger. It
was the last thing I saw before the darkness covered everything
again.

"ALIVE!" Yao Shouted above the din. "I NEED THEM
ALIVE!"

Frenetically, I crawled away through the trees, counting on
the darkness for cover and seeking to put as much distance
between myself and the cliff's edge. But the sound of heavy
boots to my left and right indicated that I was not going fast
enough. Desperately, I began looking around. There was a low
branch directly overhead. Quickly, I reached up and hoisted
myself upwards. I disappeared into the thick foliage as lighting
flashed, illuminating once more, the ground below. I saw a man
come rushing through the very spot where I had been lying just
seconds ago. And then it was dark again.

"Quick, do something," he whispered harshly...

"HE IS HERE SOMEWHERE!" It was Yao's voice. "FIND HIM," he shouted into the night, "AND USE YOUR DAMNED FLASHLIGHTS IF YOU HAVE TO."

Simultaneously, several flashlights were turned on, throwing shafts of bluish white light into the dark and rainy forest.

Up to this date, I am not exactly certain as to what happened after those flashlights were turned on, except that it probably gave away Yao's position to some government troops who had been manning an adjacent hill. I just remember that there was a sudden volley of rapid machinegun fire that took everyone on the ground by surprise. A moment later, all four flashlights were lying on the wet grass, projecting streams of light at angles that suggested the bearers were no longer in possession of them.

The chatter of machinegun fire continued for another full minute, the time it took for all four bulbs to be shot out, and for whoever was firing to realize that there was no return fire.

With the firing at an end, I waited for another ten minutes without moving. There was no sign or noise from the ground, that is, apart from the fighting that was obviously raging on at the bottom of the cliff.

When I was satisfied that it was safe to venture down, I began the process, with all the care and silence that the world could afford, gingerly letting my body slide down the wet tree stem until my feet felt the ground.

When the moon showed its face again I saw that there were bodies all around. Even Yao had been shot several times. I rushed over to Jean who was lying on his face by the edge of the cliff. Carefully, I turned him over and he grunted. He was wounded, almost unconscious, but he was alive.

Quickly, I raised him to a sitting position, and then to standing.

"Abanda," he whispered weakly, falling against me. "You have to leave now. I will slow you down too much." He was already breathing with difficulty. "Tell my children that I love them." He began to wilt, and I had to prop him up.

"You are coming along with me buddy," I said to him. He did not hear me. He was already unconscious.

With his full weight leaning against me, I felt a new sense of apprehension. I knew that I was strong by most standards, but these circumstances were anything but standard. My whole body was still aching and we were still a long way from civilization. Would I be up to it? I knew that Yao's successor was sure to take it as a personal vendetta to bring to book those who had caused the rebel leader to venture out of his camp to a sudden death, namely me. Apart from that, recapturing me will cement his position as the new leader of the rebel army. Plus, just like Yao, he would also love the publicity that holding me would bring. With Jean, I would be very lucky to make it out alive.

Bending low, I picked him up, balanced his weight over my shoulder and turned to walk away, when my eye noticed something.

Yao had fallen on his back, and in the process his shirt had ridden up to cover his bloody face, exposing his bare chest. Around his neck was the hand shaped necklace that I had glimpsed a few days ago in the tent. Instinctively, I went down on one knee, grabbed the necklace, and pulled sharply. It held. I tugged harder and there was a little click. The fastener gave, and the necklace came free.

With the weight of Jean's body on my shoulder, I limped off into the dark, rainy forest. The hyenas would be here soon. I wanted to be as far away as possible when they came.

$\mathcal{M}$any hours later I reached the Manyu River. It was over-flooded from the incessant rain, and I knew that crossing it with Jean on my shoulder was going to be quite a task.

That is, if I decided to continue with him.

I was exhausted and in too much pain to continue bearing his weight. Plus, I was becoming certain that if I did not leave him behind both of us were going to die. Some men, I suspect from Yao's camp, had picked up my trail, and were not far behind. Once or twice I even heard noises indicating that they were closer than expected. Or maybe it was the hyenas. Whatever the case, it was obvious that I had run out of time.

So, why not leave Jean here? It wasn't as if I had a lot of alternatives. The decision could be the difference between life and death. But could I abandon a man and be able to live with myself? I could argue that my action was well grounded in reason. Did that cancel the fact that he had risked his own life to save my country from war? Or that I would have crashed to my death at the bottom of the cliff if he had not been there? And I was thinking of repaying him with abandonment.

Desperately, I scanned the riverbank. I had to be careful as well. Manyu river was noted for crocs, hippos, snakes and probably a few other things that I was not aware of. Getting trapped by a hungry python was not something I wanted to experience.

About twenty meters downstream there was a tree with some big rocks around its base. It's thickly foliaged, low spreading branches would provide some shade and keep us out of sight. It was not the best spot for a rest, but under the circumstances it would have to do. I was in too much pain to go about finding something better.

I limped over to the tree, choose the most convenient spot beneath it, and lowered Jean onto the wet ground. He grunted unconsciously and lay still.

The relief on my back was immediate. What a difference! I leaned back against one of the rocks and stretched. Oh God. That felt so good. I took a series of deep mouth breaths, feeling the air go all the way down into my abdomen, and savoring the feeling. Then I got up from the stone and winced. My right ankle was on fire. Tentatively, I transferred my weight to the other leg, not knowing what to expect.

"Don't move," a voice said behind me. I was too tired to do anything else, anyway. "Are you alone?" Where had I heard that voice before? Yao's camp? Probably.

Silently, I cursed my luck, hoping that, somehow, this was just a bad dream. But the more I waited to wake up from sleep, the more it dawned on me that this was real. I was not going to get up from sleep because, the voice, the rain, the rain forest, the wounded man,... were all real.

Whatever it was, be it destiny, fate, chance, serendipity, badluck or just a bad decision, it had brought me to this end, and it was too late now. 'Spilled milk', as the English would say.

"Do you have any weapons?" It was the same voice.

"No," I answered still wondering about the voice.

"Turn around."

I did not argue. When I saw the man, my shock was more than total. "Sa...Sango?!" I stammered, not wanting to believe what I was seeing. It was Sango, alright! My neigbor from back home! He was cradling an AK 47 that was pointed at my stomach.

"You?" he whispered. "What are you doing here?" He was obviously shocked to see me as well, and for a moment we just stood there, staring at each other. The AK was still looking at me.

The last time we had seen each other, his wife had been dying and I had given him the money from Jean so he could take her to the hospital.

"What are you doing here?" I whispered back.

"I joined Yao's Liberation Army."

"You what?"

"Yes, I am now a member of the Y.L.A."

"But why?"

"Because it was the best thing to do."

"The best thing to do? What about your family?"

Sango looked away. "My wife did not make it," he said. "She died before they could operate. The doctor said we had wasted too much time before getting her to the hospital." His chagrin was obvious.

"And your children?"

"I sent them to the village. They are with my parents," he replied.

"But they need you, Sango. They need a father, especially since their mother is no more."

"I thought so too," he chuckled bitterly. "But I was wrong. What they need, more than ever, is an army that will stand up and fight for the soul of this country, an army that will make sure that children like mine will not die such senseless deaths anymore," he added bitterly, suddenly sounding like Yao himself.

"But Sango," I persuaded, "It is you they need more than anything else..."

"No."

"Yes, ..."

"Shut up! You are my prisoner, now," he murmured, raising the weapon. "It is people like you, who refuse to join the cause, that are making us weaker."

"Really?" I could not believe what I was hearing. Desperately, I racked my brain for something to say. "But how can you say that Sango?" I asked, taking an imperceptible step towards him. The weapon was still trained on me. "Are you telling me, that for a man to lay down his weapon in order to become a father, is a weakness? Were you a weaker man before your wife died? Is that why she died?" I took another little step forward. "And was it because you were not yet involved in Yao's war? Or because you were trying hard to be a good father to those little angels?"

"I said, shut up!" Sango hissed.

If I was going to do anything, now was the time.'Soon', would be too late. If only I could distract him... "Can you swear on your parent's life that your late wife is happy in the afterlife with the decision you have made to abandon her children?"

"Do you know what 'Shut up' means? Or do I have to spell it out?"

"Don't avoid the question." I insisted, sensing a crack.

"I said 'shut your mouth!" There was an ugly look in his eyes.

307

"Or else what? You will shoot me? In cold blood? I am sure your wife will approve as well, no?"

Just then, there was a sudden disturbance in the brushes a little way off.

"Did you find anything?" a new voice shouted from some distance. As clearly as day, I saw Sango hesitate. I could hear the seconds ticking away loudly in my head, as the moment seemed to stretch for an eternity. Then he cupped his free hand around his mouth and spoke up.

"No, nothing here," he shouted back. "I think he went upriver. I will join you guys in a minute. I am taking a shit."

My legs almost gave way from relief.

"All right, but hurry," the other voice floated back. "We don't have much time. It will be morning soon," it added, moving away. I was still free. I could not believe it!

"If you stay by the river you will be alright," Sango whispered to me, turning to move away.

"Wait, Sango!" I whispered back. "You don't have to go with these men."

"Listen, Abanda," Sango said, without breaking stride, "I have done my good deed for the day. Take advantage and leave now before I change my mind."

"I have something in my possession that is worth a lot of money," I added hurriedly, bringing Sango to a halt. "Millions probably. You could start a new life. I know your wife is no more, but think of the change that it would make in your children's future. With that kind of money, you could fight for change through avenues, other than war. Think of all the wives and children who will die if war should break out. You should not be contributing to that." For a moment Sango was silent. "And Yao is dead," I added.

"Yao is dead?" Sango raised the AK menacingly. "Are you crazy?" he snarled.

"No, I am not," I whispered. "I saw him die."

"You saw Yao die?" Sango took a step forward. "You know, Yao will cut out any tongue that dares to spread such a story about him."

"Which is why I will never dare to say something like that if it were not true. You know that I am not lying. And without him, his army will split up or simply disintegrate." I pressed in my advantage. "Even before his death, Yao's cause was not getting any real attention. That is not going to change much. As we speak, his army is in dire need of weapons." Sango was silent. "That is not going to change as well." I persuaded. "Get out now while you can, Sango. Please. Think of your sweet children."

The man studied me for a long minute "And this thing in your possession. The one that is worth a lot of money. What is it?" he asked, hesitantly. "Can I see it? Can you tell me more about it?"

I had searched Jean and found Yves's list, with its accompanying map tucked away in his belt. I took it out now .

"This is a map that will make us rich. See, right over here," I whispered, with my forefinger on the map, "is a small, unknown, diamond field in the eastern province, that will belong to us. And if that is not what we want to do, we can pursue other options. I know people who will pay a lot of money for this piece of paper," I said. "But we need to get out of here first. With him." I concluded, pointing at Jean.

Sango thought about it for a moment. I could see his mind weighing the options. Finally the need to reunite with his children won. "Okay, but we have to hurry. There are more men heading this way, and it will be day soon. If they find us it will be over for me. Abandoning the YLA is a crime that is punishable by death. Lets go."

"Okay," I agreed, realizing once more that chance,... no, wait, destiny, or was it God, had taken care of the situation. For the first time in several hours, I felt real hope. With Sango to help, it was beginning to look as if my death had actually been postponed for real. Wordlessly, I offered a prayer of gratitude as we picked up the unconscious French man and set out into the dark and wet rainforest.

Los Angeles, California

*T*he Los Angeles international airport was a far cry from the one I had left in Douala. First of all, it looked cleaner, even smelled clean, and to my greatest surprise, police and immigration officers were actually polite.

The complex was big, busy and just as noisy. There were people and luggage everywhere. But everything seemed to be running efficiently. It was so efficient that within my first hour on the ground, my passport, which had sailed right through

Charles de Gaulle, was detected as a fake, and I was pulled off the line to be processed 'differently'.

"Is this your first time in L.A.?" the driver asked eighty hours later, as he sent the Chrysler surging away from the airport.

"First time in America," I answered, pulling the jacket tighter around my body and buttoning it up to the neck.

"First time, and you breeze in with a fake passport? What were you thinking?"

I took a deep breath. "I am sorry for any inconvenience that this situation may have caused." I only had wanted to get out of Cameroon. "So, where are you taking me and what can I expect to happen to me at this point?" I asked looking out the window. "Will I be deported?"

Before he could answer me, a phone in the car began ringing. He touched a button on the dashboard and spoke into what I assumed was a microphone. "We have just left the airport complex. We should be there in about a half hour if there is no more crazy traffic."

"And the subject is with you, I assume?" the voice at the other end asked.

"Yes," the driver answered, before fingering another button on the dashboard as he glanced at me through the rearview mirror.

"I am taking you to where you will be staying," he said to me. "In the meantime, the immigration department will check your story to make sure that you are the person you are claiming to be." He paused. "And if the results prove beyond reasonable doubt that you are telling the truth, you may be put in a queue for people waiting to get a work permit, a social security number, a green card and a status that could well set you on your way to naturalization as a US citizen." He paused again. "But if your story is found wanting, you will be on the next plane back to Cameroon."

I shuddered at the thought, thinking of the situation that I had left behind.

Running into Sango in the forest had transformed my predicament. With his help, it had become easier to get the wounded Frenchman out of the jungle. Together, we carried him, hiding during the day, moving at night, and even building a raft at one point, a device on which we floated downstream all the way to Difa, a tiny village, which boasted a shaman.

Luckily the villagers had not been sympathetic to Yao or his penchant for war, which made everything much easier. The village shaman had cleaned Jean's wounds, dug out part of a bullet that had been lodged below a broken rib, and filled up the opening with foul smelling poultices that left me gagging. Then, accompanied by a deep nasal, sonorous chanting, the wounds had been bandaged. And through it all, Jean had slept *the sleep of almost death*.

It had taken two full days for the man to come back into his body. And then another week before he could sit up.

Once out of the forest, I had also learned about the investigations that Charlie had carried out, and about him getting shot. Luckily, he had been rushed to the hospital just in time to manage a miraculous survival. Back on his feet, he proceeded to stubbornly pursue the rest of the investigation with a vengeance.

But only after combining his findings with some insights from Jean did a clearer picture begin to appear. It turns out that the Cameroonian government had been pestering the French for some time now, asking for additional military support to beef up positions on the oil rich Bakassi peninsula that Nigeria also was claiming. As usual, the French had been reluctant to make any sacrifices, but then the situation had changed when they realized that Cameroon was turning to China for support. Not only did that force France to act, Yves saw it as an opportunity to get a shipment of weapons into Yao's hands. Which is exactly what happened. With the shipment in the country, the weapons were separated from the construction stuff, and handed to a Cameroonian military delegation, which then was expected to convey the goods to the disputed oil rich Bakassi peninsula. But Yves put tracers in some of the boxes so as to be able to pinpoint the exact location and progress of the convoy at all times, which is how he was able to tip off Yao and get him ready for the ambush.

It was quite a story, and it caused a real sensation when it was printed. Especially, since, it theorized that the only reason why the U.S. Secretary of State had not been assassinated was because the planners had failed to get Yao's prints onto the intended weapon. A few other papers had also carried articles on the story, a fact that had further aggravated some of the parties concerned.

Paris had turned livid red, and denial after denial had been issued. One statement went so far as to regret the fact that Cameroon was doing nothing to protect its long friendship with

France. It urged the Yaoundé government to *do something* about *that irresponsible drunk of a cartoonist, whose baseless accusations were rubbing the good French name in mud, and using lies to cause problems among friends'.*

Overnight, even to my own government, I became a *Persona non grata*. I had known that Paris would not rest until I had been successfully portrayed as a conspiratorial lunatic, whose real place was within the walls of some asylum. And in the process, I learned another sad truth, which was that even if it wanted to, the Cameroonian government did not have the wherewithal to protect me, or any of its citizens from French wrath. The pressures of political blackmail seemed overwhelming. Especially in a situation like this. No wonder the ideologies of men like Mugabe and Ghadaffi were so popular on the continent. Both of these men would have stood up for me, I felt. Instead, I had gone underground, and here I was in Los Angeles asking the US government to protect me from the French.

"And you do not deny that your passport is fake, do you?" the officer asked again, coming to a stop as the lights changed to red on a busy street corner. Hanging over the street, from a metal pole, was a green sign with white letters that said 'Wilshire'.

"No, I do not," I answered. "It is a fake document and I take full responsibility for choosing to use it."

Just then the lights turned green, the driver shifted into drive and we made a left into the wide boulevard.

"Who is that?" I asked, pointing at a huge poster of a Hispanic lady. The poster had been mounted on the side of a fifty-foot building. In the picture, the lady, who seemed to be speaking from some kind of stage, was talking into a microphone. At the bottom of the poster were the words: *Africa: as I see it. Saturday, June 3rd from 6pm.* It was a month away.

"She is a professional speaker, I would think," the driver replied, leaning forward and craning his neck to examine the poster as we drove past.

"If I am not put on the next plane back to Cameroon, can I go to that?"

"I cannot give you a definite answer at this time because I do not have the authority. It would depend on what happens between now and then," he concluded. "And call this number if you have any other questions." He handed me a piece of paper over his shoulder.

The poster had been mounted on the side of a fifty-foot building.

CHAPTER THIRTY

$\mathcal{T}$he man adjusted his flowing robes, picking up the hem from the tiled floor as he stepped onto the crowded airport escalator. As usual he attracted a few stares, mainly from people who were not used to seeing a man on stilts, which of course was almost everybody.

Not that he cared. People were stupid like that and he had lived long enough to know it. If they were not staring at him for one thing, then it was another. It was either the stilts, the turban, or the robe, but especially his skin. The staring had been really bad before the surgery, so bad that he had not been able to walk about without throwing a fright into some poor soul. Because of that, he had become a nocturnal being, missing the sun, yet shunning it for the light it shone onto his deformed features.

In due course, medical technology had evolved to the level of aesthetic plastic surgery, and he had employed the very best and the most expensive team of surgeons that money could buy. He had flown them in, and in the comfort of a palatial home, they had given him a new face, a face that allowed him to go out during the day without shocking people.

He got to the top of the escalator and stepped off. To the right was another escalator. He turned left, almost bumping into a group of tourists with tons of bags. Airports were always interesting like that, and although he did not particularly like them, he conceded that they made transportation and communication faster. It was the reason he was here. He needed to pick up an envelope that had been mailed the night before from across the Atlantic. He was so impatient to have it that he'd found it difficult to wait until it got to his mailbox.

He scanned the many signs that were the hallmark of all big airports and finally found the one he was looking for. It was a mailing agency that specialized in super fast, express parcels, and there was a young girl sitting behind the desk.

"Good evening sir," the girl flashed a fake smile. "How can I help you today?"

"I am here to pick up a parcel from London."

"And what is your name?" she asked turning towards a flat screen on the desk.

"Mr. Enoch," the man said. "Mel Enoch." The girl peered at

the screen for a moment.

"Oh, here it is," she said. "It was mailed late last night and got here about half an hour ago," she added, getting off her stool and disappearing into a back door that said 'Employees only'. When she came out, she was carrying a thin UPS envelope with the words 'SUPER EXPRESS' stamped across it.

"You have to sign for this, sir," she said, placing the envelope on the desk. "You will need a picture ID."

He nodded, produced one of his many passports and handed it to her. She glanced at it, handed it back, and slid over a pen and a sheet of paper with a designated signature line. He scrawled an illegible signature, pushed the sheet back at her, and picked up the envelope.

As he walked away, the girl's smile slowly transformed from fake to genuine. Not many people cared to leave her a tip, and no one had ever done so with a hundred dollar bill. She grabbed it, just as Melenoc reached the escalator.

Once more he gathered his flowing robes from off the floor, stepped onto the mobile stairway and made his way down to street level. Five minutes later he was driving out of the LAX airport with the now opened envelope on the seat next to him.

Its content had not only confirmed his suspicion, it had sent his old heart racing. He had not been this excited in a long, long time.

He was now certain that the woman Semon was not to be trusted anymore. It was a shame, because she had proven to be uncommonly efficient. But to double cross him? Who did she think he was? Some stupid mortal? He wondered what she would think if someone told her that he, Melenoc, had been alive since the time of the Pharaohs, a time when Egypt was called Kemet, when its capital was Itjawy and the Nile was the Aur. Would she even believe it? Would any one believe it? Probably not, and it served his purpose perfectly.

But the truth was that he had been alive for almost four thousand years, something that had been made possible by the secret knowledge of alchemy that had been made available to him by the elusive spirit of Belial. The information had guided him into a new kind of existence. It had also opened a door into a completely different perspective of what life really was, or better still, what life could be. Needless to say, things were not perfect, at least not yet. He still needed to get the other hand of Kepharra for everything to be resolved. And he had been trying to get it for so long, it was literally the story of his long life

"Mr. Enoch," the man said. "Mel Enoch."

For him, the golden hand had become much more than an obsession. It was everything to him. It was the only thing he wanted. He had thought about it, dreamed about it, cried about it, fought for it and almost died because of it. Yes almost died, because as long as he did not yet have both of the hands in his possession, his knowledge remained incomplete. Without a full knowledge of all the steps, he could not perform the final ritual, and because of that, the spell of immortality that had been conferred on him was only partial. Of course, human blood was quite helpful, with the drawback that he could not be exposed to sunlight when he used that diet. Plus, irrespective of the quantity consumed, the painful effects of time were never too far away. That meant his body could still be subject to death, either from the curse of thirst that was permanent, or from some very serious accident like the one that had almost consumed him so long ago in the cave. Memories of that particular incident still sent shivers down his spine. But he had never given up. He had pursued the hand with unparalleled determination.

During the fall of Itjawy, in 1720 B.C, a band of survivors had staged a daring escape with the hand, by digging their way out of the Kings Prison where they had been holed up, and taken it with them southwards to Ethiopia, then to Nubia, and eventually across the Sahara. By the time Melenoc had learned of this, it had been too late and the hand had disappeared.

For a thousand years thereafter, he had roamed the African continent, still half blind, hoping for some intelligence that would lead him to the precious hand. But it had all been wasted effort. It seemed to have vanished into thin air.

Eventually, he became a trans Saharan gold merchant. And it was on one of his trips that some colleagues had talked of Sheba, an African queen who had made an expedition to visit King Solomon in the land of Canaan. She had had an unbelievable quantity of gold in her caravan, they said, and such a jewel, resembling a hand, was rumored to have been in her possession.

So, Melenoc went to Jerusalem, only to learn that the Babylonians had sacked the city a decade earlier, enslaving everyone, and carrying away huge quantities of gold.

Onto Babylon he had gone, even taking a job at Nebuchadnezzar's court. But once more his efforts did not yield anything. The trail had disappeared again. None of the courtiers had seen or even heard of the golden hand, and no matter how hard he'd tried, nothing had come up.

Then Cyrus's army marched into Babylon, destroying everything in its path, creating pandemonium and forcing Melenoc to abandon his investigations and escape into the desert. So great had been his chagrin at the time, that he'd wandered the wilderness by himself for almost a century, living in caves, mostly avoiding the sun, killing and surviving on the blood of all who came his way.

It had been a time of tribulation, a time in which he had almost died from thirst while suffering incessant torments from the spirit of Belial, nightmarish daydreams, esoteric apparitions, sleepless nights of blood curdling visions, ghoulish voices shouting in his head, telling him how inefficient he was and promising hell if he failed to find Kepharra's other hand.

Eventually, he had wandered into a strange land, which he learned was the Kapilvastu Kingdom, walked its length and width, even encountered the man Siddhartha Gautama, sat at his feet, posed several questions and listened to the answers which he found to be very enlightening but not suited for his own personal pursuits.

So once more he'd left and this time journeyed to Greece, where the whole land had been under the spell of a knowledgeable man called Socrates, a gifted thinker and very informed speaker whose political opinions had finally led to his own undoing. Melenoc met the man, but once again he had not learned anything about the hand. Summarily put, no one had seen it, no one had heard of it and no one understood what he was talking about.

Greatly disappointed, he left the Greek city-states and boarded a sea going vessel that had taken him across the Mediterranean, past present day Portugal and down the West African coast.

It was at this time that he learned of trade contacts between the West African seagoing merchants, and a land far to the west, across the great water. He tracked down some of these merchants, befriended them, and eventually convinced them to take him along on their next voyage.

The journey, undertaken in big boats of woven reed, all of them loaded with people and goods, began on a warm, moonlit night. They started off by paddling for many miles to the south, stopping only when they came across what the west Africans had referred to as 'the river in the sea, a mighty current of water that took the boats and guided them all the way to the far, far away lands of the west. After three and a half months, twenty three of the remaining boats arrived at a land that melenoc was surprised to find inhabited by a people who called themselves the Olmecs. In this new land, which was vast by any standard, Melenoc had spent many years, exploring, making enquiries, and meeting with the different tribes. He had encountered the Aztecs, the Mayan, Navajos, Apaches, Chumash, Arawaks, Cherokee, and lots of other peoples, but the hand of Kepharra, he had not found.

After two centuries of unfruitful searching in this distant land, he departed, sailing once more in the company of merchants from West Africa who were returning home. Following a tumultuous sea journey in which every one had perished, he, alone, had been washed ashore onto the coast of present day Gambia. And from there he made his way back to the Aur, and into Kemet. He had arrived into the Kingdom just in time to witness the wars that eventually transformed it into a Roman province, making servants out of masters.

What a time of great confusion that had been. The Romans had ransacked everything, destroying Palaces, monuments, libraries, schools, temples, shrines and places of worship. They had stripped the Kingdom of everything valuable, imposed the *Pax Romana* on the Kemetian people and forced them to pay huge taxes that emptied the treasury.

In this scenario, Melenoc quickly captured the attention of Cleopatra, who was queen then, by hinting that he had special knowledge as to the whereabouts of treasures that had been buried with the Kings of earlier times.

When his word prove true, the queen was so impressed that she gave him full access to the palace, never once suspecting that Melenoc himself had selected the site of Neferhotep's burial, all those years ago when he had been the High Priest of Kepharra.

From then on, it was just a matter of time before he met Julius Cesar of Rome. The epileptic emperor had been so infatuated with Cleopatra that he spent most of his winters in the Kemetian court. It was during one such visit that the great man had been seized by a fit of the humiliating malady. Luckily for him, Melenoc was on hand to prescribe an effective herbal remedy that he had learned from the Olmecs.

Caesar had been so grateful that he took Melenoc to Rome and rewarded him with the title of *Physician to the Emperor*. The title carried enough weight to open most doors in the empire and Melenoc used it to scour the land in the hopes that, perchance, the plundering and far-reaching fingers of the Roman army had somehow encountered the golden right hand. He had even announced an impressive reward to anyone who would furnish information about the object. But alas, his authority in the empire came to a sudden halt when Julius Caesar was assassinated by a conspiracy of Roman senators. This had happened on the fifteenth day of March, exactly forty-four years before the birth of the man Yeshua, later to be called Christ.

With Caesars death, Rome was thrown into a wave of confusion that forced Melenoc to return to the relative safety of Cleopatra's court. But nothing was to be the same. Caesar's successor, Mark Anthony, soon came to visit, and just like his predecessor, he also fell in love with the beautiful African

Queen.

Mark Anthony was a man that Melenoc had met when Julius Caesar was alive, and they had never liked each other. When Anthony soon realized the magnitude of Melenoc's influence with the queen, his dislike became open. He'd made it clear to Cleopatra that Melenoc's presence at court was not welcome anymore. The Queen, who, by this time was pregnant with Anthony's twins, had had no choice but to listen. Bitter and angry, Melenoc was forced out of the royal circle. He had left the capital city and resettled in Avaris. It was there that he met Jesus Christ as a boy of six, an episode that he remembered with alarming clarity, not because of the encounter itself, but because of what had transpired soon afterwards.

A rowdy group of boys had been playing with a rolled ball of cotton on a busy market street. They had all been kicking and chasing after the ball when Melenoc came walking around the corner. Oblivious to his presence, one of the boys had kicked the ball, which came flying directly at Melenoc. He caught the ball in mid stride, and holding on to it, he continued walking along as if nothing had happened.

"Give back my ball," a little voice called after him. Too shocked to believe that one of the children actually had the courage to make such a demand on a grown man, Melenoc turned around to see a little dark face staring up at him in defiance.

"What is your name?" he asked.

"Give back my ball," the child repeated stubbornly, shaking black locks that reminded the ancient High Priest of sheared wool.

"Who is your father?" Melenoc asked in a slightly more threatening tone.

"Give back my ball," came the child's answer.

By now a few passers by were becoming curious, and not wanting a scene, Melenoc acquiesced and let go of the ball, wondering what had caused him to want to keep it in the first place.

He took a disguised sip of water, nervously adjusted the golden right hand that was permanently worn under his robes and turned to leave, as the child went for the ball.

"I am Yeshua," the child's voice floated after him. I am not afraid of you, and you do not know who my Father is." Surprised by the boy's words, Melenoc walked away, irritated that even a child could now challenge him. He'd made a mental note to find the child later.

That night, the spirit of Belial came to visit.

The spirit had been whispering in urgency, using the ancient tongue of the dead to warn Melenoc about the consequences of ever trying to find the child again. He was not to even think of it. That had left him a little confused. Why was Belial protecting the child when he would usually encourage the High Priest to indulge himself. And then it dawned on him that Belial was not trying to protect the child. The spirit was protecting itself from the child! The realization had made him even more curious. Who was this child?

Twenty-five years later, when news that a man called Yeshua was teaching multitudes, healing the sick, giving sight to the blind, and providing answers to the greatest mysteries, instinctively Melenoc knew that it was the same Yeshua that Belial had warned against.

He'd thought long and hard about it, but ultimately, greed had won. So he went to Jerusalem, to the temple of David where the Man was teaching.

"Where is the hand? If you tell me how to find it I will worship you." Melenoc had asked without any waste of time.

Yeshua stared at him for a full moment. "No one can serve two masters; for either he will hate the one and love the other, or else he will be loyal to the one and despise the other. You cannot serve God and Belial."

"But I need it. Do you not claim to be the King of peace? Why deny me this trinket if it will pacify my soul?" Melenoc challenged.

"Come to Me, all you who labor and are heavy laden, and I will give you rest." Yeshua had replied.

"Empty words," Melenoc retorted. "You are just another charlatan who is claiming to be something he is not. If you were truly the Son of God, then you would know where it is. Do you? Where is it?"

"It is written, you shall not tempt the Lord your God."

"What nonsense!" Melenoc answered back. "You can't really do much, can you?" In the silence that followed, the man called Yeshua looked at him with a small smile, and then he'd said:

"Take My yoke upon you and learn from Me, for I am gentle and lowly in heart, and you will find rest for your soul, for My yoke is easy and My burden is light..."

"Nooooooooooo!"

Later that night, the spirit of Belial visited Melenoc once again. Its wrath had been so great it filled up the whole house, smashing furniture, breaking walls and tossing everything up in a terrible whirlwind that left Melenoc with two broken arms.

"This is the second time you are disobeying me," the spirit had growled, freezing Melenoc in terror, as images of himself in the cave fire flashed through his mind. "For this you will pay dearly. Yes, you will. I will take your legs away from you."

"Noooooooooooooooooooooooooooooo!!"

But the curse would not be fulfilled until twelve hundred and fifty years later when Melenoc embarked on a distant journey to the eastern Kingdom of China, still on the tracks of the lost hand.

He'd met a Chinese man who purported to know about the golden hand. The man claimed to know a person in whose possession the artifact had been seen. Melenoc had not believed his ears. That was the first person that had actually said 'yes', in what, a thousand years?

Excitedly, he befriended the man, showered him with gifts, and interviewed him at length about the long lost artifact. The man had insisted on the veracity of his story; namely that, the possessor of the hand was a wealthy merchant, retired now and living in the ancient city of Xi'an.

That was when Melenoc made a serious mistake.

Keeping in mind how long and perilous the journey to China was going to be, he sought to ascertain, beyond reasonable doubt, the veracity of the man's story before committing to it. To that end, he let the man take a look at the other hand. The man confirmed that the object was identical to the one in the possession of the merchant in Xi'an, except for the fact that it was not a right hand, but a left. Excitedly, Melenoc made hasty preparations before setting off on the long journey. But he never got there.

After many days of travel, the Chinese man manipulated the guides and led the whole caravan into an ambush. Luckily, the attack had occurred along a rocky mountain path, with lots of crevices and little caves. Melenoc had barely had time to hide the golden hand before he was taken captive.

His captors led him into the presence of their liege, a Mongolian conqueror by the name of Temujin, who was determined to be the King of the world. Just thinking about the episode made him cringe.

Temujin had been told of the one hand in Melenoc's

possession and he wanted it. But Melenoc had not revealed its location, even when his legs were sawed off. He had decided that death was preferable at that point than to give up something for which he had already suffered so much, and for so long. Plus, growing new legs would be quite easy once he found the other hand.

Luckily for him, the Mongolian's Kingdom grew to become the most extensive to ever exist on the face of the earth, bigger than Rome, -all the way from china to Western Europe. Obviously, he had bigger fish to fry, so he lost interest in the rumors about the necklace's power. He also stopped paying close attention to the legless man. Thus, when Melenoc managed to escape a decade later, no one had bothered to give a determined chase.

He had retrieved the right hand from the crevice into which he had hidden it. And he had kept it, always worn under his clothes, up till this day. But the left hand, he had never found.

He shifted gears now, stepped on the accelerator and sent the white van speeding along the Pacific Coast Highway. When Yerba Buena road came up, he turned onto it, drove about twenty miles before turning into a dirt road with a huge sign that read 'PRIVATE! CARNIVOROUS DOGS ON PATROL! TRESSPASS AT YOUR OWN RISK!'

Ten minutes later, the dirt road came to an abrupt halt at the base of a rugged cliff face. With a long and bony forefinger, he touched a button on the dashboard and an opening materialized at the base of the cliff. He drove into it.

This was one of his homes. It was an extensive underground mansion that had been built with state of the art technology, afforded all the privacy that he could want, and was very well protected. Hurriedly he parked the van, jumped out, and rushed up to his office with the UPS envelope in his clutch.

When he turned on the projector, the picture from the envelope appeared on the opposite wall. At the sight, his heart jumped painfully, missing another bit.

It was a picture of the missing left hand, and he could not believe that he was actually looking at it. With shaky fingers, he reached for the right one around his own neck and gently caressed the metal. After four thousand years the other hand had finally surfaced. Even the first words of the sacred script were partially visible on the projection. Instinctively he began mouthing the words as he tried to read them.

"ILA ...A'M ...AN SA... ROHU SEI... G... GI..." But that

was all he could see. Damn! He needed the object itself.

For a moment, he closed his eyes and savored the intensity of energy as the power of the words coursed through his veins. There was power in those words alright. Imagine what it would be like when he could finally hold both hands of the necklace and perform the final ritual. Imagine all the healing he would get from the stone and the Elixir. His body would be completely rejuvenated. And he would be fully immortal; like God.

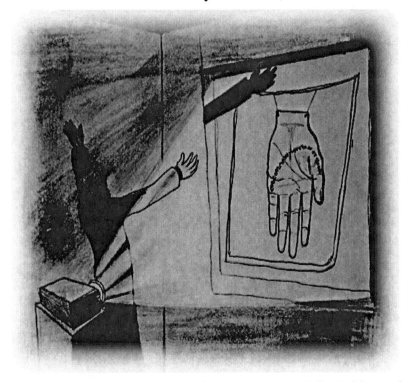

Even the first words of the sacred script were partially visible on the projection

When he opened his eyes, he could have sworn that his vision had improved! Yes he could see a little more! His age-old struggle was coming to an end. It was definitely an emotional milestone. Quickly, he blinked several times, successfully fighting off the tears. It had been more than seven hundred years since the last time he'd cried. The process, although beneficial for moistening his arid eyeballs, was physically very painful for him.

He turned away from the projected image and walked to the

other end of the room. He just had to be patient now. His struggles were finally coming to an end. And what a struggle it had been! Suffering from one mishap to the next, derided through the ages, alienated by different peoples, tortured into disfigurement, and tormented by bouts of severe hopelessness. Luckily an unexpected set of events had changed everything;

After another century of aimless wondering he had ended up in Machu pichu, 8000ft above sea level, in the courts of Pachacute, wealthy Emperor of the Inca. The land had been flooded with gold, but not the gold hand of the god.

What a time of torment! He'd isolated himself from people, killing and drinking the blood of all who ventured too close, including a whole party of explorers from the European nation of spain. It had definitely been the worst time in his life. All those questions that did not seem to have answers, living in constant pain, tormented by nightmares, thirst, doubts, fear, blindness...and when he thought it could not get any worse, the situation had spiraled into an even deeper abyss.

Machu Pichu…

On the same dark morning that the man had decided to get really drunk and end it all, Belial, who had not shown up in nine hundred years, had made his presence felt. The spirit came whispering in the tongue of the dead, about the virgin albino whose spirit was imprisoned into the necklace. Apparently, her second reincarnation into the earth plane was due after three and a half millennia, and as expected, she was to come with the special energy that had the capacity to unearth and attract the long lost, left hand!

Melenoc's depression had evaporated like a mist. He had become ecstatic at the news. All he had to do at that point was to ascertain her point of entry into the world, and be present when she was born. His quest was suddenly reduced to a simple game of waiting and surveillance. If he could follow her, she would eventually lead him to the hand. It was as simple as that.

While waiting for her to be born he celebrated his newfound hope by resurrecting himself as a series of colorful characters with the most famous becoming Jose Gaspar Rodriguez de Francia.

Selena had been born to peasant parents in the village of Humaita, in the southern tip of Paraguay. Sure enough the ancient High Priest, going by a new name, was there, albeit secretly, to welcome her into the world.

Humaita, being a place where everybody knew everybody, turned out to be not so ideal for the ancient man who wanted nothing more than to be incognito. In order to stay in the town and keep a close eye on the young girl, he reinvented himself as a fisherman tour guide, who served Piranha to the tourists who were interested in viewing the ruins of the old church, Itapunta, Corupayty, and Estero Bellaco. The concept caught on, and he had eventually been accepted as a local.

And as long as the girl had stayed in the village, the 'Piranha tour guide' had stayed as well. But as the girl began maturing into a beautiful young woman, it became harder to keep an eye on her without giving the game away. You see, the ancient High Priest believed that the power within Selena's aura would vanish if she lost her virginity, meaning she would also lose the power to attract the long lost left hand of Kepharra, - something that was absolutely unacceptable to the ancient man.

He did what he needed to do: killing off any and all potential suitors who may have stood a chance of sleeping with her. He went about it with the zeal and ruthlessness of a man who would not allow anything to get in his way.

The girl had been traumatized, but she never suspected the reason behind all the deaths. Ultimately, she was not able to live with the local rumor that she was cursed, so she ran away from the little village of her birth and resettled in Asuncion, the capital city, 370 kilometers away. But the 'curse' had followed her like a shadow.

Against her will, she became a local phenomenon, feared and misunderstood, pursued by the local newspapers and shunned by the people. Everyone had wanted to know if she was really a witch. The persistent insults, enquiries and rumors had ultimately pushed her to start speaking out against unfounded superstition, injustice, and other issues related to the human condition. But the newspaper interviews that she had done did not really help. They had instead transformed her into a reclusive national mystery.

The pressure of becoming popular as 'La maldecida', or the cursed one, became too much. In exchange for a US visa and a flight ticket, she agreed to do the first and only television interview with a local network.

In the US the game changed.

It became even more difficult to follow her without arousing suspicion. Melenoc had had to start depending on others.

For the first ten years, he used Zigfred Von Shtok, a restless, wiry ball of energy, who was so efficient that Melenoc had been truly impressed. The man took efficiency to new heights, going the extra mile to meet all the demands that the ancient High Priest had at hand. This had piqued Melenoc's curiosity, and he tested Zigfred even further, as he sometimes did with those that caught his fancy. He pushed the man to impossible limits with the same result. The man had taken instructions, executed them to the letter, always reporting back everything, and on time.

He had also begun to hope that, maybe... just maybe... Zigfred was the first of Belial's subjects who had been sent in with a singular mission to assist, the first mortal who would benefit from the gift and cross into the other side of time; the first of several creatures who would serve the ancient High Priest and facilitate the reestablishment of the Kingdom.

But then, like most men, Zigfred, with time, became greedy, even thinking himself better than Melenoc, whom he had no idea had been alive for longer than all. Neither had he known that the High Priest was planning to get rid of him. Or that he would end up as bottles of blood in the man's refrigerator. This made room for Semon, who was his most recent hireling. He had contracted her to replace Zigfred.

Just like him, she was to report everything that Selena did; every single person she met, irrespective of who they were, what they looked like or where they came from. She was also expected to take care of any 'trouble' that came too close to the woman. But most of all, she was to keep everything absolutely secret.

For three months everything had worked just fine. Semon, nothing anywhere near Zigfred, was dependable enough for things to be stable. Melenoc had given her several early tests, many of which she had passed, sometimes displaying a vicious ruthlessness that had impressed Melenoc, like taking care of Markus Franken. That had been a definite plus. It had seemed like a good start. In fact, Melenoc had actually been hoping that she would find Paulie soon and take care of him as well, -the way Zigfred would have done it. Oh, how he missed Zigfred.

But it did not matter any more because he had found out that, just like Zigfred, the woman Semon was already corrupted by sin. She was trying to double cross him!

Not only did she fail to report about Selena's new friend from Cameroon, she was actively trying to find a market for the golden hand that the Cameroonian had in his possession! She had even gone so far as to contact a few people abroad, which was how Melenoc became alerted about the resurfacing of the missing hand. A contact had sent him a copy of the scan that Semon had mailed out, the same image that was presently projected on the wall.

Zigfred Von Shtok…

CHAPTER THIRTY-ONE

I paid the Pakistani driver, tipping him generously even though my funds were running low. Making sure that the street was clear, I crossed, waving back at the cabbie who was executing a one handed, tire screeching u-turn. He had taken me on a painstaking tour of different pawn shops all around the city, and it had required all afternoon to find what I considered a convenient one, -one that was owned by someone who was willing to, not only give me a loan without asking too many questions, but also hold onto the necklace for up to a year before selling it.

I had left Africa with about three thousand dollars in cash, which in Cameroon is a lot, but not so much in the US, as I found out. Here, everything costs money. Especially, since I did not yet have a legal status so could not get employed. Before I knew it, I was running low.

I had known that I would eventually run out, which was why I had made plans to make transfers from bank accounts in Equatorial Guinea and Nigeria. What I had not factored into the equation was the headache that it would be to actually do the transactions from within the United States, without any form of US issued Identification card. The terrorist attacks of 9/11 had ushered in new banking laws, and no bank was willing to break them for me. Since I was not sure how long it would take for the immigration department to process my application for political asylum, I had to think of something else. Which was how I came up with the idea of borrowing money on the necklace in the first place. It was gold, so I had been pretty sure I could find someone who would be willing to go along.

And I did. Miguelito, the owner of the pawnshop, an Argentinean immigrant with a permanent false smile glanced at the necklace and turned to his partner. *"Es Oro"*

And his partner turned to me. "We cannot gib yo more than fibe tousand dalas." I wanted thirty. Which made me wonder if I should just wait for a little while more. Why not?

"Let me think about it."

"C'mon *amigo*, you are here now, the cash is right here... well... maybe we can do seben, but daz it. *No mas.*"

"Seven is not good enough."

"Well then maybe you really do need to think about it. Come back Friday morning."

Come Friday morning, Miguelito, who had not been willing to come to my terms had doubled the amount in his offer.

"Here is the money, he said. "Where is the necklace?"

"I don't have it with me. I did not expect you to double the amount." Which was true.

"C'mon amigo. This is not a game." He said starring at me. "Ok. This is what I will do for you. Come back in an hour with the necklace and I will give you what you originally asked for it. I left, feeling suspiscious for no reason, but with the promise to come back.

Now, I was having second thoughts altogether. What was it about the necklace that was making me hesitate? All I had to do was decide the date on which I wanted the cash, call the pawnshop the day before, and then show up with the necklace. It was not like I was selling it. I was just using it as a collateral to borrow some money until my situation thawed out, so why was I suddenly not sure? What were my alternatives? Talk to Selena? I was on my way to see her, so why not? Probably because I did not like the idea of asking her for money.

I stopped at the flower stand, got the best bouquet and walked off with a whistle and a dance, imagining her in my arms, as sweet flora smell enveloped my senses. A few minutes later, I turned into the gated community where she lived.

...imagining her in my arms...

$\mathcal{I}$ peeled off my t-shirt and flung it across the room, as Selena, looking like a voluptuous goddess, hair still damp and wrapped in a big white towel, stepped into the room.

She had gone for a swim in the pool, leaving me alone in her apartment to tweak the many quick sketches I had done of her. Even now, with her face screaming shock, all I could see were beautiful lines. Instinctively, I almost reached for my pencil, but stopped myself just in time.

"You okay?" I asked instead, taking a step towards her. Immediately, her arms shot out defensively, keeping me at bay. "What's going on?" I asked.

"Oh my God!" She was staring at me in disbelief. "I must be imagining things," she said, speaking to herself.

"What? What do you mean?" Her eyes were glued on my necklace. "Oh this?" I unclasped it from around my neck and held it out to her. "I was actually trying to make up my mind if I should talk to you about this."

"Noooo!" she screamed in panic, jumping backwards and stumbling over the bed. She lost her balance, rolled onto the floor and she began sliding away, backing off. "WHERE DID YOU FIND THAT? WHERE DID YOU FIND IT?" She was screaming.

"Calm down." This was alarming. "Its just a necklace," I offered, frantically searching for a possible explanation for the sudden change.

"NO, IT IS NOT!" she answered tersely "Where did you get it?"

"Is something wrong?"

"WHERE DID YOU GET IT?" She was now near hysterical, and the fact that we were just getting to know each other made it even more alarming.

"You are screaming," I said as calmly as I could.

"WHERE DID YOU GET IT?"

"Will you stop screaming and tell me what this is about?" Instead she grabbed her clothes and rushed into the bathroom.

"You need to leave. I mean right now." She said from within the bathroom.

"Will you tell me what the problem is?" I asked, walking toward her, but she slammed the bathroom door in my face.

"Did I do something?" I was becoming impatient.

"Just leave, ok?" She said again. "It has nothing to do with you."

"Nothing to do with me? Are you joking?" I asked. "I think we need to talk."

"About what?" She asked

"Us."

"Us? Are you kidding? There is no *us*. We've barely kissed. I don't even know you."

"But you enjoy hanging out with me," I insisted. "You know that our connection is real. You know that we have potential. And I like you. Very much."

"You know nothing about me."

I took a deep breath. Although it felt as if I had known her for all my life, I could not really argue with that. I had attended her lecture on Africa, met her after the talk, and we had just clicked, or so I thought. At the end of the evening, I'd asked for her number, gotten it, and called her the next day. And here we were two weeks later, on the verge of a break up. This was definitely life on the fast track.

"Okay," I said. "I will leave if you tell me what my necklace has to do with it."

After a very long moment I heard the lock turn, and then the door opened. She peeped out. "Promise?" Her voice was cold.

"Promise," I echoed, not quite sure what to expect.

"Let's sit down," she said, drying her eyes and walking out of the bathroom.

For the next two hours, Selena told me the story of her life. She told me about her childhood in Paraguay, about the *curse* that she was believed to have been born with, all the men who had somehow died from taking a more than platonic interest in her, and finally the dreams about the necklace. And through it all I was transfixed, especially the part about the necklace.

"And how do you know that it is the same one?" I asked. "It could just be a coincidence."

"I wish you were right, but I don't think you are."

"How can you be so sure?"

She was silent for a moment. "Is there some kind of script written across the centre of the palm?" she asked quietly. "Curving from the base of the little finger to half-way-up the thumb?"

God! How could she possibly know that? "Is there?" she asked, looking up at me. "Is there?" There were tears in her eyes. "I think you should leave now."

"But why didn't you say anything about this before now?"

"I planned to," she sobbed. "but I was so scared. I am sorry, I should have... but seeing that,..." she was pointing at the necklace. "Seeing that, tells me you should leave now. I don't want anything to do with you....to happen to you…"

"Nothing will happen to me."

"Don't say that. Just leave. Please. And promise you will stay away." She was crying now. "You know, I really like you, but can you imagine what it feels like for me? The guilt? Just from liking you? You are the first man that I have... looked at, since I moved here. I was desperately praying that, somehow, my past had stayed behind in Paraguay, that those days were truly over, but I am not that lucky, am I?" she sobbed, blinded by tears, backing away. Without thinking, I reached across the chaise longue, fighting off her slaps, blows and scratching fingers, until exhausted, she collapsed into my arms. Which was good because I had already made up my mind to stay. Curse or no curse I was going to stay with this woman. And for some reason, it felt like the right thing to do. Plus, were curses and spells actually real?

Semon took a last drag on the cigarette, crushed it in the full and overflowing ashtray and got to her feet. She was tense and she did not like the feeling. A lot depended on what she was about to do, and she could not afford any slip-ups, especially with the recent development.

She pulled out the pictures and studied both of them again, side by side, looking for clues, asking questions, searching for answers. One of the pictures was of Selena, and she was not alone, which in itself was rare. She was lounging by a pool in the company of a thirty something year old black man. The word was that he'd been in the country for less than a month.

Thoughtfully, Semon studied the picture. She had never seen Selena like this. The woman actually looked happy. But what was most arresting was the object in the other picture, an impressive looking necklace, formed in the shape of a left hand. Its golden hue was perfectly set off by the chocolate background. Miguelito had taken this other picture. He had needed a little persuasion, but the Argentinean had realized that it was a gun that was looking him in the eye. He was not being asked if he could do it. He was being told to do it, and get handsomely paid, or else...

Upon seeing the picture, Semon had instinctively known that the necklace was of significance. It had to be. It looked right and it was a hunch she was not going to ignore. She had scanned the picture, enlarged the necklace, made a few copies and mailed them out to certain very discreet contacts she kept in the art and antique underworld. As it turned out, none of her contacts had ever seen or heard of the piece. Except for the Siberian Jew in London. He faxed an immediate reply, claiming as well that he even had a client who would pay thirty million! Now, that was real money. Thirty million! With that kind of money, not only would she be able to retire if she wanted to, she would have enough resources to muscle her way into the lucrative Colombian scene, if she wanted.

So, the decision to keep these new developments to herself had not been a hard one to make. Her highly secretive employer was paying her a drop in the bucket anyway. But thirty million! Now, that was real bread indeed. So tonight, she was getting the necklace. She had to. For some reason the African had failed to drop it off at Miguelito's. The Argentinian had even offered the man what he had originally wanted, but the man had not even called back. It was definitely time to make her move. She would get the necklace, pay off everybody on her team, check out of the hotel, and vamoose.

She extricated the garment from the box that was sitting on the dresser and inspected it. It was a circus clown garment that she had made, so it could not be traced. She slipped it on and turned towards the mirror. Next, she donned the wig, glued on the mustache, and finished by slapping the multi-color paint all over her face. Yes, she looked like a clown. And she would fit right in with the Halloween crowds out on the street. It was perfect.

She adjusted the dark wig, hid her eyes behind some equally dark shades, took a deep breath and stepped away from the mirror. Everything would be fine, she told herself, as she took the lift down to the garage level. A clown is what everyone would remember when the cops show up later. And if she took longer steps and swung her arms just right, everyone would think the person in the costume was a male. That should throw the cops off and buy her enough time.

The red Mercedes was waiting in the underground parking

as she expected. It had been delivered by a rental agency. She had left an envelope of cash for the driver at the front desk, with instructions to leave the keys under the driver seat. She walked up to the car, got in, and retrieved the keys. As she backed out, she did not notice the man who pulled out a cell phone and began dialing.

"She is dressed as a clown and she is in a red Mercedes," he said.

"Good," Melenoc croaked at the other end.

Yes, she looked like a clown

$\mathcal{P}$aulie sat up with a jolt as the image of a clown appeared on the computer screen. Immediately, all of his senses went to high alert. A clown? Of course it was Halloween, but what was he doing at Selena's door? Shouldn't he be on the street? What could a joker want with the woman? Or was he there to see her new Cameroonian friend? But what about?

He felt a sense of apprehension as the clown knocked on Selena's door again. Something was not right. He peered at the image of Selena as she opened the front door.

"What the hell!" Paulie swore at the screen as Selena was forced backward at gunpoint. Then the door was shut. Frantically Paulie punched a button on the keyboard and the view on the screen moved to the inside of the apartment just as Selena's Cameroonian friend walked into the living room. Paulie saw him raising his hands in the air as he became aware of the gun. Shit, Paulie swore again, wishing that he could hear what was being said in the apartment.

Then, as he watched, the Cameroonian reached behind his neck and unclasped a necklace that he'd had on. It was a necklace that Paulie had noticed on him before, but it had not meant anything to him. But now as the man held it out to the clown, a light bulb went off in Paulie's head. It dawned on him with sudden clarity that the object was the reason why Marcus 'fuckin' Franken had died. It was the reason behind all the surveillance that had put Selena under a microscope. Which meant that it was the same prize that he himself was searching for.

He jumped out of the car and ran across the street with his tie billowing in the wind behind him.

CHAPTER THIRTY-TWO

When I stepped out of the bathroom and into Selena's livingroom, the sight that met my eyes was more like a movie scene than reality. Selena was standing in the middle of the room but she was not alone. There was a clown standing just inside the door and he was holding a gun.

"Where is it?" the clown demanded in a funny, almost effeminate voice.

"I....I..." Selena stammered.

"There he is," the clown whispered in the same voice as he noticed me.

Instinctively, I knew he was talking about Yao's necklace. "What are you talking about?" I asked, feigning ignorance.

"I don't have any time or any patience for that matter," the clown said. "Hand it over and make it easy on yourself." There was a hard edge to the voice that I recognized. He would not hesitate to kill both of us if I did not do as he asked.

The necklace had never been mine anyway. I had taken it off a dead man and worn it for a few months, but it was definitely not worth dyeing for. Maybe I should have left it with Miguelito. Then, at least, I would have gotten some money. In silence, I unclasped it from around my neck and held it out.

"Put it on the table and step back," the clown said, waving the gun at me. I did as he commanded, hoping that he would just take the necklace and leave. But it was not be.

"Pick it up and bring it to me," he said to Selena.

At that precise moment the door of the apartment burst open.

"Freeze!" Screamed the man who stepped in. "Drop your gun, keep your hands where I can see them, and don't you mess with me!" The clown did not argue. He let his weapon fall to the floor as the other man took another step into the room.

"You don't want to do this," the clown said, raising both hands in the air. "I will find you."

"Shut your funny face before I shoot your stupid ass," Paulie snapped.

He picked up the necklace, slipped it into a brown paper bag and began backing out of the room. At the door he pointed the gun at Selena.

"Come with me."

"Me? Why?"

"Shut up and do as I say," he screamed, pointing the gun at her. She did not argue either. As she stepped out of the apartment he turned to me.

"Freeze!" Screamed the man who stepped in.

"You keep this fool here," he said. "If I see you or him outside this door any time soon, your sweet lady will get one in the neck. Understand?" I nodded.

Then the door swung shut. At the same time, the clown lunged for the gun that he had been forced to drop. I had anticipated the move and was waiting for it. My foot connected with his torso and for a moment he was forced to forget the gun. With a feline snarl he came at me, jumping on the table and using it as a springboard. The impact of both feet on my abdomen was stunning and I was thrown hard against the wall. With a grunt he lunged at me once more. I moved to the side as a knife-bearing arm sliced through the air, missing my stomach by inches. He swung again, and once more I barely managed to avoid the blade. I jumped off, grabbed the outstretched arm and pulled sharply. The clown lost his balance and stumbled forward into my left fist. It was followed by a solid right and he went down. I pushed the bookshelf over, burying him in a sudden avalanche of books, wood and dust. As he struggled in vain to lift the weight off, I picked up his gun and ran out of the apartment.

I burst out into the street, gun in hand, and came to a sudden halt. There were a few 'halloweeners' around but neither Selena or her captor were in sight.

"SELENA!" I called out, but there was no answer. "SELENA," I called again.

Then I heard a car start up behind me. I spun around just in time to see a Ford SUV pull out of the curb with screeching wheels and come charging at me. I only had a second so I jumped in the air to avoid the full impact. I landed on the car's hood, rolled over the windshield onto the top and fell hard on the ground as it sped off.

"Are you okay?" A man was standing over me. His white Volvo was parked just a few steps away in the middle of the street. The engine was running and the driver's door was open.

"Thank you for asking, but you will have to forgive me," I said getting to my feet and limping into his car.

"Hey! What are you doing?" The man shouted. "That is my car."

As I sped off after the disappearing taillights of the SUV, I glanced at the rearview and saw the clown getting into a red Mercedes. What a tenacious soul!

About a quarter mile ahead I saw the SUV slow down and make a right turn. I shifted gears, stepped on the gas and the Volvo surged forward. A moment later I came up on the same street and also made a right. It was a relatively smaller way, with cars parked on both sides, but the SUV did not slow down.

With horns blaring I stayed behind it.

Momentarily, the street emptied into an intersection, and the SUV roared through it as the lights turned to yellow. I gritted my teeth and stepped on the gas. The Volvo zipped through the intersection as yellow went red. Then, there was a loud crash. I glanced at the rearview mirror, and saw the intersection go up in a ball of fire as a pick up truck that was trying to avoid the clown's Mercedes rolled over and slammed itself into a huge crane-transporting vehicle with 'oversize load' signs plastered all over it. The Mercedes did not even slow down.

By the time our convoy of three speeding cars got to the next intersection, a cop on a bike had appeared behind us. But he was not to be there for long either. The sound of screeching tires filled my ears as the clown stepped suddenly on the brakes.

In a bid to avoid the Mercedes that had abruptly stopped in front of him, I saw the cop swerve to the right, narrowly missing the car. But the swerve was too sharp. He lost his balance, crash onto a parked automobile and go flying through the air.

...and go flying through the air...

Selena twisted in pain as the SUV careened around the corner, throwing her up against some equipment that had been set up where the back seat should have been. All kinds of electronic gadgets came tumbling down. A laptop landed on her head, almost knocking her out. She tried once more to raise herself up to her knees but it did not go well. She ended up flat on her face as the car bounced through an intersection. If only she could find a way to untie her hands, she thought.

Frantically she began looking around. With all of this equipment flying about, surely there must be something she could use. She rolled onto her back, and after a few attempts, succeeded in raising her body and leaning against the side of the car.

"Did I ask you to sit up?" Paulie snarled from the driver's seat. "Lay your ass down. NOW!" Selena ignored him. Instead she craned her neck and peered outside.

"I said lie down!" Paulie shouted over his shoulder. But it was too late. She had already noticed the Volvo and recognized Abanda behind the wheel. In excitement she got to her knees without realizing how she managed it.

"In here!" she shouted, as Paulie threw the car around a sharp curve. She crashed against the rear window, crying out in pain as glass particles exploded all around.

"Damn!" Paulie screamed in frustration. But there wasn't much he could do. His best bet was to lose his pursuers now and deal with her later. There was the option of putting a bullet in her, but that was not something he was willing to do. He had a few questions of his own about the necklace and he was counting on her to provide some answers.

He glanced at the rearview mirror and swore. The Volvo was gaining on him. And just behind it was the Mercedes. He had to do something soon or else he would be in trouble.

In frustration, he spun the wheel and sent the SUV racing down a busy double street dotted with coffee shops and bars. Hopefully, no pedestrian would choose to cross the street now, he thought. And if they do, then they'd better be ready for the next world because he was not going to stop.

It was at that moment that he saw the man.

What! Was he dreaming?

No, he was not. It was a face that he would recognize anywhere.

Very calmly, he floored the brakes and the SUV screeched to a painful halt that threw Selena forward with brutal force. She cried out as her body slammed into the back of the driver's seat. Paulie did not even hear her. Neither did he notice the Volvo that collided into the back of the SUV.

All of a sudden he was in a world of his own, -a world where the only things that mattered were the painful memories of his childhood and the man who had caused them, the same man whose face he had just seen on the sidewalk.

With a zombie-like glaze in his eyes he picked up the gun that was lying by the paper bag, on the seat next to him, threw open the car door and stepped out into the horn blaring confusion on the street.

Eleven cars behind, Semon watched Paulie step out of the SUV. Immediately she pulled over, jumped out of her car and began running ahead to the SUV.

Paulie did not even look at her. Ignoring the loud horns from other motorists, he marched directly to the door of the barber's shop where he'd seen the man enter. As he pushed the door open, a little bitter smile stole across his features. Today the justice that had been denied him for all those years was about to be served. The very man who had repeatedly abused him as a helpless child in the orphanage was in the shop. And with or without his priestly cassock the time had come for that man to answer for those crimes. Paulie had replayed this scenario in his mind at least ten thousand times and he knew exactly how it was going to end. How it must end.

"DO YOU REMEMBER ME?" he screamed in rage at the man who was just settling down into the barber's chair.

Johnny Letgo was a man who was finally learning at the age of sixty, what it really meant to forgive. It was a concept that he had heard about vaguely, but it had not really meant anything to him. He had been too busy dreaming about the revenge that he wanted to exact someday on all those people who had picked on him, making his life into such a wreck, especially his own brother who was now hiding his sinfulness in a cassock. Of course, one could argue that his brother had turned out to be so messed up as a result of the incesant abuse that they had both suffered at the hands of their alcoholic parents. But still…

Then without warning, Johnny had found God, or better yet, God had found him. And that had changed everything.

For the first time in his life, he had been able to seriously consider the possibility of forgiving not only his dead parents, but his brother as well. For the first time he was acquiring a deeper and more meaningful understanding of what it really meant to *let go*. And he was liking it. The feeling of freedom and peace that came with forgiving people had totally taken him by surprise. It was as if he was the one who had just been forgiven.

He closed the bible, glanced at his watch and rolled out of bed. He had just enough time to clean up and get a haircut before heading to the airport. He was flying to Italy to meet with his brother, who was now a Cardinal in the Vatican, and he was excited about the conversation they were going to have. It felt as if he'd been waiting his whole life for this day.

Twenty minutes later he pushed open the door into the little shop, said hello to the barber and shook hands all around. Then, as he settled into the seat, the door flung open and a man holding a gun walked in.

"DO YOU REMEMBER ME?" the man screamed raising the weapon.

"OH NO! YOU ARE MISTAKEN," Johnny began, "IT WASN'T ME."

"LIAR," the man shouted as the first shot rang out. "I knew you would deny it. Coward that you are." And he fired again. "May you burn in hell!" Another shot.

"It wasn't me…," Johnny stammered coughing up blood. "My brother…" He slumped forward. "Twin brother… Please forgive him… as I forgive you…" Johnny muttered, and he collapsed to the floor.

"Oh God, no!" Paulie whispered, backing away as the gun slipped from his fingers. He turned around and ran out of the barber's shop, rushing blindly past the sidewalk and into the street. The blaring horns of the big blue bus was the last thing he heard as its huge tires came bearing down upon him.

CHAPTER THIRTY-THREE

When the SUV screeched to a sudden halt, it took me by surprise. I stepped on the brakes, spinning the wheel at the same time but I was going too fast. The Volvo crashed into the back of the SUV and all of sudden I was almost suffocating under the pressure of an airbag.

As I extricated myself from the car, I saw Paulie step out of the SUV and cross the street into a barber shop. I did not have time to figure out what was happening. I just wanted to make sure that Selena was all right. I rushed forward to the SUV.

"Abanda!" She cried out in relief as I took her into my arms. "Oh I love you, I love you so much," she said, tears welling up in her eyes. I wanted to tell her that I loved her too but I got distracted. In the reflection of the cracked rear window of the SUV I saw the clown sprinting in our direction, gun in hand.

As God would have it, Paulie had left the engine running. I jumped into the SUV and I stepped on the gas just as the clown came running along side. The car took off with screeching tires as a gunshot rang out.

"Can you see him?" I asked

"Faster, faster, faster," Selena said. "He's coming after us."

"Is he? Shouldn't he be staying with the other guy who has the necklace?"

"No. The other guy who had the necklace left it on the seat next to you."

Oh God!

Melenoc leaned over the complex looking dashboard, fidgeted with the controls, and the tiny chopper banked to the right, flying directly into the wind. It was a beautiful machine, fitted with the much more efficient coaxial rotor system, and he loved it. He had had it custom built according to very strict specifications by Wieland Helicopters and he felt that it was totally worth it. Although it looked small and deceptively fragile, it was one of the toughest helicopters that had ever been manufactured. It had been put through very rigorous testing, was adapted to fly in terrible weather, was loaded with state of the art technology, yet was surprisingly easy to fly. It had also been equipped with an ultra modern weapon system that had been developed in Israel. It had cost a fortune. But after test-flying it, he had gotten on the phone and placed an order for a second one. That was how much he loved the machine.

Just then there was a little beep. It was a call he had been expecting, a call that no one else could listen in to. He touched a button and the police officer came in clean and clear.

"Sir, just reporting that no object of that description was identified on Paulie."

"And you are sure about that?"

"Yes."

"Good," Melenoc paused. "A red Mercedes will be involved in an accident on the 210 E. I suspect the driver is wanted by interpool. See to it."

"Thanks for the tip, sir."

And Melenoc ended the short exchange.

Far below he could see both cars on the 210 free way. The SUV was still ahead but was losing ground to the red Mercedes. Not that it mattered. At this point the most important thing was the fact that the necklace had shown up and he was not going to let it out of his sight until he took possession. He had waited too long to be cheated out of that now. Just thinking about it sent his heart beating wildly in his chest. It was not everyday that a man had the power within his grasp to make the nations of the world to bow down before him? Yes, the whole world will bow to him. Eventually. After he had dissolved all boundaries and unified all governments. Then he would crown himself King. And his great vision for humanity will be implemented. And nothing, repeat nothing, was going to stand in his way. Not the government of the United States, not the government of China, not the Russians, not the United Nations, not Selena, not her boyfriend, and definitely not the ungrateful, doublecrossing daughter of a dog, who called herself Semon.

He touched a button on the lit dashboard. An image of the car chase far below suddenly appeared on a screen in front of him. In a moment, both cars will be on the bridge that was coming up. He touched the screen, and Semon's red Mercedes became centralized between the crosshairs of the advanced weapons system. With a smile he reached forward and double-tapped the image of the car. The complex onboard computer translated the instructions and a tiny, silent, pen-sized missile was discharged.

On the screen, Melenoc followed the short and precise flight of the weapon as it zoomed in on the Mercedes. A moment later there was a small flash and the car was flung into the air. It rolled over several times, crashed, broke through the protective railing on the bridge, went over the side and disappeared into the water below with a loud splash.

That should suffocate the ungratefulness out of her, Melenoc thought with satisfaction. In his Kingdom there would be no room for dissent. He would be a King whose authority was rooted in strength. Weakness will not be tolerated.

Now all he had to do was follow the SUV until it stopped or ran out of gas. Then he would go down and collect his necklace. With both hands in his possession, the world would be his for the taking. It would mark the unofficial beginning of King Melenoc's endless reign. Just the excitement of thinking about it was making his mouth dry. Instinctively, he reached out for the bottle of water. And froze.

It was not there! It was not there! There was no water! Melenoc could not believe it. He had forgotten to bring water? He, Melenoc, had actually forgotten to bring water!

The rage that seized him was like a monster in pain. Here was his precious hand, so close, and he had forgotten to bring water! His body began trembling in a wave of self-directed anger. He felt like banging his own head against a wall hard enough to explode it. How could he forget something so vital? Was he dreaming?

Then, he broke out in cold sweat.

He did not have any water! The panic that fused into his anger was barely held in check, and only by years and years of survival, in situations where his own very existence had come close to,...no, those were not good thoughts. Quickly, he wetted his thumb with spit and stamped an imprint on his warm forehead.

Frantically, he looked around, trying at the same time to keep the little helicopter steady. A hurried scan of the little cockpit quickly confirmed that Melenoc did not have any water! Oh God, no! Please, not this time! His old heart was already beating too fast.

Nervously, he tried to swallow but his mouth was too dry. And it was getting dryer by the second. Even his body temperature was already rising. Suddenly the SUV and its precious contents paled in importance. What an irony! Who would have known? With his heart racing, and his body heating up, he sent the chopper speeding downwards.

Water was the only thing on his mind now. Did he have enough time? No, the river was too far behind already. Best to head to the ground directly. Water!

He had to get some by any means necessary or else it would all be over. He would be dead, and if that happened, then even the hand would not matter. In fact, he was dying right now. Oh God! His heartbeat was beginning to slow. And it would keep on slowing until it stopped, after four thousand years, -almost like a piece of machinery that had run for so long and gathered so much momentum that it needed a little time to finally stop going. He was running out of time!

Possessed by a frantic desperation, he worked the controls, mentally willing the chopper to become an eagle and swoop to a perfect landing on the rapidly rising ground. But it was just a piece of very advanced aeronautic technology. It whined in protest, suddenly unsteady in the hands of panic.

Less than a hundred feet away was the earth and it was rising quickly. Too quickly for the landing to be safe. Already, people on the street were screaming and rushing for cover as the chopper descended. The screams. The noise. The wind.

It crash-landed in the middle of a busy intersection, forcing an over loaded eighteen-wheeler to make a sharp swerve. The truck lost control and flipped over, spewing out merchandize, rolling several times and causing extensive damage to other cars before settling on top of a small gas station. Momentarily, the siren of a fire truck filled the street, as the station exploded into flames.

$\mathcal{A}$s I lay there in the motel room with Selena in my arms, I

realized that there was probably no one else I'd rather be with. Was she the woman of my life? The feeling of deep contentment and peace that was stealing over my thoughts was the deepest I had felt in a long time. But was it going to last, I wondered. What other craziness was waiting around the corner? I still had Yao's necklace with me, wrapped up and out of sight. Selena preffered it that way.

Looking at the necklace gave her headaches. Plus, she called it an evil omen, which I found funny.

Effortlessly, I pushed away the thought. The world in which we live sometimes seems to be full of unexpected factors. A good example was something I had seen that very morning in the news; a man had crash-landed a helicopter in a busy city street, and then, bloodied, limping, but very much alive, he'd rushed into a corner store just to buy water! Think about it! All for water! Who on that street could have seen it coming? Strange, but it was the world in which we lived. So, I was not going to fret about anything. Why should I? Who on this earth was going to add a minute to their life by worrying about the future? There were too many good things to focus on right now: Just being alive was a big one. Getting up to a new day, everyday, was a miracle in itself. Being able to experience the mystery of it all, was another one. And for now, I was with this wonderful woman, and we were safe. So, why should I let my mind to dwell on the fearful possibilities of the future, or the depressing mistakes of the past when I could focus on the 'now', on good and happy thoughts, while leaving the rest to God and his arrangement of destiny.

Dallas Public Library
950 Main Street
Dallas, Oregon 97338

CPSIA information can be obtained at www.ICGtesting.com
Printed in the USA
LVOW11s2334081014

407967LV00001B/118/P